A TRAITOR'S LOVE

For a long moment, Philip stared at her. "Would it make you feel better to know I support the cause?"

Gillian's eyes flashed in anger. "What kind of fool do you take me for? Leopards don't change their spots and neither do Tories. You're just as you've always been: a traitor!"

"You really don't want to marry me, do you?" Philip mused quietly. "And that day you came to my house.... You didn't mean any of it, did you?" He grabbed Gillian by the shoulders and began to shake her. "It was all to coax me into aiding Thomas!" He released her, then picked up his hat. "Very well. I made you an honorable proposal of marriage. It was a mistake I will not repeat." He began to walk away. "When your grandmother returns, I will explain the situation to her."

Gillian watched him go with mixed feelings. Of all the men in New York, in the colonies, in the world, why did she have to be attracted to this one? Her body might accept a traitor, but she, herself, could not.

To Richard and Helen Edwards

Book Margins, Inc.

A BMI Edition

Published by special arrangement with Dorchester Publishing Co., Inc.

If you purchased this book without a cover you should be aware that this book is stolen property. It was reported as "unsold and destroyed" to the publisher and neither the author nor the publisher has received any payment for this "stripped book."

Copyright © 1993 by Helene Lehr

All rights reserved. No part of this book may be reproduced or transmitted in any form or by any electronic or mechanical means, including photocopying, recording or by any information storage and retrieval system, without the written permission of the Publisher, except where permitted by law.

Printed in the United States of America.

FOREWORD

Your Gloria Diehl Book Club selections are chosen by an independent review board with members all across the United States. Board members are carefully chosen to represent all backgrounds, views, and reading interests. Any romance novel which bears the imprint *Gloria Diehl Book Club Selection* has been reviewed and recommended by the committee for its originality, reading interest, plot, and character development.

Chapter One

From Gillian's Diary:

> *September 20, 1776*
> *Five days have passed since the British landed at Kip's Bay. The Americans have left Manhattan. All that remains now are the British and the Tories. I hear the rejoicing in the streets, and I wonder in my heart what there is to rejoice about.*

The Blue Swan Tavern was almost empty. Only three British grenadiers were gathered around a table, drinking applejack and laughing loudly at a ribald joke. From the sound of them, one would have thought a crowd was in attendance.

Seventeen-year-old Gillian Winthrop's gray eyes viewed the soldiers with distaste. She wished they'd go outside to celebrate with the rest of their comrades.

Helene Lehr

One of them had left the front door open, and she now went to close it.

The Blue Swan was on the corner of Berkley and Broad Way, the latter now crowded with people. Some were carrying torches; most were carrying bottles of rum.

The civilians were Tories, loyal to the Crown. Gillian's stomach churned with acidic resentment as she viewed them. Loyalists prudently had vacated the city during the time the Continentals had occupied New York. Now they were back, celebrating with uninhibited joy.

"Death to the rebels!" someone shouted.

The cry was immediately taken up by soldiers and civilians alike. Mouth tight in anger, Gillian slammed the door shut. It didn't do much good.

With a sigh, Gillian raised a hand to tuck a wayward curl back under her white mobcap. Her hair was the color of honey, and so fine it kept slipping out of the chignon so carefully fashioned at the start of each day.

"Gillian?"

She turned to see her brother-in-law, Thomas Carmody, coming toward her. Although Tom had yet to reach his thirtieth year, his light brown hair was already sprinkled with silver at his temples. His tall, wiry body appeared almost thin in his tight-fitting cotton breeches, but his shoulders were broad and muscular beneath his white shirt.

"You may as well go back to the house. Edwina has already gone upstairs." At Gillian's look of hesitancy, Tom smiled, lightening his normally serious demeanor. "Go along. I don't think we'll be doing much business tonight."

Gillian returned the smile. She very much liked this man her sister had married. "I know they're

The Passionate Rebel

drinking," she said with a nod in the direction of the grenadiers, "but sooner or later they might want to eat."

"There's plenty of roast beef left in case one of them gets hungry," he called cheerfully over his shoulder as he headed back to the long bar.

Going to the rear of the large, rectangular room, Gillian entered the kitchen, warm now due to the fire in the wood burning stove. There was also a hearth with a bake oven on one side, and it, too, was emanating heat, though its fire had been banked for the night. The living quarters of the Carmodys were on the third floor, the second being comprised of those rooms Tom rented out when the occasion presented itself. It wasn't often. The Fraunces Tavern was the one that drew most customers. Now that the British were back in town, half their junior officers were billeted there.

Gillian removed her apron, revealing a dress of dark blue cotton, the bodice laced tightly over a white lawn shift. Hanging the apron on a peg, she nodded to Ella Bishop.

There had been a time when the Carmody household had been fully staffed. Most of the servants, however, indentured or not, had fled the city during these past months. Some were merely frightened at the sight of the numerous warships in the harbor, their guns pointed menacingly at the very heart of Manhattan. Others had simply used the occasion to escape their bonds, joining the exodus in the confusion of the moment. Now, the only servant who remained was Ella Bishop.

Gillian stood there a moment, hands on the small of her back, and stretched. She wasn't used to standing for such extended lengths of time. She'd only been helping out in the tavern, which Tom owned, for the past two weeks.

"Not much traffic tonight?" Ella asked as she emptied the contents of a pot of stew into a wooden bowl. She was a thin woman who looked considerably older than her 40 years. A widow and childless, Ella was alone except for a sister who lived in Savannah.

"No," Gillian answered. "Just a few stragglers—" She broke off as the thundering sound of gunfire seemed to shake the walls.

"Lord have mercy!" Ella exclaimed loudly, dropping the wooden bowl she was holding. The contents went splattering across the clean floor. "What was that?"

Gillian tilted her head. All that could be heard now was the high-pitched laughter of a woman who sounded more than slightly intoxicated. A whore, most likely, Gillian thought to herself. There were many of them in the city—homeless, desperate women who had no other means of survival. Gillian saw them frequently in the tavern. They laughed—too loudly at times—but in their eyes she saw only sadness and could never find it in her heart to censure them.

"Just the redcoats, celebrating their victory," Gillian declared at last. Glancing at Ella, she saw that the woman was as white as a sheet. Gillian patted the thin shoulder. "Go on up to your room," she said kindly. "I'll clean this up."

After Ella had left, Gillian put the bowl in the sink, then mopped up the floor.

Finally, with a sigh, she picked up her shawl from the back of a chair and donned it. A moment later, she let herself out the back door. Her grandmother's house was less than a block away, a pretty Georgian-style structure fronted by a generous lawn decorated with oak trees that were now beginning to shed their leaves.

The Passionate Rebel

The September evening was cool, but not uncomfortable. It was clear, and a pale crescent moon shed just enough light to illuminate her way.

Gillian avoided the street, choosing instead to walk through the apple orchard that separated the house from the tavern. The trees were heavy with fruit, which was not yet ripe enough to eat.

Normally, when she traversed this relatively short distance, Gillian felt as if she were going home. Tonight, she wasn't so sure. It was an unsettling feeling, knowing that most Americans had left Manhattan. Friends and neighbors she had known all her life had fled the city when the British had landed at Kip's Bay.

They had no business being here! Gillian thought angrily, kicking at a stone in her path. She had been so elated when she had read in the newspapers that the Continental Congress had declared the colonies to be independent of the Crown. That was when the British should have left! Instead, King George had sent more than 30,000 soldiers to invade New York. Word had spread quickly when the army had landed on Staten Island. Everyone knew then that it was only a matter of time until the British seized New York. And now, they had.

Gillian stepped up onto the back porch and entered the kitchen. Polly, a black woman in her late fifties, was preparing the dough for the next day's bread. With one exception, the Wharton household was staffed with black servants. The one exception was Katie Kendell, Gillian's personal maid, who was indentured.

Polly looked up as Gillian closed the door.

"Still got some coffee left," she said, plopping the dough into a pan. "Did you have supper?"

"A bit," Gillian replied. "I'm not very hungry."

Grabbing a towel, Gillian picked up the pot of coffee from the stove and poured herself a cup. Even at this distance the sound of the revelers was annoyingly audible.

"Listen to them out there," she muttered. "They seem to think they've won the war."

Polly sighed. "They sure raisin' a ruckus, all right." Carefully, she placed a clean cloth over the pan. By morning it would be ready for the bake oven.

Gillian drained her cup. "Where's my grandmother?" she asked.

The question was answered by another woman who was just now coming into the kitchen. "Miz Wharton in her room. Says the noise givin' her a headache." Drucilla nodded as she offered that piece of information. She was Alice Wharton's personal maid, an attractive, cheerful woman of 47, with skin the color of tea.

Having rinsed the cup in the basin of water that Polly kept in the sink, Gillian decided she had best retire too. Tomorrow would be another long day, she supposed. Both she and Edwina were working in the tavern, what with help being as scarce as it was.

Katie had just turned down the bed when Gillian came into the room. Short and plump, Katie was not much older than Gillian, having just turned 19. Dark auburn hair framed a rather pretty face that was enhanced by a flawless complexion.

Gillian murmured a greeting and handed her shawl to Katie, who immediately went to hang it up.

Except for the rosewood writing table, positioned by the single window, all the furniture was constructed of sturdy oak and included a wardrobe, several

The Passionate Rebel

small tables and a large chest of drawers. The floor was uncarpeted, the wood buffed to a dull sheen by the heavy use of beeswax.

Now that she was here, Gillian found herself to be wide-awake. Going to her writing table, she opened her diary and stared moodily at the last entry. Americans have left Manhattan, she had written. But that wasn't true. She was still here, and by all that was holy, she was an American and a patriot.

"Miss Gillian, it's getting late." Katie fluffed the pillow. Straightening, she viewed the young girl, who seemed to be lost in her thoughts.

Having received no answer, Katie walked to the window to close the shutters, then caught her breath at the scene that greeted her eye. The sky was gold and orange, glowing with the sinister beauty that only a huge blaze can produce.

"Fire!" The word caught in her throat.

Instantly, Gillian was at her side. "Oh, God, they're burning the city!"

Hoisting her skirts, Gillian ran from her bedroom and down the curving stairs that led to the front hall.

"Wait!" Moving quickly, Katie grabbed the shawl she had just hung in the wardrobe and hurried after Gillian. As quick as Katie was, Gillian was already out the front door when her maid got downstairs.

Katie caught up with her young mistress about a block away, where she had paused on the corner of Broad Way and Partition Street. Before the girl could move again, Katie draped the shawl around the slim shoulders.

Gillian pointed. "The wind is carrying the flames south."

The streets, already crowded, were becoming more so, filling with people who were either running or gawking. Wagons and drays ground to a standstill, unable to circumvent the sudden surge of humanity. The conflagration was spreading fast. Spires of gold and red and yellow, flanked by dark columns of smoke, reached for a sky no longer black.

Gillian began walking at a fast pace, paying no mind to Katie's protestations.

Finally, they halted. The fire was a flaming barrier. Sparks flew into the air and rained down like a deadly spray of fireworks. Wherever they landed, a new blaze took hold. The soldiers had already formed a bucket brigade, but it was as effective as a drop of water on an inferno. Above the sharp crackling and the dull thud of falling trees, the night was filled with the sound of hoarse shouts and terrified screams.

Claudia Dunham was screaming. Displaying a frantic haste born of terror, she was vainly trying to remove the fiery beam that had crashed down on her six-month-old son.

Flesh seared, but she paid no mind.

By her side, Claudia's mother was just as frantically trying to pull her away.

"It's no use, Claudia!"

Her mother's shrill voice only barely penetrated. In dumb anguish, heedless of her injured hands, Claudia continued to grapple with the flaming wood.

The older woman cast fearful eyes upward. The roof was a huge torch, the heat incredible. She knew that only seconds remained before disaster struck. With a strength born of desperation, she wrapped her arms around Claudia's waist and actually lifted the young woman off her feet.

"No!"

Claudia's plea had no effect. Nearing the front door, her mother put both hands on her back and

The Passionate Rebel

roughly shoved her outside. Claudia landed on her stomach and gasped as the air was propelled from her body.

Getting to her knees, she watched, horrified, as the roof caved in. She knew that her mother and her son were lost, but the knowledge didn't prevent her from trying to get back inside. The flames did that.

Defeated and dazed, Claudia Dunham sank down on the front lawn, not hearing the screams or the sounds of the bucket brigade that could not control, much less prevent, the spread of the fire that raced eagerly to consume each house in its path.

About a quarter of a mile away, Katie was pulling on Gillian's arm. "Let's go back! It's not safe here!" She gave a frightened yelp as an ember landed on her sleeve. Quickly, she brushed it away and emitted a small groan when she saw the singed hole in her dress.

Gillian turned her head to look back up Broad Way. Her grandmother's house was in a direct line with the blaze. If the wind changed direction...

"Come on," she said to Katie. "We've got to warn my grandmother."

The two young women hurriedly retraced their steps. As they approached the house, Gillian saw the elderly woman standing on the front porch. She was dressed in black, as she had been for the past seven years, ever since her husband had died. The frail appearance did not deceive Gillian. She knew very well that beneath it was a will of iron.

"Are you all right?" Gillian called out, climbing the four steps to stand at Alice Wharton's side.

"Of course I am!" the old woman snapped. Gray hair, hidden now beneath a white cap, was the only outward sign of her 62 years. Her back was straight, her step unhesitating, and her blue eyes alert and intelligent. Right now, however, those eyes were sparked with anger as she viewed her rebellious and impulsive granddaughter.

"I think we ought to leave until the fire is under control," Gillian began.

"I have no intention of going anywhere."

"The fire is just a few blocks away," Gillian protested. "If the wind shifts . . ."

"If it does, I'm well-prepared for it." She pointed to the roof. "William is up there. The rest of the servants are filling buckets with water in case they are needed."

Gillian sighed. William was Polly's husband and nearing 60. She could only hope that it would not become necessary for him to scramble about on the pitched roof, chasing embers.

"Get into the house," Alice said before Gillian could again speak. "Don't you know how dangerous it is out here?" Her brusque tone gave no indication of the alarm she had felt when she'd discovered Gillian's absence.

The look of concern, even masked as it was by anger, was not lost on Gillian. She rushed forward and threw her arms around the older woman's neck. "Oh, Gram, I didn't mean to cause you worry. It's just that—"

"You never stop to think," Alice interrupted, refusing to be mollified. "And you, young woman!" She glared at Katie, who hung her head. "I would think that you would have more sense than to allow your mistress to race off into the night."

"Gram!" Gillian protested. "That's not fair. Katie—"

"Enough!" Alice stepped back and gave Gillian a sharp nudge. "In the house. And I forbid you to go

The Passionate Rebel

down there again!" She followed Gillian into the foyer. "Remain in your room, unless I summon you. I'm sure the soldiers have the situation well in hand."

"Probably it was they who started it," Gillian grumbled as she climbed the stairs.

"Nonsense!" her grandmother retorted, angry again. "It's inconceivable that the British would burn the city after they have taken possession of it. More likely, it was your precious patriots. They ought to hang every rebel they catch!"

The glow on the horizon was easily seen from Harlem Heights, where the Continentals were encamped.

Two men stood on a ridge, contemplating the fiercely beautiful glow in the sky. The taller of the two was garbed in a blue and buff uniform. He needed no epaulets to mark him as a general. All his men knew him by sight.

"Do you think they are really burning New York?" General George Washington turned to view his companion, who was wearing the uniform of a lieutenant.

"I wouldn't want to second-guess General Howe, but I doubt it."

"So do I. However, I suppose we'll learn soon enough." He paused a moment, then spoke in quiet tones. "I have an assignment for you. I want to stress, however, that it is voluntary. If you are caught, you will be hung."

The young man viewed his commander-in-chief with quizzical eyes. There was only one reason he could think of that would prompt the British to hang a captured soldier.

"You want me to be a spy?" he asked at last, a bit startled by the idea.

Gravely, the general nodded. His gaze once more drifted across the sky. If anything, it was brighter, and he wondered just how much of the city was in flames. Finally, he again spoke. "We sorely need someone in New York at this time. Someone who can not only live among the British, but someone who will be accepted by them."

The lieutenant released a long, drawn-out breath. Short of actually joining the British army, he couldn't imagine how to accomplish that. "That will take some doing," he mused, his brow creased in a frown.

"Indeed it will," Washington agreed. "It is not an easy thing I ask of you. Take some time to think about it."

There was no hesitation. "I don't need any time, sir. I'll leave tonight."

Washington nodded in approval. "I'm not sure how long we can hold our position here, but at any rate we will soon be crossing the river to winter at Morristown. You will be able to reach me there." He held out his hand. "Good luck, my friend. And God go with you."

Chapter Two

From Gillian's Diary:

> *September 22, 1776*
> *It is worse than I feared. The fire destroyed fully a quarter of Manhattan. Chimneys sit amid a pile of ashes where once hundreds of houses stood. Makeshift tents are already being erected. With winter soon to be here, one wonders how these people will survive. Not content with the devastation wrought upon our city, the British have been cutting down with ruthless force any man who looks suspicious to them. Nor is the carnage likely to end soon. This morning a gibbet was erected in front of the Dove Tavern, and a young patriot was hung. His name was Nathan Hale.*

The carriage rolled slowly down the cobbblestone street. In deference to the overcast and chilly day both Katie and Gillian were wearing heavy wool shawls.

Katie snapped the reins, urging the horse to a faster walk. The sooner they got there, she reasoned, the sooner they could go home again. She had tried to dissuade Gillian from making this trip, but, as usual, Gillian would have her own way. She turned to look at Gillian, seated beside her.

"Your grandmother's not going to like this," she grumbled, giving vent to her own unease.

"There's no reason she has to know," Gillian replied, not sounding the least bit concerned. "And if she does discover that we've left the house, I'll tell her you and I went shopping."

That occasioned a laugh. "On a day like this? With public hangings and half the city in ashes?" Katie couldn't for a moment accept that Alice would believe a tale like that.

Gillian grimaced. She knew that crowds had gathered in front of the Dove Tavern, and she wondered how many had cheered to see the death of a brave young man whose only crime was that he believed in the freedom of his country.

"Not so unusual, after all," she finally muttered darkly. "With the British back in the city, there will be the usual round of parties. Entertaining is one thing they seem to do very well."

Both young women fell silent as they reached the burnt ruins.

Feeling a great sense of loss, Gillian climbed down from the carriage. It was a depressing sight that greeted her eye.

Trinity Church was gutted. From Whitehall Slip to Broad Way and continuing west to St. Paul's Chapel, the fire had consumed everything in its path. Except for the brick chimneys, there literally was nothing left. Gray ash covered the ground, swirling and eddying like leaves in an autumn breeze.

"I didn't realize it would be this bad," Katie murmured, coming to stand beside Gillian.

The area was far from deserted. Men, women and even children sifted through the ruins, presumably hoping to find at least some of their possessions. Canvas tents were being affixed to what remained of the chimneys in an effort to provide at least a semblance of shelter.

"How could this have happened?" Gillian lamented.

There was no answer, and Gillian knew it. Whether the fire had happened by accident or intent, it hardly mattered now. In the midst of her despair was a core of furious anger, frustrating because she did not know where or at whom it should be directed.

Plunging a hand beneath her shawl, Katie removed a handkerchief from the pocket of her apron and held it to her nose. There were bodies among the ruins, and the stench was beginning to be noticeable. The bodies were, for the most part, not those victims who had perished in the fire. Rather, they were those unfortunates whom the British saw fit to execute for acting in a suspicious manner.

"Have you seen enough?"

Solemnly, Gillian nodded. She wanted to weep, yet her eyes were dry with a despair that went beyond tears. "Let's go home. There's nothing we can do here."

Gratefully, Katie followed her mistress back to the carriage.

Helene Lehr

They had gone only a few blocks when a flash of color caught Gillian's eye, and she turned to see a woman crawling from an alley. Though crawling was not the right word. She was on her stomach, propelling herself forward with her elbows.

Even as Gillian watched, the woman slumped down and lay still.

With a gasp, Gillian started to leave the carriage. Swallowing the muttered oath that rose up in her throat, Katie tugged on the reins with all her strength, only barely halting the horse before Gillian jumped to the ground.

Now grumbling openly, Katie quickly wrapped the reins around the post that held the whip, sighing deeply when she saw that Gillian was not injured. Aside from the fact that she was truly fond of her mistress, Katie had no desire to face the wrath of Alice Wharton. For some reason, entirely inexplicable to her, Alice Wharton was not beyond blaming her granddaughter's maid for the wrongdoings of her granddaughter. It was as if, because she was two years older, Katie should know better.

"As if I have a say," she muttered to herself. Gillian was like a fast-moving stream; one had to be quick to follow the sudden twists and turns.

Gillian was kneeling beside the prone figure. "She's alive." Gingerly, using her thumb and forefinger, Gillian took hold of the woman's wrist and couldn't prevent a shudder at the sight of the hand she was viewing. It needed only a glance to tell that the other hand was in the same condition. Both palms were scorched, in some spots so severely the skin was burned to the bone.

Katie knelt beside Gillian, then frowned deeply as she saw the woman's torn clothing. She pushed the skirt higher and drew a sharp breath. "This one's

The Passionate Rebel

had more than fire to contend with."

Gillian had been trying to bandage one of the woman's hands with her handkerchief and only now glanced down. The woman's underclothes were gone, torn off probably, and her inner thighs were streaked with blood. Hastily, Gillian pulled down the skirt. Made of peach grosgrain, it had several deep rents in it and was blackened in places by soot.

"Help me, Katie. We can't leave her here."

Between the two of them, they managed to carry the woman to the carriage. Though she moaned once or twice, she did not appear to be fully conscious.

"You can't take her back to the house," Katie said when they were finally on their way again. "Your grandmother would know for sure where you were, and she forbade you to come down here."

Gillian sighed, knowing the truth of that. She had no wish to be confined to her room, possibly for days. That was her grandmother's favorite form of punishment. Then she brightened. "We'll take her to the Blue Swan. Edwina will know what to do."

Katie nodded, and some of the tension left her body at that suggestion. She had a great deal of respect for Edwina Carmody. Unlike Gillian, Edwina possessed more than her fair share of common sense. And she was discreet enough not to mention her sister's disobedience to their grandmother.

The streets were filled with soldiers; they far outnumbered the civilians. Gillian frowned and turned away when she saw several blue-coated Hessians emerging from a grogshop. If she despised the British, Gillian absolutely loathed the soldiers the King had imported from Germany. All of them were fierce-looking men who spoke in a gutteral language not even the British could understand.

Katie turned up Berkley and drove the carriage

to the rear of the tavern. Before they could alight, Edwina came out onto the porch. Though she was four years older than Gillian, she was a full inch shorter, with chestnut-brown hair that was now barely visible beneath her white cap.

"Gillian? Where have you . . . ?" She gave a gasp as she spied the woman. "Good heavens," she exclaimed. She moved quickly forward to assist Gillian and Katie.

The combined efforts of the three of them made it an easy task to lift the woman. Inside, however, at the foot of the narrow stairs, they were defeated, and Edwina had to summon Thomas to help them. The woman was slim, thin almost, but she was a deadweight. Thomas easily lifted her in his arms and took her to a rear bedroom on the second floor.

"Katie, heat a basin of water and fetch some clean cloths," Edwina instructed, shooing her husband from the room.

Carefully, so as not to touch her burned hands, Edwina and Gillian undressed the young woman. She was beginning to stir now and gave indication of returning to her senses.

"Oh, God," Edwina murmured, seeing the blood-streaked thighs.

Claudia Dunham opened eyes that were a startling shade of green, fringed by thick, short lashes as black as her hair. For a moment, she stared blankly, then gave a cry of fright. She began to strike out wildly, and Gillian grabbed her wrists.

"It's all right," she said. "You're safe now."

Gradually, Claudia quieted, though she still regarded them with wariness. When Gillian released her hold, Claudia moaned as a new pain made itself known. Gingerly, she went to put a hand beneath her breast, but Edwina's hand was faster.

The Passionate Rebel

"You've at least one broken rib," she declared with a shake of her head. "Gillian, help her to sit up. I'm going to have to wrap her tightly."

Just then, Katie entered carrying a basin of water and with strips of white cloth draped over her arm. Gillian took the basin and placed it on one of the bedside tables. Edwina grabbed the cloths. Quickly and efficiently, she bound the woman's rib cage, then eased her back on the pillow. With a gentle touch, she then began to sponge off the blood.

"I'll get a nightgown for you," Edwina said as she finally drew the quilt up over the woman's naked body. "First, let's tend to those hands." As she worked, Edwina glanced down. Despite her disheveled state, the woman was lovely. "What's your name?"

"Claudia Dunham." She winced as Edwina fastened the bandage at the wrist.

"Would you like to tell us what happened?"

The green eyes flew open as the memory of the fire came rushing to her mind, producing a sickening awareness. She let out a thin, keening wail that sent a shiver down Gillian's spine.

"It's all right," Edwina tried to soothe. "You don't have to speak of it now."

Helplessly, Gillian and Edwina watched as the woman began to sob uncontrollably. There was little they could do until she regained control of herself.

At last, sheer exhaustion overcame her. She seemed to have lost the strength even to sob, though the tears still streamed from her closed eyes.

Edwina looked across the bed at Gillian. "Where did you find her?"

"In an alley off Broad Way. Obviously, she was caught in the fire. Either she made her own way out, or she was carried out by someone."

"There were three of them...." Claudia's voice was ragged, and she began to cough. The effects of the smoke and her own screams had combined to produce a throat that was excruciatingly sore.

Edwina motioned to Katie. "Go downstairs and tell Ella to heat some broth. You make a cup of tea and put a heavy dollop of honey in it."

Edwina and Gillian sat in an uneasy silence until Katie returned. Claudia was quiet, her eyes closed again. However, it was obvious that she was not asleep. Her lovely face held an expression that suggested she was reliving a nightmare.

"Put the tray on the bedside table," Edwina instructed Katie. Going to a chest in a corner of the room, she removed another pillow, then went back to Claudia. Raising Claudia's shoulders, she plumped the two pillows. Holding the cup of tea to the pale lips, she said, "Try to drink some of this. It will ease your throat."

Claudia dutifully sipped, and hunger was suddenly a gnawing reminder that she had not eaten for the better part of two days.

When the tea was gone, Edwina began to offer the broth, a spoonful at a time. Claudia could not hold the bowl or the spoon, but Edwina patiently fed her until this, too, was gone.

"Is there someone we can notify of your whereabouts?" Edwina asked when the bowl was empty. "Do you have a husband?"

Claudia shook her head. "My husband was killed at Brooklyn Heights. And my mother and my son died in the fire." She was strangely calm now. The pain in her hands was becoming more acute, a throbbing, searing ache that she felt up to her elbows. Claudia almost welcomed the pain, feeling as though it was a retribution for her failure to

The Passionate Rebel

save her baby. It was an atonement, and she bore it stoically.

"How did you come to be in the alley?" Gillian asked hesitantly, fearful of setting off another outburst of hysterics.

"The fire ... It happened so fast." In a halting voice, Claudia proceeded to relate the fate of her mother and son. "The heat was unbearable," she went on. "I finally got to my feet and started to run away from it. There was so much noise and confusion. A soldier grabbed hold of me and began to propel me along. At first I thought he was trying to help me. But when we were a few blocks away from the fire, he dragged me into the alley. Somewhere along the way, two more soldiers joined us. They threw me to the ground and they ... they took turns." She gave a strangled sob.

"Hush." Edwina wet a cloth in the water, wrung it out and mopped Claudia's brow, now dampened with perspiration. "That's enough. What you need now is rest. Try to sleep. I'll look in on you from time to time."

Quietly, Edwina, Gillian and Katie filed from the room and went downstairs. At the back door, Gillian turned to her sister, and her face was flushed with fury.

"I knew the redcoats were despicable," she said through clenched teeth. "But I hadn't realized what bast—"

"Gillian! That won't help matters," Edwina admonished. She sighed. "Not that I don't agree with you, but your careless words could easily get us all hung." She placed a hand on her sister's slim shoulder. "Don't worry about Claudia. Despite what she's gone through, she's strong and appears healthy. She can stay here until she's fully recovered."

Helene Lehr

"Will that be all right with Thomas?" Gillian asked worriedly.

Edwina patted her shoulder. "Thomas is a good man. He will do what needs to be done."

Over the ensuing weeks, Gillian visited Claudia at least once a day. Physically, her recovery was steady, if slow. But her spirit seemed crushed, her will to live a mere flickering flame that threatened on more than one occasion during those first days to extinguish itself from sheer lethargy.

Chapter Three

From Gillian's Diary:

> *January 4, 1777*
> *We have suffered one crushing defeat after another. White Plains, Fort Washington, and Fort Lee are now in British hands, as is the entire state of Rhode Island. More than 2500 American soldiers have been taken prisoner.*

Snow covered Manhattan. Though the sky was clear and sunny, producing a dazzling brilliance that hurt the eye, the wind had a bite to it.

Gillian drew her cloak closer about her as she made her way to the tavern. She avoided the orchard because the snow was too deep.

She was almost there when a wagon pulled abreast of her. Pausing, Gillian smiled shyly at the man who was driving it.

Robbie Clayton jumped agilely from the front seat. He was a tall lean man of 29 with curly brown hair worn unfashionably short. Gillian had known Rob all her life, though by the time she was ten, he was a man grown and married. His wife had died in childbirth, the baby stillborn. Rob had never married again. It was a loss from which he had never recovered.

Gillian glanced at the firewood piled high in the rear of the wagon. "That will be most welcome," she noted.

"It brings a good price," he responded, then frowned. "But with the roads closed and guarded as they are, it will soon be in short supply."

Gillian gave him a perplexed look. "How can that be? The country is heavily wooded."

"Now," he agreed. "Unfortunately, each day we are going farther and farther afield for trees to cut down. Both the British and the Continentals are cutting them down one after another. Once a tree is cut, it's gone. This winter hasn't been too bad so far, but if we get a hard one next year, I fear wood will grow scarce." He grinned down at her. "You got the prettiest eyes I ever did see."

In spite of the cold, her cheeks warmed to pink. "You always say that, Robbie."

"Only because it's true," he responded cheerfully. "Ahh, if you were only ten years older, I might marry you."

"I'm almost eighteen," Gillian retorted primly.

He nodded. "Which, by my calculations, makes you seventeen right now."

Gillian's soft lips tipped up in a smile. She couldn't refute that. She stared at the man before her. While she might have the prettiest eyes he'd ever seen, he had the nicest face she'd ever seen. It was calm;

The Passionate Rebel

there was no other word she could use to describe it. His brown eyes were, perhaps, a bit sad as they viewed a world not quite up to his expectations. Gillian couldn't ever remember seeing Rob angry. It was as if he knew the deficiencies of people and automatically made allowances.

Gillian sniffed, aware that he was still viewing her with what she considered to be an amused smile. It annoyed her that Rob always treated her like a child. Though she had been just last year, she wasn't now, and she wondered why he didn't notice it. "At what age do you suppose a girl becomes a woman?"

"I'd say that varies from female to female," he answered with a grin.

"And, in your opinion, I've not yet attained that exalted state?" She spoke huffily and tossed her head in what she was certain was a provocative way.

Throwing back his head, Rob laughed. It was not the reaction Gillian had hoped for, and she frowned at this display of untoward hilarity.

Seeing her expression, he immediately sobered, but his mouth still twitched with repressed amusement. "Not yet, you little vixen," he said finally. Then he grew serious. "However, I have an idea that it won't be long. One day soon, you'll begin a trail of broken hearts, Gillian Winthrop."

Turning from her, he began to unload some of the wood, carrying it to the back of the tavern.

Gillian followed. She was still miffed, but she couldn't stay angry with Rob for any length of time.

The walkway from the street to the back door had been shoveled clear of snow, though treacherous patches of ice glinted beneath the sun, and Gillian made her way carefully.

Helene Lehr

When he had stacked the wood in a neat pile, Robbie straightened and looked about with a careful eye.

"Do you have any news?" he asked in a low voice.

Gillian sighed. "Not a thing." She brightened. "However, Tom has a bag of coins for you to take on your next trip." Her brother-in-law faithfully set aside one of every ten coins he received from the British as his contribution to the cause.

"Good. The Continentals need all the money they can get. When the army evacuated Fort Lee, they were forced to leave behind their cannon, their blankets and much of their food." He gave a short laugh. "I wonder what General Howe would say if he knew British gold was finding its way to Washington's army."

"Who cares what he thinks," Gillian retorted heatedly, then lowered her voice to a whisper. "Did you see General Washington on your last trip?"

"I did, indeed. Have you heard what happened at Trenton?" When she shook her head, he spoke with unabashed pride and enthusiasm. "They caught the Hessians napping on Christmas day. The Americans crossed the Delaware late at night. It was no easy journey, I can tell you. The river was clogged with ice, the snow so thick they couldn't even see the banks."

Gillian frowned in an attempt to picture the whole army trying to cross the river at once, dodging ice floes in the blinding snow. "Why didn't the general wait until the weather cleared?"

"Because it had to be on Christmas night," Rob explained. "You see, to the Hessians, Christmas is a festive occasion. They party all day long to celebrate it, and the general knew this."

Gillian couldn't quite imagine people partying on

The Passionate Rebel

Christmas, but she said, "Well, thank goodness they all got across safely."

"That they did. Thanks to the regiment of fishermen from Marblehead. That's in Massachusetts," he added in answer to her unspoken question. "Those men know how to handle their boats in all kinds of weather." Rob gave a short laugh. "The Hessians were so drunk they never knew what hit them. Their Colonel Rall was killed. Lord Cornwallis was already on board a ship scheduled to sail for England within the hour, but when he heard of our victory at Trenton, he went scuttling back to Brunswick."

Gillian smiled in delight. "You think it will be over soon?"

"Of course." The words were spoken with quiet confidence. "The British have already lost the war; they just refuse to admit it." He glanced toward the street and saw two redcoats passing by. "I'd better get going. I'll stop by on my way home to pick up the coins."

As she entered the warm and cheery kitchen a short while later, Gillian sniffed appreciatively at the delicious aroma of freshly baked bread, which Edwina was just now removing from the bake oven.

In a corner of the room, a young black woman sat on a stool, working the butter churn. Her name was Mandy, and she was a black indentured servant Thomas had recently acquired to help Edwina, now pregnant with her first child.

Gillian removed her cloak, then frowned when she saw her sister hoist a heavy cast-iron pot from the trivet.

"Where is Ella?" she asked, as she dropped her cloak over the back of a chair. Stepping forward, she took the pot from Edwina's grasp and placed it atop the stove.

"Packing," came the short reply. "She's going back to live with her sister in Savannah."

Gillian gave a sound of disgust. "She can't leave you now."

Edwina shrugged and wiped her hands on a towel. "She's a free woman." Seeing Gillian's scowling expression, she asked, "Do you know the MacNievers?"

Gillian thought. "Yes. That is to say I've met Mary MacNiever. She's a friend of Ella's."

"A close one," Edwina said with a nod of her head. "Last night, her husband Ned was tarred and feathered." She folded the towel and placed it on the rim of the sink.

Gillian put a hand to her lips. "Oh, no! What happened?"

"Someone painted an *R* on their front door. Rebels or not, the whole family's been run out of town."

"Were they rebels?"

Edwina shrugged again. "If they were, they didn't go around telling anyone about it. That's a thing best kept quiet in this city."

"Maybe I can talk to her," Gillian said, heading for the stairs.

"Talk all you like," Edwina called after her. "It'll do no good. She's made up her mind."

Ella Bishop was indeed packing. When Gillian entered her room, the woman was removing her clothes from the wardrobe and stuffing them none too neatly into her worn portmanteau.

"I'm so sorry to hear about what happened to your friends," Gillian said. She bent over to pick up a shawl that had fallen to the floor.

Ella paused a moment to look at her. "They were no more rebels than I am."

The Passionate Rebel

"Do you know what happened?" She put the shawl on the bed.

The woman closed the doors of the now empty wardrobe. "'Course I know. Ned had a fight with one of his neighbors. Those two been on poor terms for years now. Never could agree on anything. Last week, they got into one hell-raiser of a fight."

"And you think it was this man who painted the *R* on the MacNievers' door?"

"Who else?"

Gillian correctly assumed that Ella Bishop was afraid. Yet where, in these perilous times, could one find a haven of absolute safety? "Will you be coming back?" she asked after a moment.

"I doubt it." Her movements brisk, Ella began to clear the dressing table of her personal toiletries. "Things are only going from bad to worse. A woman's not safe in the streets anymore."

Gillian bit her lip. She couldn't understand why Ella was leaving New York. The woman had always seemed to favor the British. "I . . . thought you were a loyalist."

Ella made a sound of annoyance. "You and your family think everyone's either a loyalist or a patriot." She paused long enough to view Gillian with a stern eye. "That's not true. There are a lot of people like me who just want to live in peace. It never used to be like this. The soldiers never bothered us before." She retrieved the shawl Gillian had placed on the bed, folded it and packed it away.

"Ella, you must stay," Gillian pleaded. "My sister needs you."

Although Ella looked uncomfortable, her jaw was set at a stubborn angle. "I don't deny that. Still and all, I'm going home. At least until this is all over. Somebody paints an *R* on your door, and you're done for. A person can't live that way. It's unnatural." She secured the straps on the portmanteau. "The coach leaves in an hour. I'm going to be on it!"

Quickly, as if fearful that Gillian would persist, she donned her cloak and picked up the portmanteau.

Watching her leave, Gillian sighed. "Good luck to you," she called half-heartedly.

"Nowadays we all need a healthy dose of that," the woman muttered without turning.

Gillian followed at a slower pace. Downstairs, she went to see if Thomas needed assistance. Seeing that the taproom was not yet busy, she went to help Edwina in the kitchen.

Later that day, Gillian again went upstairs, this time carrying a tray with Claudia's supper on it. Mandy usually did this in the morning and afternoon, but Gillian had fallen into the habit of bringing Claudia her evening meal. Though Claudia was six years older than Gillian, the two of them had become fast friends.

Halfway across the room, Gillian paused in surprise when she saw that Claudia was not in bed. Wearing a robe over her nightgown, she was sitting in a chair. Her hair had been freshly washed and shone blue-black. Gillian suspected Edwina's ministrations, for Claudia had shown a shocking lack of interest in her appearance.

"What are you doing out of bed?" Gillian put the tray on a table and viewed her friend in concern. In the glow from the single lamp, Claudia's face was pale. Despite the chill in the room, beads of perspiration dotted her white brow.

"I felt well enough to get up, but I had no idea I

was so weak." With a sigh, she leaned back in the chair.

"Of course you are." Gillian grabbed one of the blankets from the bed. "You must take it slowly." She arranged the blanket across Claudia's lap and wrapped it around her lower limbs. "After more than three months in bed, you cannot expect to jump up and immediately have your full strength."

Claudia sighed. "I've imposed on your family long enough." She smiled weakly and viewed Gillian with as much fondness as she could muster from her now empty heart. "God knows what would have happened to me if you hadn't come along. As soon as my strength returns, I will leave."

"Where will you go?"

Claudia shrugged. "It doesn't matter." Raising her hands, she viewed her scarred palms, the only outward sign of her ordeal. Her ribs had mended, and though she had bled for days after the cruel assault on her womanhood, that, too, had finally healed. At first, she had wanted to die. Her young, strong body had refused her that solace. But though she was alive and her body healed, Claudia had neither forgiven nor forgotten.

"If I can ever repay them, I will," she murmured, letting her hands fall to her lap again.

Gillian was uncertain as to whether Claudia was referring to the Carmodys or the British. She decided not to ask. She moved the small table on which she had placed the tray closer to Claudia.

"Eat the soup before it cools," she urged, nodding in satisfaction when Claudia dutifully picked up the bowl and began to spoon the broth into her mouth. She ate mechanically, without seeming to taste it.

When she was done, Claudia put the empty bowl back on the tray, but waved aside the pie Gillian held out to her. "I'll eat it later," she murmured.

Gillian put the plate down again. "Claudia," she said slowly, "I know that Tom will employ you in the tavern. He's already said you can stay here, have this room for your own. And Lord knows we can use the help now that Edwina is pregnant." At Claudia's doubtful look, Gillian reached out and touched her shoulder. "Even if you want to go elsewhere, you'll need some money."

Claudia looked up at her. "It's just that the thought of serving those redcoats... Maybe one of them might be the one who attacked me!" She shook her head. "And the horrible thing is that I wouldn't even know it. I can't remember what any of them looked like."

Gillian clasped her hands at her waist and walked to the window. It had begun to snow again, giving the landscape a curious luminosity that was at odds with the lateness of the hour.

"I admit that to wait on them does not sit well with me either," Gillian admitted finally. She turned her head slightly and gave Claudia a sidelong look. "But you know, Claudia, tea drinkers though they are, the British consume oceans of rum." She giggled. "For the most part they handle it badly. It loosens not only their inhibitions but their tongues as well."

Looking up, Claudia viewed her with sudden interest. She wasn't smiling. Instead she was staring at Gillian intently. "You mean they speak of things they shouldn't?"

"Exactly. And the Continentals can only benefit from such indiscretions."

Claudia looked confused. "But how do you pass such information along to them?"

Moving from the window, Gillian sank to her

The Passionate Rebel

knees in front of Claudia and spoke in a whisper, though they were quite alone in the room.

"There are more patriots in New York than you think. One of them is a farmer named Kiley Clayton, who lives a few miles outside of the city. Once or twice a week he sends his son Rob into town with a wagonload of produce or firewood. On those occasions when either Tom or I have any worthwhile news, Edwina opens the shutter on the front bedroom. That is the signal for him to stop at the tavern."

"Isn't it dangerous?"

Gillian sobered. "The danger is there, yes," she agreed, pursing her lips. Then she viewed Claudia in all seriousness. "But someone has to do it. The time for ambiguity is over. One either supports the cause, or one does not. If the Continentals can risk their lives for what they believe in, I can do no less."

Claudia leaned back in the chair, considering this. Her heart-shaped face, so long expressionless, now seemed to harden with a purpose that Gillian did not understand. Her hands gripped the arms of the chair until the knuckles whitened. They were fine hands, slender, with tapered fingers. The backs held no signs of the scars Gillian knew etched the palms with ribbed unevenness, puckering in spots with angry color.

"Claudia?" Gillian murmured uncertainly, growing alarmed by the intense look she was seeing.

"You pick up this information just by listening?" Claudia asked at last.

"Yes," Gillian responded, then gave a short laugh. "Sometimes it helps to flirt with them. It's amazing how gullible some of them can be."

A thoughtful gleam came into Claudia's eyes. "I'll wager a man's tongue would loosen even more if he had his head on a woman's pillow," she mused.

Gillian blinked. Her mouth fell open in shock as she realized what Claudia was saying. "Oh, no! Don't even think like that!"

Claudia sat up straight again, mouth grim. "But I *am* thinking like that." She stared at Gillian, who was still kneeling on the floor in front of her.

Gillian thought of those women with the sad eyes, yet in Claudia's green eyes she saw no sadness. She saw something worse—hate. The force of it made her shudder. "But what if it's one of them?" she cried. "How would you know?"

Claudia shook her head sharply. "One thing I do know—none of them were officers. And if one wanted information, they would surely be the best source." A sudden excitement caused her eyes to sparkle with animation. "Oh, Gillian, you've given me a reason to live again."

Dismayed, Gillian felt herself being embraced. She felt sure that neither Tom nor Edwina would approve of this. She also knew that New York teemed with whores. The soldiers seemed to attract them like moths to a flame.

Claudia got shakily to her feet, and Gillian assisted her back to bed.

"You tell Tom I'll be ready to go to work before another week passes."

"Claudia, you can't do this," Gillian protested. In her frustration, she wrung her hands. This whole thing was impossible. "What would your family think?"

"I have no family. Not anymore," she added grimly as she pulled up the blanket. Seeing Gillian's expression, she sighed, and her expression softened. "Don't worry. I will be very selective."

That didn't appease Gillian. Selective? she thought

with a small shudder. Was a whore less a whore if she was selective? "But if you should ever decide to marry again..."

"Marry?" Claudia sounded incredulous, and the short laugh that followed was no less so. "Who would marry me now?" She sank back against the pillow and closed her eyes, as if to put an end to the debate.

Shoulders slumped, Gillian turned away.

For the second time that day, Gillian left a room in defeat. Her step was slow as she descended the stairs. Laughter and singing combined to produce a discordant sound that blanketed the taproom.

The noise went unnoticed by Gillian as she reached the hall and headed to the rear of the building. Why had she ever brought up the subject of spying? she wondered, chewing her lower lip. And yet, how could she possibly have known what Claudia's reaction would be? Gillian shivered in distaste at just the thought of having one of those soldiers touch her in an intimate way.

In the kitchen again, Gillian sent Mandy on a hastily contrived errand that drew a perplexed look from Edwina. When they were alone, she told Edwina of her conversation with Claudia.

Gillian waited, certain that her news would cause an immediate reaction. Much to her surprise, her sister was silent for several minutes.

"It is not for us to judge her," Edwina said finally in a curiously detached voice. "Claudia's been through a lot, and I know her well enough by now to know that she has a very determined nature. She feels she must strike out, and this is the only way open to her." Seeing Gillian's dismayed look, Edwina smiled softly. "Perhaps, when the time actually comes, she will be unable to go through with her plans."

Having said that, Edwina did not for a moment believe her own words. She rested a hand on her still-flat abdomen, and instinctively she knew the extent of Claudia's loss.

Chapter Four

From Gillian's Diary:

> *November 2, 1777*
> *The war grows ugly. Less than two months ago an incident of such savagery took place I am hard pressed to believe that civilized men could so conduct themselves. On the night of September 20th, a regiment of Hessians under the command of British Major General Charles Grey attacked the Americans where they were encamped at Paoli. Outnumbered and overwhelmed, the Continentals tried to surrender. General Grey ignored their raised hands, ignored the fact that they had thrown down their weapons and were defenseless. What followed was sheer butchery. Grey's men indulged themselves in an orgy of slaughter that resulted*

in the death of more than 300 Americans on the battlefield.

The Blue Swan hummed with noisy activity. In deference to the increased business he was doing, Thomas had hired two more barmaids. One thing about the British: they paid in coin. Conversely, Congress had begun to print paper money called continentals. When funds ran short, they printed more. It was becoming so worthless, even patriots were disinclined to take it in payment. Very little of the paper currency, however, found its way to British-held Manhattan, and when it did, it was disdainfully torn to shreds.

Gillian walked to the bar and gave her order to Tom. Eighteen now, her body had matured into a well-rounded slimness that caused many a man to cast a second glance at her. These days, she usually worked in the taproom only in the early evening, when an extra hand was welcome. Claudia, together with Delia and Chastity, the two new barmaids, easily handled the trade the rest of the time.

"Here, Gillian," Tom said, putting the pewter mugs on the tray.

Gillian took the tray to a table occupied by three men, two of whom were officers. Both Colonel Harcroft and Captain Bennicot were regulars. The third man was a civilian, a stranger whom she had never seen before. He was handsome in a rugged sort of way. She couldn't tell what color his hair was because he was wearing a white powdered wig. Judging from his brows, however, she guessed it to be dark. He was dressed rather flamboyantly, his blue brocade jacket embroidered along the edges with silver thread. As she approached, she heard Colonel Harcroft speak.

The Passionate Rebel

"And you, Mr. Meredith?" he was saying to the civilian. "Were you here during the occupation?"

The man raised a hand, as if to fend off the very thought. "No. I would not set foot in New York until the rebels left." His expression grew hard as he added, "And if they return, I will once again take my leave."

"Oh, don't worry about that," the colonel said smoothly. "Just the sight of our cavalry sent the rebels into such a panic, they were climbing over each other in their haste to leave." As he spoke, his thumb brushed against the neat mustache that covered his upper lip. "Believe me, there is no way that a handful of ill-equipped militia can defeat the British Empire."

"I do hope you are right," the man called Meredith murmured with a sigh. He picked up the mug Gillian had placed before him and took a healthy draught.

"Rest assured that His Majesty's forces are here to stay." The colonel spoke soothingly. He looked up at Gillian. "Ah . . . Miss Winthrop! I must say you are a treat for these old eyes." He raised his cup. "To the prettiest barmaid in the colonies."

Gillian smiled saucily at the compliment. "I'll bet you say that to every barmaid you meet." Turning, she regarded Meredith, and the smile faded from her lips to be replaced with a prickle of indignation at the way his insolent gaze slowly traveled the length of her.

"I've not seen you in here before," she said, not bothering to smile.

Leaning back in his chair, Meredith arched a dark brow, viewing her now as though it had been impertinent of her to address him. Quite brazenly, he stared at her. Her beauty had been easy enough to discern at first glance. Now he took the time to study the details. Her mouth was wide, the upper lip narrow and extending beyond her lower lip which was full and luscious. Her eyes exceeded beauty; gray and heavily lashed, they were at once guileless and intelligent, sparked with a light of spirit that set her whole countenance aglow.

"Don't fret, lovely lady," he drawled finally. "I have an idea you will be seeing a lot of me. Now that I know what a delectable dessert is offered at the Blue Swan, you can be certain that I will return again."

A mischievous smile drifted across his mouth, and he gave her a look Gillian assumed was supposed to be admiring. She was not at all charmed, and her expression left no doubt of it. Had he been a redcoat, she would have at least pretended since one did not gain valuable information by being surly. But the man was only a civilian—and a cocky one, at that.

"I'm liable to give you indigestion," she retorted archly.

He leaned forward to tweak her cheek. "A condition I would gladly endure if you were the cause."

Captain Bennicot, an engaging man in his late twenties, let out a delighted chuckle. "My dear Gillian, I advise you not to parry words with Philip Meredith." He patted her arm in a fatherly way that did not for a moment put Gillian off her guard. "He's only recently returned here from England, having received a law degree from Oxford. And, I must add, he is rapidly becoming New York's leading lawyer."

"Really?" Gillian retorted, obviously unimpressed. "And does his license to practice law include a provision for being arrogant and overbearing?" she inquired sweetly.

Bennicot threw back his head and laughed. "That is the first time I've heard those words used to describe you, Philip." He grinned up at Gillian.

The Passionate Rebel

"Most of the ladies find Mr. Meredith incredibly attractive," he confided.

Gillian raised a brow. "Some women are easy to please, Captain Bennicot," she remarked huffily as she walked away.

Her back stiffened as she heard them all burst into laughter with her departure. Gillian had no doubt at all that she was the cause of their merriment, and the idea made her furious.

For the next hour Gillian did her best to ignore Philip Meredith. She didn't exactly know why she did this; she only knew that she felt uncomfortable around him. Those dark eyes seemed to be undressing her, layer by layer.

The supper crowd was beginning to thin now; only the serious drinkers remained, determined to stay until the tavern closed.

Gillian removed her apron. She saw Claudia having an apparently congenial conversation with a British officer, her lovely face wreathed in an animated smile that Gillian knew was only a facade.

She sighed. Claudia had not, as Edwina supposed, changed her mind. She offered herself for information, and though Gillian was reluctant to admit it, the woman did her job very well. Almost every bit of information that had any worth came to them from Claudia; moreover, any money given to her was scornfully dropped in the bag Thomas kept in a cupboard in the kitchen, there to join the funds that eventually made their way to the coffers of the Continental army.

Claudia, Gillian thought as she walked from the room, seemed to have an uncanny knack for choosing the right man at the opportune moment. Weeks, even months would go by before she admitted an officer to her room. More than one of them had tried to talk her into a permanent alliance; Claudia always refused. Oddly, this never seemed to generate any hard feelings on the part of the man. There was an elusive quality about Claudia, a certain charisma that set her apart from other women. So much so, that the men treated her with a degree of respect that was out of proportion to what she was and did. One look from those emerald eyes seemed to entrance most men that felt their impact.

In the hall, Gillian decided to go upstairs to see her sister before going home. Edwina seldom went into the taproom now, dividing her time between the kitchen and caring for her two-month-old daughter.

Edwina was in the bedroom, nursing the baby. The only light came from the blaze in the fireplace.

Gillian smiled as she entered the room. "I was hoping she'd be awake."

"Only barely," Edwina said. Lowering her head, she viewed her daughter with unabashed pride. They had named her Constance.

"She's looking like Tom more and more each day," Gillian noted.

Edwina laughed softly. "That's what Gram says." She wiped a droplet of milk from the corner of the child's mouth, then handed her to Gillian. "She's asleep again."

While Gillian rocked her niece in her arms, Edwina buttoned her bodice. She watched her sister fondly.

"You do that well," she observed. "You ought to get married and have a few of your own." She took the baby again. Crossing the room, she placed her gently in the wooden cradle.

"I don't think I shall ever get married," Gillian declared morosely. Picking up a poker, she stoked the fire. The blaze flared higher.

The Passionate Rebel

Edwina tucked the blankets securely around her daughter. "Melanie Cartwright and her mother have invited you to countless parties," she said. "You always decline. I'm sure if you went, you'd meet a nice young man."

"You sound like Gram," Gillian complained as she propped the poker to the side of the hearth. "The Cartwright house is filled with redcoats and Tories. Just as ours is," she added grumpily. "It's bad enough I have to see them here every day." She paused, then cried, "Oh, Edwina, when do you think this war will be over?"

Edwina sat down again. She viewed Gillian a long moment before she spoke. "What if the British win, Gillian?"

The girl shuddered. "Don't even think like that!" Bending forward, she kissed her sister's brow. "I'm going home now."

Downstairs, she was about to leave; then, on an impulse she could not explain, Gillian went into the taproom again. Perhaps, she reasoned, it could have gotten busy during her absence. Perhaps Tom needed help.

The table occupied by Colonel Harcroft and his party was empty.

Well, she was glad he was gone, Gillian thought as she fetched her cloak. She had enough problems dealing with the redcoats; she certainly didn't need a cocky Tory to complicate matters.

Outside, it had begun to snow. Thick, heavy flakes swirled through the air, prodded by a cold wind. Gillian drew her cloak closer about her and quickened her steps.

In her room a while later, Gillian allowed Katie to help her undress. Then, in her flannel nightgown, she headed for her writing table.

Katie carefully hung Gillian's clothes in the wardrobe. Then she sighed, watching Gillian as she began to write in her diary. What on earth could the girl find to write about? she wondered. No young man came to call on her, and Gillian flatly refused to go to a party unless her grandmother all but dragged her there. And Gillian was so pretty, she thought, with those gray eyes and that mass of golden hair. One would think the girl would turn her attention to finding a husband instead of furthering what she called The Cause. Gillian was fierce in her support of the patriots, a stance that infuriated her grandmother, who was just as ardent in her support of the British.

For herself, Katie didn't care which side won. It was all the same to her.

"Will you be needing me for anything else?" she asked, heading for the door.

Gillian only shook her head, not even noticing when Katie left the room. When she was through, Gillian closed the book, put it in a drawer, then crawled into bed.

She lay there, listening to the sound of the wind. Like an animal in distress, it began to howl around corners, sending the bare branches of trees into a frenzied dance.

Finally, she fell asleep.

The storm raced across Manhattan, dumping a foot of snow in the process. By morning, it had passed, leaving behind a watery blue sky and a landscape studded with crystal icicles that threw out prisms of light beneath a weak sun.

Chapter Five

From Gillian's Diary:

> *February 17, 1778*
> *Last night, a Tory who had infiltrated the encampment at Valley Forge described the horrors he saw there in gleeful tones that chilled my heart. The sufferings of our brave men are not to be believed. Their beds are of straw, their one blanket poor insulation from the bitter cold. Even nature seems to contrive to aid the enemy. More than five feet of snow on the roads has prevented the delivery of life-saving provisions. Food shortage is so severe they are forced to eat the bark of trees, and they faint from weakness on that meager sustenance.*

A bright blaze burned in the great fireplace in the taproom. The structure was of such a height that a man could easily stand upright in it, and it was so wide that it could accommodate the largest of game on its spit and still have room to spare.

Tonight, however, there was was no meat of any kind on the spit. Only huge logs crackled within the hearth, pervading the air with the pungent smell of cedar. That, together with the oil lamps, made it reasonably warm. Nevertheless, windows were lined with silver tracings of frost, and a blast of cold air entered each time the front door opened.

At the far end of the taproom, Claudia was wiping off the table where only minutes ago three British soldiers had eaten.

It had been a long day, and she was glad it was almost over. It was not this busy in the summer. The war seemed to heat up and cool down with the weather. Redcoats were disinclined to leave their warm fires and even warmer mistresses during the winter months. Claudia suspected they hoped that nature would defeat the rebels.

A sharp gust of wind rattled the windows, and she paused, looking up from her task.

Maybe they were right, she reflected moodily. A dog couldn't survive out there on a night like this. What chance did a man have, even fired with his convictions?

Her attention returned to the table she was cleaning.

"Pigs are cleaner than these two-legged swine," she muttered under her breath. The rag she was using was hopelessly mired in ale and gravy. She couldn't imagine how the combination had gotten from tankard and bowl to the tabletop. Of course, they were drunk, as usual. She seriously doubted the British did anything but drink and eat and rut. From

The Passionate Rebel

their generals to the meanest foot soldier, they were all alike.

Glancing down at the floor, Claudia grimaced. Heaven only knew what that mess was. That would have to wait.

Claudia stacked the dishes and tankards on a tray and now hoisted it.

She was about to take the tray into the kitchen, when she paused, seeing Captain Bennicot just now coming into the taproom. He stood there a moment, stamping his booted feet and brushing the snow from the shoulders of his cloak. Another man was with him, but Claudia paid him no mind.

With a thoughtful look, she motioned to Gillian, who immediately came to her side.

"Isn't that the young captain who is always with Colonel Harcroft?"

Unobtrusively, Gillian's eyes sought the man in question.

"Yes," she said in a low voice, then caught her lip in her lower teeth. "Come to think of it, I haven't seen the colonel in here for more than two weeks now."

The tray was growing heavy, and Claudia shifted it so that its weight was on her other arm. "Why don't you see what you can find out?" she suggested.

Gillian nodded as Claudia proceeded on her way. She was halfway to the table when she noticed the man with Captain Bennicot was Philip Meredith. Since that night in November, some three months ago, she had not seen him and had no desire to do so now.

She was about to turn around and let Claudia wait on them, but it was too late. Captain Bennicot had caught her eye and was now beckoning to her.

"Gillian, my sweet!" he called out cheerfully. "You

53

have a customer who is about to expire from thirst."

Resigned, Gillian moved forward. Neither of them wanted supper. Both of them ordered rum, and Gillian went to get it.

When she returned a few minutes later, she smiled invitingly at the captain. He had removed his hat, and his unpowdered brown hair was tousled. He would have been handsome, Gillian thought, if it wasn't for a slightly receding chin and ears that were a bit too prominent.

"I haven't seen Colonel Harcroft lately," she said, putting his drink in front of him. "I hope he's not ill." She fluttered her lashes and toyed with the fichu tucked into the neck of her lime green bodice. "He's one of my favorite customers. So polite, and always such a gentleman." Her gaze flicked over Philip Meredith. Onyx eyes were viewing her with that air of arrogance she had noticed the first time she had seen him. A thoroughly British trait, she thought to herself, wrinkling her nose and turning away.

The captain grinned up at her and took a sip of his rum. It was obvious to Gillian that this was not his first drink of the evening.

"I can personally assure you that the colonel enjoys the best of health," he declared expansively. "He had to leave town for a few days. Orders, you understand."

Gillian pouted prettily. "I don't believe you. No doubt he's at Fraunces Tavern."

"Oh, no!" Bennicot raised a hand to partially cover his mouth, but didn't bother to lower his voice. "Have you ever seen their barmaids?" he asked with a smile that didn't make it past a leer. "Believe me, there's no competition." He got to his feet, putting a hand on the table to steady himself. Then he draped

The Passionate Rebel

an arm about her shoulder. Gillian tried not to recoil from the rum-sodden breath as the captain whispered in her ear. "If you can keep a secret, my lovely, the colonel went to join General Howe in Philadelphia."

Gillian sniffed and appeared disinterested as she deftly eluded the unwanted embrace. At that moment, she happened to glance at Meredith, startled to see the smoldering expression in his dark eyes.

For a moment, Gillian was at a loss. His large, strong hand was wrapped around his pewter cup so tightly, Gillian wouldn't have been at all surprised if it got bent out of shape. That he was upset was easy to see, but about what? And why was he staring at her as if he wanted to throttle her?

Then Gillian suddenly realized the meaning of the look she was seeing. Meredith was angered with the captain for revealing his superior's whereabouts. She would, she decided, edging away to a safe distance, have to be more careful when Philip Meredith was around.

"Pretty little wench, isn't she?" Bennicot commented when Gillian was out of earshot.

That she was, Philip thought to himself, taking a sip of his drink. And a flirtatious one, as well. His jaw tightened as he watched her lithe figure flitting from table to table. Surely her hips didn't move like that of their own accord.

Philip gave himself a mental shake, annoyed with his own reactions. Why the hell should he care if she went around wiggling her hips and batting her lashes at every man in her path?

A low growl of exasperation escaped him. Like it or not, the girl stirred something deep within him, something he had not felt in a long time. He had resisted it the first time he had come in here. New York had an excess of taverns, grogshops and barmaids. A man could drown himself in more ways than one in this British stronghold. Still, he had found himself irresistibly drawn back to the Blue Swan.

Bennicot noticed that Philip didn't seem to be able to take his eyes off Gillian. Leaning forward, he tapped Philip's wrist.

"Don't waste your time with that one," he chuckled, then nodded in the direction of Claudia. "See that luscious black-haired beauty? A first-rate whore, I've been told." He sighed and drained his glass. "Trouble is, she's partial to high ranking officers."

Philip had only glanced at Claudia. His attention was centered on Gillian. "Is she indentured?"

"Who?" Bennicot asked, drawing back in some surprise. He'd never heard of an indentured whore.

Philip gave the captain an annoyed look. "The pretty little wench we have been discussing."

Bennicot shook his head. "Oh, no. She's the owner's sister-in-law."

Meredith searched his mind for the owner's name but came up with a blank. The girl's name, however, he remembered—Gillian Winthrop. He had forgotten neither her face nor form.

About an hour later, Gillian saw Captain Bennicot get up and shrug himself into his cloak. After a few words to his companion, he headed unsteadily for the front door, bumping into chairs and people alike on the short journey.

Gillian glanced back at the table, prepared to clear it as soon as Meredith left. Instead, he turned in her direction and snapped his fingers at her.

Snapped his fingers! Gillian felt angry color flood her cheeks. When she didn't move, he did it again,

The Passionate Rebel

this time accompanied by a brusque "You! Come here!"

Who the devil did he think she was, a dockside strumpet?

Gray eyes blazing, Gillian went storming over to his table.

"What is it you want?" she demanded, making no effort to be civil.

He quirked a brow and spoke in a sharper tone than he had intended. He was unused to women treating him as though he were a nuisance.

"You sell food and drink here, don't you? What else would I want?"

"Do you want to see a bill of fare?" Gillian asked in the same tone.

"That won't be necessary." He leaned back in his chair. She was every bit as lovely as he had remembered her to be. For a moment, his eyes rested on the fullness of her breasts beneath the tightly laced corset of her dress. With some effort, he tore his gaze away. "What do you recommend?" he asked finally.

"Dinner at the Fraunces Tavern?" she suggested sweetly.

Philip stared at her a moment, then turned his head to view the table next to him. "What are they eating?"

Gillian followed his gaze. "Oyster stew."

"That's good enough." He pushed the empty pewter mug toward her. "And fill that with hot tea. Put a small amount of rum in it. Not too much, mind!"

Gillian picked up the mug, gave a fleeting thought to bouncing it off his powdered wig, then thought better of it.

She was still seething when she returned to his

table carrying a tray that held the stew, the rum-laced tea and thick slabs of hot bread.

Carefully, she put the bread and tea on the table, then picked up the bowl of oyster stew. As she went to place it before him, Gillian gave a start, feeling a pinch on her well-rounded rump. The stew slopped over, spread across the table and dripped onto Meredith's lap.

Angrily, Gillian turned to confront the man who had pinched her, just in time to see him exit through the front door.

"Do you usually throw the food at your customers?"

She swung her head back to Meredith and, for a moment, stared blankly at the spilled liquid.

"Ohh!" She reached for the towel at her waist and began to mop up the white broth. "I'll get you another..."

Pausing, Gillian watched as he plucked a handkerchief from his pocket and began to apply it to his breeches, mumbling something about clumsy barmaids.

She gritted her teeth. "I said I'll get you another. You needn't act as if I did it on purpose."

"It wouldn't surprise me in the least, if you had," he murmured, still engrossed in the spot on his silk breeches.

She put her hands on her hips. "Count yourself lucky I didn't dump the whole bowl in your lap."

"I thought you had." He dropped the sodden handkerchief on the table as if it were a dirty napkin, then gave her an annoyed look.

With a toss of her head, Gillian turned away, only to find herself impeded when he grabbed her hand.

"On second thought, I'll have whatever fish is available." He glanced down at his sodden breeches.

The Passionate Rebel

"I've had enough oyster stew for this evening."

She jerked her hand away. The tremor she felt when he touched her was just anger, she told herself.

"I'll have it sent to your table," Gillian said stiffly, wanting to put as much distance between this man and herself as she could.

In the kitchen, Gillian checked the pots and pans. "Is there any flounder left?" she asked Mandy, who was drying dishes and stacking them neatly in the cupboard.

"No, ma'am," the girl answered without pausing in her task. "Only got some crab."

Gillian grinned wickedly. "I can't think of anything more appropriate," she muttered under her breath.

Not trusting her temper, Gillian gave the plate to Delia and told her to take it to Philip Meredith's table.

Even so, Gillian caught herself casting covert glances in his direction. He seemed entirely engrossed in his meal.

The third or fourth time she caught herself looking at him, Gillian took herself firmly in hand and resolved not to do it again. Lord knew the last thing she wanted that man to think was that she might be interested in him.

She was, therefore, taken off guard when some 30 minutes later, he suddenly appeared at her side.

"Once I finally got a chance to eat it, the food was very good."

Gillian just eyed him warily.

"My only regret is that I don't have time for . . . ah . . . dessert." He put on his hat, then chucked her under the chin, tilting her face toward him. "Perhaps next time."

Her earlobes felt hot, and Gillian sincerely hoped her cheeks were not crimson.

"I hope there is no next time," she sputtered angrily, jerking her head away from his warm fingertips. That little tremor had again flashed through her with his touch. It seemed to happen each time she got angry with him, and she seemed to be angry each time she talked to him. But then, Tories always provoked that reaction from her.

"Oh, there will be a next time," he countered, and his smile was lazy and infuriatingly confident.

He turned to go, then gave her another glance, as if a thought just struck.

"Oh, by the way. Don't fret if I'm late tomorrow night. Sometimes business delays me more than I would like."

Watching him saunter away, Gillian was now certain that her cheeks were a fiery red.

Fret? she fumed indignantly, gritting her teeth. She wouldn't fret if she never saw that man again. His absence would only inspire relief.

Philip Meredith did return the following night—and the next. Gillian always made certain she was busy, even retreating to the kitchen when it seemed she was the only one left to wait on him.

He said nothing, nor did he make a scene or even seem to notice that it was not Gillian who served him. In some irritation, Gillian watched Delia and Chastity fawn over him. They seemed to vie for turns when it came to his table. She could hear them giggling with delight when he teased them.

"He's a fine one, he is," Delia exclaimed breathlessly one night. Her face was flushed, and her eyes were sparkling as only a woman's can be when she has received a compliment. "He told me my hair was like spun gold."

The Passionate Rebel

Gillian made a face. "Did he?" Involuntarily, her hand went to tuck a strand of her own golden hair back under her cap. As far as she could see, Delia's hair was a light brown. True, it did have a few streaks of yellow in it.

"And he also said," Delia gushed, "that my waist was so tiny, he'd wager his hands could span it with no problem at all."

Gillian sniffed at that. If Delia weighed 90 pounds, it was a lot. Of course her waist was tiny. How foolish could she be? Gillian wondered, feeling unaccountably disgruntled. Nevertheless, she managed to smile in agreement at the happy girl.

As Delia walked away with a light step, Gillian couldn't help casting an irritated glance in Philip Meredith's direction. Annoyingly, he seemed not to notice.

For the rest of that evening, and those that followed, Gillian found herself being unusually curt to anyone who had the misfortune to speak to her.

By the first week in March Gillian had managed to push Philip Meredith to the back of her mind as the break in the weather helped her outlook. While still cold, it was no longer freezing. With satisfaction she noted how the snow melted with each passing day, leaving behind only stubborn patches in shaded areas where the sun had no access.

Less satisfying to Gillian were the signs of increasing privation she saw in her beloved city. Goods were so scarce everyone was making do with what they had.

Even food was in short supply. For as long as Gillian could remember, pigs and goats had freely roamed the streets, eating refuse and garbage. Day by day, Gillian could see the number of animals growing smaller as hunger made itself felt among the less privileged inhabitants of the city.

The refuse grew. So did the garbage.

Chapter Six

From Gillian's Diary:

> *March 30, 1778*
> *How I had hoped that the war would be over by now. Even King Louis of France has acknowledged our independence. Yet, King George remains as stubborn as ever. Surely his Majesty must know by now that the Americans will never retire from the battlefield until they are victorious in their struggle for freedom. Yet he persists, not realizing that an army, no matter how well equipped, cannot fight something as intangible as an ideal and win; for even in defeat the ideal will remain unconquered.*

When Gillian awoke, she was pleased to see the blue cloudless sky. It had been raining, on and off, for the past two days. She and Claudia had decided to go to Hanover Square today, if the weather permitted, and it certainly looked as though it had.

With some haste, Gillian donned a yellow silk gown and was fumbling with the ribbons on her bodice when Katie came in.

"You're up early," she exclaimed, coming forward to assist Gillian.

"Late, actually," Gillian countered. "Claudia and I are going shopping today. I told her that I would be by at nine, and here it is, after ten!"

Katie unbraided Gillian's hair. "I'm sure the shops will still be there," she noted as she picked up a comb.

Gillian bit her lip as she sat down at the dressing table. She knew why she had overslept. It had been past midnight by the time she had finally fallen asleep. She had been thinking about Philip Meredith, wondering where he was. For the past week now, she hadn't seen him. Not that she minded, of course. Frankly, she didn't care if she ever saw him again.

It was just that his departure had been so abrupt. Night after night, he had been in the Blue Swan; then, suddenly, he was gone.

Business? she wondered. What kind of business would take a lawyer out of town?

Or had he finally realized that she wanted nothing to do with him?

That was more likely.

Well, in that case, she should be relieved, Gillian told herself. Certainly it was no cause for her to toss and turn on her bed at night.

Gillian gave a start as she heard Katie speak.

"I said, do you want me to come with you?"

"Oh, no." Gillian jumped up and grabbed her shawl, ignoring the puzzled look in Katie's eye. "Is my grandmother downstairs?"

The Passionate Rebel

"No." Katie shook her head. "She went out early, right after breakfast."

"Well, when you see her, tell her where I've gone," Gillian said as she hurried from the room.

A while later, breathless from running across the orchard, Gillian knocked on Claudia's door.

"Are you ready?" she called out.

It immediately opened to reveal a smiling Claudia. "That's hardly the word," she responded, motioning Gillian inside. "I've been looking forward to this all week." She picked up her shawl. "I'm so tired of wearing the same few dresses over and over."

Gillian nodded in sympathy, though she really couldn't imagine having to do that. "Still and all," she sighed, viewing Claudia, "you look better in that than I ever did."

Gillian meant what she said. The dress Claudia was wearing had originally belonged to Gillian. It was a simple outfit: a dark green corset-bodice laced over a white cotton shift. A fichu of white lawn was tucked into the top of the bodice. The skirt, also of cotton, was striped in green and white. The color accented Claudia's emerald eyes and emphasized her long-waisted figure.

Shawl in place, Claudia was ready to go. The thought of refurbishing her wardrobe was a happy one to contemplate. With the exception of the torn and soot-blackened dress she had arrived in, her whole wardrobe had been lost in the flames. Both Edwina and Gillian had contributed a few dresses, and Tom had advanced her a moderate loan to purchase the essentials she needed. After the loan had been repaid, she had begun to save money. Now she wanted to spend it.

Helene Lehr

As the two young women emerged outside, Gillian asked, "Shall we take the carriage?"

Claudia glanced up at the cloudless sky, feeling the warmth of the sun on her face. "No, no! It's too beautiful a day. Let's walk."

In Hanover Square, they went happily from shop to shop, selecting and rejecting materials, laces and ribbons. At the drapers, Claudia viewed bolt after bolt of fabric, until Gillian was certain they had seen every one New York had to offer. From there, they went to the seamstress, who took careful notes of Claudia's measurements. The next stop was the cordwainer, where Claudia's dainty feet were outlined in charcoal on soft leather, so that she could be fitted with shoes that would match her new gowns.

It was already midafternoon when they paused, breathless, in front of a milliner's to view the assortment of hats and bonnets.

"I have enough money left for one more purchase," Claudia said happily. "After that—"

"Good afternoon, Miss Winthrop. An unexpected pleasure."

They both turned to see Philip Meredith coming toward them. He touched the brim of his hat.

"You've picked a fine day to go shopping," he offered with a winning smile.

Color rushed to Gillian's face. In an attempt to cover this rise of unwanted emotion, she hastily introduced Philip to Claudia.

Philip nodded amiably in the face of Claudia's stony acknowledgment. A lovely woman, he thought, in a frozen sort of way. He recalled Bennicot's saying she was a strumpet. Since he had also heard it elsewhere, he assumed it was true. There was a look in her green eyes that sent a shiver up his spine, an aloofness that went beyond cold. It would, he speculated, take a special kind of man to break through that barrier of reserve.

He turned to Gillian again, wondering what she was doing in the company of a woman like Claudia Dunham. He didn't like the idea.

"My carriage is not far," he said, making a vague gesture that could have encompassed a block or a mile.

"We are not yet finished with our shopping," Gillian replied, composure returning.

"I would be more than happy to wait."

Claudia raised a winged brow. "Is your time so inexpensive that you can afford to waste it, Mr. Meredith?"

Philip ignored the sarcasm. "Not really," he confessed. "It was simply a ruse to enjoy the company of two lovely ladies."

"We really must be going," Gillian murmured, giving him a quick look. Obviously, he was not out of town.

"Nonsense!" Philip said easily. "You both look as if you could do with some refreshment."

Without waiting for a response, he took hold of Gillian's arm and began to lead her to the café across the street. Gillian cast a helpless look over her shoulder to see that Claudia was following.

Philip looked down at her with a grin. "I hope you didn't fret too much in my absence." Bending over, he whispered in her ear. "I assure you, only the most pressing obligations could have kept me from your company."

Feeling his warm breath on her neck, Gillian drew a sharp breath. She stumbled, and his grip tightened in support. "You flatter yourself, Mr. Meredith," she retorted with as much coolness as she could muster. "I hadn't even noticed your absence this past week."

That drew a soft chuckle. "This past week?" he echoed musingly. He gave her arm a gentle squeeze. "If you didn't notice, then how do you know it was a week?"

Gillian was acutely conscious of the imprint of his touch on her arm and pulled away from him. "I don't. It was . . . just a guess."

"A good one," he murmured, still smiling.

Approaching the café, Philip opened the front door and almost collided with a British officer.

"Sir!" he exclaimed. "My apologies."

Gillian exchanged a disgusted glance with Claudia as Philip stepped aside to allow the officer the right of way.

"Why did you move aside for that man?" Gillian inquired in a low voice as they were seated at a table.

Philip took the time to order before he replied. "Courtesy is never out of fashion, Miss Winthrop," he noted sardonically. "I cannot see that bad manners will rectify any problem."

Gillian fumed. Claudia turned away.

A black waiter brought their order—coffee for Gillian and Claudia, tea for Philip.

"What would constitute an occasion for discourtesy?" Gillian asked casually as she sipped, well-aware of what Claudia was thinking. Perhaps she should have been polite to the soldiers who attacked her! Gillian was sorry now that she had allowed herself to be drawn into this little tête-à-tête. And why had she? She stole a glance at the man seated across from them. He always seemed to be dressed for a banquet. Today was no exception. His dark green

The Passionate Rebel

brocade jacket sported mother-of-pearl buttons and velvet cuffs. His neck band was a froth of white lace.

"I can think of no occasion that would prompt such behavior," Philip answered easily. He looked faintly surprised at such a prospect, but Gillian had the distinct impression that he was trying to bait her. Certainly she had seen him act rudely before. He leaned across the table and spoke in a low, conspiratorial tone. "Am I to understand that you consider His Majesty's troops intruders to be treated in an uncivil manner?"

"I'm certain Miss Winthrop meant no such thing," Claudia interjected smoothly before Gillian could fire off the heated retort that lay poised on the tip of her tongue. She pushed her cup aside and stood up. Gratefully, Gillian followed suit. "There is no need for you to escort us home," she went on when Philip got to his feet.

"As you wish," he replied politely, deferring to the firmness in her voice. He watched as the two women gathered their packages, a slight smile curving his lips as they left the café.

"I don't know what it is about that man that so annoys me," Gillian muttered when she and Claudia were outside.

"He's obviously a loyalist," Claudia noted as they crossed the street and made their way back to the shop where Philip had found them. She gave Gillian a speculative look. "You really ought to curb your tongue when he's around."

"I try," Gillian responded defensively. "It's just that . . ." She sighed, unable to explain even to herself the unorthodox reactions she was having when in the company of Philip Meredith.

Claudia was right, Gillian decided. She would simply ignore the man.

But that was easier said than done, for the next few weeks, Philip Meredith seemed to have developed the habit of eating his supper at the Blue Swan. Sometimes he was in the company of one or two British officers; sometimes he was alone. On those occasions, Gillian made certain that one of the other girls waited on him.

As always, Gillian was happy to see April arrive at last, bringing with it the usual showers one expected at this time of year. It seemed to her that almost overnight the land began to green, trees masked their brown winter coat beneath tiny emerald leaves, and flowering bushes put forth their first buds.

It was past ten on a Saturday night toward the end of the month when Gillian left the tavern. Although Philip had come into the taproom earlier in the evening, he had left immediately after eating. Obviously, he was getting the message that she wanted nothing to do with him.

She had gone only a few steps from the back porch, when someone grasped her arm. Gillian gave a gasp of fright.

"You've been avoiding me," Philip said, having stepped from the shadow of a tree. He was wearing a dark cloak and, except for his white wig, seemed to blend with the night.

Recovering quickly, Gillian glanced at her arm, then glared up at him. "You've got your nerve," she exclaimed indignantly. "You scared the life out of me!"

"At least I've gotten a reaction," he noted with a lazy smile. "The way you ignore me, one would think I've become invisible. Is it me you're ignoring, or is it your own feelings?"

The Passionate Rebel

Gillian wrenched her arm free. "I don't know what you're talking about." She started to move forward, but he stepped in front of her.

"Somehow I think you know very well what I'm talking about." With a fingertip, he stroked her cheek. Her skin was satin smooth. "I knew it would be," he murmured, more to himself than to her.

"What?" Gillian knew she should leave but felt mesmerized. Even in the dim light she could see his eyes move over the curve of her breast. A delicious heat stirred her blood, and she shivered with the provocative feeling. With a hand that trembled, she drew her shawl closer about her. Yet there was no fear, only wonder that her senses could so easily be invaded.

He didn't answer. Instead, in a fluid motion that was not at all hurried, Philip reached for her and drew her close to him. Gillian tried to pull away, but his strong arms held her easily and without effort. In the same unhurried fashion, he bent his head and kissed her.

The kiss went on for a long time. Gillian felt as though she were spiraling off into space. Without her being aware of it, her lips parted beneath his. She felt his hand cup the softness of her breast. His thumb gently rubbed her nipple, and the resulting tautness increased the delicious warmth that had already stirred within her.

When at last he released her, Gillian swayed and put a hand on the trunk of a tree to steady herself. As far as she could see, Philip Meredith's composure was not at all shaken.

"Why . . . Why did you do that?" she demanded in an uneven voice.

Tilting his head, he regarded her with amusement. "Haven't you ever been kissed before?"

Gillian wasn't about to answer that. His cocky grin washed over her, dousing the flame that had so unexpectedly engulfed her. The heat came again, this time in the form of anger.

"Well, haven't you?" he asked again.

Her breathing had calmed. "Don't you ever come near me again. If you do, I'll ... I'll have you arrested!"

A brow shot up. "Really? Have I broken the law by kissing a pretty barmaid?" Slowly he turned his head. They were standing no more than ten feet from the tavern. The kitchen window was open. He looked at Gillian again. "It seems to me," he speculated quietly, "that if you wanted help, you had only to call for it."

Gillian's chin rose. "And so I will, if you touch me again." Despite her words, she made no move to go. She wasn't about to turn her back on him.

Philip glanced toward the dark and deserted street. "Where do you live? I'll escort you home."

Gillian drew herself up to her full height. "No, thank you. I'd rather be accompanied by a redcoat than the likes of you."

As she turned, he grabbed her arm and spun her around to face him. "What do you mean by that? Is there something you find objectionable about redcoats?"

Gillian gulped and swallowed. For a moment, she had forgotten to whom she was talking.

"I meant soldiers," she said quickly. "Any soldiers. You know how they are."

He released her but held her fixed in place with a dark, brooding stare. "Actually, I have no idea," he murmured.

"Well, they can be familiar, at times." She adjusted her shawl, which had slipped from her shoulder.

The Passionate Rebel

"I didn't think that bothered you."

Gillian gave him a quick look. "What do you mean by that?"

"From what I've been able to see, you deliberately invite those familiarities."

As the meaning of his words penetrated, Gillian gasped, and her eyes widened in outrage. Raising her hand, she went to slap the smirk from his face, but he easily caught her wrist.

Gillian wrenched away. "Well, I don't recall inviting you."

Turning on her heel, she began to walk quickly to the house, half-expecting him to follow her. When she cleared the orchard, she paused and turned around. There was no sign of Philip Meredith.

In her room a while later, Gillian dismissed Katie, wanting to be alone. She was shaking with repressed fury. Her mind in a turmoil, she undressed, throwing her clothes carelessly on a chair. Her breast still felt warm and tingly from the unexpected caress it had received. Tentatively, she touched it. Her skin felt cool. There was no outward evidence of the throbbing heat she was feeling in that one spot.

Katie had already turned down the bed and laid Gillian's nightgown at the foot. Gillian grabbed the garment and hastily slipped it on.

Seating herself at her dressing table, she loosened the pins that held her hair. It fell almost to her waist.

Was it normal for a woman to get weak in the knees after she had been kissed? she wondered, still feeling shaken.

Once, many years ago, when her parents had given a ball, a young lad had stolen a kiss from her while they were walking in the garden. She had been 12; he, no more than 14.

Gillian recalled the incident clearly, for it had sent her into a paroxysm of giggles. The boy—what was his name? Seth. Yes, that was it. Seth had been affronted by her reaction and had stormed away, leaving her alone in the moon-drenched gardens.

Philip had wanted to know if she'd ever been kissed before. Technically, she had been, at least once. Gillian discounted those few occasions when she hadn't moved fast enough and a drunken soldier had managed to plant his lips on her cheek. The only reaction that had ever provoked was a shiver of distaste.

But in her heart, Gillian knew that she had never been kissed until tonight.

She had not giggled, nor had she found it distasteful.

Yet she couldn't stand the sight of the man!

Picking up a brush, Gillian began to apply it with vigorous strokes, as if she could just as easily brush aside her thoughts.

Chapter Seven

From Gillian's Diary:

> June 27, 1778
> I cannot see that we are any closer to winning this war. Nor has the recent resignation of the British Commander-in-Chief, Sir William Howe, made any noticeable difference. General Howe has been replaced by Sir Henry Clinton, a crafty scoundrel who is trying to enlist the aid of the Indians to his unworthy cause.

Gillian and Edwina were both sitting in the Carmody parlor on this Saturday afternoon. Constance, now 11 months old, played happily on the blanket Edwina had placed carefully to catch the warm sun streaming in through the open window.

Edwina, chestnut-brown hair covered beneath her white cap, sat in a straight-backed chair, her feet tucked beneath her yellow and green striped skirt. With neat, tiny stitches, she was mending one of Tom's cotton shirts.

Watching her sister, Gillian couldn't help but admire Edwina's expertise with a needle. It was a talent Gillian had long ago given up hope of possessing. She glanced down at the small quilt she had been working on for months now. It was for the baby's cradle, if she ever finished it.

"Constance will be grown by the time I'm done with this," she muttered as the thread broke.

"You are using too much pressure," Edwina advised. She didn't bother to look up as she spoke. It wasn't necessary. Gillian had no patience at all when it came to sewing or embroidering. "You mustn't jerk the needle out."

Gillian only sighed. She knew that was not true. It was obvious to her that the thread she was using was inferior to the one her sister was using. "Did you see the ships that arrived this morning?" she asked as she rethreaded the needle.

Edwina nodded. "More Hessians."

Gillian let her hands fall idle. "It's all Clinton's doing."

"He is not as sympathetic as was General Howe," Edwina observed.

Gillian looked startled. "Sympathetic?" She almost choked on the word.

Edwina's sewing was not interrupted. "Why do you think he was replaced?"

"He was lazy and inefficient," came the swift reply.

"Yes," Edwina agreed slowly. "But was it by accident or intent?"

Gillian's brow knitted. "What do you mean?"

Making a knot, Edwina bit off the thread and put

The Passionate Rebel

the shirt aside. Then she placed the needle in her enameled sewing box. "Do you remember the day the British drove the Continentals from Manhattan?" At her sister's nod, she went on. "Do you realize that on that day we could have been defeated, once and for all? The Continentals had less than five thousand men. General Howe had close to twenty thousand grenadiers, not to mention his fifty warships. Yet, when the Americans began to retreat, Howe made no effort to pursue them."

Gillian was unconvinced. "Doubtless the man was anxious to return to the bed of his mistress." She plunged the needle into the linen, remembering to draw it out slowly.

Edwina smiled. "You may be right. Howe did seem to spend more time with Mrs. Loring than he did with his officers." She leaned forward. "By the way, have you heard that Melanie Cartwright is getting married?"

Gillian looked up from her handiwork when Edwina offered that bit of news. "No," she answered. "Who is it?"

Edwina gave a short laugh. "None other than Captain Bennicot."

"A redcoat?" Gillian made a sound of disgust. But then, she supposed it was to be expected. James Cartwright was an avowed loyalist. She was about to speak again, when she saw Drucilla enter the room. A feeling of alarm shot through her. Her grandmother's black maidservant rarely came here.

"Grandmother . . . ?" Her voice emerged as a squeal.

"No, no, Miss Gillian. Your grandmother's jus' fine," Drucilla said quickly with a bright smile. "She sent me here to tell you to come home. There's to be guests for supper tonight."

Gillian expelled a breath of relief. "Of course. We were just about done anyway. Tell her I'll be right along. Oh, Drucilla," she called as the woman turned. "Will there be more than one guest?"

She nodded. "Yes, ma'am. But I'm not sure who."

Gillian bit her lip. She hoped her grandmother hadn't invited any British soldiers; she had been doing that a lot lately. Be that as it may, she would obviously have to change her clothes. She gathered the quilt and her sewing box, then viewed Edwina. "I'll try to get back."

"No, no," Edwina protested. "I'm sure the girls and Claudia can handle things." Her brown eyes twinkled as Gillian got to her feet. "Who knows? Gram may have invited a nice young man to supper. You may be in for a very interesting evening."

Gillian just shook her head and sighed as she left the room. If her grandmother had indeed invited a "nice young man" Gillian had no doubt but that he would be wearing a scarlet coat.

When she entered the house a few minutes later, she poked her head into the parlor, but Alice was nowhere to be seen.

"Gram?" she called out.

"Your grandmother's upstairs, gettin' dressed, Miss Gillian," William said, looking up from the hall table he had been dusting.

Gillian nodded an acknowledgment. As she passed the dining room, she stopped a moment to view the table. Five settings. That information, however, told her nothing about their guests.

Hoisting her skirts, she ran lightly up the stairs to her room, calling for Katie as she did so.

"Do you know who our guests are this evening?" she asked, when Katie entered the room a few min-

The Passionate Rebel

utes later. Without waiting for assistance, she began to disrobe.

Katie checked a smile. "Your grandmother doesn't tell me things like that." She gestured to the dressing table. "There's water in the basin, if you'd like to wash." She handed Gillian a cloth and watched as she headed for the porcelain ewer.

While Gillian washed, Katie took a gown from the wardrobe and laid it carefully on the bed.

Gillian picked up the towel, then paused when she heard Katie humming a gay little tune. The young woman was now on her knees in front of the wardrobe, hunting for the slippers that matched the gown.

In some wonder, Gillian studied her maid, noting the secret little smile that played about her lips.

"You certainly seem to be in a happy mood today," Gillian commented with a small frown of puzzlement. She couldn't ever recall seeing Katie like this before. She positively glowed with some sort of hidden excitement.

Having found the slippers, Katie now came forward to assist Gillian.

"Sorry." Though the apology was swift, Katie didn't sound at all contrite.

Gillian laughed. "Don't be. I'm glad to see you looking so happy." Out of her petticoats now, she gave Katie a sharp look. Even her brown eyes seemed to be smiling. "All right, out with it!" she demanded. "You're fairly bursting with some sort of news."

Katie actually blushed, her cheeks approaching the color of her hair. "I didn't think it was so obvious."

"It certainly is. And I insist you tell me."

"Well . . ." Katie cleared her throat and toyed with the hem of the white apron that she wore over her brown cotton dress. "There's this young man I met."

"I knew it!" Gillian exclaimed triumphantly. Grabbing Katie's hand she led her to the bed. Carelessly pushing aside the gown, she seated herself and pulled Katie down beside her. "Who is he? Where did you meet him? Do I know him?"

Katie laughed at the barrage of questions. "His name is Edward, and he works for the bootmaker in Hanover Square. A couple of weeks ago, Polly asked me to pick up William's boots when I went shopping. And it was Edward who gave them to me. Of course," she added quickly, "I didn't know his name then."

"But you found out?" Gillian asked with a grin.

Katie nodded. "Yes. The next time we met, we exchanged names."

"The next time?" Gillian inquired with a lift of her brow. "How many pairs of boots does William have?"

Katie stifled a giggle with the back of her hand. "I have no idea. You see, on my next day off I just happened to be walking by the shop."

"And he just happened to see you." Gillian hugged Katie. "I'm so pleased you've found someone. And I certainly hope it works out."

Through the open window came the sound of an approaching carriage, and both young women got hastily to their feet.

A while later, Gillian came down the stairs in a much more sedate manner than she had ascended them. Her gown of eggshell blue taffeta was worn over whalebone hoops that were flat both in the front and back and flared out almost six inches on either side of her waist. The square neck, low enough to offer a delightful view of the swell of

The Passionate Rebel

her young bosom, was delicately embroidered with silver thread.

At the foot of the stairs, she gave a final pat to her hair, which had been drawn back and arranged in ringlets that cascaded from the crown of her head to her shoulders.

Hearing voices coming from the front parlor, Gillian headed in that direction. She paused on the threshold. Most of the furniture in the room had been shipped from London, graceful pieces in the Queen Anne style, lavishly upholstered in silk and damask.

Taking a step further into the room, Gillian drew a sharp breath at the sight of the tall, elegantly dressed man standing by the hearth.

"Gillian, my dear." Alice looked up from where she was seated on the settee and smiled. "Come in. I'd like you to meet Mr. Philip Meredith."

He came forward and offered a sweeping bow that would have done credit to a courtier.

"A pleasure, Miss Winthrop." Philip's low tone gave no indication of the jolt of astonishment that shot through him like a bolt of lightning. Since he had begun to handle the affairs of Alice Wharton some three weeks ago, she had, once or twice, mentioned her granddaughter, but never by name.

Gillian raised her fan slightly and briefly nodded her head at the introduction. She couldn't have been more shocked than if her grandmother had invited General Washington to be here this evening.

The knocker sounded and William went to answer it.

"Excuse me, while I greet our other guests." Alice got up and went into the foyer, her black silk skirt rustling softly across the carpet.

In a graceful movement, Gillian sat down, back

straight. She wasn't about to give Philip Meredith the satisfaction of seeing her surprise. The only thing she wanted to convey was disinterest.

"So, there's a bit more to you than meets the eye, Miss Winthrop," Philip said when they were alone.

"What do you mean, sir?" She moved the fan slowly back and forth in front of her face.

"To see you sitting there, one would take you for a prim and proper lady . . . instead of the flirtatious little wench who bats her eyelashes at every officer in her path."

Gillian snapped the fan shut and let her hands fall to her lap. "How dare you speak to me like that!"

"I dare because I strongly disapprove of your conduct, as I know your grandmother would," he replied.

"I don't care whether you approve or disapprove," she said hotly.

"As for your association with Miss Dunham," he went on as if she had not spoken, "that, too, is unseemly. Unless, of course," he speculated, hands clasped behind him, "you and Miss Dunham share more in common than mere friendship." He lowered his head and stared at her from beneath dark brows. "You see, I know very well what the lady in question does for a living."

The blood drained from Gillian's cheeks. She cast a nervous glance at the door. If her grandmother ever heard this conversation, there'd be the very devil to pay. As far as Alice was concerned, Claudia was a poor, unfortunate woman who had lost her family and now worked in the Blue Swan to support herself. All true—as far as it went.

Gillian stood up, and her eyes blazed dangerously. "You know nothing!" she spat.

Philip shrugged and seemed unconcerned by her

The Passionate Rebel

outburst. "A man is known by the company he keeps," he observed. "Why should it be otherwise for a woman? Besides, I've seen with my own eyes how you like to wiggle those delectable hips of yours at any man who catches your eye."

Gillian's nostrils flared. "Well, you can be certain of one thing, Mr. Meredith," she said in a low voice, aware that her grandmother and her guests were nearing the room. "You are not a man who catches my eye."

"Strange," he drawled sardonically. "I thought I had."

Before Gillian could comment, Alice returned with two British officers in tow.

"Colonel Harrington and Major Rowen, may I present Mr. Meredith and my granddaughter, Gillian."

Philip immediately stepped forward to shake hands with the officers.

"Colonel Harrington and I are already old friends," he said to Alice; then he turned to the major. "But I am pleased to make your acquaintance, sir," he said politely.

Gillian fixed a smile on her face and hoped it would remain in place.

William appeared with a bottle of Madeira on a silver tray and set about serving the men. Alice had a glass of port, which she preferred. Gillian declined refreshments and sat stiffly in her chair, wishing for the evening to end.

Major Rowan, a short, plump man in his late thirties, sat down in a chair directly opposite from Gillian and quite brazenly stared at her breasts.

Irritated by the man's lustful gaze, Gillian raised her fan and waved it slowly in front of her.

Shifting her own gaze, she saw that Philip, still

standing by the hearth, was also watching her. He was, however, staring into her eyes in a most disconcerting way. What the devil was he doing here anyway? She stared back at him defiantly. If it was in his mind to intimidate her, he had another thought coming.

Gillian released a sigh of relief when Alice finally got to her feet and ushered them all into the dining room.

Philip gallantly offered Alice his arm. Before either of the officers could make a move in her direction, Gillian walked with undue haste toward the table.

While they ate their first course, a savory clam broth, Gillian listened with only half an ear to the conversation, until Major Rowen's grating laugh caught her unwilling attention.

"Naturally, the king is willing to be reasonable," he was saying. "If the rebels would make their wishes known, I feel certain that something could be worked out."

"I would say they made their wishes known in Boston," Gillian remarked tartly.

"Ah . . ." He waved his spoon at her. "There is a case in point. Dumping all that tea into the harbor. Acting like boys, venting their fury in a most unproductive manner." He shook his head. "What a waste."

"I understand that the French are planning to send troops to aid the rebels," Philip commented before Gillian could again speak.

The colonel laughed. "So they are. In my opinion, King Louis is badly advised. At the rate he's going he'll bankrupt his country and have his own revolution on his hands. It wouldn't surprise me in the least if the French decide to provide the Continentals with their own navy."

The Passionate Rebel

"Well, they need every ship they can get," Major Rowen noted. "Their navy's getting smaller by the day."

Gillian averted her eyes. The man had the manners of a pig. Even as he spoke, the major continued to spoon the broth into his mouth, sucking his teeth when a morsel of clam detoured on its way down his throat.

A black serving girl began to clear away the empty soup bowls. Lobster appeared next, together with a brace of duck and Polly's expertly concocted corn pudding.

"I spoke with General Clinton this morning," Colonel Harrington remarked as he began to eat. "He told me that the Continentals are not faring too well. Seems as though they've had a number of deserters, more than three thousand by our latest count. One of their regiments—Pennsylvania, I believe it is—now consists of only two officers."

Meredith laughed in a way that set Gillian's teeth on edge. "After last winter, I'm surprised that Washington has enough men left to defend his headquarters." Raising his napkin, he lightly pressed it to his lips, then placed it beside his plate. "But in all fairness, gentlemen, we must be generous. After all, the Continentals are in no way to be judged as an army."

"Certainly they're not being paid." Major Rowan guffawed as he gnawed on a lobster claw.

"Exactly!" Philip agreed with an engaging smile. "The Continentals are just a bunch of farmers, more equipped to handle a hoe than a musket. They enlist for only one year; then they go home."

"I wish they would all go home," Colonel Harrington put in with a sigh, sounding as if his appetite had suddenly left him.

Helene Lehr

Philip chuckled. "From all reports, I'd say you will soon get your wish, Colonel. The American army is the only one that seems to lose more men than it enlists." He sounded highly amused by his own observation.

Mouth tight, Gillian raised her head. She'd had just about enough.

"You seem to forget, Mr. Meredith," she pointed out icily, "that as soon as there is a call to arms the Americans respond." She offered a deceptively beguiling smile. "They will never desert the cause. They will fight to the end."

"Gillian!" Her grandmother spoke sharply. "That is quite enough."

The major stopped eating long enough to observe Gillian. "Good heavens, are we in the company of a rebel?" His admiring look said he didn't care if he was.

"Not at all," Alice interjected quickly with a scowl at her granddaughter. "Like most young women, Gillian is afflicted with foolish, romantic notions. She has no conception of what the real world is like."

Gillian lowered her head. Her cheeks were flushed, frustration and anger combining to produce the crimson color. It was useless to talk any sense to these people. She decided not to make any more comments. Her resolve, however, could not prevent the invasion of inanities that assaulted her ears.

Listening to the officers was bad enough, but listening to the senseless prattling of the Tory seated across the table from her was really too much. As far as the British were concerned, Gillian could understand them. The Hessians—well, they were, after all, only mercenaries.

But Tories! They were traitors! Gillian excluded

The Passionate Rebel

her grandmother from that select group. Alice was old, set in her ways.

Supper concluded, they all adjourned once more to the parlor, where the men had a brandy.

Just when Gillian was certain that the evening would never end, the officers took their leave amidst much praise for the excellent meal they had been given. Alice beamed in pleasure at their profuse compliments.

Gillian stared at Philip Meredith as if the sheer force of her will could drive the man out the door.

Instead, he sat down at Alice's invitation and had another brandy.

And that was finally too much for Gillian. Feeling an overwhelming need for fresh air, she went out onto the front porch. The night was cool, but she relished the fresh feel of it.

She sighed and leaned on the wooden railing. Through the open window came the voices of her grandmother and Philip Meredith, engaged in spirited conversation. Gillian had never heard her grandmother speak in such an animated way. Each time Alice pointed out a glowing virtue of the Crown and Mother England, it was promptly topped by Philip.

God, they really were two of a kind!

Gillian angrily plucked a wisteria leaf from the bush that entwined around the railing and tore it into shreds.

Well, manners or no, she wasn't about to go back in there. She'd had just about enough of Philip Meredith this evening—and for all evenings to come. She would wait here until the Tory decided to go home. Once her grandmother began to nod, he'd get the message.

Raising her head, Gillian stared up at the sky,

trying to calm her frazzled nerves. The moon was full, an ivory globe so perfect it appeared to have been deliberately placed in its setting.

Feeling more relaxed, she inhaled deeply of the fragrant air. The breeze was no more than a whisper as it sighed through the trees. Around her, cicadas offered a musical accompaniment to a night perfumed by roses and wisteria.

"This has been a most enjoyable evening."

Gillian gasped when she found Philip standing so close to her. She had not heard him come out onto the porch, had not heard the cessation of voices that might have warned her that he was finally taking his leave.

"I'm glad someone enjoyed it," she murmured, recovering, now annoyed that he had interrupted her solitude.

He sensed her surprise, even though she tried to hide it. "I didn't mean to startle you."

"You didn't, really. I thought you were still speaking with my grandmother."

"She's a remarkable woman."

"The two of you seem to have a lot in common," she said in a voice laced with sarcasm.

Meredith smiled, taking a moment to enjoy the sight of her golden tresses lit now by the silvery glow of the moon. Her skin was like warm ivory.

"There is no doubt of that," he responded finally with a nod of his head.

Gillian gave him an annoyed look. He was not wearing a wig tonight; instead, his dark hair was drawn back and tied at the nape of his neck. The moonlight accented the angular planes of his face, and, grudgingly, Gillian had to admit that he was damnably attractive.

The Passionate Rebel

He took a step closer. "Why do you work at the Blue Swan?"

Surprise flared in her gray eyes. "Why shouldn't I?"

He shrugged. "I know it isn't necessary. Certainly I don't feel it is appropriate for a young lady such as yourself to be employed in a tavern."

She took a deep breath. "For your information, Mr. Meredith, I began working in the Blue Swan to help my sister and her husband. I've stayed because it gives me something to do with my day besides embroider. And, I might add, I am there with my grandmother's consent." She straightened. "Furthermore, I cannot see that it is any business of yours what I do."

"Not now, perhaps," he retorted softly. "But the day will come when it is very much my business."

She gave a short laugh. "I assure you, sir, that day will never come."

He made no response, just stared at her with an expression she could not fathom.

The silence lengthened, but Meredith made no attempt to break it. After several minutes went by, Gillian became uncomfortable. Was he just going to stand there and stare at her?

"I think I will retire," Gillian murmured at last.

How had she gotten into his arms? Gillian wondered, feeling his lips against her own.

There it was again. That feeling of sailing above the clouds. Her mind told her one thing; her body, another. Her mind said: pull away! Her body, against her volition, pressed against his and felt the hardness of his arousal.

At last he drew back. This time, he looked as shaken as she felt. When he finally spoke, his voice was husky.

"You are interfering with my sleep, Miss Winthrop, invading my dreams at night. No woman has ever done that to me before."

She jerked away. "A glass of warm milk before you retire would probably solve that problem," she tossed back tartly.

"Offhand, I can think of several things that would do a better job."

"I'd just as soon you did not elaborate for me," she said hastily.

He grinned, taking her by surprise. Reaching out, he touched a silky curl. "I love you, Gillian Winthrop," he said quietly. "It's only fair to tell you that I intend to make you mine."

Startled, Gillian gave him a searching glance, unable to believe what she had just heard. In spite of his cocky grin, she could see that he had spoken in all seriousness.

Well, she would put a stop to this foolishness right now!

"And it's only fair to tell you that you are wasting your time."

"Pursuing something worthwhile is never a waste of time," he observed.

"You are a Tory," she accused. "Do you deny it?"

He pursed his lips, as if considering that. "I cannot deny it. But then, just about everyone in New York is a loyalist."

"I'm not," she shot back.

"If I were you, I'd take care about making that fact public."

She raised a brow. "Are you going to paint an *R* on my front door?" she taunted.

"That would be unfair to your grandmother."

"Let's leave my grandmother out of this."

He grabbed her again. She felt his fingers dig

The Passionate Rebel

painfully into the softness of her arms; but for some reason, she did not draw away.

"Don't make the mistake of trying to fight me," he whispered.

Tightening his hold, Philip pulled her even closer, so close that Gillian was painfully aware that only mere strips of cloth separated her body from his. The strength of the man astounded her. His arms were like bands of steel. He could easily crush her, if he had a mind to do so.

Then his lips claimed hers in what was now a savage kiss. Try as she might, Gillian was powerless to remain passive. She tried to fight the feeling of languor that swept over her and even clenched her fists, intending to pummel his broad chest. Instead, to her chagrin, her arms crept around his neck.

After what seemed an eternity, Gillian found the strength to pull away from him.

"I will never be yours," she proclaimed angrily.

"Oh, but you will," he countered, staring deeply into her eyes.

The audacity of the man was not to be believed. "Tell me, Mr. Meredith, would you change your allegiance if I were the prize?" she challenged.

His hands fell to his sides, and he was no longer smiling. "No," he stated bluntly. "I change my allegiance for no one."

Gillian's chin tilted upward. "Then I can only repeat what I've said, Mr. Meredith. I will have nothing to do with the likes of you."

Turning on her heel, Gillian stormed back into the house, slamming the door behind her.

Chapter Eight

From Gillian's Diary:

> *June 28, 1778*
> *Ten days ago, for reasons known only to their commander in chief, the British evacuated Philadelphia; so, too, did the loyalists and their families. It has been said that their baggage train alone was 12 miles long. On route to New York, they were intercepted at Monmouth by the Continentals under the command of General Washington. The ensuing battle, fought beneath a blazing sun with temperatures in excess of 100 degrees, was clearly an American victory.*

The morning was warm, heavy with a humidity that gave fair notice of a day that would turn out to be hot and uncomfortable.

The Passionate Rebel

Gillian came listlessly down the stairs, her hair already in damp tendrils on the slender column of her neck. Sunday was not a day she could dress casually. Hoops, petticoats and satin all combined to weigh her down even more than her thoughts—and God knew, they were heavy enough. She was still unsettled from the events of the night before. She was so shaken, in fact, that sleep had eluded her until the eastern sky had at last begun to lighten.

Alice, her black morning gown unadorned save for a small pearl brooch given to her by her late husband, was already in the dining room. She looked cheerful and well-rested. Gillian was certain she herself looked neither.

"Good morning, my dear," she said brightly as Gillian came into the room and seated herself.

Gillian sighed but managed an appropriate greeting, leaning back in her chair as a bowl of cereal was placed before her.

Damn the man! she thought, picking up her spoon, again thinking of what had taken place the night before. Annoyingly, her anger kept getting sidetracked with the remembered feeling of his warm, insistent lips pressed against her own. "You will be mine," he'd said. And that was utterly ridiculous! Well, he was arrogant and overconfident; she'd known that all along.

Looking up, Gillian viewed her grandmother a moment before she spoke.

"How did you meet Mr. Meredith?" she asked casually, moving the back of her spoon through the porridge in her bowl.

"Mr. Bissel introduced us," Alice answered readily, giving Gillian a look that suggested she should have known that. "Henry, as you know, has long been our family lawyer, but he's been ailing for months. Edith tells me it's the gout. Of course, he's seventy-two now." She smiled wistfully. "The same age as your grandfather would have been."

"Mr. Meredith..." Gillian prompted as she watched the indentation caused by the spoon fill in and level out.

"Oh, yes." Alice poured cream into her bowl. "He's joined Mr. Bissel's firm. Henry highly recommended him. Mr. Meredith was educated in Oxford and graduated with honors. He is a fine young man. Don't you agree?" Alice scraped her bowl clean.

"He's a Tory." Gillian pushed aside her bowl. She really didn't like oatmeal.

"Oh, Gillian, don't start that again. I cannot imagine where you get your ideas. Of course Mr. Meredith is a Tory. So am I. So is anyone in his right mind. Good heavens, we cannot separate from the Crown. Who do you think has protected the colonies from the Indians all these years? I'll admit that the king has occasionally acted unjustly, but that is only because His Majesty has been misinformed by his advisors. Even your grandfather, loyal as he was, was enraged by the Stamp Act." She leaned back in her chair with a faraway look in her eye. "My, he was in a fury for the longest while. However, he was never foolish enough to espouse separation."

They both remained silent while a servant removed the bowls and placed a platter of ham and poached eggs before them.

Gillian fidgeted and poked the eggs with her fork. This morning nothing appealed to her.

"Why do you need a lawyer anyway?" she grumbled. "Surely your affairs are not that complicated."

The Passionate Rebel

Alice Wharton laughed as she buttered a biscuit. "Let us say that they are more complicated than you may suppose. Your grandfather, as you may remember, was a factor. The wheat, rice, tobacco and corn raised here in the colonies was sent to London on Wharton ships. When they returned, they were filled with many goods that are unobtainable here." She paused to take a bite of the biscuit, then continued. "It was a very profitable business. Now, of course, we can no longer ship our goods to London." She shook her head sadly. "Even trade with France and Spain is difficult because of the blockade, not to mention our own privateers."

Gillian's brow creased in puzzlement. "You mean you continued the business after Grandfather died?"

Alice Wharton nodded. "For a while, I did—with Mr. Bissel's help, of course. I had hoped that your father would involve himself. Unfortunately, that was not to be. Now, Mr. Meredith is assisting me in dissolving what remains of the business." Seeing that Gillian was not eating, she frowned. "Do hurry, Gillian. We'll be late for church."

With a sigh, Gillian pushed aside her plate and stood up. "I'm ready."

A few minutes later, Gillian and Alice emerged into the bright sunshine and climbed into the carriage.

Gillian was quiet on the relatively short trip, mulling over the things her grandmother had told her. If Philip Meredith was now to be the Wharton lawyer, it would seem that she was going to see more of him than she wanted to. The prospect did not brighten her day.

Finally, the carriage halted, and William came around to assist them from the vehicle.

Helene Lehr

Trinity Church, no longer bearing the ravages of the fire that had almost destroyed it two years ago, was crowded on this warm summer morning. The color of scarlet was predominate to the point of overshadowing every other hue.

As she settled herself, Gillian happened to glance across the aisle and met the eye of British General John Burgoyne. The man winked at her, and Gillian hastily directed her eyes forward. Gentleman Johnny, as Burgoyne was affectionately called by his peers, was a notorious ladies' man. Gillian was not flattered that she caught his eye; any female would receive the same attention.

Someone now moved into the pew, and Gillian automatically shifted herself closer to her grandmother to make room for the newcomer.

Leaning forward, Alice peered across Gillian and smiled.

"I'm so pleased you've changed your mind, Mr. Meredith," she said in a low voice.

Only then did Gillian turn her head to see Philip seated beside her.

"The invitation proved irresistible, Mistress Wharton," he murmured. Although he addressed Alice, his dark eyes were on Gillian.

The services began, and Gillian tried to focus her attention on the proceedings, though, in truth, she found herself unable to concentrate. She was too conscious of the broad warm shoulder pressed against her own. She very much wanted to move away, but there was no place to go. Another few inches would have put her in her grandmother's lap.

Gillian was vastly relieved when the service was at last over. Her relief was, however, short-lived. It appeared that Alice's invitation included Sunday dinner.

The Passionate Rebel

"Do you play cribbage, Mr. Meredith?" Alice asked when they all got into the carriage.

"Very well," Philip answered with a smile.

"Not as well as I," Alice smugly rejoined.

Gillian winced. It was going to be a long afternoon.

And it was. Dinner conversation swirled between Philip and Alice. Gillian wondered why she didn't have anything to say. That had never been a problem for her before. Every time Philip looked at her, his eyes seemed to be saying, "You will be mine."

As for her own eyes, Gillian hadn't the faintest idea what they were saying, if anything. In any event, she couldn't seem to maintain eye contact with him for any length of time. In spite of herself, her gaze kept slipping down to his lips, remembering how it felt to have them pressed against her own.

When dinner was over, Gillian sat and worked on her niece's quilt, while Alice and Philip played cribbage. Their good-natured banter grated on her nerves.

"We must do this again," Alice said when the game was at last over.

"I should hope so," Philip exclaimed with a laugh. "I have never been so thoroughly trounced in all my life. I want a chance to get even."

"You shall have it," Alice assured him.

Gillian frowned and jerked the needle through the cloth with a vigor that snapped it in two. Hearing someone at the front door, she heaved a sigh of relief. It was probably Edwina. She usually brought Constance here on Sunday afternoon.

A moment later, Edwina came into the parlor, holding Constance by the hand. The little girl immediately toddled forward to the outstretched arms of her great-grandmother.

Edwina started to smile, then caught sight of Philip, who had politely gotten to his feet when they entered.

"Oh," she exclaimed to Alice, "I'm sorry. I didn't know you had company."

"Nonsense," Alice said, then introduced Edwina to Philip.

"I've seen you often in the Blue Swan, Mr. Meredith," Edwina said with a smile.

"Indeed," Philip agreed. Seeing Constance coming toward him, he bent down and hoisted her high before settling her in his arms. The child squealed in delight and clung to him. Philip again looked at Edwina. "You must be the one responsible for the excellent food I eat in your establishment," he said. "My compliments."

Edwina blushed prettily. "How nice of you to say that, Mr. Meredith," she murmured.

Gillian made a face. The man could charm the birds out of the trees when he put his mind to it.

That night, in bed, Gillian tossed and turned, overcome with a restlessness she had never before experienced. This man, this Tory, had come into her life, and there seemed to be no way to get rid of him.

The clock downstairs chimed one, then two.

With an irritated movement, she finally got out of bed and padded across the room, dragging her blanket with her. Drawing a chair close to the window, she sat down and stared moodily into the black night. There were no stars, only a hazy outline of a moon trying to shine bravely through clouds that were growing thicker even as she watched.

Soon, she knew, it would rain.

By the time the first drops fell, more than an hour later, Gillian had begun to nod. The rain was a gentle metronome that lulled her finally into a deep and dreamless sleep.

Claudia Dunham walked slowly across the polished floor of her bedroom. She had come to think of this small room in the Blue Swan as home, the only one she had now.

Staring out the window she saw that the morning had dawned gray, the rain now a mist that had saturated the air and coated leaves and grass with a shiny patina that deepened their color.

Behind her, stretched out on the narrow bed, a British major snored peacefully. Turning, she stared at him, her heart-shaped face impassive. If one looked closely, however, it was easy to see the hate that glittered in her green eyes. She was only 25 years old, but already it seemed to her as if she had lived a lifetime.

In a weary gesture, she brushed a jet black curl from her forehead. Her hair, long and luxurious, fell loosely about her shoulders. She had not yet dressed and wore only a light silk robe over her nightgown.

It had been a wasted night. Major Winters had told her nothing of importance. She had already searched the pockets of his uniform and had come up empty-handed there, too.

She had endured his loathsome touch, his ineffectual rutting for nothing. Clenching her small hands into fists, she again stared out the window, watching the droplets of water trickle down the pane of glass. The drops reminded her of all the tears she had shed in these past years, endless tears that had done nothing to assuage the grief in her heart. It was still there, frozen now into a knot of anger and hate, a heavy weight in her breast. Once, she had been happy with a family, a husband and a six-month-old son.

All gone now. Ashes.

The snoring had ceased. Claudia turned to face the man on the bed. He had thrown the blankets aside and was now sitting up, feet on the floor. He was no more than 40 years of age, but his scalp shone pinkly through the remaining wisps of hair that covered his head. His nude body was as pale as the belly of a cod.

Claudia's eyes lowered, and she viewed his flaccid member with contempt. The major had consumed a great deal of rum the night before, and though he had pumped and strained and groaned, he had been unable to attain his satisfaction.

Claudia remembered when the physical coupling of herself and her husband had been a joy. Charles had made it so. Simply seeing the expectation in his eyes had made her feel weak with longing.

Now she wondered cynically if she would ever feel that way again.

"What time is it?" Major Winters mumbled, rubbing the back of his neck.

"After ten o'clock," Claudia replied, handing him his breeches.

He looked up at her with a sheepish expression, but Claudia didn't smile.

Chapter Nine

From Gillian's Diary:

> *July 22, 1778*
> *Indian raids are occurring with chilling regularity now that the Mohawks, one of the five tribes that comprise the Iroquois nation, have joined the British. They are led by a chief named Thayendanegea, a man whom the British call Joseph Brant. These savages have massacred hundreds of people in the Wyoming Valley of Pennsylvania. The plight of those poor settlers whose only crime was that they were loyal to their country is too gruesome to put into words. The fact that the Indians were, I am ashamed to say, aided by Tories, only reinforces my contempt for this despicable group of traitors.*

Helene Lehr

Alice arranged the roses in the vase, frowned, then repositioned the lush flowers. She didn't have the talent her sister had been gifted with; there was no question about that. Bertha had only to put flowers into a vase, and they suddenly became a work of art.

A small sigh escaped her lips as Alice thought of Bertha, who lived with her husband in Halifax, Nova Scotia. They had been so close as children and even as young women. Though they corresponded regularly, almost two decades had passed since they had last seen each other.

Stepping back, Alice viewed the roses. One side seemed to be drooping in despair. "Let it be," she murmured, resigned.

Someone coming down the stairs now caught her attention. Tilting her head, Alice listened. That light step could only be Gillian. Something was troubling her granddaughter. Though Alice had tried to discover what the problem was, Gillian stubbornly insisted that nothing was wrong.

Moving into the foyer, Alice took note of the way in which Gillian was dressed. Her gown of primrose yellow, worn over a bell-shaped hoop, was not the sort of outfit she wore to the Blue Swan. Her hair, too, was dressed fashionably in a high chignon and adorned with green silk ribbons.

"Gillian? Where are you going?"

"To visit Melanie Cartwright. Edwina told me she's to be married, and I want to offer my congratulations."

Alice smiled her approval. "You'd better have William drive you."

Gillian shook her head. "No, I'd rather walk."

Alice frowned. "I don't like the idea of your going

The Passionate Rebel

out unattended. At least take Katie with you."

Gillian laughed. "Oh, Gram, it's only three blocks. What could possibly happen? Besides," she added ruefully, "there are plenty of soldiers out there to protect me."

"Gillian, there have been at least two separate incidents in this past week involving unescorted women."

"Only with those women foolish enough to leave the safety of the streets," Gillian retorted quickly. "I have no intention of doing that. If a redcoat has a mind to attack me, he will have to do so in full view of everyone." At the sight of her grandmother's distressed look, she was immediately contrite. "It's broad daylight," she added.

Before Alice could offer further argument, Gillian hastily took her leave.

Though she was walking quickly when she left the house, before she had gone a block, Gillian's steps slowed. If the truth be told, she really didn't want to see or congratulate Melanie; they were friends only by virtue of the friendship of Alice Wharton and Florence Cartwright, Melanie's mother. Still, it was the polite thing to do, and she had been postponing this visit for weeks now.

As she made her way along the street, Gillian eyed each passing soldier with suspicion, ready to take flight if they so much as looked at her for too long a time. In spite of her flip words to her grandmother, Gillian knew very well that both the redcoats and the Hessians were becoming more bold in their confrontations with women. Rape was becoming common. Any lone woman was considered easy prey.

Gillian contented herself with the realization that the two incidents Alice had referred to had taken place at dusk and in the more secluded areas of town. Even the British weren't yet so brazen as to drag a woman from the crowded streets in broad daylight.

When Gillian arrived at the two-story brick structure, the butler ushered her into the front parlor. It was a large room with pine paneling painted a soft ivory. A fireplace framed with walnut molding and delft tiles now had a brass firescreen in front of it to conceal the black and empty grate.

Gillian had just seated herself on the cushioned sofa when Melanie swept into the room, garbed in a satin gown of pale blue. At 18, she was plump and pink-cheeked with a small mouth that could pout charmingly, something she did rather frequently. Her light brown hair was parted in the center and drawn back into a tight chignon. Two horizontal curls above each ear softened the severity of the coiffure.

"Gillian!" Arms outstretched, she lightly embraced her visitor. "How nice to see you. It's been such a long time." Turning to a hovering servant, she instructed the woman to bring refreshments. Then she seated herself in a chair opposite Gillian.

"Edwina told me of your engagement," Gillian began.

"Oh, isn't it exciting? Captain Bennicot is so charming. His father is a member of Parliament, you know." She paused as the servant put a tray of small cakes on the low table between them, then filled two crystal glasses with champagne. Melanie raised hers and took a dainty sip. "I know my mother will be disappointed to have missed your visit. How unfortunate that she is not at home."

Gillian picked up her glass but declined the cake. "I should have sent word."

"Not at all," Melanie countered graciously.

The Passionate Rebel

Gillian cleared her throat. "When is the wedding to be?"

"February 28th." She gave a deep sigh and straightened the folds of her skirt to a position more to her liking. "I wished it could have been sooner. Seven months seems like an eternity, but Richard's regiment is being sent to the Carolinas. He expects to be there at least until the end of the year." Her white hand made an irritated gesture. "I really don't understand what all this fuss and bother is about."

Gillian raised a brow. "It's about independence," she offered dryly.

"Oh, Gillian!" Melanie gave a helpless little laugh. "You're positively stuffy about this whole thing. Richard says that all rebels should be hung for treason."

"And what do you think?" Gillian was sorry now that she had come. It would be rude, however, to leave before she had stayed at least an hour. She finished the champagne and had no sooner set the glass on the table when the servant stepped forward to fill it again.

Melanie blinked. "Why, I agree with him, of course. It's about time this silly fighting was over and done with. It's much more fun to have parties, to dance, to be gay. If the Americans win, Richard says we will return to London. And I, for one, would be glad of it."

"Is it treason for a man to fight for his freedom?"

"Freedom?" The charming pout appeared. "Oh, don't be absurd. His Majesty's loyal subjects serve him of their own free will."

Gillian sighed and again drained her glass. Seeing the servant approach with the bottle, she raised a hand. "Oh, no," she protested. "No more, thank you."

"Gillian, it's only wine," Melanie said with a laugh that sounded condescending to the ears of her guest. "Besides, you've not yet toasted my engagement."

Resigned, Gillian picked up her glass and drank it down rather quickly, reasoning the sooner she finished it, the sooner she could go.

Finally, she got up, feeling a little unsteady on her feet.

"You will be coming to the wedding?" Melanie said as she walked Gillian to the front door. "I shall never forgive you if you don't."

"Yes, of course," Gillian murmured. Her head was beginning to spin. What she needed was fresh air.

Outside, she inhaled deeply. It didn't do much good. She should never have had that last glass of champagne, she thought, annoyed with herself. Pausing, she leaned against a fence, hoping her head would clear. She rarely drank wine, and when she did, she consumed no more than one glass. Obviously, three glasses in one hour had made her tipsy. Best to walk until she felt better, Gillian decided.

Thirty minutes later, she found herself on Queen Street, not far from the wharves on the East River. She wasn't feeling much better; in fact, she felt worse.

The street teemed with soldiers and sailors. A jumble of color swam before her unsteady gaze—scarlet jackets, blue coats, white shirts, the searing glint of sunlight on a bayonet.

A sailor came stumbling out of a grogshop and plowed right into her, almost knocking her off her feet. For a moment, it was difficult to tell which one of them was supporting the other.

Finally, Gillian pulled away and began to head

The Passionate Rebel

back to Broad Way. She had taken only a few steps when she felt a hand go around her waist. Though she tried to free herself, the sailor ignored her struggles. The man never spoke a word; though from the reek of rum emanating from him, he might well have been beyond coherent speech.

Dimly, Gillian realized that he most likely took her to be a dockside whore.

"Let go of me!" she cried, beginning to pant with her exertion. His mouth was on her neck, feeling wet and hot. Gillian screamed and pummeled his back with her fists.

Suddenly, his weight was gone, and Gillian stood there, dazed.

"Get going! You must have better things to do," said the man who pulled the sailor away.

Gillian stared at Philip Meredith, wondering why she felt no surprise at seeing him. But after finding him in her own parlor, she was half-expecting to see him every time she turned around.

The sailor began to spout profanities. Philip never said a word. He simply took a step forward and raised a massive fist, stopping just below the man's nose.

"Hey, now!" the sailor sputtered weakly. "No need to get upset." He backed away as quickly as he could.

When the sailor had gone a distance up the street, Philip turned and confronted Gillian squarely.

He was angry, she surmised, but she didn't care. Who asked him to be here at this particular minute on this particular day?

"What the devil are you doing, roaming the streets unattended?"

Well, he had his nerve! Questioning her comings and goings. Gillian's hands reached up to straighten her white cap before she remembered she had not worn it.

"What are you doing here?" Philip repeated in a sharper tone.

Gillian rubbed her neck, still feeling the imprint of the sailor's mouth on her flesh. "I was walking," she said lamely.

None too gently, Philip took hold of her arm. "I suggest you find a better part of town to walk in." He gestured with his free hand. "My carriage is here. I'll drive you home." He paused, noticing her glazed look for the first time. He had smelled the alcohol but assumed it had come from the sailor. The sailor was gone now; the odor remained.

He cocked a brow. "You wouldn't be just a bit inebriated, would you, Miss Winthrop?"

Gillian swallowed. "I'm no such thing," she declared with as much dignity as she could muster. "I was visiting a friend and toasted her engagement with a glass of champagne."

Making a face, he nodded at the small hiccough that punctuated her statement. She stumbled, and his grip tightened on her arm as he assisted her into the carriage. After giving his driver instructions, he climbed in beside her.

"Mr. Meredith . . ." Gillian spoke slowly, as if she were choosing each word with care. "It really isn't necessary for you to drive me home. I walked here, and I can walk back."

Exasperation overcame him. He turned, so that he was facing her fully. Gillian's hair, a glorious mass that gleamed gold even within the confines of the carriage, was in total disarray. Wispy tendrils floated around her face, prodded by a soft breeze that quickened slightly as the vehicle rolled along. Her chignon was askew, off-center from the slender

The Passionate Rebel

column of her neck. Back straight, she was not even leaning against the back of the seat. She looked so prim and adorable that Philip wanted to crush her in his arms.

Anger intruded. His voice emerged as a shout.

"Don't you realize that sailor was about to attack you?"

She gazed at him blearily. "Was he a friend of yours? You seem to be on good terms with the whole British Empire." She giggled, finding the idea funny, then slumped back against the seat. "I think I'm going to be sick," she declared solemnly.

"Oh, Lord!" Philip called to the driver to stop.

Gillian got out of the carriage and stood there uncertainly. After a moment, her stomach seemed to settle down of its own accord. She smiled sheepishly at Philip, who was watching her intently.

"I . . . guess I'm all right," she murmured.

In the carriage again, Gillian gave a shuddering sigh. In spite of her words, she felt dreadful. When Philip put his arm around her and drew her to him, she felt too weak to resist. Her head rested against his chest, and she could feel the warmth of his hand on her neck. It felt comforting, until his thumb brushed against the lobe of her ear. A sharp dart of feeling shot through her, and her eyes flew open. His cheek was resting on her hair now, and she could feel his warm breath down the back of her neck and, it seemed to her, to the tips of her toes.

She stayed still, trying to sort out these disturbing sensations.

Philip's other hand now slid down to cup her breast. With a gasp, Gillian raised her head to admonish him for this familiarity.

The words never came. How could they when his

mouth covered hers in one of those long, lingering kisses at which he seemed to be a master?

The carriage rolled over the cobblestones, rocking gently from side to side, but Philip's strong arms held her secure.

When she felt the tip of his tongue probing at her lips, Gillian stiffened. The pressure grew more insistent, and Gillian opened her mouth. She heard him groan as he gained entrance to the velvet recess.

She had thought the feeling of his kiss would be familiar, but nothing prepared her for the jolt she felt now. It was almost painful in its intensity.

With great effort, she tore her mouth away from his.

"You! You take advantage every chance you get." She knew her voice wavered; doubtless it was the champagne.

Philip took a deep breath. The ache in his loins was not allowing him to think clearly.

"I suppose you're going to tell me I was batting my eyelashes at you," she said, glaring at him.

Philip stared out the window and shifted his weight. There was no comfortable position.

The remainder of the trip was made in silence.

When they arrived at their destination, Philip got out of the carriage. As quick as he was, Gillian was faster and alighted before he could assist her.

"I'll thank you not to mention this incident to anyone," Gillian said to him. "It would upset my grandmother."

"I had no intention of doing so."

"I'll also thank you to stop following me around."

Philip raised a brow at the accusation. "I assure you, I did not follow you. It was quite by accident that I was on Queen Street when you had your encounter with a member of the Royal Navy."

"I don't believe you." She sniffed as she turned away.

Philip grasped her upper arm, halting her progress. "I told you not to fight me," he said softly. "It will do you no good."

Her fierce and angry expression drew only an amused look from him. She slapped his hand away. "Damn you!" she hissed. "If this is some sort of a game you're playing, I'm not interested."

"Oh, it's no game, Gillian Winthrop," he answered easily. "I am a man who usually gets what he wants." His voice turned husky. "And I want you."

Shaken by the intense look in his eyes, she gathered her skirt with her hand and hurried into the house.

Gillian was certain she would be unable to go to work that night, but after she had bathed and eaten, she felt much better.

She cast an apprehensive eye about the taproom when she entered. To her vast relief, Philip Meredith was nowhere in sight.

Business was brisk, and Gillian was grateful. She was kept so busy that she didn't have time to think. By nine o'clock, things had calmed down, and Gillian poured herself a cup of coffee, seeing Claudia come toward her.

"I've just learned that General Grey is on his way to Dartmouth," Claudia whispered. She gave a slight nod in the direction of a table where four dragoons were sitting. "They were discussing it when I put the food on the table." She paused and peered closer at Gillian. "You don't look too well," she noted with a frown. "You're not ill, are you?"

"No, no." Gillian wondered if she looked as pale as she felt. It was an uncommonly warm night. The closeness, the smell of stale ale and pungent rum had all combined to revive the queasiness she thought had been conquered. "I guess I am a bit tired." She smiled weakly as she put down the cup. "I didn't sleep too well last night."

"Go on home," Claudia urged immediately, giving her a gentle nudge. "It's after nine, anyway. I'll see to it that the shutter is opened first thing in the morning."

Gillian made no argument. Nothing seemed so inviting to her right now as sleep.

Claudia stood there a moment, then picked up the empty cup Gillian had left behind. As she made her way to the kitchen, she saw the Hessian sitting by himself at a corner table. This was the fourth night in a row he'd been in here. He was, as he always seemed to be, watching her. Claudia made it a point to ignore him. He was tall, blond and good-looking, but Claudia wanted nothing to do with the Germans. Only a few could speak English, and even fewer had any worthwhile information to impart. They were rough, brutal and inconsiderate.

Besides, the Hessian lieutenant always seemed to remain sober. She had never seen him drunk. Intoxication was the main criteria Claudia used when she made the decision to invite a man up to her room. It served two purposes. They were inclined to speak more openly, and they were usually unable to complete the act of sex before they passed out. By morning, they felt too wretched to be amorous. Though she had taken many officers to her room during the past year, Claudia had actually submitted to less than a handful of them.

"Good evening, *Fräulein*," the Hessian said to her as she passed his table.

The Passionate Rebel

Claudia viewed him coldly, not bothering to correct his term of address.

Though the shutter on the bedroom window remained open, Robbie didn't show up until two days later.

"I almost didn't come into town today," he said as he climbed out of the wagon.

"I don't even know if it's important," Gillian said.

"Everything's important," he stated firmly and listened intently as Gillian related what Claudia had overheard.

When she was through, Robbie nodded in satisfaction. His mouth stretched into a wide smile that Gillian found appealing. What would it be like to have his lips pressed against her own? Gillian suddenly wondered. Would it be the same as when Philip kissed her? It just might be that all kisses were alike.

Gillian decided it was time she found out. She took a step closer and placed her hand on the lapel of Rob's shirt. Slowly, she raised her head to look at him.

For a long moment, their eyes met and held. Robbie was no longer smiling, for he sensed the change in her manner.

"Gillian," he breathed softly as his hands went around her slim waist. "You tempt a man beyond endurance."

Her luscious lips parted, and he needed no further inducement. His kiss was gentle, a mere brushing of lips. Gillian waited expectantly for the surge of excitement she had experienced with Philip, but there was nothing.

When they finally drew away from each other, Gillian was vaguely disappointed.

"I think that 'one day soon' has finally arrived," Rob mused and couldn't help but be saddened. It appeared that his days of easy friendship with this spirited girl had now come to an end. He brushed a knuckle across her chin. "But take care, you little vixen. Not every man will stop at one kiss."

Gillian blushed deeply, ashamed that her actions had been so obvious.

With a wave of his hand, Robbie climbed back into the wagon, snapping the reins to prod the horse forward.

Pensively, Gillian watched him go. Perhaps, she reasoned, a kiss between friends was not the same as a kiss between . . .

Between what? she wondered, now thoroughly confused as she walked back to the house.

Entering the front door, Gillian was about to make her way upstairs, when she heard her grandmother call to her.

"Gillian? Come in here, dear. I was just about to have some tea."

Gillian entered the room but waved away the tea.

"I have just received a letter from your father." She settled herself and put on her spectacles. "I don't know how you are going to take this. Nor Edwina, for that matter. It seems that your father is planning to marry again. In fact, since this letter is three months old, I would venture to say that he has already married."

Gillian's gray eyes were wide with shock. "Married? How could he?"

"Oh, my dear," Alice said, laughing at the expression she was seeing. "Your father is not an old man. He's in his forties. You cannot expect him to go through life alone now that your mother has died. He loved my daughter dearly. She was very happy, you know." She removed a rather official-looking paper from the envelope. "He also sent this document appointing me your legal guardian until such time as you reach the age of twenty-one or marry."

Gillian only nodded at that, her mind still on her father's marriage. "I guess that means he is not planning on returning."

"I would imagine that he will stay in London," Alice agreed. Then she brightened. "I almost forgot. He also sent you a present." Getting up, she left the room. When she returned, she handed Gillian a box.

"Oh!" Gillian exclaimed in delight when she opened it. "It's a fashion doll."

"There are two. One is for Edwina. Now, you must write to him and thank him for his thoughtfulness." She looked up as she saw William.

"Mr. Meredith is here. Says he's got some papers for you to sign."

"Splendid." Alice moved forward to greet her guest. "Do come in." She smiled at Philip.

As he entered the room, Philip nodded at Gillian. "Miss Winthrop. How nice to see you looking so well."

The underlying mockery in his voice caused Gillian's cheeks to flush. "I'm going to take these to Edwina," she said. Gathering the dolls, she got quickly to her feet.

"Very well, dear," Alice said. "Give your sister my love. And tell her to bring Constance by more often. I don't see nearly enough of that child as I'd like." She turned to Philip. "Now, Mr. Meredith. I believe the tea is still hot. Will you join me?"

"It would be my pleasure, Mistress Wharton," Philip responded with a smile. "And if you have the time, there is a matter of great importance that I would like to discuss with you."

Chapter Ten

From Gillian's Diary:

> *November 10, 1778*
> *Congress has formally rejected the ineffectual overtures of Parliament and have now ended negotiations with Great Britain. They will not resume until our independence is acknowledged and the king withdraws his fleets and armies. So far, no move has been made in this direction. It would appear they have yet to realize that America is a nation on the course of liberty, and nothing will deter us from that course.*

Although two people currently occupied it, the parlor of the Wharton house was, at this moment, silent. It was not a comfortable silence.

Outside, the day was overcast and dismal, a perfect frame for Gillian's thoughts at this moment.

The Passionate Rebel

"I cannot believe that you do not give me credit for recognizing a suitable marriage for you when I see one."

Alice glared at Gillian, who was standing by the hearth, gray eyes defiant.

"Philip Meredith is wealthy," Alice went on when she received no response. "His family owns a tobacco plantation in Williamsburg, one which he will one day inherit. He is twenty-five years of age, well-educated and charming."

Gillian's lip curled. "He's a Briton!"

Alice's color deepened above the high neck of her black dress. In a rustle of silk, she got up from the chair in which she had been seated and stood there, hands clasped tightly at her waist. "May I remind you that I was born in England?"

"But I was not," Gillian shot back. "I'm an American."

"I am well-aware of where you were born," Alice snapped.

Gillian bit her lip, now sorry she had spoken so sharply, but it was true. She and Edwina had both been born right here in Manhattan. When their mother died three years ago, their father had returned to England, leaving Gillian with her maternal grandmother. Edwina was, at that time, married to Thomas Carmody, and the question of her leaving the colonies had not even arisen.

"Mr. Meredith was born in Virginia." Alice said that as if her point had been made.

"I don't care where he was born," Gillian retorted. "I will not marry him." With a toss of her head she began to leave the room, then paused as her grandmother's voice came at her. The tone was flat, edged with a finality that left Gillian feeling chilled.

"I would caution you against making a hasty decision. You would do well to give this proposal the serious consideration it deserves." She fell silent as Gillian turned.

"That will take no more than a minute of my time." Going to a chair, she sat down heavily, feeling as though she were being backed into a corner. She didn't like the feeling at all. "Do you really expect me to seriously consider a proposal from a man who goes sneaking behind my back, forcing me into a situation I want no part of?"

"Sneaking? What a foolish thing to say. Mr. Meredith acted in all propriety in first gaining the permission of your guardian before speaking to you. If your father had been here, you know very well that he would have to be consulted before any gentleman could formally approach you."

Gillian raised her head and viewed her grandmother through narrow eyes. "Exactly! And after that step was taken, I would then have the right to accept or reject the offer."

Too agitated to remain still, Gillian got up and moved around the room.

"Well, if you reject this offer," Alice grumbled, "I sincerely doubt you will ever receive another."

"But I do not love him," Gillian protested.

"Love?" Alice echoed incredulously. Her brows, as gray as her hair, dipped into a frown of censure. "Love is a state a man and a woman attain *after* they are wed. It's disgraceful to even think of such things beforehand. We are discussing marriage, a suitable union whereby you will be taken care of for the rest of your life. And, I might add, your father is in full accord with what I have done. When Mr. Meredith approached me some months ago, I told him that while I was personally delighted by his overtures, I felt it only right to contact your father."

The Passionate Rebel

From her pocket, she withdrew a letter. "This is for you. It was enclosed in the same envelope. As you will see, he has not only given his consent, he is greatly pleased and impressed by my reports of Mr. Meredith's character."

Gillian automatically took the proferred letter but made no attempt to read it. She just stared at her grandmother, unable to believe this was actually happening.

Her spine stiffened. "If you force me to marry him, I will never forgive you."

"Perhaps, one day, you will thank me," Alice murmured, unmoved by the threat. "Now, my dear," she went on, sounding suddenly businesslike, "it was not my intention to deny you a voice in this matter, and if there were other suitors—suitable ones—I would not have taken the direct action that I did."

"Other suitors!" Gillian said heatedly. She raised both hands, then let them fall to her sides again. "In the past two years I've seen no men in this house who weren't British."

"Be that as it may," her grandmother responded, unperturbed. "The fact still remains that you have no prospects for a husband that I can see. It's about time you settled down. At your age, I do not see that you are in a position to carelessly reject an offer of marriage, certainly not one from a man of Mr. Meredith's caliber. Bah!" She waved an irritated hand. "I should never have agreed to let you work in the tavern."

"But you did," Gillian said quickly. "And you cannot go back on your word. If I did not work, I would expire from boredom."

The blue eyes narrowed. "All the more reason for you to be married. Once you have your own household to run you will not need outside distractions to deliver you from tedium." She took a step closer, and her voice sharpened. "Do you think I am unaware of what you've been doing?"

Gillian stared blankly. She really had no idea of what Alice was referring to.

"You've been passing along information to the rebels in a most clandestine manner."

Gillian's mouth tightened. Damn Philip Meredith, she thought, gritting her teeth. She had known from the first he was not to be trusted. She had no difficulty in recalling the angry expression in his dark eyes when she had wheedled information from Captain Bennicot.

"If you've known that, why have you allowed me to work in the tavern?"

"Gillian, I may be old, but I am not stupid. Removing you from the tavern would not guarantee an end to your activities. A person can pick up information in many ways—at the market, at a banquet, in the street. What your sister and her husband do is their own affair. I would not presume to interfere in Mr. Carmody's business. But you, Gillian, are my business. Your father left you in my custody; therefore you are my responsibility. It's obvious that I cannot curb your tendencies, however detrimental to your welfare they may be. You are no longer a child. I can no longer confine you to your room."

She was pacing now, working herself into a fine snit, Gillian thought.

"It is time and more that you were married." Alice paused to view Gillian with a stern eye. "With a husband and a family, these foolish notions would be laid to rest." Seeing the stubborn set to Gillian's mouth, Alice felt a prod of desperation. "Good God, child!" she exclaimed, really frightened now. "Don't you realize that you could be hanged for what you are doing?"

That question went unanswered. "Did Mr. Meredith tell you all this?" Gillian demanded, wishing she could wring the man's neck. Her hands clenched at the delicious prospect of such an event.

Her chin drew in, and Alice looked surprised. "Mr. Meredith? Whatever gave you that idea?" She sniffed. "It is only to be hoped that he is unaware of your disgraceful behavior."

Gillian's gray eyes clouded with confusion. "But then, how did you find out?"

"Servants, my dear," Alice retorted dryly. "They love to gossip among themselves. Polly has made the acquaintance of a young black woman named Mandy." A vague gesture of a ringed hand concluded her statement.

Gillian sank into a chair. She felt cheated, somehow, at learning that Philip had not been her betrayer, felt robbed of a logical reason for her still-simmering anger. From beneath her lashes, she viewed her grandmother. Gillian loved her dearly, but not enough to submit to this. How dare that man simply walk into her life and seek to attain ultimate control over her? He hadn't even had the decency to court her. Not that it would have made any difference, she told herself, once again feeling righteous in her anger.

At the sight of Gillian's face, Alice spoke crisply. "Now, don't be childish. The world has no use for spinsters."

"I'm only nineteen," Gillian protested.

Alice raised a brow. "And soon to be twenty," she observed scathingly. "Your sister married at seventeen. I was married a year younger than that."

"I will not marry him," Gillian stated, refusing to be intimidated.

Alice took a deep breath, annoyed again. "Now hear me, Gillian! I will say this only once; then the subject is closed. You will marry Mr. Meredith, or I will be forced to send you to England to live with your father until you come to your senses."

Gillian searched her grandmother's face in an attempt to gauge the seriousness of her ultimatum. Even seeing the implacable expression, she couldn't believe it.

"You can't do that," she cried.

"Ah, but I can." Alice folded her arms across her bosom and looked supremely satisfied.

Gillian paled. "You would send me away, Gram?" She held her breath; this couldn't be happening.

"I would indeed," her grandmother affirmed. "All this patriotic nonsense that is filling your head with sedition is dangerous, not only for you but for your family as well."

Feeling a bit numb, Gillian went to the window and stared outside. Behind her, save for the ticking of the clock on the mantel, the room was again silent. Gillian's mind was working at a fast pace. She needed time.

"Gillian, Mr. Meredith will be here at four o'clock for your decision."

Wetting her lips, Gillian turned and regarded her grandmother for a long moment before she spoke.

"Very well," she said at last. Coming closer, she reached out a hand to rest on her grandmother's arm, as if to assure herself that she had the complete attention of the older woman. "But I make one condition."

Alice scowled but waited.

"The marriage is not to take place for one year."

The Passionate Rebel

"No!"

"One year! I insist upon it." Seeing the hesitation, she pressed her point. "Gram, surely you agree it would be wise for two people to at least know each other before such an important step is taken. I've never even spoken to Mr. Meredith in private." She bit her lip against the lie.

Alice gave her a sharp look but saw only a girl's youthful concern. She relaxed, her good humor restored. "Well, if Mr. Meredith has no objection..."

Hearing the knocker sound loud on the front door, Gillian braced herself. A moment later, Philip Meredith entered the room.

Surreptitiously, Gillian studied him with more care than she normally did. It was no use. Her eyes came to rest on his lips, and there they stayed. She was judging a man by his lips, by his kisses! How foolish could a woman be?

Alice headed for the decanter. "May I offer you some wine, Philip?"

"Thank you," he said, then turned to Gillian.

She stood there, stiff and proud in her gown of amber silk, patterned with roses embroidered in dark crimson. Elbow-length sleeves ended in a froth of ivory chiffon. The square neck was cut low, but a cream-colored fichu hid the swell of her bosom.

"How lovely you are," he said admiringly, then turned to accept the glass of Madeira from Alice, who raised her own glass in a toast.

"Well," she said with a broad smile. "It's all settled. Gillian has accepted your proposal."

"You do me great honor," said Meredith with a smile at Gillian.

"However," Alice concluded, "she has requested that the marriage not take place for one year. Do you have any objection to that?"

Meredith turned to Gillian and nodded his head to a point just short of a bow. "Not at all," he said easily. "A year's engagement is quite acceptable to me, if that is what Gillian wants."

Alice beamed. "I knew you were a sensitive man the first time I saw you."

Gillian repressed a smile of satisfaction. Anything could happen in a year. If, at the end of that year, she hadn't worked herself out of this impossible situation, she could always go to live with her father until she was 21. And then she would be free! The thought made her feel better. One thing she did know. She would never marry Philip Meredith!

Philip drained his glass and took his watch from a vest pocket. "I do hope you will forgive me," he said to Alice. "I have an appointment."

"Of course," Alice said graciously.

He turned to Gillian. "May I call for you on Sunday? Perhaps we can go for a drive."

Gillian hesitated, but her grandmother's frown told her what her answer must be. "I would be delighted," she murmured, lowering her eyes demurely.

When Philip left, Gillian went upstairs to her bedroom. Katie was shoveling ashes from the fireplace and dumping them into a pail. She paused in her task as Gillian entered. Having heard the raised voices coming from the parlor, she gave her mistress a sympathetic look.

"Is it set then?" she asked, knowing that Gillian would not mind the question.

"So they think," Gillian muttered.

Katie shoveled the last of the ashes from the hearth. Straightening, she rubbed her hands on her apron. "When is it to be?"

The Passionate Rebel

Gillian bit back the word "never" and instead replied, "Not for a year." She plopped herself down on the edge of the bed in an attitude of utter dejection.

Seeing that her mistress was in no mood for further conversation, Katie quietly left the room. After a few minutes had passed, Gillian reached into her pocket and withdrew the letter from her father. Settling herself more comfortably, she read it.

My dear daughter,

I have received your letter and am pleased that you and your sister enjoyed the fashion dolls.

Your grandmother has written to me of your impending marriage. Having been informed that Mr. Meredith attended Oxford, I have taken the liberty of speaking to his professors. Their very favorable reports only confirmed your grandmother's description of this fine young man, and I readily give my blessing to this union. It greatly relieves the apprehension that beset me when I left you behind in the colonies. Though I realize that it was your own decision to remain with your grandmother and your sister, I confess I would rather you had returned to England with me. I draw a measure of comfort during this time of conflict to know that you are safe in New York, for I know that the British will never relinquish their stronghold.

My wife, Evelyn, is at this time expecting our first child. I know that you will be as overjoyed with our good fortune as we are.

My love and thoughts are with you always,
Your Loving Father

Getting up, Gillian crumpled the letter in her fist. How nice that everyone was in agreement as to what course her future should take!

No wonder she had been seeing Philip Meredith here at the house virtually every Sunday afternoon. Playing cribbage with her grandmother indeed! She should have known there was more to it than that.

Gillian threw the crumpled letter on her writing table. And how polite he had been—no more stolen kisses, no more unwanted overtures.

A more conniving devil never lived!

With a deep sigh, Gillian smoothed out the letter and put it in a drawer. Then she hurried from the house, anxious to talk to Edwina.

After relating the news contained in their father's letter, Gillian told Edwina about her unexpected betrothal.

If she had expected sympathy from Edwina, Gillian was sadly mistaken. Edwina was once again pregnant and was viewing the world and all it held with a rosy smile.

"Mr. Meredith?" Edwina giggled. "Somehow I didn't think he was coming around so often just to visit Gram. He's such a nice man."

"There is no such thing as a nice Tory," Gillian snapped. "I will not marry him."

Edwina moistened her lips. "Gillian, if he was a redcoat, I'll admit that I would march right back to Gram's with you this instant in an effort to change her mind. But, on the face of it, she's made an excellent decision."

"Edwina!"

"She has," her sister persisted. "I've seen Mr. Meredith often enough to know that he is a gentle-

The Passionate Rebel

man. Certainly, he's good-looking. And I'm willing to wager that Gram has verified the fact that he's prosperous."

Gillian's shoulders slumped. She cast an accusing glance at her sister. "Did you love Tom when you married him?"

Edwina looked surprised. "Gracious, no. I hardly knew him."

Gillian gritted her teeth. "I don't believe you. I know you too well to believe that you would entrust yourself and your future to a man you didn't care for."

"Oh!" Her brown eyes widened. "You didn't ask me if I cared for him. You asked me if I loved him."

"Edwina!" Gillian was exasperated.

"It's not the same thing," Edwina insisted. "You must believe me, Gillian. Truly, it's not the same thing." Her glance turned sly. "Somehow, I don't think I'd be wrong if I said you cared for Rob Clayton."

Gillian stared at her sister. "I . . . do care for Rob."

"Of course you do. He's a fine man. But what else is there?"

"Edwina, you are talking in circles. I really don't appreciate it."

"Well, take a moment to think about it."

Gillian fumed and waited until the alloted time had passed. "All right, you said it. Caring and loving are two different things. Fine! You also said you 'cared' for Tom. So . . . ?"

"I wasn't in love with anyone else," Edwina pointed out mildly. "I married a caring, sensitive man, and in time it turned to love."

"And if it hadn't?" Gillian demanded sharply.

Edwina grinned, something rare for her. "Then I would be married to a man I cared for, one I consider a friend. Hardly an unbearable situation."

Gillian thought it was.

Edwina saw and understood. "Oh, Gillian, what do you expect from marriage?" When she received no reply, she answered her own question. "It is a commitment two people make to each other. One that says you will not only be faithful, but that each one of you remain first in each other's thoughts. Can you honestly say that I have not remained first in the thoughts of my husband?"

"But that's different," Gillian protested. "Tom loves you."

"Of course he does. He wouldn't have approached Father if he hadn't—any more than Mr. Meredith would have approached Gram."

Gillian narrowed her eyes and viewed her sister squarely. "Tell me, Edwina. If you hadn't considered Tom to be caring, and if you had not regarded him with fondness, what would your reaction have been to his proposal?"

Edwina spoke without thinking. "Why I never would have consented." She drew a sharp breath, and her eyes reflected a sudden dismay. "Darling . . ."

Gillian stood up. "You've answered my question," she said in a sharper tone than she had ever before used to her sister. "I cannot imagine you accepting a traitor. Why should I?"

"When this war is finally over, there will be no more Tories or rebels," Edwina pointed out quietly. "Hopefully there will only be a people united as a nation." Seeing Gillian's implacable expression, she bit her lip. "Oh, Gillian, do you really have such a strong feeling against this man?"

"I do."

Edwina's smile was sad but resigned. "Then stand by your convictions, my dear." She clasped Gillian to her in a fierce embrace. "Don't listen to anyone who thinks they know better than what your heart tells you." She drew away. "Including me."

As Gillian turned to go, Edwina's voice halted her.

"Just make certain that you don't ignore whatever your heart does tell you."

Feeling dispirited, Gillian went down to the kitchen, deciding she would have a bite to eat before she went into the taproom. Claudia was at the table, finishing her supper. Without a word of greeting, Gillian sat down in a chair.

After a few minutes of silence, Claudia said, "Do you want to talk about it?"

Gillian made a face, then told her friend about her impending marriage.

"Ahh..." Claudia's white teeth caught her full lower lip, and her eyes narrowed in speculation. "There is something about that one."

Gillian's brow furrowed, sensing that Claudia was not referring to the fact that Philip was a British sympathizer. "What do you mean?" she asked.

Claudia gave one sharp shake of her head. "There is something deceitful there, something I cannot put a finger on."

Gillian laughed, although the sound held no mirth. "I can't argue with that. The man went sneaking behind my back to speak to my grandmother, to propose marriage before he even considered what my feelings would be on the subject."

"And what are your feelings?" Claudia asked as she got to her feet. Picking up her plate, she put it in the sink.

Gillian blinked as if the question had taken her totally by surprise. "Why . . ." She waved a hand, then tightened her mouth. "You know how I feel about Tories. Swine are more agreeable to me."

Claudia pursed her lips to keep from smiling. She herself had little use for Tories, but her feeling in no way matched that of her detestation for the redcoats.

"What if Mr. Meredith was a patriot?" she asked finally. "Would that change your feelings about him?"

Gillian sniffed at the idea. "Somehow I doubt it. I've never met a man who so irritates me. Besides," she added with a sigh, "the fact remains that he is a loyalist, and I have no intention of marrying such a one."

With a soft smile, Claudia walked from the room while Gillian stared after her in some perplexity. Of all people, she had been certain that Claudia would be the one who would commiserate with her plight.

In the taproom, Claudia paused as she saw the Hessian just now entering. He was late tonight. As he always did, the man headed for the corner table.

Claudia glanced around. Both Delia and Chastity were otherwise occupied. With a sigh, she moved to the bar and filled a cup with ale.

The man smiled as she approached, but Claudia saw no need to do the same.

"It was so crowded earlier in the evening," he said to her when she stood before him, "I decided to wait a while before I came in."

Claudia just stared at him. Did he really think she cared? she wondered.

"I am more or less stationed in Manhattan permanently," he went on conversationally. "I work in the supply depot, you see."

In spite of herself, Claudia viewed him with curiosity. He was, as she had noticed before in a quite dispassionate way, good-looking, even handsome. His features were strong, the nose aquiline. His skin was smooth and clear, but his eyes were easily his most striking feature. Claudia had never seen eyes that were such a piercing, pristine shade of blue. No hint of gray or green marred the clarity of color.

"You speak English very well," she commented at last.

"I have been in this country for more than two years now," he said. "It seemed foolish not to learn the language."

"Doesn't seem foolish to your cohorts," Claudia remarked, unimpressed. "I presume you want the same?" She put the cup on the table, then turned away, startled when she felt his hand on her wrist.

"Do not judge me by my companions." He held her wrist a moment longer, marveling at how fine-boned she was. Then he released it. "Will you have a drink with me?"

"I'm not allowed to do that."

"Then a late supper elsewhere?"

"No."

"Please. I only want to talk to you."

"What is it you want from me?" she demanded.

His smile revealed white, even teeth. "I'm not sure a man needs a reason to talk to a beautiful woman."

Claudia turned abruptly and saw another customer beckoning to her. With relief, she hurried away.

When she had gone, the Hessian stared morosely into his cup. He never drank enough to get drunk, just enough to assure his place at this select table. Although the rest of the room was adequately lighted, the ceiling-hung oil lamps cast only a glimmer of light into this particular corner of the room. It allowed him to watch the other occupants without being obvious about it.

What had happened, he wondered, to so change his ideas, his feelings, his goals? A few years ago, life had been simple. Now, all that had changed.

Maybe it was the fact that he was growing older. He would be 30 on his next birthday. Not a great age, really, but one by which a man assumed his life would be settled.

His was not.

His long, sensitive fingers traced an aimless pattern on the wood table, and his blue eyes again sought Claudia.

She knew it, even though she had her back to him. Her voice shook as she gave Tom her order, and he viewed her sharply.

"Are you all right?" he asked.

Claudia nodded. "It's just that Hessian."

Tom's eyes narrowed as he viewed the lieutenant. "Christ, I'd throw him out on his blue-coated rump, if I could. But he never does anything. He just sits there, eats, has a few drinks . . ."

" . . . and watches me," Claudia observed tonelessly.

"Yes, he does." Tom sounded worried. "Look, Claudia, maybe it would be wise for you to move up to our apartments for a while. I'm sure Edwina . . ."

"No. Thank you, Tom. Thank you for all you and Edwina have done for me. This is something I must do. There's a debt to repaid, and I'm the only one left to do it."

Tom put the drink on the tray. "A debt, Claudia, or revenge?"

She stiffened. "Maybe it's the same thing."

Chapter Eleven

From Gillian's Diary:

> *November 15, 1778*
> *The United States of America! How fine it feels to pen those words and know they have meaning. The Articles of Confederation, adopted by our Congress one year ago today, have now been signed by delegates from ten of our newly formed sovereign states: Connecticut, New Hampshire, Pennsylvania, Rhode Island, Massachusetts, New York, Virginia, South Carolina, North Carolina, and Georgia. It is expected that the rest will follow shortly.*

The ironclad runners of the horse-drawn sleigh slid easily over the slick surface of the street.

The day had dawned clear, with a bright sun that

set the snow to sparkling with an intensity that dazzled the eye.

The fair weather left Gillian disgruntled. She had hoped it would snow, hoped there would be a blizzard. Even a strong wind would have given her an excuse not to go out with Philip.

Still, she supposed it was better than being trapped in the parlor with him.

For a while they drove in silence.

The sight of her beloved city always filled Gillian with sadness these days. The New York of today was vastly different from the one she remembered from her childhood. It was now a garrison town, and evidence of it was everywhere. Bad enough were the barracks and fortifications of the British Army; bad enough, too, were the charred ruins of the fire that had destroyed almost a quarter of the city, producing what people now called Canvas Town. But what Gillian found especially intolerable were the trees. They were almost all gone now, having been cut down for firewood. And no wonder, when a cord of wood cost as much as ten pounds!

As if all that were not enough, in Wallabout Bay—if one cared to look—were the prison ships. Dank and foul-smelling, they were a constant reminder of the war.

There were jails on land, too, buildings that were former sugarhouses or warehouses. But these, though only fractionally better than the ships, were filled to capacity. In all, better than 10,000 American patriots struggled against sickness and starvation in an effort to live until the end of the hostilities.

With a start, Gillian realized that Philip was speaking to her.

"On the way back, I'll drive by my house," he was

The Passionate Rebel

saying. "I'm certain you would like to view your new home."

Gillian just stared at him. Inside her muff, her hands clenched, and she was unable to contain her anger.

"What kind of man are you?" she demanded. "Have you any idea of how presumptuous it was of you to speak to my grandmother before you sought my feelings in this matter?"

"Love does strange things to a man," he murmured, ignoring her bristling demeanor.

"Love!" She spat out the word like a cat unpleasantly awakened from a peaceful doze. "Doesn't it bother you that I feel no love for you?" She shifted her weight in agitation.

He smiled, infuriating her further. "I have every intention of changing that."

Reaching out a hand, Philip's fingertips trailed a slow path down her cheek. Gillian jerked away as a sudden spark shot down her spine and settled in that most private part of her. It was so unexpected, she drew a breath and held it until the feeling passed. It had not been unlike the sensation she had experienced when Philip kissed her. She couldn't understand her reaction. The gesture he had just made was in no way to be considered intimate—untoward perhaps, but not intimate.

Philip was smiling at her, but his eyes held a puzzled look at her reaction. And so they might, Gillian thought. She herself was no less puzzled.

When she spoke, her voice was cold. "I have no intention of marrying you, you know."

A brow arched upward. "Indeed?" he murmured. "Your grandmother led me to believe that it was all settled."

"For her, it is, but not for me." She directed her eyes forward and modulated her tone. "A year is a long time. Perhaps you will find someone more suitable."

"I doubt it."

Annoyance creased her brow and tugged at the soft corners of her mouth. Nothing worked. The man certainly didn't know how to take a hint. Doubtless he thought her a foolish female incapable of knowing her own mind.

"Would you care to tell me why you find the idea of marrying me so objectionable?" He spoke so matter-of-factly it was a second before his question registered.

"I would find the idea of marrying any Tory objectionable."

Meredith sighed. "I fear that subject will remain a source of contention between us until the matter is settled, one way or the other. Who knows? The Continentals may actually win their war."

Gillian made no comment. They were riding up Maiden Lane. Redcoats were everywhere.

Two British officers on horseback came riding down the street. As they neared, Gillian stiffened. One of the men was Major General Charles Grey. Gillian sincerely wished the general would fall off his horse and break his neck. Ever since the massacre at Paoli, she had hated this man, as did every patriot who knew of his infamy.

The two officers were now abreast of the carriage. To Gillian's horror, Meredith waved a friendly hand.

"A good day to you, General," he called out and was rewarded by a friendly greeting in return.

"My God," she exclaimed in outrage, "how can you even speak to such a one?"

Now Philip looked annoyed. He gave the reins a sharp snap, and the startled horse sprinted forward.

The Passionate Rebel

"Gillian," he said in a tight voice, "I feel it necessary to inform you that after we are married, you will not be permitted to contradict me at every turn."

Gillian turned away. "Pompous ass," she muttered under her breath.

Jaw set, Philip snapped the reins again, and Gillian was pushed back against the seat with their forward movement. Well, she thought in satisfaction, at least the drive would be over sooner than expected. At the rate they were traveling, they would cover the whole of Manhattan in no time.

Philip did slow down in front of his house. Gillian gave it a brief look, then directed her eyes forward. After they were married! Gillian thought with a sniff, remembering the reason for the detour. Since that day would never come, there was no reason for more than a casual glance.

Some ten minutes later, the sleigh halted in front of the Wharton house and Gillian got out before he could assist her.

"There is to be a banquet at Governor Tryon's house this Saturday," Philip said before she could walk away. "I will expect you to accompany me."

Gillian sighed. "That would be nice," she said listlessly. Without waiting to see him drive away, she went into the house.

Feeling exhausted, Gillian went to her room and threw herself on the bed. Taunting visions of the future plagued her. She could remain husbandless—unthinkable. She could live in England for a year—intolerable.

Or she could marry Philip Meredith.

None of the choices were enticing.

She didn't think she had slept, but when next she became aware, Gillian was surprised to see that it was already dusk. Hurriedly, she left the house.

Outside, it had begun to snow again, and Gillian pulled up the hood of her cloak.

She was halfway to the Blue Swan when she heard her name being called. Turning, she saw Rob Clayton riding toward her.

Approaching her, he halted his horse and dismounted. He wasn't wearing a cap, and the snow dotted his brown hair with glistening flakes.

"What are you doing in town?" she asked, a bit surprised to see that he wasn't using the wagon.

"I came to say good-bye," he answered.

"Oh, Rob!" Gillian cried. "Where are you going?"

"Both me and Pa have signed up for one year. We're joining the Continentals in New Jersey."

Gillian drew a breath of dismay. "But I don't understand. Who will take your place here? How will we get word through without you?" She was upset, never having expected this. Aside from Edwina and Tom, there was no one she trusted more than Rob.

He shrugged impatiently. "There are plenty of people around who can carry notes as well as I can." He put his hands on her shoulders. "Oh, Gillian, don't you see? I want to be a part of it. I want to fight for my country. I'm tired of sitting on the sidelines while other men do the real work."

Gillian bit her lip. The decision had been made, and she knew she could not change it. "I'll miss you," she said plaintively.

"And I, you." Releasing her, he grinned. "Don't break too many hearts while I'm gone, little vixen. No man is safe when you turn on your charm."

Her eyes glistened with unshed tears. "You always have been . . ."

The Passionate Rebel

Rob laughed, then sobered, his expression almost sad. "The time was never right for us, Gillian. But if you ever need a friend, you know where to find me."

She smiled bravely through her tears and watched as he mounted his horse, turning to wave at her. "Rob," she called out. "You will take care?"

"Don't worry about me. Those lobsterbacks won't stand a chance once I join the fray."

Gillian stood in the snow-covered street until Rob was gone from view. Then, with a deep sigh, she continued on her way.

The taproom was crowded. Smoke from the hearth and from the pipes the men were smoking created a blue haze that hung there like a false sky just below the ceiling.

Gillian tied an apron around her waist and went to work, grateful for the distraction.

Claudia came out of the kitchen, carrying a tray piled high with dishes and bowls of food. She had already set them at their assigned tables when she saw the grenadier. With a gasp, she whitened. She had thought she would never recognize any of the soldiers who had so brutally attacked her, but she was now looking at one of them. The memory of the leering face looming over hers rushed forward, leaving her nauseous.

Weakly, she leaned against the bar. For a moment, she couldn't move, felt paralyzed.

"Claudia?" Gillian's voice was low, giving no indication of the alarm she felt when she saw her friend's distress.

Slowly, Claudia turned. She looked like a lovely marble statue. "It's . . . him! One of them," she qualified and only now began to tremble.

"Are you certain?" Gillian asked, immediately catching Claudia's meaning. "You said . . ."

"I know what I said," Claudia responded in a harsh whisper. "It's like . . . I blocked it from my mind. It's him! He's the one who helped me get away from the fire. 'Come along,' he said to me. 'You'll be safer away from here.'"

Gillian regarded the man in question. He looked to be somewhere in his mid-thirties. Since he was seated, she could not see how tall he was, but he was barrel-chested, with muscular arms that not even his jacket could hide. A peculiar bump on his nose gave indication that it might at one time have been broken.

Claudia's hand now curled around the knife resting on one of the plates, and Gillian's hand quickly flashed out to cover hers.

"No! You'd never get away with it," she hissed. "They'd take you outside and hang you."

"What matter?" Claudia demanded.

"No!" Gillian pried the knife from the rigid fingers. She turned to look at the man again. He was drunk but not sodden. However, a few more drinks might alter that state. Going behind the bar, she filled a cup with rum. "Here, put this in front of him. When it's empty, give him another."

"What . . . ?"

"Do it!" She turned and went to converse with Tom, whose jaw tightened, but he said nothing and only gave her a short nod.

It took three more drinks for the grenadier to slump over the table. They left him there until the tavern emptied.

"What are you going to do with him?" Claudia asked, watching as Tom and Gillian dragged the man to the kitchen. She wanted to help but was powerless to do so. If she touched him, she knew she would kill him.

The Passionate Rebel

Edwina was in the kitchen. As soon as she saw them, she dismissed the servants. In a few quick words, Thomas explained the situation. Edwina nodded, then left the room. When she returned a few minutes later, she handed Tom a piece of paper.

"This should do it," she said.

Thomas read aloud the words that his wife had penned: "British troops are moving toward Savannah. They plan to attack the city in full force."

"Good," he said, then stuffed the paper into the grenadier's shoe. It was the first place the patrols looked. "We will not be telling the British anything they don't already know," Tom said shortly. "But when the patrols find this information on him, they'll cart him to the nearest gibbet."

With the help of all three women, Tom removed the soldier's uniform, then dressed him in an old shirt and a worn pair of breeches. After that, they carted him outside and put him gently into the back of the wagon. The man groaned once or twice but did not awaken.

"I'll be back as quickly as I can," Tom said to Edwina, giving her a quick kiss.

Claudia's eyes were brilliant with tears as they trooped back into the kitchen. "If anything happens to Tom, it will be my fault."

"Nothing will happen," Edwina asserted firmly, though she was greatly concerned. Then she sighed. "Thomas has placed himself in jeopardy since this war started."

"And you?" Claudia peered intently. "I have nothing to lose, but you . . ."

" . . . have everything." Edwina smiled. "And I want to keep it intact for my children. It would be unforgivable for either of us to deny them their future."

There was no sleep for any of them. Prudently, Gillian returned home, lest her grandmother become suspicious. She did not, however, get into bed. Instead, she sat by her window until, some 40 minutes later, she saw Tom's wagon return. Only then did she sleep.

The following day they learned that their plan had worked with only one unexpected development. The grenadier, who had quite belligerently protested his innocence with raised fists, had been shot instead of hung.

Chapter Twelve

From Gillian's Diary:

> *November 21, 1778*
> *Once again, winter has cast a blanket of inactivity over the war effort. Only the profiteers are indefatigable. The weather does not deter them from selling a pair of boots for 20 pounds or a horse for 200 pounds. They prosper and grow fat, dozing in front of their warm fires while our poor soldiers shiver in the snow and long for a decent meal.*

Saturday night, for Gillian, came all too quickly. She was able to summon no more than a weak smile in the face of her grandmother's happy anticipation of the banquet to be held in the governor's house. Philip had invited Alice to join them, and she had readily agreed.

As she dressed, Gillian kept glancing at the hairpiece on the wig stand. She wondered if it was as heavy as it looked. Alice had personally brought it home from the wigmaker only this morning.

And what a lavish creation it was.

It was fashioned into a tall, rather wide pompadour with a saucy ringlet on each side and curls arranged down the back.

"I'd better not lower my head while I'm wearing that," Gillian muttered to Katie. "It's for sure I'll pitch forward, flat on my face."

Katie laughed as she helped Gillian into an undergarment of pearl-colored satin. The pointed, tightly fitted bodice flared into a bell-shaped skirt.

Over this, Gillian slipped on a loose, flowing gown of turquoise silk. This was fastened beneath her bosom with a black velvet ribbon but was open from that point down to reveal the undergarment. On her feet she wore turquoise silk slippers.

That accomplished, Gillian sat at her dressing table while Katie positioned the wig in place.

"It needs something," Katie commented with a small frown. She rummaged through Gillian's jewel case and brought forth an onyx comb. The top was fan-shaped and fitted with minute silk roses of a deep crimson color.

Gillian checked a smile, not at all surprised at the choice. Katie seemed fascinated by the delicately constructed accessory and always seemed disappointed when Gillian declined to wear it.

"Oh, my," Katie breathed when she was through. "You sure do look splendid."

Getting up, Gillian viewed herself in the mirror, a bit surprised to see that she really did look splendid. Slowly, she moved her head from side to side. The wig was even heavier than she had thought it would be. How ridiculous, she thought, to put hair on a head that was already adequately endowed.

"Here." Katie handed her mistress a lace fan. "There'll be no one there tonight prettier than you." She cocked an ear, hearing voices from downstairs. "Seems like Mr. Meredith's arrived." Picking up a fur-lined cloak, she draped it around Gillian's shoulders. "Will you tell me about it?" she asked, smiling wistfully with the request.

Gillian paused at the door, realizing that Katie had never in her life been to a ball. For a moment, impractical as it was, she wished they could trade places for the evening.

"Oh, Katie," she sighed, "if you could only go in my stead."

"Now that would set them on their heels," Katie exclaimed in delight. She pirouetted around the room, lifting the coarse muslin of her skirt in an exaggerated display of coquetry. "Who do you think would ask me for the first dance?"

Gillian smiled softly. "In the dress I'm wearing, just about every man in attendance," she remarked quietly as she left the room.

Coming down the stairs, she saw Philip and her grandmother conversing in the hall.

Not even an occasion of this magnitude had prompted Alice to forego wearing black. The gown, however, was a stunning creation of lace over heavy satin, and while the lace overskirt was black, the satin underskirt was cream-colored.

As Gillian approached, Philip turned to her.

"I've never seen you look more beautiful," he exclaimed admiringly. His eyes twinkled softly as he added, "I have an idea that I will be the envy of every man at the banquet."

"Thank you," she responded coolly.

Helene Lehr

In spite of herself, Gillian considered the appearance of elegance he so casually projected. From the silver buckles on his blue-heeled shoes to his elaborately detailed silk brocade jacket, Philip wore his finery with ease and no hint of affectation.

Philip now opened the front door and escorted them both to the waiting carriage.

As they drove along the snow-covered streets, Gillian listened to Alice and Philip as they engaged in a lively repartee. Though they tried to include her in their conversation, Gillian could summon no more than a nod. The thought that she would have to spend hours in the company of redcoats and Tories left her feeling depressed. How she wished for the evening to be at an end!

Just before they arrived at their destination, Alice raised her fan and whispered, "Gillian, I do not want to hear you voice any seditious remarks this evening. Please, try to conduct yourself with propriety. You will do neither me nor your intended husband any credit if you do otherwise."

Gillian sighed. "Yes, Gram." But, she thought to herself as she stared out the window, that doesn't mean I can't listen. She perked up with the idea. Perhaps the evening would not be a loss, after all. She just might pick up a piece of worthwhile information.

The large, three-story mansion was ablaze with light when they arrived a while later.

The estate was one of the largest in Manhattan. To the rear were the stables, the carriage house, over which were the servants' quarters, and the summer kitchen. While the plight of most New Yorkers ranged from small privations to outright poverty, here in the mansion General Tryon, the Royal Governor, had commandeered for his personal use,

The Passionate Rebel

one saw only richness and plenty. Servants almost tripped over each other as they hurried to attend the guests.

Though she tried not to be, Gillian was impressed. When she had been a child, her father had often spoken of the splendor of the King's Court. Gillian was convinced that this was what it looked like.

The ballroom was large, the floor tiled in pink and gray. Tall white columns that had been crafted from marble delineated the dance floor. Around this perimeter were positioned armless chairs upholstered in crimson velvet, their backs carved and gilded.

On a balcony at the far end of the room, a 25-piece orchestra offered music. The musicians were garbed as elaborately as were the guests. On the opposite side of the room were long tables, piled high with a variety of food Gillian hadn't known existed. One whole table was devoted entirely to pastries, cakes and pies. One table held only fish; another, meat and game; and still another, various spirits. A row of liveried servants stood behind each table, ready to serve the guests.

Alice caught sight of Florence Cartwright and hurried off to join her friend.

Gillian stayed at Philip's side as they meandered through the crowd at a very slow pace. Philip seemed to know everyone, including the Royal Governor. William Tryon had been appointed by the Crown as both Governor of New York and General in the armed forces. He was a tall thin man with a narrow face that seemed to have been carved into a perpetual frown. Gillian rated him only below General Grey, insofar as her antipathy was concerned, and the distance was marginal.

They were standing at the buffet, and Gillian was

listening with only half an ear as Philip and Tryon were conversing.

"General Clinton feels that Washington will remain at Elizabethtown for several months yet," Tryon commented at one point.

Meredith frowned. "Perhaps it isn't wise for the general to make such an assumption. You must remember what happened at Trenton."

The Royal Governor gave a short laugh that held no humor. "We are not likely to forget, but good God, man, it's positively uncivilized for a general to move his troops on Christmas night. In fact, it's uncivilized to fight a war in the dead of winter. Of course, it was the fault of the Hessians. To them, Christmas is a convivial affair. It was only to be expected that they would spend the day celebrating."

Gillian nibbled at the tidbits on her plate. It was outrageous, she thought, for Tryon to label Washington uncivilized. She turned away.

Perhaps, she thought, once more viewing the elegance around her, it really was a lost cause. How could they defeat a nation like Great Britain? How could people like herself, ordinary and inexperienced, defeat an empire that had been many years in the making? They had the guns, the soldiers, a navy that was unexcelled.

And what do we have? she wondered. Militia that was ragged, ill-equipped, underfed and underpaid. Only a promise of better things to come.

Gillian put down her plate. The fanciful food seemed suddenly like refuse.

Was it worth it? Worth all the heartache and privation?

Only one thing beckoned at the end of the road—freedom!

The Passionate Rebel

Gillian smiled and straightened her shoulders. It was, after all, a carrot too tempting to ignore.

When Philip turned to ask her to dance, Gillian was still smiling.

"It pleases me to see you looking so happy," he remarked as he stepped backward then forward in time to the minuet. "It's not often that I see that radiant smile of yours. May I assume that it is my company that is producing such a charming display of euphoria?"

Gillian gave a trilling little laugh but remembered not to toss her head. "You may assume anything you like, Mr. Meredith."

Although it irked him that she refused to use his first name, Philip did not comment on it. Instead, he said, "Then I choose to assume that I am the cause, Miss Winthrop."

The dance ended, and Gillian saw Melanie Cartwright and Captain Bennicot coming toward them.

Melanie threw her arms around Gillian and gave her a brief hug. "Your grandmother's just told us of the wonderful news," she gushed.

Gillian blinked, wondering what on earth Melanie was talking about.

"When is the wedding to be?" Melanie asked, clasping Gillian's hand as though they were best friends.

Gillian stifled a sigh. Oh, she thought to herself, that news! "Not until next year." The words caught in her throat, and she withdrew her hand from its unwanted captivity.

Melanie offered one of her cute little pouts. "That's not far away. I do hope you are not planning on marrying before me. I shall be terribly upset if you beat me to the altar."

Gillian laughed. "I assure you, there is no chance of that happening."

"Actually, I confess to being surprised when your grandmother told us of your engagement," Melanie confided as they headed back to the buffet, Philip and Bennicot trailing behind them. "I was beginning to despair that you would ever have a beau, much less a husband."

Gillian felt a prickle of annoyance. "May I ask why?"

"Well, you hardly ever come to a social event, and when you do, you're so standoffish. Men don't take kindly to that attitude, you know."

"I wasn't aware that you were such an expert on what men like," Gillian retorted dryly.

"Oh," Melanie laughed and waved a plump hand. "It doesn't take an expert to know that a man likes to have a woman look up to him, to give him her undivided attention, to be cheerful and agreeable."

"I once had a pet dog who could do all of that," Gillian muttered under her breath as she moved away.

Philip immediately followed. "Did I hear Miss Cartwright expressing surprise that you've captured a man?" he teased when they were out of earshot.

Gillian gave him a look filled with irritation. "Melanie Cartwright is a spiteful little witch without a brain in her head."

"What an unkind thing to say," Philip murmured, revealing a great deal of amusement.

"Well, it's true," Gillian sniffed.

Putting a hand on her elbow, Philip guided her behind a tall malachite vase to a window embrasure. Then he put his arms around her and drew her close to him.

"I can tell you one thing," he whispered huskily, "you've captured my heart."

The Passionate Rebel

Ignoring her gasp and the nervous look she cast into the ballroom, Philip kissed her soundly.

"Are you mad?" she hissed when he finally released her. "People will see us."

"At least there will be no doubt in their mind that you've caught a man," he remarked with a grin as he led her back to the dance floor.

Though she had been determined not to, Gillian enjoyed the ball at Governor Tryon's house. Regretfully, she had picked up no information whatsoever. Still, she was young enough to have been impressed by the gorgeous gowns of the ladies, the extraordinary food and the gaiety of the music.

Sunday dawned gray and cold. Despite the fact that they had arrived home after three o'clock, Alice insisted that they attend church as usual.

Gillian only barely remained awake during the services and was vastly relieved when it was over.

When their carriage turned onto their street, Gillian looked out the window to see Claudia. She instructed William to stop, then stuck her head out the window.

"Where are you going?" she called.

Claudia came closer. "For a walk. Would you like to come along?"

Gillian groaned and shook her head. "I plan on doing nothing more energetic than taking a nap."

Claudia smiled as the carriage continued on its way. Then she took a deep breath. The air felt clean and refreshing.

She walked aimlessly, not having a destination in mind, enjoying the peace and quiet of the Sunday afternoon. When, some ten minutes later, she caught sight of the blue-coated Hessian, Claudia's step faltered. She knew his name now—Franz Heideman.

Hastily, Claudia crossed the street in the hopes that he had not seen her.

But, of course, he had, and he immediately headed in her direction. Touching the brim of his hat, he fell in step beside her. Claudia rebuffed his polite words of greeting and quickened her step. Undaunted, he continued to walk with her.

"Why does it upset you to be in my company?" Franz asked, sounding genuinely puzzled.

Claudia didn't attempt to answer that; she didn't quite understand it herself.

"If I have said or done anything to offend you, please allow me to apologize."

For reasons she could not explain, the man's politeness grated on Claudia's nerves. She could have easier dealt with a churlish clod.

"You've done nothing to offend," she said shortly, annoyed to see his face lighten with her words. "It's just that I have so little time to myself, I enjoy my few moments of solitude."

He nodded slowly. "I can understand your need, for it is one of my own."

She paused, expecting him to leave then, but he didn't. As if he had sensed her thoughts, his blue eyes reflected amusement.

"You will, I hope, forgive my persistence. For a woman to travel the streets unescorted is an open invitation to trouble. If you will allow me to walk with you, I promise I will not intrude upon your thoughts."

Claudia arched a brow. "And what assurance do I have that *you* will not cause me trouble?"

"My word," he answered in all seriousness.

Claudia sighed and resumed walking. She wasn't about to waste any more of her precious time off having an inane conversation with a man she hardly

The Passionate Rebel

knew. Franz fell in step beside her, not too close, but close enough to signal to the casual onlooker that they were together.

True to his word, Franz remained silent. He never once even looked at her.

Claudia, however, was unable to resist stealing a few glances at her self-styled escort. She couldn't determine exactly what it was he wanted from her. He was a strange man, unlike any she'd ever known. Even his speech, at times, sounded odd and stilted, somehow. Though reason told her that this was because he probably formed his thoughts in German before speaking them in English. She couldn't figure him out. He was always alone. That in itself was unusual. The Hessians traveled in groups, like sheep.

A movement caught her eye, and Claudia turned to her left to see a group of people ice-skating. Leaving the road, she headed in their direction. The pond, thick with ice, wasn't large; in fact, it reached no more than a three-foot depth at its deepest point. A thin stand of poplars lined its far bank. The other three sides were relatively flat with only a few scraggly bushes to break the expanse.

It was crowded with skaters. Most were children, but there was a scattering of adults gliding along the hard surface. One woman, bundled up in a fur cloak, was skating with her mittened hands resting on the back of an armless chair, which she was propelling before her and which offered her balance.

"It looks like fun, doesn't it?" Claudia murmured after a while, watching the fur-clad woman.

"It is," Franz agreed, for the first time breaking his self-imposed silence. "Have you never skated?"

Claudia shrugged. "Once, when I was a child. I was not very good at it."

"I could teach you, if you would like to learn how to do it properly. People in my country learn to skate almost as soon as they learn to walk."

Claudia turned her head to look at him, suddenly uncomfortable with the turn of the conversation. "I don't have the time for that."

"People make time for whatever is important to them," he observed.

"Well, skating is not that important to me," she replied tartly as she headed back to the road.

He fell silent again, not speaking until they arrived back at the Blue Swan.

"May I have the privilege of taking you to supper this evening?" he asked then.

Claudia gave him an annoyed glance. "You may not," she answered shortly, ignoring the hurt look that clouded his blue eyes.

Before he could try to persuade her to change her mind, Claudia hastily went inside.

She closed the door firmly behind her, took a step, then halted. Turning slowly, she walked to the window and peeked out, careful not to reveal herself.

Franz was still standing there. He was staring down at the ground, almost as if he had lost something in the snow.

And why did she care if he was still there? Claudia thought in annoyance, moving away.

Foolish man, she thought, looking at the closed door. I have nothing to give you.

Chapter Thirteen

From Gillian's Diary:

> *December 31, 1778*
> *The year has come to an end, but there seems to be no end in sight insofar as the war is concerned. We are entering the fourth year of bloodshed, of battles that are won or lost without deciding a clear victory for either side. Where will it all end?*

Gillian sighed and threw the copy of the *Royal Gazette* she had been reading to the floor. Mr. Rivington was such an ardent Tory that his newsletter read like an advertisement for the virtues of the British. According to him, they could do no wrong.

Moodily, Gillian looked around the parlor, toying with the fringe of the shawl she was wearing over her blue cotton dress. Patterned with narrow yellow stripes, the dress was a simple creation, of the sort she wore in the Blue Swan. The skirt was looped up to her hips, fastened in place with knots of black ribbon. Both the exposed underskirt and the fichu tucked into the top of her bodice were of fine white lawn.

Early afternoon sun streamed through the window in the parlor, bronzing wood and highlighting colors. In the hearth, a fire burned brightly.

Gillian found the sight depressing. The house seemed so empty, she thought, a bit surprised by her feeling. In the kitchen, Polly's voice rose as she chided William for some misdemeanor. Faintly, she could hear Katie humming a gay little tune as she went about her chores. Katie had been doing that a lot since she met Edward.

But her grandmother wasn't in the house, and that made it empty. Alice had received a letter from her sister Bertha. Having taken a fall, Bertha had suffered a broken hip. Although the woman had not requested it, Alice had immediately packed and made arrangements for herself and Drucilla to travel to Nova Scotia to stay with her sister until she recovered.

With a sigh, Gillian got up, stoked the fire, then sat down again.

From the hall came the sound of the front door being opened, followed quickly by the sound of running feet.

Startled, Gillian again got up from her chair. Whoever it was hadn't even bothered to knock.

At that moment, Edwina burst into the room. Her face was so pale, even her lips seemed to be white. Though the day was cold, she was not wearing so much as a shawl over her brown woolen dress.

The Passionate Rebel

"Edwina!" Gillian didn't even know she had screamed the name of her sister, who clutched at her.

"Thomas . . ." Her voice was ragged. "He's been arrested!"

"Oh, my God." Gillian put her arms around Edwina, who was shivering so violently that her teeth were chattering. "Where did they take him?" Gently, she eased the distraught woman into the chair nearest to the fire. Removing her own shawl, she draped it around her sister.

Raising her tearstained face, Edwina seemed at first unable to speak.

"The *Jersey*," she managed at last, then gripped Gillian's hands so tight that it was painful. "He will die. Just like all the others, he will die!"

Feeling weak, Gillian sank down on the floor in front of her sister. "What happened?"

Edwina released her grip and covered her face with her hands. "I'm not sure. Nowadays, it takes no more than for a person to paint an *R* on your door."

"Did that happen?"

"No! Oh, Gillian, I don't know what it was."

"Did they close the tavern?"

"No, they didn't do that. The Blue Swan is one of their favorite places," Edwina said bitterly.

Gillian got up. Clasping her hands at her waist, she forced herself to think of alternatives. No one had ever escaped from one of those prison ships. Someone would have to intercede for Thomas. Her grandmother—there was a possibility. God knew, she entertained the British enough. But it would take weeks for the post to reach Halifax.

Philip! Her expression lightened. "Yes," she murmured, unaware that she had spoken her thoughts aloud. "Philip."

Edwina raised her head, her expression now eager. "Will he help? Can he?"

"Yes, I'm sure he will." Gillian kept her voice calm. She had never seen Edwina so agitated. Edwina had always been the calm one, ready to take charge in an emergency.

Even sitting close to the fire, Edwina's small body was still being racked by shuddering spasms. Gillian knew it was fear rather than cold that was producing this reaction. Going into the dining room, she headed for the sideboard, where the liquors were kept. Selecting a bottle, she poured a small amount into a glass and took it back to Edwina.

"Drink this," she instructed quietly. "Please, you must try to calm yourself."

Gillian watched with a worried eye as her sister dutifully sipped the blackberry brandy. Edwina was now five months pregnant. All this could be doing her no good in her condition.

The glass was empty, and Gillian took it from Edwina's unresisting hand. She did seem to be quieter, and Gillian drew a breath of relief.

"Stay here for a few minutes. I'll send Katie down with a cloak. She'll see you home. And please try to rest. I know that's difficult for you right now, but you must think of the baby."

Edwina nodded absently, as though her mind was on a more important subject. Looking up, she asked, "Do you know where Mr. Meredith lives?"

"Yes. It's not far. He's on Chambers Street. He pointed it out to me when we went for a drive."

"You will let me know?" Edwina's brown eyes pleaded.

"I will. I promise." She gave Edwina a searching glance to assure herself that she was now in control of her emotions. Then she hurriedly left the room.

Upstairs, she gave Katie a few instructions. She did not take the time to change her dress or even replace her shawl. Donning a cloak and picking up a fur muff, she hastily went downstairs again to find William.

A while later, her carriage drew up in front of Philip's residence.

The door was opened by a tall, thin black man. White shirt and stockings contrasted sharply with his black jacket and breeches.

Gillian recognized the man, whose name was Matthew, as Philip's driver. It didn't strike her as odd to see the man performing the duties of a butler; in her house, William did the same.

"I would like to see Mr. Meredith. Is he at home?"

"No, ma'am," Matthew said, sounding regretful. He recognized Gillian and knew his employer would like to see her. "But he should be soon. Would you care to wait?" He swung the door wider.

Gillian released a deep sigh; however, she didn't see that she had any choice. She stepped over the threshold and into the entry hall.

With a dignified step, Matthew led her into the library. A huge fire was burning in the grate. The room was warm and cheerful.

Gillian removed her cloak, and Matthew immediately stepped forward to take it. She put her muff on the table beside one of the two settees that were positioned in a parallel line before the fireplace.

"When do you expect Mr. Meredith?" she asked as she settled herself.

"He should be comin' home soon," Matthew offered encouragingly. With a respectful nod, he left the room.

Soon, Gillian thought, making a face. That could mean five minutes or an hour.

She glanced around. The room was longer than it was wide. The wall at the far end was paneled in wood and shelved from the ceiling to the floor. There were no books on the shelves, though; obviously, Philip wasn't much of a reader.

The furniture was of good quality, lavishly upholstered, for the most part, in damask and velvet. A square, brightly colored Persian rug covered the area in the immediate vicinity of the hearth, with the two settees and several tables positioned on its expanse. The rest of the floor was bare. There were two windows, the brocade draperies now drawn against the chill day.

Gillian was growing restless. Getting up, she headed for the door. Just then, Matthew appeared, tray in hand. Her passage effectively blocked, Gillian returned to the settee.

She had no sooner sat down when she heard the sound of a horse.

"That be Mr. Meredith now," Matthew said. He poured tea into two cups and put them on the low table, setting the teapot beside them. Then he went outside, knowing that Philip would want his horse fed and watered.

Gillian stared at the steaming cup in front of her and sighed. Tea. Discounting spirits, she had never seen Philip drink anything else.

Restlessness was beginning to turn into nervousness. She had been so glib when she had assured Edwina that Philip would help Thomas. What if he didn't? Couldn't? Wouldn't?

A few minutes later, Philip strode into the room, cheeks pink from the cold. His dark hair was drawn back and tied at the nape of his neck. He had

The Passionate Rebel

removed his jacket, and his shirt gleamed white above his dark green breeches.

"Gillian!" he exclaimed, and his delight at seeing her was evident. "What a pleasant surprise." He paused before the fire to warm his hands. "If I had known you were here, I would have come home sooner—"

"Please," she interrupted him, and for the first time he noticed her pallor.

"What is wrong?" He spoke quietly against his sudden unease.

"Something awful has happened." Sudden tears welled in her eyes, and she dashed them away, annoyed at this intrusion. "I . . . need your help."

"Tell me what this is all about."

Walking to the door, Philip closed it so that her words would not go beyond this room.

"My sister's husband, Thomas Carmody, has been arrested. Unjustly," she added quickly. "I swear to you, it was a mistake."

Philip made no immediate response, and Gillian's voice sharpened. "They said he was to be taken to the *Jersey*."

Without sitting down, Philip picked up a cup and sipped from it. "That's unfortunate."

"Unfortunate?" Gillian sprang to her feet. "It's a death sentence." Immediately, she brought herself under control. "I know that you are acquainted with many British officers, even General Clinton himself." Her composure broke. "Oh, please . . . please see what you can do."

"Why was he arrested?" He put the cup back down on the table.

"Do they need a reason?" Her voice had risen again, and Gillian swallowed. "I don't know," she said in a quieter tone. "Apparently they have the misguided idea that Thomas is a rebel. Now, you know that's foolish. It's all a mistake. My sister is expecting her second child. A situation like this could be of the utmost harm to her."

"Now, now, calm yourself." Somewhat awkwardly, Philip patted her shoulder. "Of course, I will look into this matter. The British are a most reasonable people."

Gillian couldn't believe he said that. There were many words she would use to describe the redcoats; reasonable wasn't one of them.

"For God's sake!" she cried. His apparently unconcerned attitude was making her nerves taut. "Thomas will die on that ship. You know it."

"Yes, yes. I do not mean to minimize the danger. I only mean that, as soon as they learn the truth, the British will release him." He peered intently. "What *is* the truth?"

"I told you, I don't know!" She moved close to him. "Philip . . ." she whispered, for the first time using his given name, "I promise you, I will be most grateful."

He enfolded her in his strong arms, and she leaned her head on his chest. At this moment, Gillian felt almost fond of the man. He held her for long moments until, finally, she felt herself relax.

"Gillian?" His voice was a husky whisper. Her nearness was taking its toll on him in no uncertain terms.

Raising her head, Gillian studied his rugged face. She could easily see the desire in his dark eyes, and she shivered, drawing an unsteady breath as his hand caressed the slender column of her throat. Tenderly, he bent his head to kiss her, his tongue probing gently at her velvety lips.

The Passionate Rebel

Without conscious thought, Gillian's arms went around him. She had not planned this, but she was now powerless to dam the surge of feeling that flooded her body.

"Please . . ."

Was her cry a plea for him to stop or to continue? Even Gillian couldn't answer that. All she knew was that the tension inside her was becoming unbearable. He was undoing buttons and ribbons. Then her dress was in a crumpled heap on the floor, followed quickly by her undergarments. This time, there was no turning back, and Gillian didn't want to.

She barely heard his murmured endearments over the pounding of her heart, sounding loud in her ears. His lips blazed a trail of fire across her bare flesh, and Gillian shuddered with the delicious sensations that set every nerve in her body to tingle with anticipation.

"I knew you were lovely," he breathed, "but I had no idea how exquisite you are." His eyes seemed to hungrily devour her creamy flesh. The firelight flickered across the length of her golden beauty, creating amber shadows beneath her high, full breasts.

Gillian was only vaguely aware that Philip's clothes had joined hers on the floor. When his warm body covered hers, Gillian's eyes flew open, and she gasped with the contact.

Gently he parted her thighs and positioned himself between their softness, his fingers caressing that most private part of her. Instinctively, Gillian's legs straddled his lean hips. She moaned and clutched him to her. Philip sensed her silent plea and surrendered to the spell she wove about him, no less real because it was intangible.

Philip entered the tantalizing moist warmth of her. He moved slowly, prepared for the barrier he knew he would encounter, trying to spare her as much pain as he could, though his own raging need threatened to destroy his resolve. But Gillian's legs tightened about him, urging him on, and she arched her body upward in an effort to receive all of him.

Conscious thought was beyond her now. Gillian was riding the crest of a wave of excitement that seemed to have no apex. Higher and higher it went, carrying her along until she cried out her pleasure.

Dimly, Gillian felt the pain as the last vestige of her maidenhood was relinquished. Then the wave soared even higher, taking her with it. The climax, when it came, left her body trembling in its aftermath, and she clung to Philip, panting.

He buried his lips in her hair and held her close until she quieted. He had known that she was spirited, had suspected that she was sensual, but the extent of her passion amazed and delighted him.

Finally, he drew away, brushing a wayward golden strand from her still damp brow.

"Rest a moment longer," he whispered, covering her with his shirt.

He began to dress, and Gillian closed her eyes. She heard him leave the room, closing the door behind him. She sighed deeply, feeling utterly content, and began to drift into a light doze.

A while later, Gillian awoke to find Philip gently sponging her body, dipping a soft cloth in the basin of warm water he had brought back with him.

Somehow, the procedure seemed to her to be more intimate than the act of love they had recently completed. Embarrassment swept through her, and she tried to cover herself with her hands.

His dark eyes sparkled in amusement. "I can't imagine why you would try to hide anything from

The Passionate Rebel

me now," he murmured, trying not to smile and not succeeding in his effort.

Gillian sat up, legs pressed together and arms folded over her breasts, trying to look dignified. She was now shocked at the way in which she had behaved so wantonly.

"Would you . . . would you please turn around while I dress?"

"Of course," he said, striving for a solemn tone. Picking up her clothes, he handed them to her, then walked to one of the windows. Parting the draperies, he stood there surveying the scenery that he knew by heart.

When he judged enough time had passed, Philip turned to find her fully clothed, trying to smooth her hair back into place with her hands.

Catching his gaze, her cheeks flamed again at the remembered intimacy they had shared. She had no idea what he must think of her.

"I must be going." Her mouth felt dry. "Edwina . . ." She drew a sharp breath. Thomas! How could she have forgotten? "You will do what you can?"

"Yes," Philip assured her. "I will do everything I can." Taking her arm, he led her to the front door, where Matthew was waiting with her cloak.

Gillian entered the waiting carriage and instructed William to drive directly to the Blue Swan, knowing that Edwina was waiting for any news she might have.

It was, Gillian reflected dourly, precious little.

Claudia was every bit as upset as Edwina and Gillian. She liked Tom, respected him as a man and a friend. Though she had been in the taproom when Tom was arrested, she could shed no light on the cause. One moment, a grenadier had been slouched over his table; the next, he had jumped to his feet, accusing Tom of being a rebel. The soldiers at the bar hadn't bothered to ask questions. They had immediately grabbed Tom and dragged him outside. Only because she had known one of them was Claudia able to find out where they were taking Tom.

She now stood quietly, her green eyes scanning the room.

Claudia wasn't even aware that each time she entered the taproom, her eyes immediately went to the corner table. He was there, quietly sipping his ale. Since the day she had rebuffed his invitation for supper, Franz had been treating her with a politeness she found unsettling.

Glancing up just then, Franz saw her, and his face lightened with a welcoming smile. Each time he saw her, it seemed to Franz to be the first time. She was wearing a simple muslin dress patterned in a floral design; on her, it looked like the finest silk. He raised a hand and beckoned her toward him.

Claudia was so upset on this night that when Franz urged her to sit down she did so without even thinking about it.

The taproom was almost empty. Whether this was because of Tom's arrest or because of the stepped-up actions of the war, she didn't know.

She realized that Franz had been talking to her for several minutes now. More in an effort to ease her troubled mind than anything else, Claudia began to listen.

". . . and since there were four of us, it seemed the wisest thing for me to do was to join the army."

She raised her head to look at him. "Four of you?" she repeated absently.

The Passionate Rebel

"Yes. My brothers. As I just explained, my father owns a bakery shop in Hanover. With three older brothers, I knew there would be little room for me in the business."

Claudia tilted her head. "Aren't you from Hesse?"

He laughed and shook his head. "No. I'm a Hessian only by virtue of the uniform I am wearing. My home is in Hanover."

Claudia nodded. Why was she sitting here, talking to this Hessian? She should get up and leave. Having thought that, Claudia made no move to do so.

"You don't look like a baker," she murmured idly. Though she made the observation, she wasn't looking at him; in fact, she wasn't giving much conscious thought to her words.

His blue eyes twinkled in amusement, though Claudia didn't notice.

"I suppose it is difficult, at first glance, to tell what anyone is or does." Franz grew somber and viewed her with a thoughtful expression. "You, for example," he said slowly. "I know enough by now to know that you are not what you pretend to be."

Now her attention was caught. "What makes you think you know so much about me?"

"Why does the idea disturb you?" he asked mildly. He finished his ale and pushed the tankard aside.

"I don't want to talk about this." Claudia's emerald eyes blazed like green fire.

They were silent for a time; then Franz asked, "Where is Mr. Carmody? I have not seen him in a few days. Is he ill?"

"He was arrested. Taken to the *Jersey*." A deep frown creased the Hessian's brow, and he issued a sigh that was so obviously sympathetic, Claudia looked at him with sudden hope. "Do you . . . do you think you could help him?"

"I could try," he said, then frowned. "Is Mr. Carmody a . . . friend of yours?" Though the question was posed casually, it pained him to ask it.

"A very good friend," Claudia asserted quickly. "As is his wife. They offered me help and shelter when I badly needed it."

He smiled slowly. "Reason enough for me to do whatever I can."

"Thank you, Lieutenant."

"Franz," he said. Reaching across the table, he attempted to take her hand, but she pulled away.

"Lieutenant," Claudia repeated firmly.

Chapter Fourteen

From Gillian's Diary:

> *January 13, 1779*
> *Indian raids have continued at an alarming rate, the most recent in Cherry Valley, not 50 miles from Albany. Settlers of the entire village were herded into a huge bonfire, there to die in agony. The savages are encouraged by British gold and incited by British rum. Even the frontiers of New York are no longer safe.*

The man halted his horse as he entered the camp at Morristown. The palisades were covered with snow, and yet more was coming down. A persistent and, it seemed, never ending wind swept over these highlands, adding to the discomfort.

And, Christ, it was cold, he thought, nudging his horse forward.

Helene Lehr

Around him, he saw the tents that housed the soldiers, and it sickened him to see the poor shelters when he knew that the British were gathered around their warm fires.

A soldier stumbled into the path of the rider, and the man reined in quickly. The soldier, a threadbare blanket over his shoulders, never looked up; indeed he seemed not to notice either the man or the horse.

When the way was clear, the man proceeded, stopping by the only house in the area. Dismounting, he tethered the horse and hurried inside.

It was only marginally warmer. The wind was so unremitting, the snow so powdery, that the white stuff actually seeped in through the windowsills.

When he entered the room to which he had been directed, he smiled at the young man seated behind the desk. Approaching, he leaned over the desk to shake the outstretched hand.

"Alex . . ."

"Lieutenant! Sit down." Alexander Hamilton, who was Washington's chief aide, motioned his visitor to a chair. He was 22 years old, with a thin frame that gave him a somewhat patrician appearance. His brown hair, pulled back and tied, was heavily powdered. Though he dressed and acted like an aristocrat, he was in fact the illegitimate son of a French woman and a Scotch peddler. He was also brilliant and a staunch supporter of the cause.

"Is the general here?" the lieutenant asked as he sat down.

"No," Hamilton replied. "He went to West Point. Can I help you?"

The lieutenant rubbed his chin wearily. "I hope so." He explained about the arrest of Thomas Carmody.

The Passionate Rebel

"Carmody..." Hamilton mused. "That is the innkeeper who has been so helpful to us?"

The other man looked startled. "You know him?"

Hamilton shook his head. "I've never met him, but he has been channeling information and money to us for quite some time now. Are you a friend of Mr. Carmody?"

"Not really. I was told of his predicament and asked to help. I had no idea of his activities."

"That's not surprising. Our sympathizers, especially in New York and Philadelphia, tend to keep a low profile. And with good reason, as you know."

"Well, apparently Carmody's been found out. It's a wonder he wasn't hung."

Hamilton nodded in agreement, then said, "Certainly we cannot abandon such a valuable asset to the cause. I feel certain we can effect a change of prisoners. I'll see what I can do. It will take time, though. Do you know where they have taken him?"

"He's on the *Jersey*."

"God be with him, then." Hamilton's blue-gray eyes darkened. "More than four thousand of our brave countrymen have lost their lives aboard those hulks. And, from my reports, the *Jersey* is the worst of the lot."

At that moment, Thomas Carmody would have wholeheartedly agreed. Like everyone else, Tom had heard stories of the wretched conditions aboard these ships, but it hadn't prepared him for the reality of the squalor. The stench was overwhelming, the food barely enough to keep a child alive.

He had been here almost two weeks now, and during that relatively short time, 11 men had died.

God, he thought to himself, how could he have been so careless?

A redcoat had stopped by the tavern. Tom knew him to be a courier, for he had been in the Blue Swan before. As usual, the young man had consumed a great deal of applejack. Before too long, he was slumped over his table. Tom thought he was asleep. On the pretext of settling the man so that he would not fall down, he went through the grenadier's pockets. The man, however, had not been asleep. He had suddenly jumped up with an outcry and begun to accuse Tom of treason. Tom had been arrested on the spot.

With a deep sigh, Tom now seated himself, hearing the sound of the grating being fastened over the hatchway.

The air was so foul, he found himself taking shallow breaths, as if that could somehow minimize the disgusting vapor that seemed to have insinuated itself into the very plankings of the deck. With some longing, he cast his glance toward the airholes, wishing he could obtain a spot close to one of them. There was not so much as a foot of room.

Resigned, he settled himself as well as he could and fell into a fitful doze.

A dim, gray light announced the following morning.

Tom sat up, feeling every bone in his body protesting the hard surface on which he had slept. The guards would not, he knew, open the hatches until eight o'clock, and he wondered what time it was now.

Most of the men were beginning to stir; some would never move again. The bodies were removed only once a day, and that was in the morning. After that, any corpse stayed where it was until the following day. There was, of course, no burial, no attempt

The Passionate Rebel

at ceremony; they were simply dumped into the bay.

As miserable as he felt, Tom felt sympathy for the wretches who were his fellow prisoners. Their clothes hung in tattered rags about their skeletal frames. They looked shrunken and pallid, and Tom knew it was only a matter of time until he became one of them.

Escape was out of the question. No one escaped from the *Jersey*.

The light increased as the sun finally rose.

There were, Tom saw, at least two new cases of smallpox, and he wondered uneasily how long it would be before the disease afflicted him.

"Have you had it?"

Jarred out of his morose contemplations, Tom turned to the man beside him. His name was Silas Peabody, and he owned an apothecary shop in Philadelphia. He had been aboard this black hulk for more than five months, having been taken prisoner during the battle of Butts' Hill in Rhode Island.

"The pox," Silas said when Tom made no immediate answer. "Have you had it?"

Tom only shook his head.

"Then you'd best do something about it." He fumbled in his shirt pocket with a hand that visibly shook. Finally, he brought forth an ordinary pin and handed it to Tom. "You will have to inoculate yourself. There are no physicians here." At the look on Tom's face, Silas pointed to a small scar on the back of his hand. "See? This is the only reason I'm alive after all these months." He looked around. "That one." He gestured to a man not far from where they were sitting. "His ulcers have begun to erupt. It takes only a bit to be effective." He nodded at the pin Tom was holding, somewhat gingerly between his thumb and forefinger. "Make certain you give yourself a scratch deep enough to draw blood. Put some of the matter into the wound; then tie your hand with your handkerchief, if you have one."

Tom grimaced. "Does that work?"

"You will know by tomorrow. If your wound festers, then it has worked."

"But what if it gives me the disease?"

That occasioned a shrug. "You'll get it either way," came the philosophical reply.

As much as he was loathe to approach the sick man, Tom followed Silas's advice. In only minutes, it was done. Tom did not have a handkerchief, so he tore a small strip of cloth from his shirt and carefully bound his hand.

By the time he was through, the hatches were finally being opened and, gratefully, he surged forward with the others, anxious for a breath of fresh air.

"Stand back!" the guard shouted as two sailors descended the ladder. "The fish need to be fed before you damned rebels." This was accompanied by a hearty laugh as the guard watched the sailors remove any prisoner who had succumbed during the night. Today there was only one, and the job was accomplished swiftly.

After that, they were allowed on deck, 50 men at a time, to receive the first of the two meager meals allotted them.

Wearily, Tom trudged with the others to the galley, located under the forecastle. All food was prepared in two huge copper boilers. One contained a thin, watery oatmeal, to which had been added the unlikely accompaniment of peas—their morning fare. The other contained the boiled meat that would be served for supper.

The Passionate Rebel

Tom glanced longingly at the latter but dared not eat it when it was served. While the porridge was cooked in fresh water, the meat was boiled in salt water, drawn up from alongside the boat, a process that had long since corroded the copper.

"A dish of poison," Silas had contemptuously announced on Tom's first day.

So at night they both contented themselves only with a biscuit and the pint of water allotted each man at that time. The biscuits were barely palatable, being slathered with oil instead of butter.

Having collected their bowl of cereal and a tin cup filled with tea, they moved to an unoccupied space on the deck and began to eat.

Glancing across the bay, Tom saw three so-called hospital ships: the *Scorpion, Hunter* and *Strombolo*. They were not, of course, in use to administer aid to the sick and starving men that rested in their foul-smelling holes. They served the same purpose as the *Jersey*.

A small boat pulled up alongside the *Jersey*, and a rope ladder was thrown over the side. Several more prisoners were being brought aboard. When they reached the deck, Tom saw a British officer approach them, speaking in earnest tones. He knew what the conversation was about, having received the same pitch when he arrived. The officer was giving the newly arrived men the opportunity of taking the oath for the king. If they did, they would be released.

Tom smiled grimly as he saw the men vigorously shake their heads in denial. A moment later, they were led away.

When Tom and Silas had broken their fast, they were once again herded below, there to spend the weary and tedious hours that stretched through the day until six o'clock, when they were served their sparse evening meal.

That night, when Franz entered the taproom, Claudia rushed toward him, for the first time happy to see him.

"Have you any news about Tom?" she asked quickly, before he could speak.

Removing his hat, Franz sat down heavily. "He is indeed aboard the *Jersey*."

Claudia sat down across the table from him, unmindful of the fact that she was the only one on duty at the present. Gillian was upstairs with Edwina. Both Delia and Chastity had quit the day after Tom's arrest. Claudia couldn't blame them. Those officers who were still coming to the tavern had a hard look of suspicion in their eye.

"Is there any way we can get him released?" she asked.

"I've made inquiries, spoken to my superior, but I must be honest with you. If something can be arranged, it will take time."

Claudia's shoulders slumped, knowing this was information she would have to pass along to Edwina. She wet her lips. "How long do those men survive on those prison ships?"

"I can't answer that," he replied softly. "Some men are stronger than others."

"Do you think an escape could be arranged? Those ships are anchored only two miles offshore." She was taking a great risk in talking like this to a Hessian, and Claudia knew it. Yet the situation was grave enough to warrant such action. "Perhaps a small boat at night could get close enough. And if someone could get word to Tom, tell him to jump overboard at a certain time . . ."

The Passionate Rebel

Franz was shaking his head before she was half through presenting her plan.

"Those guards shoot at anything that moves. I should know," he added with a sigh. "Most of them are Hessians. To my knowledge, no one has ever succeeded in escaping. Even if a man managed to jump over the side, there are many loyalists who would gladly turn him back in once he reached shore. And after a few weeks on board, it's doubtful that even a man who is a good swimmer would have the strength to swim that distance."

"Are you saying they are not well-fed?" Despite her words, her eyes pleaded for denial.

Seeing that, Franz was sorely tempted to lie. Instead, he said, "They are fed barely enough to keep them alive." He pursed his lips in a thoughtful manner. "Now that is something I can do," he mused. "I promise I will try to get food to him."

"That would be appreciated," Claudia said, somewhat surprised by the generous offer.

He was staring at her in that intent way that always made her uncomfortable. Claudia found herself unable to meet those probing blue eyes. She moistened her lips, knowing she should not ask the question she was about to pose, but the compulsion to do so was irresistible.

"You once said that I was not what I pretended to be. What did you mean by that?"

"You present yourself as a woman of easy virtue," he answered easily. "But you are not."

She flushed. "That is a foolish observation," she said lightly. "I am exactly what you see."

He was silent a moment, his look thoughtful. "I think not."

Hastily, Claudia got to her feet, sorry now that she had given in to her impulse.

Helene Lehr

* * *

The January days grew colder as they slipped by, one by one, beneath unremitting gray skies. Ice began to appear in the river, and ponds froze solid. During these weeks, Gillian saw Philip regularly. There was, however, no further attempt at intimacy; Gillian saw to that. She was nervous, on edge, worried. Edwina seemed to be fine, but Gillian didn't know how much longer that could go on. Day after day, she listened with feigned patience to Philip's vague assurances that everything would turn out well.

Nothing happened.

Finally, at the end of the first week in February, her patience snapped. Philip arrived at the house in the early afternoon and responded to Gillian's inquiries in the same vague manner that he had been doing for these past weeks.

"It has been almost a month now," she cried.

"These things take time."

"Time!" Gillian almost shrieked the word. "Tom is suffering on that rotting hulk, and you talk to me about time. Perhaps your influence with your British friends isn't as great as you thought it was," she accused scathingly.

"The person I spoke to assured me that Thomas would soon be released."

"Who did you talk to?"

"I'd rather not reveal his name," Philip said evasively. "I've done everything I could."

"Well, it's not enough." Hands on her hips, Gillian viewed him disdainfully. "God knows, your insistent groveling to these people should have net you more than a vague supposition."

"I have been assured—" he began, but she interrupted him.

The Passionate Rebel

"Can't you see how unreliable they are? I really cannot understand your way of thinking."

Seeing how upset she was, Philip reached for her, and she wrenched away so violently that he was taken by surprise.

"Stop it," she said with a sharp edge to her voice. "That's your solution to everything, isn't it?"

For a long moment, Philip stared at her. Then he pursed his lips. "Would it make you feel better to know that I support the cause?"

Gillian's nostrils flared. "What kind of a fool do you take me for? Leopards don't change their spots, and neither do Tories. You're just as you've always been—a traitor!" Again he reached out a hand, and she slapped it away. "But you wouldn't want to fight, would you? You wouldn't want to get your clean hands dirty."

From the look on his face, Gillian knew she had gone too far, but anger made her reckless, and she tilted her chin at a defiant angle. She had thrown down the gauntlet. Now it was his place to pick it up.

He did so in a way Gillian would never have expected.

"You really don't want to marry me, do you?" Philip mused quietly, viewing her as if seeing her for the first time.

The sudden shift took her by surprise. So much so, that she made no immediate answer.

Philip took her silence for an affirmation.

"And that day when you came to my house, you didn't mean any of it, did you?" He grabbed her by the shoulders and began to shake her. "It was all to coax me into aiding Thomas." He released her, then picked up his hat. "Very well. I made you an honorable proposal of marriage," he went on softly. "It is a mistake I will not repeat." He began to walk away. "When your grandmother returns, I will explain the situation to her." He was amazed at the pain he felt. But why? he wondered bitterly. It had been obvious from the beginning that Gillian was reluctant to marry him. Her excuse was that he was a Tory. Yet Philip knew very well that was not the sum of it.

Gillian watched him go with mixed feelings. On the one hand, there was relief. And yet . . .

Clenching her fists, Gillian smashed them against a table, almost welcoming the pain it caused. Of all the men in New York, in the colonies, in the world! Why did she have to be attracted to this one?

Her body might accept a traitor. She, herself, could not.

Chapter Fifteen

From Gillian's Diary:

> *February 28, 1779*
> *Today, a farmer from Long Island was killed. He entered the city with a wagonload of wood for sale, setting a price so high that it enraged everyone. The people set upon him with such great force that he was fatally injured. At times, I feel this war is between Americans, rather than Americans against the British. We are sadly a people divided. It amazes me that fully a third of our citizens support the Crown; another third remain neutral. How are we to be victorious?*

Gillian paced her room in nervous agitation. At one point she paused by the window, only to discover that Katie had already drawn the shutters for the night.

More than three weeks had gone by since her last meeting with Philip. He hadn't come near her in all that time. Twice, she had almost gone to his office of employment, but her pride would not allow her to do this.

Even if she had overcome that obstacle, Gillian had no idea of what she would say. Inside, she seemed to be torn in two directions at once. She kept telling herself that she wanted to see Philip so that she could learn of any new developments in Tom's release. But at night, in the darkness of her room, her mind conjured up maddening reminders of the afternoon they had made love.

If her grandmother had been home, Philip might have shown up, if for no other reason than to talk to her. But Alice was still in Halifax.

Going to her writing table, Gillian picked up the letter she had received from Alice. It had arrived only this morning.

She sighed and put the letter down again. "I had hoped Gram would be coming home by now," she said to Katie, "but it looks like she'll be there for some weeks yet."

Katie was sitting in a chair, mending a small tear in one of Gillian's petticoats. "How is her sister?" she asked, without looking up.

"As well as can be expected, I suppose. She's still bedridden."

"Bones take a long time to heal in a woman her age," Katie offered. She held the garment closer to the lamp and critically inspected her handiwork.

"She wants me to go to Halifax and stay with her until she's ready to come home."

Now Katie did look up. "And are you going?" She

The Passionate Rebel

got to her feet and put the mended petticoat in a dresser drawer.

Gillian shook her head. "I can't leave Edwina now." But, she thought to herself, if it hadn't been for her sister, she already would have packed and been on her way.

Gillian began to pace again, knowing she would have to answer her grandmother's letter. There was no way she could avoid telling Alice about her broken engagement. Yet she hesitated. What reason would she give? She had suddenly, without warning, been given what she wanted. Philip Meredith was apparently out of her life. Why wasn't she happy about it? Why had this corrosive feeling of restlessness engulfed her to the point where she couldn't think straight?

Feeling utterly frustrated, Gillian picked up a pillow and flung it across the room.

Patiently, Katie went to retrieve it. Gillian had been acting like a caged cat these past weeks. She didn't seem able to sit still for more than a few minutes at a time. Part of the problem, she knew, was Mr. Carmody's imprisonment. That, however, was not all of it. Gillian had told her about the broken engagement, although she had offered no reason for it. An argument of some sort, Katie surmised. Given Gillian's obvious and outspoken reluctance to marry Philip Meredith, Katie had at first expected a display of elation. Such had not been the case. If Gillian wasn't a woman in love, then Katie had never seen one.

"You've changed your mind about Mr. Meredith in these last few weeks?" Katie asked slyly as she returned the pillow to its rightful place.

Gillian spun around, startled by the question. "No!"

Seeing Katie's smug smile, Gillian bit her lip. She hadn't changed her mind. She hadn't! Just because her treacherous body on occasion had betrayed her was no reason to suppose her mind had done the same.

"Maybe it would be a good idea for you to dress and have William drive you to the Cartwrights'," Katie suggested in a casual way.

"Why on earth would I want to go there?" Gillian demanded, surprised by the suggestion.

Katie rolled her eyes heavenward. "Melanie Cartwright was married today. Have you forgotten?" From Gillian's look, it was obvious she had. "There's to be a huge reception. Everyone of any importance will be there. My goodness, the town's been abuzz with it all week."

Gillian looked annoyed. "What makes you think Philip will be there?" Lord, she thought, pacing again. She really had forgotten about the wedding, had neglected even to send a gift.

Katie shrugged. "He's a friend of Captain Bennicot's, isn't he?"

Pausing, Gillian glowered at her young servant. "He's a friend of every damn officer in the British army," she muttered.

"Well, then," Katie said reasonably, undeterred by her mistress's ill temper, "don't you think you should go?"

"For what reason?" Gillian demanded.

"Why, to patch things up."

"Are you daft? What makes you think I'd want to patch things up with him?" She clasped her hands tightly at her waist and viewed Katie sternly. "I can't believe you said that."

Katie grinned and waited, taking no offense at the sharp tone. She knew the workings of Gillian's mind

The Passionate Rebel

very well. The seed had been planted. In a short time it would grow and bear fruit.

Of course, Gillian was thinking, the last time she and Philip had been together, she had spoken in anger. Even though Philip obviously had been lying to her about his sudden shift in patriotism, he had been trying to pacify her.

A new thought struck, and Gillian paled. Thomas! What about Thomas? Would all this prevent Philip from following through? Oh, God, she couldn't let that happen. She would find Philip, apologize to him, plead with him, if necessary.

"You're right, Katie. Hurry! Fetch a gown and help me dress."

"Which one?"

"It doesn't matter. Any will do." Her fingers were clumsy in their haste to undo buttons and ribbons.

Throwing aside the mahogany doors, Katie surveyed the contents of the wardrobe, then shrugged, choosing the gown that was her own personal favorite. Of smoke-gray taffeta, she thought it matched Gillian's eyes perfectly. The skirt was patterned with embroidered violets, delicately outlined with silver thread and small crystal beads.

She assisted Gillian into the frothy creation, then buttoned the close-fitting bodice, taking care not to wrinkle the box pleats that descended from the shoulder, widened at the waist and became part of the full skirt.

That done, she fluffed the deep frills of ivory chiffon on each sleeve.

Going to the dressing table, Katie then selected a pearl necklace from Gillian's jewelry case and held it up questioningly.

"Oh, I don't care," Gillian exclaimed impatiently. "Do hurry, Katie."

Katie fastened the necklace around the slim throat, then headed for the wig stand. Gillian, having picked up her cloak, was headed for the door.

"Your hair!" Katie protested, then sighed as Gillian ran from the room.

Coming quickly down the stairs, Gillian called to William to ready the carriage. The long minutes she had to wait for him to accomplish this almost prompted her to walk the three blocks. Prudently, she decided it would be unsafe at this time of night.

Finally, William had the carriage in the front drive, and Gillian almost tripped over her own feet in her haste to get inside the vehicle.

Having informed William as to their destination, Gillian leaned back and tried to compose herself. She would not for a moment confess to herself that her unsettled state might be due to the fact that in all likelihood she would soon be seeing Philip again.

What would their meeting be like? Naturally, she would give him a cool smile when first they caught sight of each other. She would, at first, be distant—not too distant, of course. Just enough to let him know she wasn't about to fall into his arms.

He would, of course, request a dance. She would accept graciously.

And then . . . ?

As they turned onto the street where the Cartwright house was located, Gillian blinked in astonishment. Both sides of the street were lined with carriages.

Good heavens, she thought, as William halted the horse directly in a line with the front walkway. It appeared that half the town was here.

Alighting from the driver's seat, William opened the door and assisted her as she got out.

The Passionate Rebel

"Wants me to wait for you, Miss Gillian?" he asked.

"No." She turned. "On second thought, maybe you'd better, William. If I don't need you, I'll send word out to you."

Inside, it was every bit as crowded as Gillian had supposed it would be. To her right was the ballroom. From inside came the sound of music that only barely concealed the sound of loud voices and laughter. It seemed that everyone was having a good time.

To her left, Gillian saw that the doors that separated the front parlor from the dining room had been opened. Both rooms held long tables, covered with gleaming white cloths that were almost hidden beneath countless platters of food.

No shortages here, she thought wryly as she handed her cloak to a servant.

Walking slowly into the ballroom, Gillian saw Melanie dancing with her new husband. Captain Bennicot was in full military uniform. Melanie looked radiant in her white satin wedding gown. From the way in which they were gazing into each other's eyes, they could have been alone in the room.

Of Philip, however, there was no sign.

Gillian gave a start when she felt someone touch her arm, then relaxed when she recognized Colonel Harcroft. He was beaming at her.

"Ahh . . ." He smiled appreciatively as he viewed Gillian from head to toe. "I've always said that the most beautiful women in the colonies are right here in New York."

"Thank you. Um, have you seen Mr. Meredith this evening?"

"Meredith? Oh, yes." Harcroft looked about him.

"Can't imagine where he went to. He was here a few minutes ago."

"It's all right," Gillian said hastily. "I'll find him. Perhaps he's in the dining room." She moved away before the colonel could ask her to dance.

Ten minutes later, Gillian still had not found Philip and was standing uncertainly in the tiled foyer. At the end of the hallway, past the curved stairs, she saw a black servant carrying a tray enter a room. After a short interval, he came out.

Curiosity piqued, Gillian carefully made her way down the hall. The door was slightly ajar. From her limited view, the room appeared to be a study. Like the rest of the house, it was richly appointed. She could see paneled walls with oil paintings breaking the expanse.

Inside, there were at least two men. One of them was Philip. The other was a major she had never seen before. As they began to speak, she moved to the side so she would not be visible.

"That has been tried before," Meredith was saying, "and bungled in a most miserable manner."

"True, true. But this time, my dear fellow, we shall not fail."

Philip's short laugh held a great deal of skepticism. "If my memory serves me correctly, the only thing you managed to kill were a bunch of chickens. How can you be so certain you will succeed now?"

Gillian heard the slurring tones of Philip's voice and suspected that he was as drunk as the major.

"Thomas Hickey failed because of an incredible piece of bad luck. And the poor devil paid for it with his life."

Rising from his chair, Philip stumbled to the table for another drink, disappearing briefly from Gillian's line of vision.

The Passionate Rebel

Cautiously, she moved a step to the side and leaned against the wall, feeling a chill of horror trace a damp path down her spine. She knew who Thomas key was. The man had been a trusted member of Washington's own guard. He had also been a Tory. One night, he had poisoned a dish of peas that were to be served to the general. The attempted assassination had indeed failed because of luck—good or bad, depending in which light it was being viewed. For reasons of his own, the general had declined the vegetables. After the meal, a servant threw the peas to the chickens in the backyard and had watched, horrified, as they had proceeded to die, one by one.

"The tobacco farmer from the Potomac will shortly have a new cook." The major spoke so low that Gillian had to strain to hear the words. "One who is, in fact, in our employ."

"You're not planning on sending one of your men, I hope," Meredith said. "He'll never get away with it."

"No, no," the major said hastily. "He's an American, a loyalist like yourself. I have every reason to believe he will be successful."

Meredith raised his glass and smiled broadly. "To victory!" he toasted.

In the hall, Gillian put a trembling hand to her lips. The British were planning another assassination attempt. Somehow she was going to have to get word to General Washington, warn him before it was too late.

As for Philip Meredith . . .

Gillian's mouth was grim as she left the Cartwright house and hurried to the waiting carriage. She would have nothing more to do with that traitor. Damn him! Damn his lies! And damn the feeling he aroused within her.

Arriving home only minutes later, Gillian hastily removed her ballgown and donned a simple gray woolen dress. This she accomplished alone, not bothering to summon Katie, who, in any event, had probably retired to her room on the third floor.

Grabbing the dark blue cloak she had worn to the Cartwright house, she hurried downstairs and out the back door. She would need a horse. The mare that William used to pull the carriage would never make it. She was well past her prime and fit only to move at a sedate pace. Tom's horse, however, would be most suitable.

Twenty minutes later, Gillian had awakened Edwina, told her of what she had learned and what she was going to do.

Edwina viewed her younger sister in dismay. Though she realized the seriousness of what Gillian was telling her, she was filled with alarm for her sister's safety.

"Gillian," she said at last, "you cannot ride a horse along the Post Road at night. It's too heavily guarded."

"I'll walk, then," Gillian said stubbornly.

Edwina made a sound of exasperation. "You can't walk to Elizabethtown. It's too far. And how are you planning to cross the river?"

"The same way everyone else does," Gillian retorted. "I'll find someone to ferry me."

Edwina chewed her lip as she saw how determined Gillian was. Then she sighed in resignation. "If you can make it to the Clayton farm, I'm sure Amy will lend you a horse when she knows of this." She went to the chest of drawers. Removing a small pouch, she handed it to Gillian. "Take this; you'll need money."

It was almost midnight when Gillian set out for

The Passionate Rebel

the Clayton farm, located some three miles outside the city. Twice she heard the patrols and quickly sought cover, holding her breath till they sped by, grateful now that she had heeded Edwina's advice. Hiding herself was easy enough, especially in the dark. Even where the trees thinned, she could conceal herself behind a bush or even flatten herself on the ground when the trees gave way to the flat expanse of a field or meadow. It would have been virtually impossible to do that with a horse in tow.

The farmhouse, built on level ground, was set about a half mile off the road.

Breathless, Gillian paused a moment to survey her surroundings. She had been here often in her childhood. Her father and Kiley Clayton had been friends, having made the trip from England to the colonies on the same boat. There had been no patrols or restrictions then, only freedom. Gillian wondered if the future that faced them all would be as rewarding.

The moon was a soft round globe, casting over the landscape a milky white sheen.

Having caught her breath, Gillian continued on her way. The road ahead of her was little more than a footpath, lined with oaks and elms that rose up like mute sentinels. The house itself was dark. Gillian hadn't expected otherwise at this time of night. She guessed it to be close to three o'clock.

Feeling a sudden pain in her foot, Gillian gasped. Bending over, she saw a small, sharp stone and realized that she had just stepped on it. Sitting down, she pulled off her shoe. Except for a slight scratch, her foot was all right. Unfortunately, the sole of her shoe was torn. The flimsy material had not been meant to withstand the rigors of a long hike.

Having no alternative, Gillian put the shoe on and

got to her feet. Summoning her energy, she moved forward.

Approaching the front door, she knocked, softly at first, then louder when she received no immediate response. Finally, through a window to the side of the door, she saw the flickering glow of a candle.

"Who's there?" a woman's voice inquired.

Gillian identified herself and waited. She heard the bolt being thrown back; then the door was cracked a scant inch.

"Lord, child!" Amy Clayton opened the door wider to admit Gillian. "What on earth are you doing out at this time of night?"

In as few words as possible, Gillian told her.

When she was through, Amy Clayton regarded her for a long moment with a worried frown that deepened the lines in her forehead. She was 57 years old, with iron gray hair that was now plaited into one long thick braid. Despite her age, she was slim, but her hands were large, heavy-knuckled and worn by work.

"Do you have a horse I could borrow?" Gillian asked into the silence that had fallen.

Amy went to the hearth and stoked the banked fire. It immediately sprang to life, casting dancing shadows along the rough-hewn walls of the large room that served as kitchen, parlor and dining room all in one. The furniture was plain but comfortable, with cushions that were obviously homemade.

"Yes, I have a horse," Amy said at last, straightening. "However, I don't think you ought to go. A woman out there, alone . . ." She shook her head.

"You know I must go," Gillian said quietly. "There is no one else." Quickly, she explained about Tom. "And with Rob and Mr. Clayton gone . . ." She gestured helplessly. "Surely you understand that this is no ordinary message."

The Passionate Rebel

The older woman nodded. "I do, but..." She broke off at the sound of harsh coughing, and a moment later drew a sharp breath as the door to the bedroom opened. "Kiley, you should not be out of bed."

"What is it?" her husband asked. "I heard voices. Is anything wrong?"

"No, no." She rushed forward to assist him to the nearest chair, and only then did Gillian see how badly he was limping.

"He took a shot in the leg," Amy explained as she eased her husband down on the cushions. "For a while we thought he might lose it, but, praise God, it seems to be healing."

Now that he was settled, Kiley viewed Gillian, demanding to know why she was here.

Again she explained, trying to hide her impatience. Soon, it would be light. Her chances of crossing the river into New Jersey undetected would be nil come dawn.

Kiley's weather-beaten face flushed with anger, and he rapped the arm of his chair with a tightly clenched fist. "They would do such a thing," he muttered. "They cannot win fairly, and so they stoop to this." He raised his head to view Gillian. "You're right. You must go!" He waved aside a murmured disagreement from his wife. "His life is more important than any of ours, woman. Help Gillian. Give her whatever she needs."

The impassioned outburst seemed to have drained him of strength, and he slumped in the chair as if overcome with weariness.

The decision having been made, Amy wasted no more time.

"You can't go in that outfit," she declared, walking from the room. When she returned, she handed

Gillian a pair of white stockings, tan breeches and a somewhat frayed muslin shirt. "They were Robert's. He's long outgrown them, but the material's good enough to use in a quilt, if I ever find the time."

"How is Rob?" Gillian asked. "Have you heard from him?"

Amy nodded. "Last word we had, he was fine." She sniffed and swallowed. "Now, you get into those. I'll help Kiley back to bed."

Quickly, Gillian changed clothes, mindful of the passing time. Surprisingly, the breeches and the shirt fit well. But her shoes . . .

Gillian was still staring doubtfully at her feet when Amy returned. However, it appeared that the woman had thought of that, too. She handed Gillian a pair of boots.

"They'll be big, I suspect. Stuff this flannel into the toes." She nodded in satisfaction as Gillian followed her instructions, then brought forth a cap, which she personally put on Gillian's head. "Tuck your hair under that," she ordered. "You'll need food."

"No, please," Gillian protested. "You've done enough already."

Amy gave a short laugh. "Don't expect the soldiers to feed you. They don't have enough to eat, as it is." She bustled about, then handed Gillian a cloth bundle. "Not much. Just some bread and cheese. You'll find plenty of water along the way." She picked up Gillian's cloak. "This'll be torn to shreds in no time. I'll get you another."

That accomplished, she led Gillian to the barn, where she quite expertly saddled one of the two horses that were stabled there.

"You know where Jeb Strunk's place is?" she asked as she worked.

"No."

The Passionate Rebel

She handed the reins to Gillian. "Head straight for the river, then turn north. About two, two and a half miles, you'll come to it. Just a shack, really. But he has a flatboat. For a small fee, he'll take you and the horse across the river."

"He's one of us?" Gillian swung herself up on the horse.

"No. But neither is he a Tory." The woman laughed, though without humor. "I suspect Jeb's only creed is money."

Chapter Sixteen

From Gillian's Diary:

> *March 1, 1779*
> *The cold weather seems to have brought the war to a standstill. The Continentals are, for the most part, wintering in Elizabethtown, across the river in New Jersey. The British do little but party in New York; each week sees a new gala event.*

The morning was raw and chill, the sun hidden by lowering clouds that threatened rain. A wind, nasty in its sharpness, swept down from the highlands with a vengeance, causing Gillian to huddle beneath her cloak. She was riding astride and finding it difficult to keep the tops of her legs covered.

The trip so far had been uneventful. For a few coins, Jeb Strunk had ferried Gillian and the horse

The Passionate Rebel

across the river. He would not, however, wait for her, and Gillian couldn't blame him for that. She had no idea how she was going to get back. Once she reached camp, though, she supposed that someone would give her information as to how to accomplish the return trip.

There were few, if any, British patrols on this side of the river. Tories, however, were another matter. And under certain circumstances, they could be worse than the redcoats.

It was late morning when Gillian heard the sound of horses on the road ahead of her.

Quickly, she led her own horse off the road and into the cover of trees, praying the animal would remain silent.

In only a few minutes she saw the riders going by. She had no idea whether they were friend or foe, but she wasn't about to place herself in danger in order to find out.

When they had passed, she waited until she could no longer hear the drumming of hooves; then she made her way back to the road. Allowing the horse to walk, she took the time to eat the bread and cheese Amy had given her.

It wasn't getting any warmer. From time to time, Gillian studied the sky. If it rained, the road would most likely turn into a thoroughfare of mud.

The terrain was getting rough and hilly now. Gillian dismounted, carefully threading her way around trees and bushes. Though she had been certain she would reach Elizabethtown by late afternoon, it was already dark by the time she finally arrived.

Through the trees, Gillian could see the campfires. Still afoot, she headed toward the welcoming glimmer of light.

Helene Lehr

She neither heard nor saw the two sentries until one of them thrust a musket under her chin. For a moment, Gillian was too terrified even to scream.

"Don't shoot," she finally managed weakly. Raising a hand, she removed her cap, allowing the golden mass of her hair to tumble about her face.

Her movement caused the other guard to grab hold of her arm. "Jesus, it's a woman!"

Gillian tried to pull away, dropping her cap in the process, but the man held her fast. The man holding the gun stepped closer.

"Who are you? Why are you skulking around in the dark?"

Gillian wrenched herself free from the man gripping her arm. "If I told you my name, it would mean nothing to you. And I am not skulking. I want to see General Washington."

They both laughed. "Got a knife in your pocket, do you?" said the man who had grabbed her.

"I've no such thing," she exclaimed indignantly.

"Well, why don't I just find out."

Before Gillian could react, his hands roamed up and down the sides of her and came to rest on the outside of her breasts.

Angrily, Gillian lashed out to box the man's ear. "You spawn of the devil!" She put her hands on her hips, watching as the man rubbed his ear. "Are you satisfied that I'm not carrying a weapon?"

He grinned sheepishly. "Can't be too careful."

"You will take me to General Washington," Gillian said through clenched teeth. "And you will do it now!" She glared at them both in turn. "I would have expected such treatment from the redcoats but not from my own countrymen."

"What's going on here?"

The Passionate Rebel

A man dressed in the uniform of a captain strode toward them, his visage stern.

The soldiers, both Massachusetts militiamen, eyed their superior with open dislike. The captain came from Connecticut. The American army might have been reasonably united under their commander-in-chief, but they were woefully divided among themselves and trusted only those men from their respective states.

"I must see General Washington," Gillian said quickly before either of the guards could respond.

The dark countenance didn't lighten. "And what business would you be having with the general?"

"I . . . have a message. Please! It's important!"

The captain hesitated a moment, as if assessing her, then nodded. "Come with me."

Gillian picked up her cap and grabbed the reins of her horse.

As she followed the captain, Gillian looked about her with startled curiosity, surprised and appalled by the overt poverty she was seeing. It appeared to her that the troops were wearing whatever clothing they had brought with them, and most of it was by now in rags. A number of them didn't even have shoes. Their feet were wrapped in gunnysacks. She glanced at the captain walking at her side. He was clad in an outfit of blue and buff and was wearing sturdy-looking knee boots.

"Why aren't the men wearing their uniforms?" she asked at last.

His quick laugh was filled with sardonic amusement. "What uniforms? There aren't any."

She frowned. "But I distinctly remember reading that Congress authorized a regulation uniform for the army."

"So they did. Unfortunately, there's no money to

pay for fancy clothes." He looked down at her. "The men aren't even being paid a wage."

"But you . . ." She gestured at his attire.

"I paid for it myself, as do all officers who can afford it." Pausing, he motioned to the two-story white farmhouse the general had comandeered as his headquarters. "Here we are." He waited a moment while Gillian tethered the horse.

They entered into a large foyer.

The captain halted before a closed door and knocked, waiting patiently until he received permission to enter. When it came, he motioned for Gillian to remain where she was.

Gillian looked about for a place to sit but found no such convenience. The only piece of furniture was a coatrack. One blue and buff jacket hung on it, probably the general's.

She tightened her lips against a sudden nervousness. What if the general didn't believe her story? She had no proof. In retrospect, though she did not approve of the unnecessary liberties taken, Gillian felt reassured by the actions of the guards. She could indeed have had a weapon secreted on her person. The British had chosen to make use of a male cook to carry out their devilish plan, but they could just as easily have decided on a woman who was supposedly delivering an important message.

The door opened, and Gillian turned quickly to the captain, who motioned her inside. When she crossed the threshold, he closed the door, remaining in the hall.

Gillian took a few steps forward, clutching her cap in both hands. Only a single lamp was lit, and this was on the desk. She would never be able to recall what the room looked like. She was too intent

The Passionate Rebel

on the man seated at the cluttered desk. With her entrance, he got to his feet. He was tall and rather good-looking, though his features were etched with weariness.

"Good evening, young lady," said General George Washington. He smiled encouragingly. "I understand you wanted to see me?"

Gillian managed a nod. The general seated himself again, watching her expectantly.

Gillian wet her lips and moved closer. As quickly as she could, she told him what she had overheard at the mansion on Broad Way.

The general leaned back in his chair and shook his head slowly, as if saddened. "How fortunate we are to have patriots of your caliber," he said quietly.

"You will take precautions?" Gillian asked anxiously.

That smile again. "You may be assured that precautions have already been taken."

Gillian looked confused, but before she could voice it, a movement in the far corner of the room caught her attention. Slowly, a man stepped forward from the shadows. The light from the single lamp illuminated him from the chest down, and Gillian blinked. The man was not wearing a uniform; he was dressed in buckskin.

As the man took another step forward, Gillian drew a sharp breath and put a hand to her breast. Her heart began to thud painfully in response to the shock she was feeling.

"The fact that this news has already been delivered to us in no way lessens its value," the general was saying as he again got to his feet.

"Gillian . . ." The low word was put forth in angry tones.

General Washington regarded the man in buckskin with open surprise. "You know this lady, Lieutenant?"

"We've met."

Gillian tried but couldn't speak. The words froze in her throat. What on earth was Philip doing here?

"Well, that will make it easier," the general went on. "She has shown great courage in traveling here alone, but it would set my mind at ease if I knew that she was not placed in any further danger. Therefore, I will assign you as her escort on the return trip."

"It will be my pleasure to escort the lady home."

Without looking at Gillian, Philip strode from the room.

Washington came forward and took Gillian's hands in his. If he noticed they were trembling, he made no comment. "My dear, don't think your efforts to be in vain. This time, two people heard of the attempt on my life. Next time..." He smiled sadly. "Will I be as fortunate?"

"Oh, God, I hope there is no next time," Gillian said fervently, shuddering at just the thought. "Without you, our cause is lost."

"There always will be someone to carry forth the banner. It does not rest on the shoulders of one man." He laughed as he led Gillian to the door. "If I fall, another will take my place. It is as it should be."

"There can be no other," Gillian protested.

The general smiled, amused and a bit saddened by this naïveté. "There are always men who believe in liberty. One can only hope that a country has them when needed."

"And you?" Gillian said, pausing on the threshold. "You do believe?"

"I do," came the reply. "We cannot lose." A large hand came to rest on her slim shoulder. "How can we, when we have patriots like you?"

The Passionate Rebel

Outside, Gillian found Philip waiting for her on the porch.

"What the hell are you doing here?" He grabbed her upper arm in a rough gesture, almost dragging her down the steps.

She jerked her arm from his grasp. "You've no right to question me," she declared indignantly.

". . . playing your little games."

"Games! Do you call warning the general that there is a plot to take his life a game?"

Philip shook his head. "Come on. We'd best be getting back." He motioned to the animal tethered to the front porch. "Is this your horse?"

"Of course. You don't think I walked here, do you?"

"I'm beginning to think you'd do just about anything," he muttered without looking at her. Untying the reins, he threw them at her. Then he began to walk away at a fast pace.

Gillian had to quicken her steps until she was almost running in an effort to keep up with his long strides. "Where are we going?"

"Back to Manhattan."

"Are we going to run all the way?" she asked innocently, still trotting beside him.

He halted abruptly and stared at her. The way those hips of hers filled out those breeches took his breath away. "Where the devil did you get that outfit you're wearing?" he growled.

She didn't bother answering. "Why was the general calling you Lieutenant? Who the hell are you, anyway? Are you really a lawyer?"

"Yes, I am. And, I hope, a good one. I am also a lieutenant in the Continental army. I have been staying in New York under orders from my commander-in-chief."

"You tricked me," she shouted. "I shall never forgive you. I hate you!"

Again, he grabbed her roughly by the arm, and she could see his anger. "Do you think I wanted to?"

"You could have told me the truth."

"And then what?" He released her so abruptly, she stumbled to regain her balance. "One word . . . and people would have died."

"I would never have betrayed you." She had never before realized just how handsome he was. The soft buckskin molded his wide shoulders and fell softly about his lean, hard waist as no brocade jacket could have done.

"Not to your grandmother, perhaps. But what of your sister?"

Gillian looked confused. "Edwina would never have told," she said, unable to understand his reasoning.

"Don't you realize what you're saying?" he demanded. "A secret between two people becomes three, five, ten. In the end, people die. I must say," he went on ruefully, "that your brother-in-law is as adept at hiding his true feelings as I am."

"You didn't know about Thomas?" She was grateful for the change of topic.

"No, I didn't. And you were a part of it, too, weren't you?" At her nod, he sighed. "Well, it seems as though we both had secrets to keep."

Having reached the area where the horses were penned, Philip led his mare out. He mounted, then waited till Gillian did the same. He made no move to assist her.

A sudden rumble of thunder made Gillian raise her head. The sky was black. Neither stars nor moon broke the endless expanse of ebony that met and melted into the horizon.

The Passionate Rebel

The first drops of an icy cold rain began to fall before they were out of camp. The wind quickened to the point where it bent young trees and set bushes into a frenzied dance.

At last, Philip reined in, and Gillian stopped her horse next to his.

"We'll never be able to cross the river in this," he shouted.

"What can we do?" Gillian was beginning to shiver.

"There's an inn about a mile west of here. We'll have to shelter there until the storm passes."

Leaning forward, Philip tightened his grip on the reins and nudged his horse to a slow walk, proceeding forward.

A while later they reached the inn. A two-story, wooden structure, it offered little in the way of architectural design to please the eye. The iron bar protruding over the front door was bereft of the usual sign that proclaimed the name of the establishment.

Philip dismounted, then glanced up at Gillian. The wind had loosened tendrils of her hair from the cap she was wearing. Curtly, he told her to push it back under the cap.

Without waiting to see if she obeyed, he hurried inside, emerging a minute later with a young black boy. After giving the lad instructions to stable and feed their horses, he motioned to Gillian.

"Keep your head lowered," he said gruffly.

Moving forward, Philip opened the door but did not allow her to precede him.

Noise assaulted her ears as they entered. All the tables were filled with men who were either singing, laughing, arguing or just plain shouting to each other in an effort to be heard.

They were a rough-looking bunch, she thought uneasily, now realizing why Philip had wanted her to conceal her feminine attributes. She moved closer to Philip, who was conversing with the innkeeper.

"I've got only one room," the man said. "The weather . . ." He gestured vaguely.

Philip smiled affably. "It's certainly not a night to spend sleeping under the stars. I'll take it."

The innkeeper scowled as Philip reached into a pocket. "I'll not be takin' any of that continental money."

Philip threw hard coin on top of the bar.

The scowl turned to a grin.

"Can you send up some food?"

"I've got nothin' left but potatoes," the man advised, not at all apologetic as he pocketed the coins.

"It'll do," Philip said, heading for the stairs.

"It's the last one on the left," the innkeeper called out.

Gillian repressed a shudder when they entered the room. Lord, she thought, the Blue Swan was a mansion compared to this. The one window had no curtain, and the glass was cracked. There was no lamp. The only light came from a small blaze that was lit in the modest fireplace. The bed held only a poor straw mattress, though a heavy-looking quilt was folded at the foot. Gillian wouldn't even let herself consider when the sheets had last been changed. A straight-backed chair and a scratched dresser completed the spartan furnishings.

Gillian moved toward the fire, then turned to look at Philip. He was hanging his dripping cloak over the back of the chair. Hearing a knock on the door, he looked at Gillian. "Turn around." When she did, he opened the door.

The Passionate Rebel

A young serving girl entered carrying two plates of steaming boiled potatoes, which she placed atop the dresser.

She smiled invitingly at Philip. "It's a nasty night, ain't it?"

Philip nodded briefly. "One of the worst."

"Cold, too," she said, taking a step closer.

"The fire will keep me warm enough," Philip said firmly. Taking her arm, he guided her to the door. When she left, he locked it. Then he turned to Gillian, who was at the window with her back to him. "Get out of those wet clothes and eat."

Gillian's mouth tightened. She was becoming irked with his dictatorial manner. Do this! Do that!

As he watched her remove her cloak, Philip's eyes narrowed. "How did you find out about the plot against the general?"

Gillian gulped and turned away from him.

"Answer me!"

She didn't. "Where is the necessary?"

He grunted in exasperation. "Outside in the back, where it usually is."

Gillian grabbed the cloak and hastened from the room before he could persist.

When she returned a while later, Philip was sitting on the edge of the bed, eating the potatoes. He jerked his head in the direction of the dresser, the top of which held the other bowl.

"You'd better eat that before it gets cold," he said after she had closed and locked the door.

"Shall I do that before or after I remove these wet things?" she asked sweetly, not trying to mask her sarcasm.

Philip just kept on spooning the potatoes into his mouth. It was apparent to him that she wasn't about to answer his question, so he decided not to pursue it. Doubtless she had discovered the assassination plot in the same manner as he did, Philip reasoned, not realizing how close he was in his assumption.

Gillian removed her soaked outer clothing, draped it on the chair with his, then moved it closer to the fire, so that it would dry more quickly. Picking up the plate of potatoes, she ate half of it, then put the plate back on the dresser.

Going to the opposite side of the bed on which Philip was seated, Gillian sat down and pulled off her boots. That done, she glanced over her shoulder.

"Are we both supposed to sleep here?" she asked.

"I don't care where you sleep or even if you sleep," he retorted. Standing up, he began to remove his clothes.

Gillian averted her gaze and wondered why she did so. But then, that afternoon at his house had been different, she told herself. Then, they had been engaged. A crimson flush stained her cheeks. Still, she'd be damned if she'd sleep on the floor. Getting to her feet, Gillian began to undress. She glanced at him several times, but he wasn't looking at her.

Philip climbed into bed. With a sigh, he drew the quilt up to his chin.

"You didn't tell the British about Tom, did you?" she inquired in a low voice.

"No. The only hope for Tom is to be exchanged."

"Will that happen?" Gillian slipped beneath the coverings, trying to position herself at the far side of the bed. The warmth of his body was too much to resist, and she settled herself closer to him. Philip didn't seem to notice.

"I have been assured that it would be," he said in answer to her question. "They are aware of how

The Passionate Rebel

helpful Tom has been." He paused, then said, "Did you know that your brother-in-law has also been sending money to them?"

"Yes," she answered. "For that matter, so has Claudia."

"And what about Miss Dunham?" he asked then. "Has she secrets to keep, as well?"

Gillian turned away. "Claudia is not entirely what you think her to be."

He gave a harsh laugh. "Are you going to tell me that she is something other than the common tart everyone knows her to be?"

Gillian swung back to him angrily. "You've no cause to say that. You don't know anything about her."

He put his hands behind his head. "Well, why don't you tell me?"

She did.

When she was done, Philip was very still while he digested the news he had just been fed. It lay heavily in his gut, like spoiled meat. He was ashamed of his rashly formed opinions. But there was really nothing for him to say, so he didn't say anything.

Aware that Gillian was watching him intently, Philip turned to look at her, a long, level look that made her catch her breath. Unaware that she did so, Gillian leaned toward him.

Did he move, or did she?

Gillian never knew, for when their lips met, all coherent thought left her mind. As his hand slid beneath the blanket and caressed her bare back, Gillian gave a soft moan. Her arms went around his broad warm shoulders, and she gave herself up to the sweet pleasure that flooded through her.

Lightning flashed outside, illuminating the room with a brilliance no lamp could match. And, it seemed to Gillian, the same force exploded within her.

When Gillian opened her eyes some hours later, it was still dark. Raising her head, she looked out the window, seeing a star-studded sky. Philip was getting dressed, and this was what had awakened her. She sat up, clutching the quilt around her, still feeling sleepy.

"The storm has passed," he said to her. "We must leave before it gets light."

Though she much preferred to stay snuggled in the warm bed, Gillian got up and reached for her clothes.

In the process of buttoning his breeches, Philip was standing with his back to her. He had not yet donned his shirt. The warm glow from the waning fire played on the hard muscles of his broad shoulders.

A delicious shiver wended its way through Gillian as she looked at him. After they were married, she thought to herself, she would be spending every night with those strong arms wrapped around her. Why had she been so foolish as to insist they wait a year? It now seemed an eternity.

Gillian bit her lip. Of course, in a sense Philip had broken their engagement, but that was only because they'd had that silly fight. If only he'd told her the truth, none of this would have happened.

And why didn't he speak now? Because, obviously, he was waiting for her to do so.

"You know," she said, clearing her throat, "I really don't think it's necessary for us to wait until November to be married. I think—"

Philip fastened his belt, then gave her a sharp look. "What are you talking about?"

The Passionate Rebel

Gillian's eyes went wide. "Surely we are going ahead with our marriage?"

Philip sat down and drew on his boots before he responded. "Whatever gave you an idea like that?"

"Well, I mean, after last night, I thought . . ."

He gave a short laugh. "It seems to me that we have already covered that ground."

"But . . ." Gillian looked puzzled.

He looked amused. "My dear Gillian," he said with exaggerated patience, "I am not made of stone. When a beautiful woman crawls into bed with me and presses her warm and inviting body against my own, I do my best to accommodate her."

It took a moment for his words to register. When they did, anger and outrage combined to produce twin spots of crimson on her cheeks.

"You . . ." Gillian almost choked on the word.

Deep inside, Philip cursed himself for this overwhelming need to hurt her as she had hurt him, but the feeling was too strong. It was a force he could not control. Gillian had not, as most women would have, accepted him at face value. Her acceptance appeared to be based on his political outlook. The thought, to him, was intolerable at this moment. Never mind that he had placed his own life in jeopardy for a cause in which he believed with an intensity that overshadowed all else. Never mind that she had, too. He realized the enormity of the decision that had prompted her to travel alone to reach the camp of the Continentals.

That, however, should have had nothing to do with her feeling for him.

"Certainly," he added ruthlessly, "it does not seem to matter to you whether it's a Tory or a patriot who serves your purposes."

Gillian's gasp was audible. She felt as though a

knife had pierced her heart. She should, she knew, refute his words. Instead, anger blotted reason from her mind. She gave a strangled cry as she lunged at him. He caught her wrists and pinned them behind her waist. Tightening his hold, he pulled her so close, she could feel the hardness of him, feel the warmth of his breath on her face. His dark eyes held her captive as he spoke.

"And anytime you'd care to crawl in bed with me again, just let me know." Almost immediately, he was contrite, but the coldness in her voice when she spoke precluded any apology he may have thought to offer.

"You insufferable beast," she ground out in measured tones that tore at his heart. "I wouldn't marry you if . . . if you got down on your hands and knees and begged me."

His smile was sardonic as he released her. "Rest easy, Miss Winthrop. I will not place you in the awkward position of having to spurn me twice. Finish dressing. We've a long ride ahead of us."

The ride was, in fact, interminable. Philip found someone to ferry them back to New York. Even though the storm had passed, the water was rough and the crossing unpleasant.

The silence between Gillian and Philip was alive with things unsaid. To outward appearances, each of them was oblivious to the other, speaking when they had to in short, clipped tones.

It was close to dawn when they arrived at the Wharton house. Though Gillian wished he hadn't, Philip escorted her to the stable. Once there, Gillian quickly dismounted. After the horse was rested, she would have William take him back to the Clayton farm.

The Passionate Rebel

Forearm resting on the pommel of the saddle, Philip looked down at her as she opened the stable doors.

"I do hope that you will not take it upon yourself to again go dashing off into the night to deliver messages. Rescuing you could prove to be a weary endeavor."

"I wasn't aware you rescued me," she retorted shortly. "I arrived at my destination safely, and I could have arrived home in the same state without your help."

Philip stared at her in a way that made her heart ache. She wasn't in love with this man, Gillian told herself. She couldn't be—not now, not when it was too late.

"Then in the future I will make certain that I do not interfere in your comings and goings." Philip straightened and spurred his horse forward, leaving her standing there in the increasing light of day.

Gillian took a step forward and almost called to him, but with anger spreading its insidious strength through her, she turned, leading the horse into the stable.

The same anger sustained Gillian in the days that followed. Soon, however, it began to dissipate, leaving behind a deep hurt that seemed to plunge her into a bottomless well of misery. She wept until she had no more tears to shed, but the ache persisted. She told herself she didn't care, was better off without a rogue like Philip Meredith in her life. Then she wept anew, knowing that she was only deceiving herself.

Chapter Seventeen

From Gillian's Diary:

> *March 27, 1779*
> *George Rogers Clark, a young lieutenant colonel in the Virginia militia, marched his men 180 miles over terrain so covered by water as to be almost impassable and, with only 170 brave men, recaptured the fort at Vincennes. For the protection of the people in the village that surrounds the fort, Colonel Clark sent word of his intentions before he advanced, giving them the option of remaining in their houses, if they were patriots, or joining the British in the fort, if they were Tories. Most stayed in their homes. The British were fooled into thinking that Colonel Clark had 1000 soldiers with him, and they hastily surrendered when the shooting began in earnest.*

The Passionate Rebel

Franz tightened his jacket as he made his way slowly down the street. It was cold and damp. The air was so thick with fog he could not see more than five feet in any direction.

When Franz opened the door to the taproom, he breathed a sigh of relief, feeling the warm air envelop him like a welcoming friend. Inside, he stood there a moment until he spied Claudia. Then, instead of going to his usual table, he headed in her direction.

When he caught her eye, he smiled. She was wearing a green dress that matched her eyes. Some of her black hair was visible beneath her cap, though not nearly as much as Franz would have liked to see. It was very fine in texture, a true ebony with no hint of red in it. Franz imagined it to be silky and longed to touch it.

"It took some doing," he said to her, "but I am scheduled to go aboard the *Jersey* tomorrow morning to deliver a supply of powder. I feel certain that I will be able to see Mr. Carmody while I am there. As I promised, I will bring food with me. Is there anything you would like me to tell him?"

Claudia shook her head. "No. However, I know his wife would like to send a message. Come with me."

Edwina was in the kitchen, stirring a pot of beef stew. At the sink, Mandy was carefully plucking the feathers off a chicken destined for soup.

When Claudia came in with Franz, Edwina viewed them both in surprise. She couldn't imagine why Claudia was bringing a Hessian into her kitchen. Wiping her hands on the apron she was wearing over a blue grosgrain dress, she smiled tentatively.

Claudia made a hasty introduction, then explained

the situation to Edwina, whose face lit up.

"Can you get food to him? A change of clothing?"

Franz had barely nodded in affirmation when Edwina hurried from the room. The kitchen was warm. Franz removed his jacket and hung it on the back of a chair.

Claudia motioned Franz to a chair at the table. "The very least I can offer you is a free meal," she said, bustling among the pots on the stove.

"That's not necessary," Franz protested, although he did sit down.

She placed before him a plate piled high with beef and potatoes.

"This is a kind thing you're doing," Claudia said after a moment, watching him eat.

"Not at all," he murmured.

In a graceful movement, Claudia sat down across from him. "Why are you doing this?"

He looked up. "Don't you know?"

She moistened her lips and turned away, relieved to see Edwina.

Going to the table, Edwina placed a parcel on its scrubbed surface.

"Clothing," she said, eyes glistening with tears. "I'll get food." Going into the pantry, she brought forth a cooked ham and began to slice it.

Having cleaned his plate, Franz stood up. He looked at Claudia, but she kept her face averted from him. He was growing used to her attitude. The moment he became personal, she withdrew. He wondered whether she was afraid of him or afraid of herself.

Edwina put the food in a clean cloth, then tied it neatly into a bundle.

"Do you think it's enough?" she asked anxiously

as she put it beside the clothing.

Franz smiled at the petite woman. It took only a glance to tell that she was well along in her pregnancy. "I am certain that it is most adequate."

"They do feed the prisoners well, don't they?" Edwina asked in a voice that was suddenly breathless.

Franz looked at Claudia. This time, she was viewing him gravely.

"Of course," Franz answered easily. "Naturally, the food is plain, and I am certain what you are sending will be a treat." He was rewarded with a soft sigh of relief. "And if there is anything you would like to tell him, I would be more than glad to relay the message."

Edwina clasped her hands. There was so much, but she didn't want to impose.

"Tell him I am well," she said at last. "He'll want to know that first."

Franz nodded and waited patiently, knowing there was more.

"And tell him that he should not lose hope. We are doing everything we can. And tell him . . ." She bit her lip against threatened tears. "I miss him so much—No!" She shook her head. "No, don't tell him that. It will make him unhappy." She looked at Claudia as if she could help.

"I'm sure Tom will know everything that's left unsaid," Claudia responded gently. Her green eyes sought Franz. "Thank you, Lieutenant."

"Yes, yes," Edwina said quickly. "Thank you from the bottom of my heart. Will you come back and tell me how he is?"

"I will be back tomorrow evening," Franz promised. Picking up the parcels, he nodded to both women.

When he had gone, Edwina said, "He doesn't seem like the others, does he?" She went to the stove, where Mandy was now stirring the stew with a wooden spoon. After tasting a sip, she waved the girl away. "It's fine. Peel the potatoes." She turned to look at Claudia again, realizing she had received no response to her comment.

Claudia shrugged. "Time will tell," she murmured noncommittally. She could not bring herself, even in the safety of her own mind, to admit to the truth of Edwina's observation. Along with her family and her possessions, it seemed as though trust, too, had been consigned to the flames.

During the endless, dreary days that comprised his confinement, Tom fought for a sense of balance, clinging to the hope that the war would miraculously end and that he would be released from this hell on earth. The scratch on his hand had festered and healed, causing him no more discomfort than a slight fever that had lasted less than 48 hours.

The diet of oatmeal, peas and biscuits, however, was beginning to take its toll. He was losing weight at an alarming rate. A bout of dysentery in his third week had so sapped his strength that he had to lean heavily on Silas to reach the galley, for no prisoner was allowed to carry food to another.

Through it all, the vision of Edwina was always with him, a beacon of light to which all his hopes adhered.

The cold, damp days of early March had given rise to sickness and disease, until virulence cut a noticeable swath in the unwilling population of prisoners aboard the *Jersey*. Now the men were dying at the rate of six and seven a day.

The Passionate Rebel

Tom and Silas had managed to secure a place close to the airholes during this upheaval, but while the air was measurably cleaner, it was every bit as cold.

It was late in the morning during this last week in March, the twelfth of his confinement, when Tom opened his eyes from an uneasy doze to see the Hessian standing before him.

"Mr. Carmody?"

The man spoke in a low murmur. He squatted down on his haunches so that he was almost at eye level with Tom, who had raised himself up on an elbow.

"I have a message from your wife. She said to tell you not to give up hope." Franz kept his face impassive, for the change in Tom was great. His hair was matted and unkempt, the gray now turning to white at the temples. His normally clean-shaven face was bearded. His cheeks were sunken, making his eyes appear too large for his face. Franz handed Tom one of the two bundles he was carrying. "This is a change of clothing."

Tom finally found his voice. "How is my wife?"

"She is well. She also sent you this." Franz gave him the other bundle. "I suggest you eat the meat first, before it spoils."

Tom's mouth watered as his trembling hands opened the package and he saw the food. He was sorely tempted to shove it into his mouth all at once. He swallowed, tore his gaze from this unexpected bounty and again viewed the Hessian.

"When you see my wife again, tell her . . . tell her I am also well." He clutched the other's arm. "Please don't tell her you've seen me like this."

Tom wanted to ask more, so much more, but the idea of discussing his wife's pregnancy with a virtual stranger was beyond him. The face of the man was familiar, of course. Night after night, Tom had seen it at a table in the corner of the tavern. However, he had never spoken to the man, and to see him now, here, was a shock beyond description. Who was this blue-coated mercenary who brought him food, brought him word from Edwina, brought him hope?

Tom was nonplussed, unable to come to terms with the fact that one of the enemy had gone out of his way to show him a kindness.

The Hessian nodded. "I will make every effort not to upset her." He stood up again. "I will try to get more food to you. Unfortunately, I cannot come aboard without good reason."

As quickly as he had come, the Hessian was gone. Only the bundle he clutched so tightly in his hand was evidence to Tom that it had not been a dream. He moved closer to Silas, pulling the bundle between them. A sigh came from both of them as they viewed the precious contents. Tom divided the meat and gave half to Silas.

They ate slowly, savoring each bite, prudently saving a portion for later in the day. There was also bread and cheese and, most glorious of all, three apples. Unable to resist, Tom ate one, then lay back with a contented sigh, feeling replete for the first time since he'd entered this hellhole.

That night, both Claudia and Edwina were waiting for Franz, ushering him into the kitchen as soon as he entered the Blue Swan.

Having heard the news from her sister, Gillian left the customer she was waiting on right in the middle of a sentence and hurried to follow them.

The Passionate Rebel

Questions flew at him from all sides, and Franz raised his hands in an effort to calm the three women. He smiled at them all but addressed his remarks to Edwina. For the past hour, he wondered what he would tell her. The truth would have been best in the long run, and he would have done this if it hadn't been for her condition.

"Mr. Carmody is in good spirits," Franz began, uncomfortable with the way in which they were all hanging on his words. "He was most relieved to hear that you are well. As for the food . . ." He gestured and offered a laugh. "He was so delighted. I have an idea he plans to share it with his companions."

Franz paused. They wanted more, and he knew it.

"How does he look?" Edwina cried, clutching his arm. "Is he well?"

"He is not sick," Franz replied carefully. "He has grown a beard. However, I am sure you can appreciate that he cannot bathe and shave as often as he likes. He is a bit thinner."

Edwina put her hand to her lips. "Thinner?" she echoed faintly. "He's not eating?"

"You must understand, Mrs. Carmody, the variety of food is most unimaginative. Boiled beef . . ."

Edwina shuddered. "Thomas is not fond of boiled beef."

"Well, there you have it. He is probably not eating as much as he would normally."

At last it was over, and Franz gratefully moved into the taproom again. Edwina had insisted that Franz not be charged for any meal he consumed in the Blue Swan. However, Franz found he had no appetite this night.

Claudia put a cup of ale in front of him. "Did you tell her the truth?" she asked quietly.

He looked up at her. Claudia was the most beautiful woman he had ever seen. She quite took his breath away. Her coldness did not deter him; if anything, it intrigued him. And her hands. How had that happened? She never made any attempt to hide their scarred palms; indeed, she never even seemed to think about it.

"Did you?" Claudia demanded, jarring him from his reverie.

Franz viewed his ale. "No. He requested that I not do that." He sought her eyes again, thinking how lovely they were. "He is like all the rest—weak and undernourished. They live on hope. If it does not materialize in time, they die."

Claudia felt weak. "Will he die?"

Franz shrugged. "How do you expect me to answer that? I have seen men survive under the most extraordinary conditions. I have seen them die from no more than a flesh wound."

Franz fell silent as he saw a British officer stumbling toward them. Anger boiled up inside him, drumming a staccato beat in his ears when the man put an arm around Claudia in a most familiar way. Franz felt a searing ache in the region of his heart when she did not rebuff the man.

Chapter Eighteen

From Gillian's Diary:

> *April 5, 1779*
> *At last, General Washington has seen fit to strike a decisive blow against Joseph Brant and his unholy savages. Four thousand men under the command of General John Sullivan have been sent into Iroquois territory to put an end to their ceaseless quest for destruction.*

"I remember the day you was born," Polly reminisced, smiling at Gillian. Then she shook her head. "Hard to believe it was twenty years ago."

Both of them were seated at the kitchen table. Gillian had discovered that she disliked sitting alone in the dining room with only her own thoughts for company.

Gillian sighed at Polly's observation. "And a fine

birthday it is," she said morosely. "Gram's not here, Tom's not here, and . . ." She bit her lip. She didn't even want to say his name.

"Well," Polly said philosophically as she got up, "birthdays come whether anyone celebrates them or not." She began to clear the table.

At that moment, Gillian glanced out the window and saw Claudia, skirts hiked in both hands, running at top speed through the orchard.

Quickly, Gillian got up and went outside.

"What's wrong?" she called out as Claudia neared.

"Edwina!" came the breathless answer. "Her time's come."

Gillian put a hand to her lips. The baby was not due for another two weeks. "Have you sent for the midwife?" she asked as they both made their way back across the orchard.

Claudia nodded, still panting from her exertion. "She's on her way."

"When did it start?"

"I'm not sure. Sometime through the night." Claudia gave an exasperated shake of her head as they entered the Blue Swan. "You know how Edwina is; she never complains. Mandy came to fetch me about thirty minutes ago. Near as I can tell, she's pretty far along."

Gillian took the stairs two at a time.

The midwife, a florid-complexioned woman named Meg Kersey, was already in the room.

"Edwina!" Gillian gasped as she heard her sister's shrill cry.

"Now, don't you worry," Meg said comfortingly, patting Gillian's shoulder. "Second one's always easier." She nodded to Claudia. "I think both of you should wait outside. Won't be long," she added as Edwina again cried out.

The Passionate Rebel

"No!" Gillian went to the bedside and clutched Edwina's hand. "I'm staying with her."

Meg shrugged. She didn't have time to argue. The baby's head was already visible. Putting a hand on Edwina's swollen stomach, she smiled encouragingly. "Push hard. Once more should do it."

Edwina's small body arched as she strained; then she fell back, feeling an overwhelming relief as the child was expelled.

"A boy, Mrs. Carmody!" Meg exclaimed with a broad smile. "A perfect boy!"

As the midwife began to clean the child, Claudia looked on with mixed feelings of joy and sadness. The lump in her throat felt as large as an apple. She supposed all babies looked alike when they were first born, but the squirming little babe so resembled her own son it was, for now, too painful for her to look at him. Coincidentally, her husband Charles had had auburn hair, and the fuzzy thatch of ginger on the infant's scalp tore at her heart.

Going to the door, Claudia quietly left, unwilling to display her emotions before the happy occupants of the room.

Slowly, she descended the stairs. She felt like an empty vessel, drained of feeling. In the kitchen, she pushed open the back door. The sweetness of spring engulfed her with a soft seductiveness. One could see summer; certainly one could see autumn and winter. But one had to "feel" spring. It invaded the senses like a lover. It was a season to be shared.

And Claudia didn't have anyone to share it with.

With a sigh that came from the innermost recess of her heart, Claudia left the porch, feeling a need to distance herself from the happiness contained within the confines of the structure behind her. She did not begrudge anyone happiness, certainly not the woman who had shown her nothing but kindness.

On the street, Claudia turned left and headed toward Broad Way. It was, as usual, crowded. She looked with some amazement at the people that swirled around her. Did they have families? Did they have loved ones?

Claudia felt she had nothing and wondered if she was the only one in this hub of activity to be so deprived.

"I am so delighted to meet you unexpectedly."

Claudia drew a sharp breath and turned to see Franz beside her. He thrust a lush hyacinth at her.

Unprepared, Claudia took it. "Where did you get this?" she asked.

"I stole it," Franz cheerfully confessed, putting his hands behind his back. He had seen her walking ahead of him and had quite unabashedly plucked a blossom from the nearest garden.

"It's pretty," Claudia allowed, viewing the delicate flower.

"All flowers are pretty," Franz observed.

Claudia viewed him through eyes darkened by sadness. Yet she was moved by the simple gesture. Compressing her lips, she moved forward.

So did Franz. "Would you rather I did not speak?" The question was posed with a seriousness that cut through her.

Claudia gave a laugh that was half a sob. "I wish," she said, biting back her tears, "that you would speak of anything that takes your fancy."

He did, but Claudia didn't listen. Clutching the hyacinth, she walked beside him, thinking of babies, of husbands, of a life she had had, and one which had been snatched from her by the relentless hand of fate.

In the bedroom, Gillian was smiling through her tears as she hugged her sister. "Oh, Edwina," she cried softly, "I'll never again have as nice a birthday present as this."

Having cleaned and swaddled the infant, Meg had put him at his mother's breast.

"Thomas," Edwina whispered as she gazed down at her son. "That shall be your name." She looked up at Gillian. "Tom will be so proud when he comes home."

"I'm sure he will be coming home within a week or two," Gillian said quickly, praying she was right.

It didn't take a week or even two. It took nine.

As the weather grew warmer and April gave way to May, Edwina refused to lose faith. But when May began to slip by without word, her spirits began to sag to a degree that made Gillian begin to fear for her sister's health.

"The British will never release him," Edwina cried. "I will never see him again. My son will never know his father."

Gillian stared worriedly at her sister. Edwina was spending more and more time in bed. She only picked at her food, even though Gillian constantly reminded her that she was nursing.

In desperation, Gillian swallowed her pride and went to see Philip at his place of business.

When she arrived, the clerk took her name and ushered her into an office.

"Mr. Meredith is consulting with a client at this time. However, he should be through shortly," the young man said.

Leaving the room, he closed the door behind him.

Gillian sat patiently until, some 15 minutes later, Philip strode into the room.

He placed the papers he was carrying on the desk, then looked at her. "Do you have a legal problem, Miss Winthrop?" he asked coolly as he sat down.

Gillian clenched her teeth against a sudden throb of anger. When one was hoping for a favor, one did not scream at the person who was expected to perform it.

"No," she said quietly. "I am here on a personal matter. I want to know if you have any further news about Tom. The strain of this endless waiting is beginning to take its toll on my sister. I'm greatly concerned about her."

Philip pursed his lips and sighed. "I had hoped it would be resolved by now," he confessed. "If Mr. Carmody was an officer, I believe the change already would have been made. I'm sure you can understand that the Continentals must give first priority to their officers."

"No, I cannot understand that," Gillian said. "Each day, each hour that passes threatens Tom's life. How long do you think he can hold out?"

Philip stood up. "I do not make the decisions," he said to her. "However, I will speak again to those who do."

Slowly, Gillian got to her feet. For all intents and purposes, they could be two strangers discussing a problem of mutual concern.

"When is your grandmother returning?" Philip asked as he escorted her to the door. A faint perfume of roses teased his senses, and his jaw tightened. It was, he knew by now, her favorite scent.

"I don't know."

The Passionate Rebel

"I miss her," he said with a smile that did not quite reach his eyes.

"I'm sure you do," Gillian replied wryly. Then she could not help adding, "Perhaps you should have proposed to her."

Philip stared at her for a long moment before he spoke.

"Things might have worked out better if I had." He opened the door.

Gillian wet her lips. No tears, she told herself sternly. She straightened her shoulders and managed to face him with unwavering eyes.

"As near as I can tell, things *have* worked out for the best."

Gathering her skirt, Gillian swept past him, chin high.

Outside, after she settled herself in the carriage, reserve fell away. Her shoulders slumped, and her eyes smarted in a most annoying way.

Once, Philip Meredith had proclaimed undying love for her. Well, it was certainly fortuitous that she had discovered how shallow his feelings were, Gillian told herself.

Not that it made any difference to her; she was well out of it. She couldn't imagine spending her life with a man who so aggravated her.

Gillian fumbled for her handkerchief and dabbed her eyes.

By the time they reached the Blue Swan, Gillian was once more in control of herself.

Going upstairs, she viewed Edwina with a frown. Though well past noon, she was still in bed, staring listlessly at the ceiling.

Gillian drew a chair closer to the bed. Sitting down, she took Edwina's hand in her own. Speaking softly, she related her conversation with Philip.

For a long moment, Edwina studied Gillian's face closely, not quite able to believe it.

"How ironic," she murmured at last. "Tom is being helped by a Hessian and a Tory."

"I told you," Gillian said quietly, "Philip is not a Tory. And you must not tell anyone about this. Anyone!" she emphasized, uncomfortably aware of what Philip had said to her about secrets being shared. Philip had been right, after all, Gillian thought despondently. In a sense, even though with good reason, she had betrayed him.

On the second Sunday in June, Gillian and Edwina were sitting on the back porch, enjoying the warm summer day. A short distance away, Constance, now almost two, was busily inspecting a butterfly hovering on the delicate petal of a rose.

For a time, Gillian watched her sister, cuddling the baby on her lap. Edwina's calm, good spirit had finally reasserted itself.

"You really should think about having young Tom christened," Gillian murmured.

"No!" The answer was swift. "He will not be christened until his father comes home and can be a part of the ceremony. And he will come home," she declared, glaring at Gillian as though she might be inclined to take exception. "I will not let myself believe otherwise."

"Of course he will," Gillian quickly agreed. "There is no question of that." But when? she thought in anguish. When?

They were silent a while. Constance repeatedly tried and failed to capture the elusive butterfly.

Her daughter, Edwina thought with a soft smile, had been aptly named. She was a constant joy, unfailingly cheerful and sweet-tempered.

The Passionate Rebel

Finally, Edwina turned to Gillian, who seemed to be lost in her own thoughts. "What do you think of the Hessian?" she asked.

Gillian took a moment to respond, which seemed odd, even to her. Only a short while ago, her answer would have been swift and deadly.

And it wasn't fair, she thought angrily. People she hated were suddenly turning into something other than she thought them to be. Nothing was as it should be. The world was becoming topsy-turvy.

"Well, Claudia seems to trust him," she said at last.

Edwina smiled. "She more than trusts him. Although I don't think she realizes that yet."

"Claudia would never become involved with a Hessian." Gillian refused to meet the sidelong glance that came her way.

"It is not a Hessian she is involved with," Edwina noted quietly. "Nor is it a Tory. I speak of a man."

"Oh, Edwina!" Gillian moved in her chair, appearing agitated. "Of course we know he is a man. What a foolish thing to say."

Edwina sighed. "Why won't you tell me what happened between you and Mr. Meredith? We used to share everything."

"I told you what happened," Gillian retorted briskly. "Philip finally realized that I did not want to marry him."

Edwina was unconvinced. "You didn't injure his pride in any way, did you?"

"What on earth are you talking about?"

"Well..." Edwina took a deep breath. "Mr. Meredith strikes me as being a very proud man, and I just thought that perhaps you may have inadvertently said something to wound his pride." Seeing the dark expression on Gillian's face, Edwina quickly added, "You do have a sharp tongue at times, and I know for a fact that at the beginning you were very outspoken in your determination not to marry him. And if you foolishly said those things to him, I imagine that would be a bit much for a man like that to swallow."

Gillian almost laughed. Someone's pride had definitely been wounded, all right, she thought ruefully. But it happened to be hers, not Philip's. She moved uneasily in her chair with the sudden thought that Edwina's analysis had been right on target. By words and by actions, she had shown Philip Meredith in many ways that she did not want to marry him. It had been only a matter of time until he believed her.

And when, ironically, Gillian had realized that she did indeed want to marry him, it was too late.

The baby was asleep. Edwina tucked the light blanket closer about the child. "Constance," she called, "come along. It's almost time for dinner."

The little girl looked up and made a face. The fascinating butterfly was still hovering, always just out of reach.

Edwina was about to repeat her command when she saw the tall, elegantly dressed man approaching them. He paused a moment to smile at Constance, then nodded politely to the two women.

Gillian felt the breath leave her body.

"Good afternoon," Philip said, doffing his hat.

"Mr. Meredith! How nice to see you." Edwina, still cradling her son, cast a quick glance at Gillian and began to go inside.

"Please . . ." Philip's voice halted her. "It's you I came to see, Mistress Carmody."

Gillian viewed her hands, clasped in her lap.

"I have news about your husband," he said.

The Passionate Rebel

At that, both women stared at him, and Gillian got to her feet.

"There is every indication that he will be released before the week is gone. I'm sorry I cannot give you an exact day. He is being exchanged, you see, and it will depend on how long it takes to transfer a certain British officer back here. If all goes well, it shouldn't take more than three days. However, I don't want you to worry if it takes a bit longer."

Unable to contain her joy, Edwina began to weep.

Gillian put an arm around her sister and looked at Philip.

She had forgotten how handsome he was. His skin was deeply tanned. Although he had placed one foot on the bottom step, he did not come any further. The hand in which he held his hat now rested on his upper thigh. His fashionable breeches were skintight, as were his white stockings, and Gillian could see every hard muscle outlined. A familiar excitement caused her breath to quicken, and she lowered her eyes, certain that he would see the sudden, unwanted longing that filled their gray depths.

"It was most considerate of you to bring this news to us," she said to him at last.

"I don't like to leave any loose ends," he retorted curtly.

Recovering, Edwina offered her thanks, then said, "There are things I must do now. I'll leave you two alone."

"That won't be necessary, Mistress Carmody," Philip said as he turned to go. "I believe that Miss Winthrop and I have said all that needs saying." He donned his hat. "Good day."

Gillian was trembling as she watched him walk away. She had already taken one step down the porch stairs when she halted. Philip was getting into his carriage, motioning the driver forward. As far as Gillian could tell, he never glanced back.

Her mouth tightened as the carriage rolled up the street. She'd be damned if she would go running after him.

"I'm well rid of him," she muttered.

And though her heart cried out at the lie, Gillian refused to listen.

Tactfully, Edwina said nothing as they went back inside. In any event, her mind was unable to dwell on anything other than the fact that her husband was at last going to be released.

Three days later, they brought Tom home in a cart, as if they were delivering a load of firewood. Ordinarily, they would not have gone to this trouble. Tom, however, had been exchanged for a high-ranking officer and, as such, terms had to be carried out.

The change in Tom was dramatic. Never a large man, his bones now shone whitely through the spare layer of flesh that covered them. Despite the fact that on two more separate occasions Franz had managed to bring food to him, Tom had lost better than 20 pounds. For a big man, that might have presented little problem. For Tom, it had the effect of reducing his body to skeletal proportions. His teeth pained him, and some had loosened.

Only Edwina was able to summon a bright smile. Gillian turned away in tears, and it was Claudia who stepped forward to assist Edwina as she helped her husband from the cart.

"It's all right, my love," Edwina crooned as she and Claudia helped him up the stairs. "Soon your strength will return, and all this will be behind you."

Tom made no comment. It would never be behind him; the degradation, the squalor, the foul smell of confined men would be with him always.

Chapter Nineteen

From Gillian's Diary:

> *June 17, 1779*
> *In their spare time, the redcoats have taken to counterfeiting continental money, passing it out with a generous hand at every opportunity. Thanks to their underhanded efforts, the currency has become all but worthless. Our soldiers had little enough to send home to their families; now, they have nothing.*

The June evening was sultry and hot. It had rained earlier in the day, and a heavy humidity blanketed the island of Manhattan.

Claudia was sitting with Franz at the corner table, fanning herself with a bill of fare. It didn't do much good. Even though all doors and windows were

The Passionate Rebel

open, the heat was pressing and uncomfortable.

"I want to thank you for all you've done for Tom," she said to Franz. Viewing him, seated across the table, her green eyes glistened like emeralds. "If it hadn't been for you, he might not have survived."

"I only wish it could have been more," he said quietly, but he was greatly pleased by her words.

Claudia put down the bill of fare, as if realizing that her efforts were a waste of time. A fine sheen of perspiration covered her face and the generous swell of her bosom above her bodice.

To Franz, her skin glowed like warm ivory. And her hair . . .

Conscious of his intense gaze, Claudia gave him a quizzical look.

"No woman should have hair as glorious as yours," he said solemnly. "It is most distracting."

Claudia shifted in her chair, uneasy with her sudden awareness of him as a virile male. "I don't know that my hair is any different from any other woman's," she retorted, feeling embarrassed by his observation.

"I assure you, it is unique."

Reaching across the table, Franz attempted to take hold of her hand. As always, Claudia pulled away from him. She had begun to realize that she was afraid of this man, afraid of the feelings he aroused in her, feelings she thought she would never again experience.

"Tomorrow is Sunday," he went on as if nothing had happened. "May I take you for a drive in the country?"

"I have no pass."

He smiled. "You don't need one, if you are with me."

Claudia hesitated. A drive in the country. A day

of relaxation. How long had it been since she had sampled those simple pleasures?

"I will call for you at ten," Franz said before she could speak. Getting up, he extended a hand to assist her in rising.

Claudia said nothing. It seemed easier right now to let someone else make the decisions.

The following morning, Claudia dressed with more care than she had displayed in a long time. She selected and rejected several outfits before deciding on a pale-green silk gown she had never worn before. Low-necked with elbow-length sleeves, it fell softly about her rounded hips, for she wore no hoops beneath it. The bodice came to a point in the front, accenting her small waist.

Viewing herself in the mirror, Claudia frowned. It looked awful; she looked awful. Quickly, she began to remove the dress.

A knock at the door gave her pause. Hearing Edwina's voice, Claudia told her to come in.

"I thought you might like to borrow this," Edwina said, holding out a white lace shawl. "Franz is waiting—" She came to an abrupt halt, seeing Claudia sitting on the edge of the bed in her underclothes.

Claudia motioned to the dress, which she had thrown at the foot of the bed. "It doesn't fit right. I look terrible in it."

Putting the shawl down, Edwina picked up the dress. "Claudia, it's lovely. Come, let me help you."

"It's not suitable for a drive," Claudia protested, nevertheless getting to her feet.

"It's perfect," Edwina said soothingly.

Resigned, Claudia allowed Edwina to assist her back into the dress.

"Come along, now," Edwina urged when they

The Passionate Rebel

were through. Picking up the shawl, she handed it to Claudia. It warmed her heart to see Claudia showing an interest in something, even if it was only the selection of a dress for a Sunday drive.

Franz was waiting at the foot of the stairs. Watching her descent, he smiled softly.

"If I did not know better, I would say I was looking at a vision from heaven," he whispered to her.

Feeling suddenly shy, Claudia allowed him to escort her to his carriage.

Although the air was warm, it was considerably drier than the preceding day. A delightful breeze kept the temperature at a comfortable level.

About three miles from the city, Franz drew in on the reins and halted the carriage.

The landscape was a patchwork of color; daffodils, blueberries and the exquisite lily of the valley bravely held their own amidst honeysuckle and rambling roses. Leaves had lost their delicate hue of green, to be replaced by the rich shades of emerald that proclaimed maturity.

Franz looked at Claudia beside him. "Would you care to walk?"

Claudia nodded, and they began to stroll slowly along a road that was no more than a footpath.

It was a beautiful day. The blue sky was marred only by a few wispy cirrus clouds. To their left, the Hudson River flowed serenely, its sunlit surface throwing out little darts of blazing light.

Franz paused and, kneeling down on one knee, scooped up a handful of dirt, letting it trickle through his fingers.

"The soil is rich." Straightening, he brushed his hands. "A man could make a good life on this land."

She looked surprised. "Didn't you tell me your father was a baker?"

Throwing his head back, Franz laughed. Claudia couldn't help thinking what a pleasant sound it was; hearty and infectious, it almost made her join him. She settled for a smile.

"Working with dough is not that much different from working the soil. They both produce good things to eat." He put a finger to her lips with a touch as light as a butterfly's wing. "This is the first time I have seen you smile," he said softly. "If anything, it makes you more lovely."

Claudia instantly sobered. "There is not much to smile about these days," she noted quietly.

They began to walk again. Hands behind his back, Franz made no move to touch her.

"Would you care to tell me about it?" he asked after a while.

Turning her head, she gave him a quick glance, uncertain as to what he was referring.

They had reached a soft rise that overlooked the river. Franz walked to a wide-trunked oak. Removing his jacket, he spread it on the soft grass.

"Come," he urged quietly. "Let us sit for a while."

Obediently, Claudia sank down, her skirt billowing about her in a pool of green silk. She watched as he sat down on the grass, legs drawn up, arms resting on his knees. Plucking a blade of grass, he twirled it absently.

The silence lengthened. Franz did not repeat his question. Claudia wondered if he had forgotten he'd asked it.

She swallowed. "I . . . was married," she began. In a halting voice, she told him about the night of the fire, told him everything, in fact. He never looked at her, and that made it easier. Instead, he stared across the water as if engrossed in the sight.

The Passionate Rebel

Finally, Claudia was through. The quiet was palpitating, accented rather than diminished by the noisy chatter of birds and the droning hum of bees.

"You loved him? Your husband?" Franz asked after a while.

"Very much," Claudia whispered, studying her hands, clasped in her lap. The burns had long since healed, but they had left behind their scars as reminders.

"I have never been married," he said, still staring at the river. "However, I do know what it is like to lose someone you love."

Claudia waited, for a moment thinking he would not continue. Then he did.

"I was very young, only seventeen. She was a year younger. We planned to marry. Then, five weeks before we were to wed, she got sick. Nothing to be concerned about, the doctor assured us. But she never got out of her bed."

Claudia released her breath in a sigh. "I'm sorry. Have you never found anyone else?"

He turned to look at her. "Not until now," he said simply.

Flustered, Claudia got to her feet. This was impossible. What was she doing here? "I think we ought to go back."

Franz got to his feet and came toward her. Putting his hands on her shoulders, he gazed down at her. "No one can go back," he said quietly. "We are given only two choices—to go forward or to stand still. Which do you choose?"

Claudia swayed, and her body made its own decision. His lips were warm and gentle on her own. His arms held her with a strength she had long been without. When he drew her down to the softness of the sweet-smelling grass, she made no resistance.

Helene Lehr

But when she felt the lacings of her bodice being undone, her hand covered his.

Drawing back, he observed her intensely. "I will stop if you want me to."

His quiet statement threw Claudia into a quandary. She almost laughed, an hysterical outbreak that had nothing to do with amusement. She, who had slept with countless men these past two years without a thought for modesty, was now feeling shy. At 26 she was no longer a young girl; however, she was suddenly, painfully, conscious of the stretch marks on her full breasts. Pregnancy had left her abdomen unlined, and it was now as taut as it had ever been. But her breasts . . . What would Franz think of these imperfections?

With a start of surprise, Claudia wondered why she cared. That she was attracted to this man—the first since Charles had died—she could no longer deny. But it could go no further. She would be foolish to deceive herself. This man was a mercenary. When his job was done, he would be gone.

Slowly, her hands went to the lacings, and just as slowly, she undid them. He made no effort to help her as she undressed.

At last she sat before him, unclothed, her head at a proud angle as his eyes feasted on her. She had loosened her hair, and it fell in an ebony cascade that contrasted sharply with her white skin, now tinted golden in the warm rays of the sun.

"I thought I had seen beauty," he murmured, and in his glistening eyes, Claudia saw truth. "But it has been withheld from me until this moment."

She had long since thought herself incapable of any more tears; now Claudia felt her eyes brim with them.

"It's kind of you to say that," she said unsteadily.

The Passionate Rebel

"But I know I'm not . . ." Instinctively, her hand covered a breast; both of them were scarred and without any beauty that she could see.

For a long moment, Franz viewed her thoughtfully. Then, slowly, he began to undress. Though not much taller than she was, Claudia saw that he was superbly built, having the hard, compact body of a soldier. Soft golden hair on his chest narrowed to a thin line that flowed like a golden stream down his flat abdomen, then flared into a triangle, only slightly darker.

Fascinated, Claudia stared, openly and unashamedly. At last her eyes found their way back to his.

Still without speaking, Franz leaned forward and took hold of the hand that still covered her breast and placed it on his left side, just below his rib cage. Startled, Claudia felt the rough outline of a scar that appeared to have come from a bayonet wound. She was surprised she hadn't noticed it; it was ragged and at least a quarter inch wide.

"We are neither of us without our battle wounds," he whispered. He smiled, and Claudia's heart gave a lurch. "Let us leave perfection to those who cannot recognize true beauty."

His hand now buried itself in the glory of her hair, and when he drew her toward him, Claudia went willingly, almost eagerly into his embrace.

Her hands slid across his back, feeling each hard muscle outlined. She hadn't realized his shoulders were so broad. Claudia felt small within his embrace and relished the feeling.

Warm sunlight slanted through the leaves, dappling their naked bodies with counterpoints of golden light and lilac shadows as they clung to each other, exploring, mouths pressed together in deep, lingering kisses that seemed to have no end.

Helene Lehr

Claudia had forgotten just how powerful a kiss could be between two people who were mutually attracted to each other. It came rushing back to her now, a tidal wave of emotion that threatened to drown her. All the pent-up passion that had found no escape in these past years now flooded her with an intensity that was becoming unbearable. The blood that flowed through her veins seemed to have turned into liquid fire.

Strong hands played about her body, summoning forth an ardor from her that had long been dormant. When his hand slipped between her legs, she whimpered.

His mouth, pressed against her neck, now moved to her ear. "Patience, *liebchen*," he whispered.

Claudia didn't understand the meaning of the second word. The first was fast becoming unattainable.

His sensitive fingers felt the tension in her, but Franz was not to be hurried.

Claudia gasped as his mouth trailed a blazing path down her abdomen to the very essence of her being. The fire that ignited every nerve in her body could not be banked.

When she at last felt his fullness inside her, Claudia clung to his rocking body as if it were a lifeline.

A sharp, breathless cry came from her lips as a hot flood of feeling released her from tension. For long minutes, they lay locked in each other's arms.

At last Franz drew away. Raising himself on an elbow, he looked down at her.

"Have you regrets?" he asked softly.

Claudia sat up. Her body felt warm and replete. Not even Charles, whom she had dearly loved, had taken her to such a pinnacle of ecstasy.

The Passionate Rebel

"No," she answered with a small smile.

With her fingers, Claudia combed her hair free of grass and the tattered remnants of leaves. Then she twisted it into a knot at the nape of her neck.

Dressed again, she viewed Franz uncertainly, still unable to believe it had really happened. Surely, now that he'd had his way with her, he would return to his duties, this pleasant interlude forgotten. He was a mercenary, after all. No place or woman could hold such a man for very long.

Her suspicions were confirmed a moment later when Franz got to his feet and assisted her in rising—polite, as ever.

"It is getting late," he said. He saw her shiver, and his brows drew together in concern. "Are you cold?" He began to remove his jacket.

"No, no," she assured, then smiled brightly against the ache in her heart. "I have a shawl."

Claudia began to walk quickly back to the carriage, willing herself not to weep. Foolish, she told herself. Foolish to have let her heart hope.

They drove back in silence. Franz looked preoccupied, his thoughts certainly elsewhere than on herself, Claudia supposed.

And why not? Why should it have been otherwise? Nothing had been promised.

It had been a pleasant interlude—for herself, as well as for him. Claudia straightened, determined that she would remember this bright and golden afternoon. Since there were so few in her life, they deserved to be cherished.

As she got out of the carriage, Claudia's smile turned genuine. She had no regrets.

Franz remained lost in thought until he reached his quarters. As a junior officer, he had a room of his own. It was small, cramped even, holding only a cot, a table and a chair. Only the latter was in decent condition, since he had purchased it himself. But small though the room was, it offered a degree of privacy the ordinary soldier did not have.

He had told Claudia that he'd joined the army, and so he had. For men that did, life was comparatively easy. They were usually enlisted as officers. But the majority of Hessians were pressed into service, beaten into submission and executed if they rebelled. A button missing from a jacket was cause enough to send a man to the hospital from the effects of a severe whipping.

Until he had come to the colonies, Franz hadn't known any other kind of life existed. Now that he did, he burned to be a part of it. This land offered a banquet he'd never known—freedom. Wild and disorganized though it was, it still offered hope for men like himself.

Franz knew he neither would be the first nor the last soldier to defect. He had seen many patriots show up in the dead of night, weak from hunger, disillusioned, ready to avow eternal allegiance to the Crown. Franz didn't blame them. A man did what he had to do. And a man with a family was more susceptible than most. Children could not eat an ideal. They needed something more substantial.

His decision had been made weeks ago. Only one thing had delayed its fruition—Claudia. From the moment he had first seen her, Franz had known that even freedom would be meaningless without her. He had fallen in love with her before he had even spoken to her. He'd known from the first that she had been taking British officers up to her room. Now he thought he knew the reason. It made it easier to bear. But it would not have changed his feeling, either way. He loved her. There was that to be said and no more.

Franz sat down in the chair and stared out the narrow, curtainless window. The first thing he would need would be clothes. Walking out of town in his Hessian uniform would be foolhardy. Perhaps Claudia could get them for him. He would speak to her of this tonight. They would have to lay their plans carefully. It never entered his mind that she would not come with him. She would; she must! Life held no meaning for him without Claudia.

And money. He had some saved—not much, but it would have to do.

If his calculations were correct, four nights hence would be moonless. That would be the best time to go.

A loud knock on his door caused Franz to jump to his feet. Quickly, he opened the door to see the sergeant-at-arms.

"The captain wants to see you immediately," the man said in German.

Franz nodded and reached for his jacket, buttoning it as he walked.

A few minutes later he stood stiffly at attention before his superior.

"We have just received word that the regiment at Dobbs Ferry is low on ammunition. They have had a few skirmishes with the damned rebels. Nothing serious, so far, but it could escalate. Take twenty men and a wagonload of shot up to them. Stay with them until you are no longer needed."

Franz hoped his dismay wasn't reflected in his face. "You want me to leave today?" he asked in a barely audible voice.

"I want you to leave now," came the barked order.

Chapter Twenty

From Gillian's Diary:

> *June 26, 1779*
> *As has happened since this war began, the warm weather spurs both the Americans and the British to greater activity. It now appears that the British are ever increasingly directing their attention to the South.*

Tom opened his eyes, tensed, then relaxed when he saw familiar surroundings. He was in his own bedroom with its well-worn but comfortable furniture. The curtains at the window had been made by Edwina, as was the lace covering atop the dresser and the counterpane, now neatly folded on a chair. He was home. Sometimes, in that split second before coming awake, Tom thought his release had been no more than a dream.

Turning his head, he looked out the window. It

The Passionate Rebel

was almost sunset. Once again, he had slept a good part of the day away. He hadn't realized that his strength had been so depleted.

The door opened a crack, and Edwina peeked in, smiling broadly when she saw that he was awake. Holding the baby in her arms, she came toward him. With a pride that shone clearly in her brown eyes, she offered the child for view. On the day Tom arrived home, Edwina had instructed the servants to move the cradle into the parlor so that the child's crying would not disturb Tom's rest.

"I brought him in to say good night," she said, sitting on the edge of the bed.

Tom sighed in contentment. A man could and would fight for what he believed in, but there was no more rewarding sight than a son to carry on.

"Thomas," he whispered, touching a tiny hand.

"A name to be proud of."

Getting up, Edwina returned the child to his cradle in the parlor, then went back to her husband.

"I have told him of your bravery," she said, "and I will continue to do so until he's able to understand." Slowly, she began to disrobe.

Tom had always liked to watch her do that. Edwina was gratified to see him watching her intently. She refused the tears that burned behind her eyes. Now was not the time. Later, when he could not see, she would weep, weep for his once strong and wiry body, now wasted. Time would cure that. Time and her own constant attention would heal this man she loved more than life itself.

Naked now, she stood there a moment. A low westerly sun sent its farewell through the window, outlining her body, tipping her breasts with warm gold, imparting to her skin the color of a ripe peach.

There was no hurry. She had waited this long; so

had he. Raising her hands, she loosened her hair, carelessly dropping the pins on the floor and allowing the thick chestnut brown tresses to spill about her shoulders. Her body, small and rounded, was in good shape, and she knew it.

Coming forward, she stood there a moment, looking at him, seeing his chest rise and fall with his quickening breaths.

"I am so proud of you," she whispered.

When she lowered herself on him, Tom forgot his weakness in the surge of desire that engulfed him.

They made love slowly, with the intimacy that can only come from being united for many loving years. It was no less sweet for all its familiarity. When it was over, they rested contentedly within each other's arms.

Edwina opened her eyes some time later, surprised that she had fallen into a light doze. Not too much time had passed, though. While the sun had set, the sky was still pale with waning light.

Gently, she disengaged herself from her husband's embrace. However, he was not sleeping and tightened his hold, sliding his hands along her satiny back.

She giggled. "It's time for supper."

"I can feast on you," he responded, nuzzling her neck.

"You're not as weak as I thought," she chided, nevertheless enjoying his caress.

In the next room, the baby began to wail, and Edwina sighed.

"It seems your son is unwilling to wait for his evening meal."

Getting up, she began to dress. Thomas displayed just as much interest in the procedure as when she had disrobed.

The Passionate Rebel

There was no time to do her hair, and Edwina merely tucked the mass beneath her white cap.

Tom sat up and put his feet on the floor.

"What are you doing?" Edwina asked in alarm.

He frowned. "Six days is long enough for a man to stay in bed." Even having said that, he made no move to get up.

"No, no," Edwina said quickly. "Give it a few more days. Please . . ."

Fetching his robe, Edwina helped him into it. Assisting him to his feet, she led him to the chair by the window.

"Now," she said when he was settled, "if you'll wait for me here, I'll bring up a tray. We'll have supper together, just you and I, by candlelight."

Tom leaned back, hating the weakness in his limbs and knowing that for the present he could do nothing about it. He smiled at Edwina and raised a hand to smooth the lines of anxiety that creased her brow.

"That will be worth waiting for," he whispered.

Taking his hand in her own, Edwina kissed it. "I won't be long."

Glancing out the window, she saw Gillian coming out of their grandmother's house. In the next room, the baby's cry was becoming more insistent. With another quick kiss for her husband, Edwina hurried from the room, hoping that little Tom had not awakened his sister.

As Gillian crossed the orchard to the Blue Swan on this Saturday evening, she inhaled deeply. Overhead, the sky was the exquisite shade of lilac that only twilight can produce, a color so ephemeral that the brush of even the most talented artist would have been hard-pressed to duplicate it.

The air was sweet and clean. No garbage here.

Edwina saw to that. The rest of the city was becoming a disgrace. Down by the Bowery the stench was so bad that people had taken to holding perfumed handkerchiefs to their noses while walking through the streets. Canvas Town was the worst of all; even scented handkerchiefs didn't help there.

Leaving the stand of apple trees, Gillian frowned as she saw Claudia seated in a rocking chair on the back porch. The gaily colored, calico print dress she was wearing was at odds with her solemn expression. Head resting against the high back of the chair, she was rocking slowly, eyes fixed on a far point only she could see.

Gillian sighed. Claudia had seemed so happy when she had returned from her outing with Franz. That had been almost a week ago.

Gillian thought she knew the reason. Since that Sunday, Franz had not come into the Blue Swan once.

Curse all men, Gillian thought in irritation as she climbed the steps. They came into a woman's life, turned her world upside down, then left without so much as a fare-thee-well.

Pausing beside the chair in which Claudia was seated, Gillian's frown deepened when she saw the dark smudges beneath the emerald-green eyes. She was willing to wager that Claudia hadn't slept again.

Gillian put a hand on Claudia's shoulder and gave it a gentle squeeze. There were no words of comfort to offer, and Gillian didn't try.

"If you want to rest," she said after a minute, "I'm sure Mandy and I can handle things."

A small sound escaped Claudia's lips which could have been a laugh that didn't quite mature. "There isn't anyone in there now." With a sigh, she got slowly to her feet. "In any event, I'm not tired."

The Passionate Rebel

Gillian believed her. Rest was not what Claudia needed right now.

With no further words, they both went inside.

A few customers had come in during her absence, and Claudia supposed that either Mandy or Edwina had waited on them.

Slowly, almost as if she was afraid of what she would see, her eyes sought the corner table. It was empty. She stared a moment longer, then turned away.

"Claudia!"

She gave a gasp as a heavy arm draped around her shoulders like a shawl of lead. Turning her head, she looked at Major Winters. Drink in hand, he was grinning at her.

"I'll bet you've been waiting for me." Releasing her, he swayed, his smile carved into place. "I saw you looking around." He wagged a finger at her in a playful manner.

How had this weak and ineffectual man become a major? Claudia wondered disdainfully. The thought came into her mind and slid away as if unworthy of her consideration. "Yes," she replied dully. "I was wondering where you were."

She felt his hand cup her breast, and she felt nothing. Even revulsion fled. Her flesh felt like the pewter cup he was holding—cold and unyielding.

"Can we go upstairs?" he slurred, his breath quickening with growing passion.

Claudia summoned her smile without too much difficulty. It was becoming automatic. "Of course," she said.

Her back straight, she began to walk from the room.

Gillian only glanced at Claudia when she saw the two of them heading for the stairs. With a sigh, she set about wiping tables; then she swept the floor.

The few customers that had come in were gone. There were no others.

Upstairs, Claudia closed the door to her room. With a grunt, Major Winters sank down on the bed so heavily that Claudia feared its structure would collapse.

He began to struggle with his boots. The simple procedure of removing them seemed to be beyond him.

With a sigh, Claudia moved forward to assist him. She was used to seeing the major in his cups; tonight, however, he was very, very drunk.

"You're a good sport, Claudia," he mumbled as she helped him out of his jacket. He fell back on the bed, arms outstretched at his sides. "I wish you would come with me. I'm going to miss you."

Claudia's brow creased as she tried to sort out the meaning of his words. He was slurring them so badly she could hardly understand him.

"Perhaps I might," she said softly. As she hung his jacket over a chair, she saw a folded piece of paper in one of the pockets.

He tried to sit up, but the effort was too much. "Would you? Would you, really?"

"That would depend," she murmured, "on where you were going."

"Conn . . . Conn . . ." he hiccoughed.

"Connecticut?" Claudia prompted. At his nod, she sat down on the edge of the bed. "That's a pretty place."

He laughed. "Won't be so pretty when General Tryon gets done with it. Pack of rebels in Norwalk!"

"I'm sure there are." Claudia began to loosen his neck band. "General Tryon will have them all arrested."

The Passionate Rebel

The major waved an arm, just missing Claudia's head. "Won't be nothing left to arrest," he declared. "We're going to burn it to the ground. Won't be nothing left."

He repeated that several times in a singsong voice, then grabbed her hand.

"Come with me."

Claudia's mouth flattened into a thin line. With difficulty, she kept her voice soft and allowed her hand to be held.

"When are you leaving?"

"In a couple of weeks."

"How many regiments is General Tryon taking with him?"

There was no answer. Seconds later, his deep snores told Claudia that he was asleep. Carefully, she disengaged her hand and got up. Going to the chair on which his jacket hung, she removed the folded piece of paper. With a glance at the man on the bed to assure herself that he was, in fact, asleep, she unfolded it. It was a map. She studied it for a moment, then quietly left the room.

Downstairs, Gillian yawned. It was a slow night, and she wished it to be over so that she could go to bed. It was after nine, a bit too early to close up. Still, she wasn't about to sit around waiting for any late stragglers to stumble in.

Going to the front door, she locked it. Then she extinguished the oil lamps.

"Gillian."

Claudia's voice was a whisper, edged with urgency. Gillian, however, had enough presence of mind to make her way casually to the darkened hall where Claudia was standing. She had seen Claudia leave with the British officer. For all she knew, the man was at her side now.

"What is it?" she asked as she approached Claudia. Her eyes swept the shadows. Claudia appeared to be alone.

Claudia didn't immediately reply; instead she took Gillian's arm and drew her further into the darkened hall. "We must get word to the Continentals right away," she whispered. "There's no time to lose. I've just learned that General Tryon is going to attack Norwalk. He is planning to burn it to the ground."

"Oh, my God. When?"

"A week, maybe two. Here..." Claudia fumbled in the pocket of her gown. "It's a map. It has nothing to do with the attack. As near as I can make out it's a compilation of weaponry and ammunitions at the supply depot."

In the dim light, Gillian looked at the map and agreed with Claudia's interpretation. Then she gave a deep sigh.

"I'll have to get this to the Clayton farm myself," she said, tucking the map in a pocket.

Claudia looked uneasy. "I don't think you ought to do that. You'd better wait until Mr. Clayton comes by."

Gillian shook her head. "That could be tomorrow or next week. His leg still pains him. Some days he doesn't even get out of bed." She smiled a reassurance at Claudia, who still looked doubtful. "Don't worry. I'm not going tonight. And when I drive there tomorrow, I'll take Katie with me." Bending forward, she brushed Claudia's cool cheek with her own.

Philip was still in his office on Maiden Lane. He was alone. Everyone else had left hours ago.

With a deep sigh, he reread the letter from his mother, delivered to him earlier in the day. His

The Passionate Rebel

father, having suffered his second heart attack in as many years, had died.

This was the third time Philip was reading the letter. Why, he didn't know; yet he felt compelled to do it.

" . . . swiftly," his mother had written. "And without pain."

Philip didn't believe that. He knew his mother was trying to lessen the anguish she knew her son would feel upon learning the news.

"There is no need for you to come home," she had also written. "By the time you receive this letter, the funeral will be over."

Over. Philip rubbed his eyes. Such a final word. He forced himself to again read the last paragraph.

"The crop is flourishing, and we hope to harvest in a few weeks. Please set your mind at rest. Everything is under control."

Philip dropped the letter to the desk. He didn't believe that, either. At least he would not until he could see it with his own eyes. Isobel Meredith knew very well what her son was doing for the cause. It was as important to her as it had been to her husband.

But not that important, Philip thought grimly, as he got up. The damned war could just wait until he straightened out matters at home and assured himself that everything was, in fact, under control.

Chapter Twenty-one

From Gillian's Diary:

> *June 27, 1779*
> *Plunder is becoming rife. The redcoats no longer seem content merely to capture a town. Now they must burn and loot. Even the loyalists are becoming vocal in their outrage. And in this, I see a glimmer of hope.*

William brought the carriage to the front drive, as he had been instructed to do. But as he waited for Gillian and Katie to come out of the house, he was unable to quell a growing unease. Instinctively, he knew that Alice Wharton would not approve of this outing.

Two young women going on a drive that would take them out of the city could only mean trouble, William thought to himself as he checked the trap-

The Passionate Rebel

pings to make sure they were tight. Yet there was no one here to dissuade his young mistress. Certainly he could offer no objection.

Satisfied that all was secure, he went back into the house, heading for the kitchen.

Polly was seated at the table. A bowl in her ample lap held fresh green beans. She was methodically snapping them into bite-sized pieces, after which she placed them in another bowl on the table, this one containing cold water.

"Don't like this at all," William mumbled as he entered the room.

Polly didn't look up from her task. "Don't upset yourself worryin' about something you can't do nothin' about."

"Wish I could write," her husband went on, ignoring the advice. "I'd send a letter to Miz Wharton right now, tellin' her to come home."

Polly shrugged. "Wouldn't do you no good, even if you could write," she noted with a sigh. "The letter wouldn't get there in time, anyway."

She broke off as Gillian came in.

"Is the carriage ready, William?" she asked.

Unhappily, he nodded. Although he had asked before, William felt compelled to do so again. "Wish you'd let me drive you, Miss Gillian."

"Nonsense," Gillian said. "Katie is quite capable. We won't be long."

As she left the room, William followed. In the hall, Gillian ran up the stairs to get Katie, and William continued outside.

"Are you ready, Katie?" Gillian asked, going into her room.

Katie nodded and held out a mobcap. "I think you should wear this."

Gillian sighed. "I suppose you're right." She sat

down at her dressing table and allowed Katie to place the cap on her golden hair. "Now, you understand what it is we are going to do?" Gillian studied Katie's reflection in the mirror. She had no wish for Katie to do this unless the young woman fully understood what was involved.

"We're to deliver a message and the map you found to the Clayton farm," Katie recited.

"And?" Gillian prompted.

"If we're stopped by a patrol, we tell them that we are going to the nearest farm to buy fresh corn."

"Exactly," Gillian said, getting to her feet.

As they headed down the stairs, Gillian checked her pocket to make certain the map was there. With a bit of luck they wouldn't even see a redcoat once they left town. The patrols were active mostly at night, reasoning that a person had no business being out after dark. Also, many regiments from New York had been sent to the South and to New England, with the result that the number of patrols had been sharply decreased.

When Gillian and Katie finally came out of the house, William frowned at the sight of their smiling faces. While he didn't know the reason behind this sudden urge for a drive in the country, he had his suspicions. If he was right, there was no cause for smiles. Like his employer, William was perfectly aware of what was going on at the tavern. Bunch of rebels, they were, and they had infected his young mistress with their ideas. For himself, William had been shocked when he learned that Alice Wharton had continued to allow her granddaughter to work there even after she had learned what was going on.

Both young women had climbed into the front of the carriage and were now fussing with their

The Passionate Rebel

full skirts as they settled themselves. Katie's blue cotton skirt was slit open in the front, exposing a flash of white petticoat. Her tightly laced bodice was of a darker shade of blue. Gillian's outfit was essentially the same style but fashioned of fine green silk patterned with bright yellow stripes.

Despite the object of their journey, both of them were in high spirits as they set out.

As the carriage proceeded up Broad Way, Gillian was conscious of being in better spirits than she had been in a long time. She had resolutely pushed thoughts of Philip Meredith from her mind. She never quite succeeded in doing this at night, but on this fine summer day, with the sun shining brightly and Katie chattering on, Gillian found herself feeling almost happy.

When they finally left the outskirts of town, Katie eased up on the reins, letting the horse find its own pace. As far as she was concerned, this mission was no more than a lark, a break in her routine.

Since Gillian seemed in a mood to listen, Katie spoke at length about Edward and the life they hoped to have together, for the young man only recently had proposed marriage.

"Of course, he was indentured, like me," she explained. "But he's already worked off his bond, and now he gets a wage." She said that so proudly, Gillian smiled.

"And . . . ?"

"Well, he's said that when my time's up we're going to be married."

"Oh, Katie!" Gillian leaned over and gave Katie a hug. "That's wonderful. When did he propose?"

"He only spoke of marriage last week."

Gillian frowned. "But your bond won't be over for another year."

"I know that. And so does Edward. But it's all right, because he plans to use the time to save money. He's very thrifty and very ambitious. Someday he plans to have his own shop." Her chin went up. "I will be the wife of a merchant."

"Well," Gillian said, eyes twinkling, "I would think that the wife of a merchant would certainly be expected to dress the part."

Katie gave her a puzzled glance.

Reaching over, Gillian gave her companion's wrist a gentle squeeze. "On the day you are married, I will give you my onyx comb. I know it's your favorite."

For a moment, Katie just gaped at her. "Oh, I couldn't accept anything as fine as that."

Gillian's laughter trilled out to blend with the chattering of the birds. "Nevertheless, you shall have it. And it would please me very much if you saw fit to wear it on your wedding day."

"I'm likely to wear it to bed." Katie laughed, still flabbergasted at Gillian's generosity.

They both fell silent at the sound of approaching horses.

A moment later, two redcoats came into view. Gillian held her breath, hoping they would just pass by without incident. As they neared, however, one of them grabbed the bit of Gillian's horse, effectively halting the animal and the carriage.

"Where are you going?"

The man who addressed them was a sergeant, and he angled his horse close to the carriage. He was about 30, with a ruddy complexion that could have been natural or could have been acquired from too much exposure to the sun. His companion was an ordinary grenadier who didn't appear to be much more than 20.

"To the nearest farm to buy some fresh corn,"

The Passionate Rebel

Katie said quickly, remembering her instructions.

"You've already passed by two of them," the sergeant pointed out flatly.

Gillian leaned forward. "Neither had any corn to sell to us."

The sergeant dismounted, and the grenadier quickly followed suit.

"Get out of the carriage," the sergeant ordered.

"For what reason?" Gillian demanded.

"Because I said so."

Katie and Gillian exchanged uneasy glances but did as they were told.

The sergeant then began to search the carriage, even looking beneath it.

Gillian and Katie were puzzled by his actions. Neither of them could figure out what the man was searching for. The sergeant, however, prided himself on being thorough. Nowadays it paid to be careful. Rebels would use most anything as a weapon if they were cornered, and the yellow-haired wench had a look in her eye he mistrusted. After several minutes passed, he appeared convinced that there was nothing unusual aboard and finally turned from the carriage.

"Did you find the cannon?" Katie asked.

The sergeant gave her a sharp look but did not respond to the sarcasm. He took note of the quality of her dress and decided she was only a servant. His eyes swung to Gillian. This one was no servant. He didn't even have to view her clothes to know that.

"Do you have a pass?"

Gillian bit her lip. That was an incidental she had completely forgotten about. "I wasn't aware I needed a pass merely to buy vegetables. See..." She withdrew a pouch from the pocket of her skirt. "I have coin."

Helene Lehr

Standing a few feet away, Katie's eyes went wide when she saw the paper flutter to the ground. It had been dislodged from Gillian's pocket when she withdrew the pouch.

The redcoat's eyes flicked over the small leather pouch, and Gillian wondered if he would accept the bribe.

Suddenly, the man moved forward. Gillian drew back, fearing she was about to be attacked. But instead of reaching for her, he bent over and picked up a piece of paper. With a sinking feeling in the pit of her stomach, Gillian saw that it was the map.

"What is that you have?" she asked shakily.

The sergeant's eyes narrowed. "Why don't you tell me what it is?"

"I . . . have no idea," Gillian said, raising her chin. "You're the one who picked it up off the ground."

He snorted. "Don't play games with me." He waved the map beneath her nose. "This came from your pocket, and we both know it." He looked at his companion. "Come on. We must take these two to the provost marshal."

The grenadier, curious now, came forward to view the map held by the sergeant. Looking at it, his eyes widened. "That's—"

"I know what it is," the sergeant snapped. Folding the paper, he put it in a pocket.

From the corner of her eye, Gillian saw Katie sidle toward the edge of the road. Thinking quickly, she bolted forward. Hoisting her skirt with both hands, she began to run up the road as fast as she could in a direction away from Katie.

As she had hoped they would, both soldiers came after her. The grenadier reached her first and clutched at her arm. With her free hand, Gillian swung at him. The blow landed harmlessly on his

The Passionate Rebel

shoulder, but it was enough to throw him off balance. As he fell, he dragged her down with him.

Her cap had fallen off, and when the sergeant caught up to them, he grabbed a handful of Gillian's hair, then yanked her to her feet.

Gillian looked back along the road. Katie was nowhere in sight.

Docile now, she allowed the soldiers to lead her back to the carriage.

"We're not taking any chances with this one," the sergeant growled. Going to his horse he took a coil of rope from its resting place on the pommel of his saddle.

A moment later, Gillian felt her hands being bound behind her.

"That's not necessary," she exclaimed indignantly.

"I'll say what is, and what's not," he retorted, jerking the knot tighter.

Lifting her up, he threw her facedown across his saddle, then mounted.

It was late afternoon by the time Katie trudged tiredly up the back steps of the Blue Swan.

She paused at the door, trying to catch her breath. She had been running for hours, and every muscle in her body ached.

Through the window, she could see Edwina bustling about the kitchen, now and again wiping her hands on the apron tied around her waist. Her face was flushed and rosy, the heat of the stove increasing that of the summer night. Mandy was at the sink, washing dishes and pots. As Katie watched, Claudia came into the room, served herself a cup of coffee and sat at the table, one hand rubbing the back of her neck in a gesture of weariness.

Katie swallowed and opened the door. It seemed to her as if all eyes swung in her direction at once. The scene was like a frozen tableau. No one moved. They just stared at her with expressions that registered surprise. Edwina reacted first, and her question went right to the point.

"Where is Gillian?"

"The soldiers took her." Katie came further into the room.

"Tell us what happened," Edwina said in a low voice. Only a slight breathlessness gave indication of how her heart had begun to thud in her breast.

Claudia asked no questions, afraid to have her suspicions confirmed. She had said nothing to Edwina about the map or told her where Gillian was going. This had been not so much a conscious omission as it was due to an underlying feeling of not wanting to cause Edwina undue concern. In fact, Claudia had supposed Gillian to have returned hours ago. It had only been when dusk set in about 30 minutes ago and Gillian had not come to work that a feeling of unease had gripped her.

Claudia turned her attention to Katie, who had been explaining how Gillian had been arrested on the Post Road.

"It's all my fault," Claudia cried out in dismay when Katie paused.

"It's no one's fault," Edwina contradicted in a firm voice. Then she looked at Katie again. "Have you any idea where they took her?"

Katie shook her head miserably. "I don't know."

Edwina turned away, trying to marshal her thoughts. Her heart slammed into her ribs with a force that took the breath from her body. How was she to deal with this? Edwina wondered frantically. She had been fully prepared for herself or

The Passionate Rebel

her husband to pay the price of their activities. Her sister, however, was another matter. Had she and Tom directed the girl into a situation she was not able to handle? The question weighed heavily on Edwina's mind.

Finally she faced the two women. "Mr. Meredith will be able to find out where she is. We must get word to him."

Both Claudia and Katie viewed the suggestion with a mixture of surprise and shock.

"He's a Tory," Claudia exclaimed.

Edwina took a breath. She knew better, but she had given her word that she would tell no one. "Nevertheless," she said firmly, "they were engaged to be married. Even if he cannot help her, he can certainly find out where she is."

"I'll go," Claudia offered. "Where will I find him?"

"His office is on Maiden Lane," Katie supplied quickly, happy to be of some help. "I heard Mistress Wharton mention that once."

"And he lives on Chambers Street," Edwina added.

Claudia nodded and headed for the door.

When it closed, Edwina gently prodded Katie to a chair. "Sit down," she said, for the first time noticing Katie's appearance. The young woman looked to be at the end of her resources. Her arms bore several deep scratches. Going to a drawer, Edwina got a clean towel, wet it and began to sponge off the wounds.

Claudia returned about an hour later. From the look on her face, Edwina and Katie knew the news was not good.

"Mr. Meredith was not there. His clerk told me he's out of town on business and not expected back until next week. I went to his house, just to make certain, but he's not there either."

Edwina sank down in a chair as if her legs would no longer support her. "Let us wait awhile," she said after a moment. "Perhaps someone will contact us."

The hours crept by. All three women were tense. It had been tacitly agreed that they would say nothing to Tom, who was still recuperating from his ordeal. Edwina and Claudia managed to keep busy. Katie only sat in the chair, wringing her hands with a feeling of helplessness.

Finally, just after eleven o'clock, Edwina gave a deep sigh. "It's too late to do anything else tonight. I suggest we all get some sleep." She began to extinguish the lamps, holding one aloft until Katie cleared the back porch and disappeared into the orchard.

Claudia went to her room, but she did not undress. There would, she knew, be no sleep for her this night.

Back and forth, she paced the floor, cursing herself, the war, the British, and Major Winters and his drunken bragging, in particular.

Oh God, she thought, feeling her head begin to throb. Where was Gillian?

Gillian was in the provost marshal's office. It was actually a house, not far from the governor's mansion.

For hours now she had been sitting on an uncushioned chair in the hall, waiting for she knew not what. No one told her anything, and her few tentative questions had gone unanswered. She was hungry, but no one offered her food.

Not far from where she was sitting, the sergeant who had brought her here stood silently, guarding her with a watchful eye.

She rubbed her wrists. They were both chafed

The Passionate Rebel

from the rope with which she had been bound during the trip back here. Thankfully, it had been removed when they entered the house.

Growing restless, she shifted her weight, causing the sergeant to scowl at her.

As if she could run anywhere, Gillian thought disdainfully, ignoring him. The front door was not only locked; it was guarded by two armed redcoats.

"How long am I supposed to sit here?" she demanded at last, glaring at her captor.

"Until the marshal has time for you. Don't be so anxious. There might be a noose waiting for you come dawn."

Gillian was properly subdued by this ominous prospect.

"Then again," he went on, seeming to enjoy himself, "you could just go to prison for a long, long time."

"For what reason?" she retorted with a show of bravado that she did not really feel. "I've done nothing."

The sergeant scratched his ear. "Well, now, that's not for me to decide." He fell silent as a door across the hall opened.

"Sergeant, bring the woman in here."

Hearing the command, the soldier immediately sobered. "Come along," he said gruffly, prodding Gillian ahead of him into the office.

Inside, Gillian viewed the man standing by the window with his back to her.

Slowly, the man turned to look at her. Gillian felt faint and bit down on her tongue so that the pain would revive her. She'd be damned if she'd show any weakness, much less any cowardice.

The man she was looking at was William Cunningham, Provost Marshal of New York. With the exception of General Grey, this man was the most hated and feared of all British officers. He was the one responsible for the deplorable conditions of the prison ships, as well as the sugarhouses, warehouses and even churches that had been converted into jails. To him went the dubious distinction of having been responsible for the deaths of more prisoners than all the soldiers who had died in battle since the war began.

And he looked the part. His visage was stern, forbidding, unforgiving. Cold eyes, the color of a windswept sea, were viewing her with no sign of mercy.

"What is your name?" he asked.

"Gillian Winthrop."

"And where do you reside?"

Gillian opened her mouth, then closed it. She wasn't about to implicate her grandmother in this.

He waited a moment but did not repeat his question. Instead, he said, "The punishment for the offense you have committed is death by hanging."

Gillian started but recovered quickly. "I've done nothing," she replied, thankful for her steady voice. Her mouth tightened until her jaw protested. If she had to die, Gillian vowed she would do it bravely, as befitted a patriot.

He walked to his desk, his boots echoing his passage. Picking up the map, he viewed it as if seeing it for the first time. "Where did you get this?"

"It does not belong to me," Gillian said quickly.

"And just who does it belong to?" Menace added a dark nuance to his voice.

Gillian waved a hand at the sergeant. "He's the one who found it. Why don't you ask him?"

"I have," Cunningham said dryly. "The sergeant assures me that this map was in your possession."

"Map? Is that what it is?"

The Passionate Rebel

The provost marshal pursed his thin lips and dropped the paper on the desk again. "You don't know it is a map of the depot, detailed to show the extent of our weaponry and ammunition?"

Gillian's chin rose. "Of course not!"

Cunningham sat down, fingers drumming an aimless rhythm on his desk. The wench was guilty as sin, he was thinking, annoyed that she was trying to deceive him. He would be well within his rights to have her hung. Not publicly, of course. Americans were unduly sensitive when it came to executing a woman. Such a situation would never occur in London. There, a woman could be hung as easily as a man, and the crowd would still treat the event as an excuse for celebrating. Even in France—barbarians, though they were—a woman could be publicly executed, and the people would only cheer at the spectacle.

But here in the colonies . . . Cunningham thoughtfully rubbed his chin. Well, there were other ways. As long as he was provost marshal the rebels would pay the price for their treason, be they men or women.

His eyes swung to Gillian again. "I am required by law to give you the opportunity of declaring your allegiance to his Majesty, King George."

Gillian blinked at the sudden change of topic. "And if I do?" she asked hesitantly.

"Then you will be released. All you have to do is swear that you are now loyal to the Crown and will remain so."

She moistened her lips. "And if I refuse?"

A ghost of a smile tipped the thin lips. "I think you already know the answer to that. You may take a moment to think about it. Coercion is not our way. The oath of allegiance must come from a person's convictions. All prisoners are offered this opportunity by the grace of His Majesty."

All prisoners, Gillian mused, thinking of the hundreds, the thousands of men who were being held captive. They must have all, to a man, refused. Even Tom.

From a drawer, Cunningham withdrew a Bible. Placing it on top of the desk, he pushed it toward her until it was within her reach.

"It is a very simple procedure," he advised.

Gillian put her hands behind her back. Not even to save her life would she swear to something in which she did not believe.

"My allegiance is to my country," she murmured at last.

"Indeed?" He seemed to find that amusing. "An interesting equivocation. Would you care to tell me which country it is that you so favor?"

Gillian lowered her head but made no reply.

"Well, it is of no matter. The oath must be taken for the king, not for a country." He waited a moment, then added, "I must warn you that your silence will be taken as a refusal."

The sergeant, who had remained impassive this while, now shifted his weight from one foot to another. He was growing uncomfortable with the little cat and mouse game. He'd served under Cunningham long enough to know the man's ruthless nature. He sincerely hoped that, if the marshal decided the woman should be hung, the man would delegate the task elsewhere than himself. Orders or no, he doubted he could kill a woman.

Cunningham looked up just then and fixed the sergeant with a stare that chilled the man's bones. The sergeant wouldn't have been at all surprised to learn that the marshal had read his thoughts.

The Passionate Rebel

"Take her to the warehouse on Water Street," the provost marshal instructed. "She is to have no special privileges."

The sergeant nodded, half-relieved and half-dismayed. The warehouse offered little comfort and less food.

Gillian was ushered outside. To her acute annoyance, her hands were bound again. In a gentler way than she had expected, the sergeant placed her in a wagon.

The streets were almost empty at this hour. The horse's hooves sounded loud in the stillness as the vehicle creaked over the cobblestones. Behind closed doors and shutters no light could be seen.

The sergeant allowed the horse to walk, as if he was in no hurry to get his prisoner to her destination.

Gillian felt her muscles tense in nervous apprehension. Having her hands tied behind her back left her feeling vulnerable. She was alone in the dead of night with a redcoat she didn't trust. If the man took it to mind to attack her, how could she defend herself? Recalling the state in which she had long ago discovered Claudia now caused Gillian to shiver in the hot and humid air that swept in from the river.

Never in her life had Gillian felt so alone and helpless as she did at this moment. The blocks, short as some of them were, seemed like miles.

At last the wagon turned onto Water Street, fronting the East River. Though she could not see around the bend to Wallabout Bay, Gillian knew the prison ships were there, and she shuddered. A warehouse, the marshal had said. At least she wasn't to be put aboard one of those hulks.

Finally, the wagon turned off the street. Ahead,

Gillian could see the warehouse. The squat, square-shaped building appeared deserted, at first. Then she saw the armed soldiers.

Inside, she was turned over to a guard. The man untied the rope with which she was bound, and Gillian sighed in relief. She rubbed her wrists, feeling a tingling up her arm. There were no windows in the corridor. Oil lamps had been hung at intervals but not close enough for the light to overlap, with the result that pools of shadow loomed every few steps.

At one point, the guard halted, picked up a tin of water from a table and handed it to Gillian. She saw that his features were coarse, his skin heavily pockmarked.

As they continued on their way, Gillian viewed the water and wondered whether she was to be given food. She hadn't eaten since breakfast, and her empty stomach was beginning to rumble in protest.

They passed by many doors. Behind each one Gillian assumed were prisoners. For the most part it was quiet, but occasionally came the sounds of cries and moans and curses. Someone begged for water; someone demanded food. The guard plodded along stoically. Gillian wondered if he was hard of hearing or incredibly callous.

Pausing before a door, the guard unlocked it and motioned her inside, apparently bored with the whole proceeding.

With a sigh, Gillian moved forward. She guessed a few missed meals wouldn't hurt her. In the light from the corridor she could see that there were three men in the room, which measured no more than ten square feet. All appeared to be asleep.

Then the door closed. At first, it seemed to Gillian that she was in total darkness. She stood very still, not wanting to move lest she step on someone. The blackness was disorienting, and she fought a sudden feeling of terror.

After a few minutes passed, her eyes began to adjust. A thin ribbon of light shone from beneath the door to break the darkness. There were no mattresses, no furnishings of any kind in the room. There was one window, but it had been boarded up.

Slowly, Gillian moved forward. Finding an unoccupied space, she sat down carefully, fearful of making any noise that would draw attention to herself. She needn't have bothered; no one moved. If it hadn't been for the deep breathing and the snores of at least one of them, she would have serious doubts that the men were alive.

It was hot to the point of being stifling, and Gillian was beginning to perspire profusely. Even her hair felt damp. Though she was hungry, a growing thirst was proving to be the most pressing need. Raising the tin of water to her lips, Gillian drank deeply. Even the water was warm. She put the container on the floor beside her.

As much as the feeble light allowed, Gillian tried to assess her fellow prisoners. All she could see were vague outlines.

She drew her knees up, crossed her wrists on them and bowed her head until her forehead touched the back of her hands. How had Tom endured all those months? Was there a secret reservoir of strength one drew upon when it was needed?

Sheer exhaustion overcame her, and Gillian finally dozed.

Chapter Twenty-two

Gillian knew it was morning. The boards covering the window were not fitted tight, and the gaps allowed a bit of light to enter the room.

It seemed that she was the only one awake. The three men incarcerated with her lay quietly in various positions. The man closest to her was curled up on his side. Mouth open, he was snoring gently. He had removed his shirt, bunched it up and was using it as a pillow. Gillian wondered how long he had been here. He was thin to the point of being scrawny. Because of that and because of his gray, thinning hair, it was difficult to ascertain his age. Somewhere in his fifties, Gillian decided.

Her gaze, at first casual, sharpened as she spied the man across the room. There was something familiar about him. She couldn't see his face, yet...

On her hands and knees, Gillian crept forward,

The Passionate Rebel

careful not to come in contact with the other two men.

Finally, she paused. The light was no better, even this close. His face was turned to the wall. She put a tentative hand on the man's shoulder. There was no response, but even through his ragged shirt, she could feel the heat of fever.

Her grip tightened on the shoulder, and she pulled him toward her.

The man rolled over.

"Oh, Rob!" she cried softly.

That he was deathly ill needed only one glance. He was burning with fever.

The other man had awakened with her cry and now sat up, viewing her with astonishment. To Gillian, he appeared to be no more than 17 years old.

She gestured to Rob. "How long has he been like this?"

The young man shifted his gaze to Rob, then back to her. "They brought him in last week. He was coughing a bit, but not like he is now. Couple days ago, he started sleeping a lot. Didn't want his food."

Gillian was aghast. "Why didn't you ask for a doctor?"

He gave her a blank look. "There's no doctors here."

"They could send for one." The apathetic look she was seeing drove her wild. Her worried glance fell on Rob again. Gillian took no comfort in the fact that he wasn't coughing now. Even her inexperienced eye told her he was unconscious.

A sob tore at her throat, and she scrambled to her feet. Going to the door, she began to pound on it with both fists.

"We need a doctor in here," she shouted as loud as she could.

Helene Lehr

Several minutes went by. Though Gillian continued to pound on the door until her hands were bruised, no one came.

The exertion left her panting and perspiring. As early as it was, it was already quite warm. Gillian wondered what it would be like by midday.

Finally, she turned away from the door.

The older man was now sitting up. "You're wasting your time," he mumbled, rubbing the sleep from his eyes.

Gillian frowned. "Where are the guards?" she asked him. "Are they here?" Perhaps, she thought, they left the building at night and didn't return until morning.

The man gave a dry laugh. "They're here, all right. They just don't pay no mind." With that, he settled himself down again and closed his eyes.

Gillian moved toward the young man. "You say he's not been eating?"

"No, ma'am. He's not been awake much." He cleared his throat, appearing embarrassed; then he jerked his head in the direction of the older man. "Me and Samuel have been eatin' his share. They'd only take it back again, you understand," he added quickly.

Gillian nodded. She did understand.

"I managed to give him some water yesterday," he went on, then shook his head. "Or maybe it was the day before."

They both fell silent when the door opened.

It was the same pockmarked guard who had brought her here the night before. He didn't come into the room but just set bowls and mugs of tea on the floor.

Mouth tight, Gillian approached. He seemed startled by this and stared at her, holding a bowl of porridge in his hand.

The Passionate Rebel

Gillian couldn't remember ever being so angry in her life. With great effort, she kept herself under control. Seeing that he was garbed in cotton breeches and a shirt that was no longer white, Gillian knew the man was not a soldier. He was a Tory, hired to oversee his fellow countrymen.

Hands on her hips, Gillian's lip curled in contempt. "How much do the British pay you for doing this?" she demanded scathingly. "Thirty pieces of silver?"

His face flushed, seeming to deepen the craters in his coarse skin.

"Nobody has to pay me to watch rebels."

Gillian didn't believe him but to argue would be a waste of time. She pointed to Rob. "That man needs a doctor." The only response she received was a laugh. She took a deep breath. "Then bring me some water."

"You get water at night," he advised shortly. As if suddenly aware that he was still holding the bowl of porridge, he thrust it at her.

Control gone, Gillian knocked it out of his hand. "He needs rich broth," she shouted. She couldn't believe the man was standing there, looking so unconcerned. "Take me to the kitchen," she pleaded. "I'll make it myself."

The guard's hand reached out in an almost lazy motion, and he slapped her cheek.

Gillian was so shocked she couldn't immediately speak. In her whole life she had never been struck in the face.

"You pig!" she screamed, finding her voice in a surge of fury. Lunging at him, she began to pummel him with her fists, kicking indiscriminately.

Suddenly, she felt herself being pulled away. For a minute, Gillian continued to struggle violently until, with a stab of surprise, she saw that it was the young man who was her fellow prisoner holding her captive.

The guard had again raised his hand, only this time it was clenched into a fist. Gillian knew that if it landed, it would probably break her neck.

"Let her be," the man said in a cajoling voice. "She's only a lass."

"She's a goddamned hellion," the guard shouted. He narrowed his eyes and brought his face so close, Gillian could smell his foul breath. "I'm not puttin' up with any more trouble from you, and I'm not about to listen to your screamin' all day. Now you either shut up and behave yourself, or I'll send both you and your friend to the *Jersey*."

Gillian paled, wondering if he meant what he said. Viewing his scowling face, she decided that he did. Even so, she might have continued her protest, but she had seen what Tom had looked like after a stay on that ship. She could not be responsible for exposing Rob to that.

The guard began to curse at her, then said, "Maybe the best solution would be to put you in a room by yourself."

That idea was even more intolerable to Gillian. Rob would get no attention at all if she wasn't here. She didn't dare dwell on the thought that alone she would be fair game for every guard in the building.

"I will not bother you again," she said in her meekest voice. "You have my word on it."

His laugh was harsh. "The word of a rebel don't mean much around here." He stared harder, wondering who she was. They seldom received a prisoner from the provost marshal. An offense serious enough to be brought to Cunningham's attention usually resulted in death. However, when

The Passionate Rebel

they did, it was recognized that the prisoner was of some importance. Obviously, this woman wasn't captured during a battle. Therefore she had to be a spy. "Guess I'd better keep you in one piece for the gibbet." He gestured to the spilled contents of the bowl he had been holding. "You can eat off the floor, if you've a mind. There'll be no more till supper."

With that, he left, locking the door behind him.

"Sorry," the young man said, releasing his hold. "I hope I didn't hurt you."

"You didn't," Gillian quickly assured. Her arms now felt as bruised as her hands, but Gillian refused to rub them. She knew the man had acted in her interest. "What's your name?"

"Lucas Brownlee." He went back to the section of the room he had selected as his own, then sank down as if his effort had drained him of strength.

The sun was up now. Sharp, narrow shafts of light thrust through the slats on the window, cutting across the room and revealing countless tiny dust motes that drifted lazily through the warm air.

Feeling disheartened, Gillian returned to Rob's side.

Lucas Brownlee was viewing her with sympathetic eyes. Gillian offered a semblance of a smile.

"Is there another guard who comes in here?" Surely, Gillian was thinking, not all of them were so callous. Her hopes were soon dashed.

"Blake's the only one who comes in here. There's others, but they work in different parts of the building."

"Blake?"

He nodded. "That's his last name. Never learned his first."

"But this Blake must have a day off," she persisted.

"Not since I've been here. I'm not sure, but I don't think the guards stay here all day. And I think they take turns staying at night."

"How long have you been here?"

He shrugged thin shoulders. "I don't know. A long time," he said vaguely.

Gillian bit her lip, wondering how to phrase her next question. "When do they let us go to the necessary?"

Even in the weak light, she saw his blush. "They don't." He pointed to a shadowed corner. "The bucket . . ." His hand fell, and his voice trailed off.

Gillian sighed and got up, grateful when the young man turned to the wall. The other man was now so engrossed in his porridge, he never looked up from his bowl.

A few minutes later, she returned to Rob's side. Removing her lawn fichu, Gillian sat down on the floor and carefully tore it into strips.

She had just finished when she looked up to see Lucas holding out his bowl.

"I saved some. You're welcome to it."

Her eyes brimmed. "Thank you. That's very kind."

Gillian took the bowl and ate some of it, saving a bit for Rob. Then she picked up the remaining mug of tea. It was now lukewarm. She took two sips to relieve her parched throat, then remembered the tin of water. She sighed in relief when she saw it was half full. Moistening one of the strips of cloth with the water, she put it to Rob's lips.

At first, there was no response. After a few minutes, however, he licked his lips and swallowed. She wet another cloth and began to sponge his fevered skin.

It seemed to her that a long time passed before Rob finally moved his head and emitted a groan.

The Passionate Rebel

Still more time passed before he at last opened his eyes and looked at her. Gillian stroked his brow. It was still hot, so much so that her hand felt cool to him. Still looking at her, he murmured something unintelligible.

"Rob . . . it's me, Gillian."

He grinned a reasonable facsimile of the smile she knew so well. "You got the prettiest eyes I ever did see."

She bit her lip but gave the expected response. "You always say that." He began to cough, painful, racking spasms that tore at Gillian's heart.

Finally, he quieted. She gave him more water and coaxed a spoonful of the porridge into him, but he was too weak to eat more.

It was growing dark again when Rob had enough strength and enough presence of mind to ask, "What are you doing here?"

In as few words as possible, Gillian told him.

"Christ," he muttered. "They have no business putting a woman in here."

Gillian smiled ruefully. Rob apparently didn't realize that the alternative could easily have been her execution. Gillian didn't fool herself into thinking she had not committed an act of treason, insofar as the British were concerned. She knew very well that prisoners of war were incarcerated and spies were hung.

Rob struggled to sit up. "We must get you out of here."

Gillian put her hands on his shoulders and gently pushed him down again. The heat from his body was like a burning sun.

"Not now," she said quietly. "We'll talk of it later. I am in no danger here, as long as you are with me."

He seemed comforted by that. Turning his head, he looked at Lucas Brownlee. Back against the wall, his knees drawn up with arms draped across them, he appeared to be dozing.

"Lucas," Rob croaked. He resisted Gillian's attempt to keep him still. "I know I cannot stay awake much longer," he managed when he had the young man's attention. "I charge you to watch over her when I am unable to do so."

Lucas Brownlee nodded solemnly. "I'll do it," he responded simply.

Could she escape? Gillian wondered, staring thoughtfully at the door. The only opportunity would be when the guard opened the door. If he could be overpowered... Mentally, she shook her head. No. There was no chance of that. Even if Rob was strong enough to help her, they would both be shot down before they got outside.

Rob again looked at Gillian. Raising a hand, he touched her cheek. "I don't know why I never asked you to marry me." He stared at her for a long moment, as if trying to focus his eyes. "If I had, what would your answer have been?"

Gillian blinked away her tears. She really didn't know, so she compromised. "I think you know what my answer would have been."

It seemed to satisfy him, and he closed his eyes. From his deep and ragged breaths, Gillian knew he was again unconscious.

Claudia's room was dark. The only sound was the creak of the rocker in which she was sitting.

She was at her wits' end. Racked with guilt and knowing that Gillian had come to her aid at a crucial time, Claudia yearned to help her friend. All her

The Passionate Rebel

efforts in this past week had been fruitless. Shamelessly, she had tried to enlist the aid of every British soldier who came into the tavern, going so far as to seek them out on the streets.

No one seemed to know anything. All the men professed shock that a woman might be held in one of their foul prisons.

Claudia spat on their denials.

The chair moved slowly back and forth as if propelled by her troubled thoughts.

Claudia heard the noise before she was aware of what it was. She stopped rocking. It came again, sounding like hail on the panes of glass.

Getting up, she went to the open window and looked outside. A summer evening, soft and clear, greeted her eye.

A few pebbles bounced off her arm, and Claudia looked down to see a man standing in the shadows of the orchard.

Even at this distance, she knew who it was—Franz.

"I'm coming up," he called to her in a controlled voice.

Claudia ran to the door and waited long moments until he entered. He no sooner did, than she threw her arms around his neck. No matter that he came later than she would have wished; he was here now. Her arms gripped him tightly.

"Oh, my love." Franz stroked her hair, delighting in the feel of her slender body pressed against his.

Though he ached with wanting her, Franz forced himself to draw away. He had returned from Dobbs Ferry only this afternoon. Rumor had it that General Clinton was preparing to move the bulk of his forces to the South before the year came to an end. Franz wanted to be long gone before that happened.

Before he could tell Claudia, she began to speak, her words tumbling out as she explained what had happened to Gillian.

"Oh, Franz," she cried, "is there anything you can do? Is there anything I can do?" She clutched at him. "I would gladly take her place. It's all my fault that she was arrested."

Franz went cold as the meaning of her words sunk in. "Your fault?" he echoed.

"Yes, yes. I was the one who gave her the map."

"And just where did you get it?" Why had he asked when he knew the answer? Why had he thought she would change her ways, just because they had spent an afternoon in heaven?

"I . . ." She put a hand to her lips.

Franz stood with his hands at his sides, fists clenched. He wasn't at all certain whether he wanted to strike her or crush her to him in a fierce embrace.

For the moment, he did neither.

Claudia was staring at him with stricken eyes. She couldn't imagine why he had asked a question to which the answer was so obvious.

Their being together had made a difference to both of them, she realized. Never before had she ever felt guilty about what she was doing. In her mind, the means had more than justified the end.

Now, however, guilt pressed down on her till she thought she might collapse from its unwanted weight.

"You slept with him." No emotion colored the statement.

"Not in the sense you mean," Claudia replied in a small voice. "He didn't . . . He never does . . . He can't . . ."

"You let him touch you."

The Passionate Rebel

Tears brimmed and spilled over. Not being able to refute that, Claudia didn't respond.

Franz finally moved. His hands gripped her shoulders, and he shook her so hard that her white cap slipped from her head.

"You are never to do that again," he said through clenched teeth. "Do you understand me?" He now held her still and stared deeply into her tear-filled eyes.

Claudia inhaled a ragged breath, then shrugged away the hands on her shoulders. She bristled with sudden anger. The man had lain with her once and now thought he owned her, thought he could dictate orders to her.

"Who are you to tell me what I can and cannot do?" she demanded. Arms folded across her breast, she glared at him.

A puzzled look shaded his blue eyes. "I am the man who loves you," he said. Both his tone and manner were quiet now.

Claudia's heart skipped a beat at that, but she wasn't ready to relent. "Why haven't you told me that before? Why did you let me think . . . ?"

His puzzlement grew, deepening the lines in his brow. "When would you have had me tell you?" A small smile tipped the corners of his mouth. "I could have told you how I felt the first time I spoke to you, but I think your reaction would not have been a warm one."

Claudia chewed on her lower lip. "That day . . . by the river . . ."

He reached for her and drew her close, cradling her head against his chest. "Oh, my dear heart," he murmured, wondering how to explain. No words had yet been conceived that could describe what he felt for this woman. "Sometimes a man's feelings are too great to be contained in a small word like love." His hand cupped her chin, and he tilted it upward. "I came here tonight to ask you to be my wife."

Claudia's eyes flew open, and she took a step away. She had wanted, needed, an avowal of love. His proposal of marriage caught her off guard. Her mind presented all sorts of obstacles. She could never join the British camp, even as the wife of a Hessian officer; she certainly couldn't envision herself living in Hanover.

"Franz," she began, "be realistic. When this war is over, you will return home."

"I am being realistic," he returned with a smile.

"What are you saying?" she cried. "I can't marry you. You're not even an . . ."

" . . . American?" he supplied. "Oh, but I hope to be. I will not be the first Hessian who has made the decision to defect, nor the first British soldier, for that matter."

Claudia felt as if the wind had been knocked out of her. "You would defect?"

"Ahh, what a word for finding a new life and new hope." He smiled. "Hasn't everyone in this new nation defected? Haven't you? When this war began, weren't your loyalties to England? Where are they now?"

"I . . ." He was right, of course. She'd just never thought of it in just that way. True, she had been born in Liverpool, brought over here when she was only five years old. Until that fateful night of the fire, Claudia had always thought of the colonies as a mere extension of Great Britain.

"Claudia," he whispered, "do you love me as much as I love you?" As he spoke, he stroked her hair. The color of a winter night sky, its fragrance filled his senses. Silk was not as soft. Silk was rough in

The Passionate Rebel

comparison to what his fingertips encountered.

Claudia felt a rippling shimmer of apprehension course through her. She was afraid and knew it. Once before, a man had spoken to her like this. The words were not the same, but the meaning was. Last time it had turned to ashes. What now would be the outcome?

In her green eyes, Franz saw her indecision and guessed the reason for it.

"Don't be afraid of love, my dear heart," he said quietly as his arms encircled her. His finely molded mouth captured her soft lips in a deep and lingering kiss.

Claudia was grateful for the security of his strong arms, for her limbs weakened beneath the tender onslaught. Held firmly against the muscular length of him, her fears began to melt like the morning mist under the rising sun.

At last he drew back to study her lovely face, waiting for her answer.

"I love you more than I thought it was possible to love anyone," Claudia said finally, and she willingly offered herself to his embrace.

Chapter Twenty-three

From within his carriage, Philip stared moodily outside. A gentle rain was falling—more of a mist, really. It served to cool and freshen the air.

Philip leaned back against the cushioned seat. He was bone-weary, having returned to New York only hours ago.

As tired as he was, however, he had been unable to sleep. Although he had wanted to stay longer, his mother had convinced him otherwise. At this time, she had told him sternly, his duty was elsewhere than Williamsburg.

At this point, Philip wasn't so sure.

The foreman he had left in charge was a good man, experienced and trustworthy, and Philip had no qualms about the running of the plantation in his absence. His mother, however, was another matter, but Isobel Meredith was a patriot and did her own duty as she saw it. She was well-aware that men all

The Passionate Rebel

over the country had left their homes, their fields and their businesses to fight this battle.

Still, even with her urgings, Philip had felt remorse at leaving at her alone during this most trying time of her life.

With a start, Philip saw Matthew open the door to the carriage, and he realized that it had stopped in front of his office building. Getting out, he addressed his servant.

"You'd better wait. If there are no pressing problems, I'll be returning home."

Matthew had no sooner settled himself back in the driver's seat when he saw Philip come running out of his office. Matthew didn't even have time to climb down, much less open the door, before Philip got into the carriage.

"Drive to the Blue Swan," Philip instructed curtly. "And do it as fast as you can."

As they moved forward, Philip unfolded the note that his clerk had given him. It was from Edwina Carmody. It contained little practical information. Only a request that he come to see her as quickly as he could. Her sister, she had penned, needed help.

Philip's hands trembled as he stuffed the note into a pocket. He couldn't imagine what sort of trouble Gillian had gotten herself into, and he didn't even want to hazard a guess.

Despite his resolve, Philip's mind proceeded to conjure up all kinds of fantasies, none of them pleasant.

Matthew was driving as fast as he could along the rain-slicked streets, but it wasn't fast enough for Philip, who urged him to hurry.

Leaning back, Philip covered his eyes with his hand. Why had he ever thought that this relationship with Gillian would work? From the start she had made it plain that she didn't want him. Why had he pressed the issue? From the beginning things had gone wrong. He had tried to correct them, but he had not succeeded. He knew that now.

If Gillian had tried to banish Philip from her mind, Philip had tried no less so to rid his thoughts of Gillian. He had been less than successful. Lately, he found himself unable to look into a fire without seeing the golden color of her hair, unable to view a clouded sky without seeing her glorious eyes, unable to view a rose without its scent and texture recalling the incredible softness of her skin beneath his hand.

With a groan, he sat up again, seeing that they were almost at their destination.

Philip was out of the carriage before it came to a full stop. He bounded up the back stairs and opened the door without bothering to knock.

Edwina spun around in startled surprise, then emitted a cry of relief.

"Thank God you've come," she said, then motioned to Mandy. "Go next door and fetch Katie," she instructed. "Bring her back here as quickly as you can."

After Mandy left, Edwina again looked at Philip.

"Something terrible has happened," she began. "Gillian's been arrested. They've taken her somewhere, and we don't know where. Katie was with her, but managed to get away."

"Has Mistress Wharton contacted anyone about this?" Philip's mouth went dry with the sudden surge of fear that coursed through him.

Edwina shook her head. "She's still in Halifax. I was going to write to her, but I decided the post would take too long. We all thought for sure we'd know something by now."

The Passionate Rebel

At that moment, Katie came in, breathless from her run across the orchard.

Philip immediately turned to her. Although he had never before seen her, he correctly assumed that the auburn-haired young woman was Gillian's servant.

"Oh, sir," Katie exclaimed, rushing toward him, "you will help us find Miss Gillian, won't you?" In her agitation, Katie forgot herself, clutching at his lapels with a force that almost threw him off balance. "You don't suppose the redcoats have put her on one of them ships, do you?"

Philip's mind was reeling. Maybe, he thought, Gillian had been abducted. People were not simply dragged off the street or out of their house without anyone knowing about it.

"How do you know she was arrested?" he demanded.

Katie's eyes widened. "I was there."

"Where?" Impatience sharpened his tone.

"On the Post Road."

Philip rubbed his chin and sighed. It would only delay matters if he asked what the hell Gillian had been doing on the Post Road. "Begin from the beginning and tell me exactly what happened."

Katie swallowed. "Well, Miss Gillian found this map, and . . ."

Philip expelled a deep sigh. He didn't need to hear any more of the details. "When did this happen?" he asked, interrupting her.

"More than two weeks ago." Her voice ended on a note of hysteria. Why was he standing there? Why didn't he do something?

Two weeks, Philip was thinking, cursing himself for not returning sooner.

Philip took hold of Katie by the upper arms and

bent his head so as to look closely at her. "Think, Katie. When the soldiers found the map, did they say anything about where they were going to take her?"

Katie shook her head sharply. "No, I told you. We don't know where they took her."

"Please, this is important. I want you to think very carefully. Take your time."

Katie stared at the fancy buttons on Philip's jacket and tried to force her mind back to that ugly incident. As soon as she had seen the map fall to the ground, Katie had known they were in trouble. So intent had she been on seeking a means of escape, she hadn't even been listening to the conversation. Only when the sergeant . . . She raised her eyes to see Philip still peering intently at her.

"Yes," she said slowly, ashamed that she had not thought of it before. "He said he was taking us both to the provost marshal."

Philip's hands fell away, and he repressed a groan of utter dismay. It must have been Cunningham's men who picked up Gillian. Had it been one of the regular patrols she probably would have been taken to their superior officer. Now he understood why no one seemed to know where Gillian was. Cunningham liked to shroud his operations in secrecy—and with good reason.

He became aware of Edwina's distraught face and gently patted her shoulder.

"I'll find her," he promised quietly. "Try not to worry."

Edwina shook her head sadly. "I'm afraid I can't grant you that, Mr. Meredith."

Ruefully, Philip nodded. "I'll let you know as soon as I find out anything."

As he headed back to his carriage, Philip's

The Passionate Rebel

brow creased in a deep frown. He knew William Cunningham only by virtue of a brief introduction at a party. Nevertheless, he knew all about the man. It would be pointless, even futile, to go to Cunningham's office. The provost marshal would release a prisoner only on the direct order of the commander-in-chief of the British Army. That man was General Sir Henry Clinton.

Ten minutes later, Philip's carriage drew up in front of General Clinton's residence. Outside, it equaled the Royal Governor's mansion in splendor; inside, it surpassed it.

Unfortunately, General Clinton was unavailable. Philip was instructed to return the following morning.

The rest of that day, Philip fretted. Though he, like Claudia, tried to discover Gillian's whereabouts, he was unsuccessful. Tormenting visions returned. What if she was injured? What if she was indeed aboard one of those ships? No! That was an altogether unacceptable thought, and he pushed it away.

The next day he again went to Clinton's residence, ready to break down the door if he was once more denied entrance.

This time, however, he was admitted by a black servant, resplendent in gray and crimson livery. A white powdered wig was perched on his head, and his shoes sported silver buckles.

Philip gave his name and cooled his heels for more than an hour before finally gaining an audience.

The room the commander-in-chief used for his office appeared to have been at one time a library. It was a large, rectangular room with tall narrow windows at both ends. There was an oval table, its surface now bare and polished, though Philip imagined it was at this table where Clinton conferred with his advisors and planned his strategy. There was also a desk, and this did have a myriad of papers strewn across its top.

Clinton himself was seated in one of two cushioned chairs positioned by a window. A low table in front of him held a pot of tea and a plate of sliced cake.

"Sir Henry," Philip said with a nod of his head as he entered, "thank you for taking the time to see me."

"Ahh, Mr. Meredith. Come in. Please sit down and join me."

While Philip seated himself, a servant poured the tea. These little social amenities grated on Philip's nerves, but he forced himself to play the game. The British were sticklers for protocol.

When the servant was done, Clinton waved him away.

In deference to the heat of the day, the general had removed his scarlet jacket. He was, Philip knew, a professional soldier, having been in the army for most of his adult life and having worked himself up through the ranks. Considering his status, Henry Clinton was a somewhat unprepossessing man. He was below average in height and had a paunch that blurred his waist and strained the buttons on his breeches. He was a man who rarely made a quick decision. He liked to think things through. War, to him, was on a par with a game of chess. All angles had to be considered before Sir Henry made a move.

Still and all, Philip much preferred to deal with this man than with Cunningham, who had both the tenacity and the instincts of a fanatic.

They spent a few minutes discussing the weath-

The Passionate Rebel

er while Philip sternly repressed his growing agitation.

At last Clinton put down his cup and asked, "Now, Mr. Meredith, what can I do for you?"

Calmly, Philip told him of Gillian's arrest. "Of course, none of this would have happened had I been here," he concluded. "I've been out of town for these past two weeks."

Clinton's sparse brows rose. "Really? Where have you been?"

"To Williamsburg," Philip replied easily. What the hell did it matter where he'd been? "My family owns a tobacco plantation there."

Clinton smiled. "I've always thought that Virginia is the loveliest of the colonies." He poured himself another cup of tea, taking a sip before he again spoke. "I have been apprised of Miss Winthrop's arrest. It was not without cause." He fixed Philip with a level look. "She had in her possession a map of the depot that clearly outlined the extent of our weaponry. I'm sure you can appreciate the consequences should such information fall into the wrong hands."

Philip shrugged that away. "Her servant told me about that. Miss Winthrop found the map. She had no idea what it was. I'm sure you know that Miss Winthrop is the granddaughter of Alice Wharton. Like myself, Mistress Wharton is a staunch loyalist. As is her granddaughter," he added quickly and, he hoped, emphatically.

"I am acquainted with the lady," Clinton murmured noncommittally.

"Then I'm sure you are also aware that Miss Winthrop is my fiancée."

A flicker of surprise. Seeing it, Philip pressed the point.

"And I can assure you, once she is my wife there will be no more of these foolish incidents."

Clinton put down his cup. "Foolish it may be, yet one wonders where Miss Winthrop was taking the map."

Philip took the time to pour cream into his tea before he answered. "Frankly, Sir Henry, I don't believe she was taking it anywhere. She was stopped on Post Road. To my knowledge, there isn't a Continental within miles of there. There are, however, numerous British patrols. If she had been on some sort of secret mission, why on earth would she be riding at a leisurely pace down a well-traveled road in broad daylight?"

Clinton sighed. "I'm sure I can't answer that, Mr. Meredith."

Philip took a sip of his tea, then placed the cup back on the saucer. "It doesn't make any sense on the face of it," he pointed out with a casual wave of his hand. He was amazed at his own lighthearted tone and easy manner; inside, his stomach was churning with anxiety. If Clinton refused to release Gillian, what then? He still didn't know where she was. "No," he said, giving a sharp shake of his head. "This whole thing is an unfortunate mistake. I know Gillian very well. We are, after all, to be married," he reminded.

Clinton brushed an imaginary crumb from his paunch. According to his reports, the woman claimed she had never seen the map, claimed the sergeant who stopped her found it on the ground. Now, here was Meredith stating that she was the one who'd found it. He wasn't lying. Clinton was certain of that. Therefore, he had been misinformed.

"Miss Winthrop refused to take the oath," he said quietly, not looking at Philip.

The Passionate Rebel

Philip gave a short laugh. "Given the circumstances, I would imagine that Miss Winthrop was too terrified to even understand what was being asked of her. It seems most unfair to expect a woman to react the same as a man would under those conditions." Philip thought that was a nice touch; next to protocol, the British were very strong in their interpretation of what was fair and what was not.

Clinton's only response, however, was a deep sigh.

Damn you! Philip thought savagely, planting a smile on his face. Where have you taken the woman I love? The only woman I will ever love!

"Where is Miss Winthrop now?" he asked as casually as he could.

"She is in a safe place," Clinton replied, without looking at him.

Safe for whom? Philip wondered bleakly. Leaning forward, he sternly repressed the urge to wring Clinton's neck. "Come now, Sir Henry. Knowing me as you do, I cannot imagine that you would believe I would be taking a rebel as my wife." He sniffed and appeared annoyed. "If you like, I will take the oath right now." And he would have. Philip was ready to sell his soul to the devil if it would help Gillian.

"That won't be necessary. Your loyalties are not in question here. As for your taking a rebel as your wife." He chuckled at the idea. "I'm willing to wager that when it comes to a beautiful woman, a man wouldn't give a fig for her political affiliations."

"I most certainly would," Philip protested, and in that, at least, he spoke the truth.

With a sigh, the general got up and went to a cabinet. Removing a bottle of brandy, he held it up to Philip in a silent offer. At his nod, Clinton poured some of the amber liquid into two glasses.

Crossing the room, he handed one to Philip.

"Cunningham is pressing to have the woman executed," he murmured in a low voice.

Like a bursting rocket, rage exploded in a red mist before Philip's eyes, and he sprang to his feet. "I will kill him with my bare hands if that's allowed to happen."

Clinton waved a hand as he again sat down. "Calm yourself, Mr. Meredith. I can assure you it will not come to that. God knows there's been enough bloodshed already in this whole sorry mess." After taking a sip of his brandy, he absently twirled the glass between his fingers. "Half the time I feel as though I am at war with my own people. No one wanted this war, least of all His Majesty. Yet, it is here, and we must all deal with it."

Philip picked up his glass and drained it in one swallow.

The general paused and gave Philip a searching look. "Are you certain you will be able to vouch for Miss Winthrop's conduct once you are wed?"

"Absolutely," Philip replied, his jaw still set in anger.

The general sank back in his chair and stared thoughtfully into space. Cunningham was indeed pressuring him to have the woman hung, and from all the evidence, he was justified. Yet Clinton knew he must not lose sight of the fact that colonists were like children; certainly the women were. They parroted their men, demanding a society that did not exist within the realm of civilized men. Freedom was anarchy. Sooner or later, they would realize it.

Being himself a civilized man, Clinton could not reconcile slaughtering people until the truth made itself known to them.

"To be honest, keeping a woman captive does not

The Passionate Rebel

sit well with me," he said at last. "Yet I cannot release her on her own recognizance." Getting up, he walked about, hands clasped behind him.

And what the hell did that mean? Philip wondered.

The general finally halted his aimless prowling and looked down at his visitor. "Therefore, I can see only one solution. Your wedding will have to take place as soon as possible. Once the ceremony is performed, the woman will then become your responsibility. And you, Mr. Meredith, will be held accountable for her actions." He fell silent at the sight of the startled look he was seeing. "You did say you were betrothed to Miss Winthrop?"

"Yes." What would he do if Gillian refused? Philip cleared his throat. "However, it had been agreed that we would not marry until November."

The general shrugged. "That's only a few months away."

"Yes. But you see, Sir Henry, Miss Winthrop's grandmother is in Halifax right now. It may be that Gillian would like to wait until she returns."

The general's expression hardened. "If she does, I can assure you that she will do so under lock and key."

Chapter Twenty-four

Gillian moaned softly. Every part of her body seemed to ache from sitting in one position all night. Rob was sprawled out, head in her lap, his weight long since having numbed the upper part of her legs.

It was morning, she guessed. She cast a quick glance at the boarded-up window, now uncertain. The light coming through the slits was gray. It wasn't dawn. Too much time had passed. Therefore, she surmised the day to be cloudy. It was not yet eight o'clock, though, because the morning meal had not been delivered.

When the door finally opened, Gillian looked up without much interest, though she was somewhat surprised that the guard had no food with him.

"You!" He motioned abruptly to her. "Come along with me."

Gillian did not move immediately. Bending her head, she viewed Rob. With a gentle touch, she brushed the hair back from his brow. His skin was

The Passionate Rebel

no longer hot with fever. It was cold, as it had been for hours. She had shed her tears. Her eyes were now dry and her voice detached as she murmured, "He's dead."

The guard frowned. "I'll send someone in here to get him. Come on!" Impatience was back. He was not a man to question the decisions of his superiors, but he was convinced that women did not belong in prison, at least not in the one in which he worked. They were too disruptive, possessing an odd mixture of weakness and strength that drove a man to distraction.

When Gillian still did not move, he went to her, rolled the man off her lap and dragged her to her feet. Gillian's legs immediately buckled, and she sank down to the floor, only to be jerked roughly to her feet again.

"Let her alone," Lucas said through clenched teeth.

The guard turned, lips drawn back in a snarl. "You don't tell me what to do, rebel. If you value your miserable life, hold your tongue."

Lucas lowered his head. He wanted to go to Gillian's aid, as he had promised he would do, but his strength simply would not support his urge. In misery, he just sat there, hoping Gillian would not see his shame.

Realizing that there would be no more interference, Blake once again turned his attention to Gillian, grasping her arm in a tight grip.

Gillian stumbled forward, each step sending sharp, knifelike pains up her limbs as feeling began to spread through her cramped muscles.

In the hall, the man released her long enough to lock the door. The oil lamps flickered, sending changing patterns of light and shadow to splash up the wall in demented shapes. In this part of the building, it seemed to be endless night.

Gillian swayed but managed to remain standing. She felt no curiosity as to her destination. Her mind refused to focus beyond the immediacy of the moment at hand. This reaction, she knew, was most likely due to a lack of sleep. For the most part, rest had eluded her since she had entered this place, and for the past 30 hours or so she had not slept at all.

"Move along," the guard growled at her.

Obediently, Gillian placed one foot in front of the other. Even the act of walking was one she seemed to need to concentrate on right now.

She was led through a maze of corridors to a room that had been set up as a kitchen. The walls seemed to have been recently whitewashed and offered a deceptive appearance of cleanliness belied by the unscrubbed and unswept floor. Two large woodburning stoves made the area uncomfortably warm. From the pots came the now sickening smell, to her, of porridge.

She was directed to a chair at the solitary trestle table. Other guards were in the room, some drinking tea, some just standing about talking to each other. None gave her more than a cursory glance.

The pockmarked guard put a cup of tea and a bowl of the hateful porridge before her. Gillian just looked at it and turned away.

"I'm not hungry," she said. Her mind was so weary, so preoccupied, she gave no thought as to why she had been brought here to eat her breakfast.

Blake frowned. "My orders are that you are to eat before we go."

Go? Go where? she wondered briefly. The thought came and went without her pursuing it to any logical conclusion. She found herself not caring.

The Passionate Rebel

With a deep sigh, she put an elbow on the table and cupped her chin in the palm of her hand. She had tried so hard, but all her efforts had been in vain. Rob had almost made it. He had rallied, appearing to get better. Then, two days ago, he had taken a turn for the worse. Last night, he had slipped once again into unconsciousness and had died in her arms. It had been a peaceful end; for that, at least, Gillian was grateful.

She gave a start when the guard laid a heavy hand on her shoulder and gave it a rough shake.

"What's the matter with you?" he demanded. Then he pointed to the bowl. "Eat!"

Listlessly, Gillian picked up the spoon.

Satisfied that his orders were being carried out, the man moved away to converse with his companions.

Despite the guard's insistent urgings, he seemed to be in no hurry to go anywhere. Time passed, and still Gillian sat at the table, the half-finished cereal long grown cold and congealed.

Finally, when she judged it to be late morning, a British sergeant strode into the room. He and the guard spoke in tones too low for Gillian to hear, but she saw both men glance at her several times during their conversation.

Then the guard came toward her.

"You're to go with the sergeant," he said.

Gillian stood up, a bit surprised by her calmness. The thought skipped across her mind that she might be walking to her own execution. Oddly, she felt no fear.

The sergeant made no move to touch her. He did, however, watch her closely until she entered the waiting carriage, his vigilance lessening only slightly as he climbed in beside her.

Helene Lehr

The day was indeed cloudy, the sun hidden behind what appeared to be one thick cloud that obscured the sky from horizon to horizon.

Gillian made no resistance. She just sat there as the vehicle rolled along, wondering where she was being taken. Edwina must be terribly upset by now, she thought with a sigh. Turning her head, she viewed the soldier seated beside her. Catching her glance, he gave her a small smile.

Encouraged by that, Gillian ventured to ask, "Would it be possible for me to send a message to my sister to let her know that I'm all right?"

Slowly, he shook his head. "I'm sorry, but I cannot carry any messages for you. Or for any other prisoner," he added in an effort to soften his refusal.

The carriage finally halted. Gillian knew the house and couldn't imagine why she was being brought here. The sergeant got out, then turned to assist her, offering her his hand.

Gillian ignored the polite overture. From somewhere deep inside her, she drew on her remaining strength, certain she would need it to face what lay ahead. No doubt they were about to question her again. Well, let them! She would tell them nothing.

Gillian squared her shoulders and lifted her chin as she entered the house occupied by the British commander-in-chief.

Inside, it was measurably cooler. The foyer was a vast expanse of black and white tile set in a diamond pattern. At intervals had been set small cherrywood tables, each one supporting a delicate porcelain figurine. A wide, carpeted staircase arched gracefully to the second story.

Halfway along the foyer, Gillian paused, catching sight of herself in a mirror. Her hair was a tangled mess; tousled and uncombed, it displayed little of

The Passionate Rebel

its normal luster. Her fingers went to her bodice. Though she could only see herself from the waist up, Gillian was shocked by how grimy and dirty she looked.

Turning from the mirror, she saw the sergeant watching her. He made no attempt to prod her along and seemed content to wait until she was finished with her inspection.

Gillian had seen enough. She followed the sergeant to an open doorway. Pausing, he motioned her inside.

When she entered the room, Gillian drew a sharp breath at the sight of Philip, not wanting to admit to the relief she felt at the sight of him. Regardless of their estranged situation, she knew instinctively that he was here to help her.

Philip had been seated in a chair, and as Gillian came farther into the room, he stood up.

Gillian saw his eyes travel the length of her, and with effort, she kept her head high.

Viewing her, Philip's jaw tightened as his feelings swung from anger to pride. He made a conscious effort to relax, knowing it was best not to reveal any emotion while General Clinton was in the room. Despite his resolve, Philip knew that if Cunningham had been in the room, he would have throttled the man, regardless of the consequences.

Taking himself in hand, Philip motioned to the chair he had just vacated. With a small shake of her head, Gillian declined. Her face was pale and drawn, and the few pounds she had lost now gave her an air of fragility that tore at Philip's heart. She looked like a lost waif. He longed to gather her in his arms and tell her how beautiful she was.

And he might have done so, had not Clinton chosen this moment to clear his throat. The general was seated in the chair by the window, the same one in which he had been seated when Philip first appeared before him on the previous day. He was now, however, dressed in full military uniform.

Clinton waved a hand at Gillian. "Come closer, Miss Winthrop. I don't wish to shout across the room to make myself heard." He waited a moment while Gillian took a few steps forward, coming to stand behind the chair opposite from him. He did not invite her to sit. "You have caused us all a great deal of problems with your untoward behavior."

The glint of defiance in her gray eyes was not lost on him. Clinton wondered what this woman would do if he demanded the oath of allegiance from her right now, but he knew very well that each prisoner was offered that opportunity before they were incarcerated. Had she sworn for the king she would not now be here, causing a most unwanted intrusion in the routine of his day.

"Mr. Meredith has informed me that the two of you are soon to be married."

Gillian's eyes widened, but she made no comment, quickly reasoning that this might be the ploy Philip was using to gain her release. In any event, the general didn't seem to expect any response from her, for he continued speaking almost immediately.

In clipped tones, he began to explain the price of her freedom.

"I have therefore sent for the clergyman," the general concluded. "As soon as the ceremony is performed, you will be free to leave in the custody of your husband."

"No!"

As she went to step away, Philip's hand gripped her upper arm. At odds with the pressure he was

The Passionate Rebel

exerting on her arm, his voice was mild, almost disinterested.

"My dear Gillian, I have already explained to Sir Henry that you would prefer to wait until your grandmother returns from Halifax. However, he feels the delay would cause problems."

"What problems?" Gillian managed to disengage herself from Philip's grasp.

In a deceptively soft voice, the general answered her question. "The problem of what to do with you, my dear. You have been arrested for a serious offense, one for which a man would be hung. However, I am willing to take into consideration your age and the fact that your grandmother is a loyal subject of His Majesty. Yet it is apparent to me that you must be placed in the care of someone who will be responsible for your actions. What better person than a husband?"

Gillian lowered her eyes. "And if I refuse?"

Leaning back in his chair, the general sighed deeply. "Then I would have no alternative but to place you aboard one of our prison ships, and I do not think you would like that. There are few accommodations for ladies. I fear you would be most uncomfortable."

Involuntarily, Gillian shuddered and looked to Philip, hoping for some sign of denial. Surely they would not put a woman aboard one of those vessels.

For a moment their eyes met. It would have been easier to read the face of a sphinx, Gillian thought glumly.

"This is foolish, Gillian," Philip said, dragging his eyes away from her lovely face. "We will be married today, and there's an end to it." He was rewarded with a look of approval from the general.

Gillian took the time to study Philip, wondering if he did indeed want to go through with this or if he was trying to save her from imprisonment.

Philip was looking at the general. "Would you permit us a moment to speak in private?" he asked in his most socially acceptable voice.

"I don't see the need for that," Sir Henry replied shortly. "Well, Miss Winthrop?" His voice was now edged with impatience. His fingers drummed on the arm of his chair.

Turning her head, Gillian stared at General Clinton a long moment before she spoke.

"Before we go any further, there is something I want done."

She stated that with so much authority that the general's surprise was overshadowed with respect. He didn't ask her what it was she wanted done; he knew very well she would tell him.

"A man died in the room in which I was held prisoner. I want his body buried decently, and I want his parents notified."

Philip made a sound that could have been impatience or a sound of warning. Gillian didn't care and didn't favor him with her attention.

Raising a hand, Clinton massaged his forehead as if to forestall the beginnings of a headache. "Prisoners die every day . . ." he began.

"Not friends of mine," Gillian retorted coldly. "A physician might have been able to save his life, yet when I requested one, the scum you have seen fit to appoint as a guard merely struck me in the face." She didn't turn away when the commander-in-chief looked up at her through narrowed eyes. "There was no decent food with which to feed him." She went on in the same icy tone which clearly conveyed her contempt. "Nor was there enough water to soothe his

The Passionate Rebel

parched throat. Tell me, General," she asked, "have you ever tried to sponge a fevered brow with your miserable tea?"

Silence danced off the walls like rain from a pitched roof.

Philip forced himself to stand still, but his mind was racing at top speed. Unobtrusively, his eyes darted toward the door. The sergeant-at-arms was standing at attention. Even if his musket wasn't loaded, the bayonet was fixed in place. He turned away. The window? There was a possibility.

Before Philip's mind could fully explore this plan of escape, should it suddenly become necessary, he heard the general speak.

"Miss Winthrop," he said at last, his words slow and strung out, "we are not the inhuman monsters you make us out to be. Men are imprisoned, and they die. This is a fact of life. No army can feed and care for its prisoners as they would like to do. There simply aren't enough provisions available. A choice has to be made between fighting soldiers and those men who are captured during battle."

His practicalities were not appreciated, and he saw it.

"His name was Robert Clayton," Gillian continued as if he hadn't spoken a word. "His family lives some three miles out of the city on Post Road."

Philip was now seriously viewing the window. Fortunately, it was open.

Clinton sighed. Like Howe before him, he felt a reluctant admiration for the patriots who fought against odds so overwhelming yet somehow managed to rise above the horror inflicted on their land in these past years. Cautious though he might be, Clinton was no fool. That this woman was at heart a patriot, he had no doubt. He could only hope that her inclinations would be curbed once she was married to a man like Philip Meredith. And if they were not? He rubbed his chin, then looked at her. She could not have had an easy time of it these past two weeks. Perhaps she had learned her lesson.

Watching Gillian, Philip knew better. That indomitable spirit was not even bent, much less broken. Though she was undoubtedly weary and most likely weak from hunger, she stood proudly, shoulders square, gray eyes steady and unafraid.

"Very well," Clinton said at last. "The man's body will be returned to his family. They can bury it in any way they see fit."

Slowly, Gillian nodded.

Clinton turned to the sergeant, standing by the door. "See that it's done," he ordered shortly. He looked at Gillian again. "Is that all, Miss Winthrop?" he inquired with wry annoyance.

Gillian bit her lip. "Actually, no."

Philip strolled to the window. Hands clasped behind him, he appeared to be studying the lush gardens. He was, he thought, near enough to grab Gillian's arm and drag her through the window, if necessary. Most likely, the guard would wait for orders. Given his cautious nature, Clinton would probably think a moment before giving any. Time enough, he reasoned. His muscles bunched with the urge to sweep Gillian off her feet and cart her out of here.

"There is a young man in that room who kindly shared his food with me," Gillian was saying, "even though there was hardly enough for him to eat. I would like to be able to send food to him and be assured that he receives it for as long as he remains there."

The Passionate Rebel

"Miss Winthrop, you may send food to every prisoner on Manhattan, if you wish. Now, can we proceed?"

She sighed, aware of the general's piercing gaze. It was now cold and gave no quarter.

Even so, Gillian hesitated—not because she didn't want to marry Philip, and not because she didn't love him. She did and now knew it. The endless days and nights during which she had been confined had provided, if nothing else, uninterrupted time to think, uninterrupted time to evaluate what was and what was not important in her life. The cause for freedom still burned brightly within her; nothing would diminish that.

And her deep and abiding love for Philip Meredith had had to be faced and recognized. That, too, would never diminish. Would she still have loved him if he had, in fact, been the Tory she had once thought him to be?

Gillian suspected she would, but the question was, at best, a moot one. The real question was whether Philip actually wanted to marry her. She couldn't tell.

Aware of Clinton's unwavering stare, she felt a sudden chill in spite of the warm, humid air that wafted in through the open window. The man was definitely prepared to imprison her if she didn't acquiesce. Her brow, having creased in a frown of which she had not even been aware, now cleared. Philip was, after all, a lawyer and by his own estimation a good one. While divorce was not easy to come by, it was not impossible to obtain.

Slowly, Gillian nodded her acceptance at the scowling face of Sir Henry Clinton.

Chapter Twenty-five

This day, Gillian thought with a sigh, would never end. The afternoon was well on its way, and they were still in the general's house.

The ceremony was over. Gillian was now the wife of Philip Meredith.

Seated in a chair, Gillian rubbed her hands together. They were clean, as was her face. The guard had, after a bit of persuasion, allowed her to wash. Though she was not as clean as she would have wished, she surmised that she was at least presentable.

Raising her head, Gillian looked about her. The room seemed to be crowded with people. Clinton had insisted that the newlyweds, as well as the parson and those officers commandeered to act as witnesses, join him for tea. To Gillian's annoyance, Philip had accepted. She knew very well that Clinton had been referring to the English high tea, an endless affair that could more easily be compared to a

The Passionate Rebel

small banquet than a cup of tea.

Servants had trooped in, one after another, carrying trays laden with cold meat and cheese, freshly baked scones and jam, and an assortment of tiny cakes and pastries. They now stood about, cheerfully serving the guests. There was much laughter and talk. Everyone seemed to be in high spirits and having a good time—except the bride and groom.

Gillian shifted her weight. Her back was beginning to ache, though she ruefully considered the fault to be of her own doing. She had spent the previous night sitting up, back against a hardwood wall. Now, she was seated straight and rigid, refusing to lean back in the chair, refusing to display any of the weariness and discomfort she was feeling.

Philip brought her a plate of food.

"Eat something," he urged quietly. Although he kept it carefully hidden, Philip was as anxious to leave as was Gillian. He knew very well it was still within Clinton's power to change his mind and return Gillian to prison. He would not be at ease until she was out of this nest of vipers. Clinton, however, was now in a jovial mood, and Philip wanted him to remain so.

Touched by his thoughtful gesture, Gillian accepted the plate. To please him, she nibbled at the food. As hungry as she was, it all tasted like sawdust.

"Well, my dear," Sir Henry said, coming to stand in front of her, "I am sorry that your family could not be here to witness your wedding vows. Yet I do hope that our little celebration here today counters that loss in some small way."

Gillian was irked by his paternal manner, but she made no comment. Beside her, Philip did.

"I'm certain my wife appreciates all you've done

for her," he offered smoothly. And if the tight set of his mouth and the dark look in his eyes countered his words, the general didn't seem to notice.

Clinton nodded and again looked at Gillian. "I have just been informed that your friend's body—Mr. Clayton, I believe you said his name was—has been returned to his parents."

Gillian raised her eyes to his pleased face. From his expression one would have thought that he had just given her a wedding present. "Thank you," she said dully. What was she thanking him for? she wondered. Doing what should have been done in the first place? Thoughts of Amy and Kiley caused her eyes to mist. Turning her head, Gillian sent a silent plea to Philip for them to leave.

Bending forward slightly, Philip took the plate from her hands and put it on a nearby table. His hand cupped her elbow, and he gently raised her to her feet.

With great dignity, Gillian smoothed her skirt and kept her head high, not seeing Philip's glance of admiration. From her regal bearing she could have been gowned in lavish silk and bejeweled to the teeth.

"I'm sure you will excuse us now, Sir Henry," Philip murmured.

"Of course." He clapped Philip's shoulder. "Doubtless you've had enough of our company and would like to be alone with your bride."

How right you are, Philip thought silently. The sight of Gillian's shimmering eyes gave his heart a painful wrench. She had never shed any tears over him. His jaw worked tightly as they took their leave amid much good-natured banter and well wishes. Gillian was vastly relieved when she was once again outside.

The Passionate Rebel

Without speaking, Philip assisted her into the carriage.

The sky had cleared somewhat, and a low sun blazed on the horizon, streaking remaining clouds with hot crimson color.

Seated beside Philip, Gillian tried to relax. It was difficult. As tired as she was, she felt keyed-up. She couldn't resist looking at her left hand. There was no wedding ring. That didn't make her any less married. She had been so sanguine about the whole thing, she thought ruefully. A marriage made; a marriage broken. Suddenly, it didn't seem so sanguine. Marriage was for life. How could she have taken this step with the thought that it might be otherwise?

"Who was Robert Clayton?" Philip asked abruptly, jarring her from her thoughts.

"Rob was the one who delivered our information to the Continentals," Gillian answered in a low voice, again feeling a sharp prod of loss.

Philip knew his jealousy was unfounded. The man was dead. Yet, whoever he was, he had prompted a surge of protectiveness from Gillian. "And he was a . . . good friend of yours," he ground out.

Gillian faced him defiantly. "The best."

Philip turned to look at her. Why did she look so beautiful to him? He had seen her gowned fit to meet a king; he had seen her garbed as a tavern wench. But he had never seen her look more beautiful than she did at this moment.

"He was fortunate to have such a friend," he said finally, directing his eyes forward.

"I should stop by Edwina's and let her know that I'm all right," Gillian murmured after a moment.

"Yes, I had planned to do that," her husband replied in an equally subdued voice.

When they entered through the rear door and into the kitchen a while later, Edwina jumped up so quickly from the chair in which she had been seated that it pitched backward and crashed to the floor. Rushing forward, she hugged her sister with such enthusiasm, Gillian felt as if the breath was being forced from her body.

"I've been so worried. Thank God you're safe," Edwina cried. She held Gillian at arm's length and viewed her carefully, as though to assure herself of the veracity of her own words. Tired, a bit thinner, in dire need of a bath—but in one piece as far as she could tell. She looked at Philip. He had removed his hat and was standing patiently by the door. "Thank you, Mr. Meredith." She reached out a hand to rest on his arm. "Not only for bringing Gillian back safely, but for your efforts in behalf of my husband." She gave a shaky little laugh. "Thank you seems so inadequate."

Philip patted her hand. "I don't regard it as being in any way inadequate, Edwina." He grinned. "I hope you will permit the familiarity, in view of the fact that I am now a member of the family."

Edwina's brown eyes, having grown wide with surprise and shock, swung back to Gillian. "What is he talking about?"

Before Gillian could answer, Claudia came into the room. Catching sight of Gillian, she emitted a happy cry and clasped her friend to her in a fierce embrace. Several minutes passed in a tearful reconciliation.

When Edwina judged that things had calmed down enough for her to be heard, she repeated her question.

"We were married today," Gillian explained. "It was a condition of my release. The only condition," she qualified. She did not look at her husband as she spoke.

Edwina took a moment to consider. She offered a tentative smile, uncertain of her sister's happiness. Gillian's expression was a far cry from the radiance one came to expect in a bride. Well, it was done. Only time would reveal the outcome.

She viewed her new brother-in-law. "Please sit down. I'll put some food on the table, and we can eat."

"No," Philip said, softening his refusal with a smile. "It has been a long day for Gillian, and I'm sure you can see that the best thing for her right now is rest."

Leaving the Blue Swan, Philip stopped by the Wharton house so that Gillian could pack the few clothes she would need until William could send the rest of her belongings. Gillian insisted that Katie accompany her, and Philip made no objection.

Dusk already embraced the land when they at last reached their destination. Wearily, Gillian followed her husband into her new home.

"I'll have Matthew heat some water," Philip said, heading for the kitchen.

Katie went with him. Gillian stood there with uncertainty for a moment. She was beginning to feel as though she could sleep standing up. After a moment, she made her way to the kitchen, her reluctance growing with each step she took. She wanted to go home. Home was not this house in which lived the man who did not want her. Why was he carrying this charade so far? she wondered. He simply could have delivered her to her grandmother's house and left her there. The thought that she would soon be alone with him caused a flutter of apprehension in Gillian's stomach. Their last meetings had not been cordial ones.

While the water was heating, Katie bustled around, opening and closing cupboards and drawers. There was a pantry, but there wasn't much in it. There was a gunnysack filled with potatoes, a basket of eggs, a cold ham and a tub of butter. Two tins on a shelf revealed flour and tea.

"Lord," Katie mumbled, "the man don't have anything in the house."

Having said that, she proceeded to use what was at hand. Both Philip and his servant left the room, and Gillian sat down at the table, feeling exhausted.

In a short while, Katie placed a steaming platter of eggs, ham and fried potatoes in front of Gillian. While Gillian ate, she made more of the same. She didn't know what Mr. Meredith was expecting for supper, but this would have to do.

No meal had ever looked or tasted so good to Gillian. In only a few minutes, she had cleaned her plate.

"Thank God it wasn't porridge," Gillian murmured as she swallowed the last bite.

Katie tilted her head. "He doesn't have any."

Gillian laughed. It was the first time in more than two weeks she had done so, and it felt good.

The water was now warm, and both Matthew and Philip carried the pails upstairs and poured it into a cast-iron tub.

Katie put the dishes and utensils in the sink. "I'll do these later. I think what you need now is a bath." She wrinkled her nose and sniffed as Gillian got to her feet.

Unable to refute that, Gillian only smiled wanly as they left the room.

The Passionate Rebel

Upstairs, in the bedroom, Katie helped Gillian to disrobe. As she draped the dress on a chair, Katie shook her head. From the looks of the garment, it was fit only for the trash. She assisted Gillian into the tub.

Going to the portmanteau Matthew had placed on a chair, Katie removed a small bottle of perfumed oil she had packed along with Gillian's clothes. Returning to the tub, she dumped a fair amount of it into the bathwater.

Immediately a light scent of rose petals drifted about the room.

"Umm..." Gillian sighed in deep pleasure as Katie began to scrub her back.

That done, Katie handed Gillian the cloth so that she could wash the rest of herself. Then she lifted a few strands of Gillian's hair, wincing at the sight of it. It was so tangled that she despaired of ever getting it combed out. She soaped the tresses and rinsed them, then repeated the process twice more before finally seeing the golden sheen she had come to expect. Glancing down, she frowned, seeing how shockingly thin Gillian looked. With her clothes on, it had not been too noticeable. Now, naked as a babe, Katie could see the distinct outline of ribs and the dominant thrust of pelvic bone.

Throwing the towel aside, she began to brush Gillian's hair. "They ought to be ashamed of themselves," she muttered. "Putting a woman in place like that and treating her like she was a common criminal."

Gillian smiled. "You're not turning into a rebel, are you?" She was well-aware that Katie had no strong feelings about the war either way.

"Maybe I am," she responded, fluffing the now dry hair. She looked down. Gillian's eyes were closed, and her breast rose and fell with the measured rhythm of sleep.

Katie sighed, wondering if she should awaken her mistress. It was for certain she could not leave her in the tub all night.

Just then, the door opened, and Philip strode into the room.

In a reflex motion, Katie stepped in front of the tub to shield Gillian.

Philip nodded briefly. "You may leave."

"I . . ." Katie knew she was blushing furiously. They were married, to be sure. However, Katie wasn't entirely certain that this gave a man the right to see a woman naked in a tub.

"I said you may leave," Philip repeated in a stronger voice. "For tonight, use the guest room at the end of the hall. With the exception of Matthew's room, none of the servants' quarters are ready for use."

Katie nodded a bit dubiously. Servants' quarters indeed! Except for that driver, there weren't any servants that she could see. In fact, there didn't appear to be much of anything in this house. It was as if Mr. Meredith was passing through, just spending the evening here.

Philip waited until Katie left the room. Stripping down to his breeches, he easily lifted Gillian from the tub. Laying her on the bed, he gently patted the droplets of water from her satiny skin.

She had awakened, but only barely. By the time he drew the sheet up over her, she was again asleep. Removing the rest of his clothing, Philip crawled in beside her and gathered her in his arms.

Gillian sighed contentedly and snuggled up against him. It had been in Philip's mind to simply hold her thus, close to his heart. Her nearness, however, had an immediate effect on his resolve, and he groaned as the familiar ache in his loins made its presence known in no uncertain terms.

He pressed his lips in the softness of her hair, and the sweet perfume of roses filled his senses.

Unable to help himself, his mouth breathed a warm trail to a pink earlobe, and he gently nibbled on its enticing softness.

Gillian made a small whimpering sound, and her arms went around him. The fullness of her breasts against him seemed to scald his flesh, and Philip's strong arms tightened their hold. When he kissed her, Gillian parted her lips, playfully nipping the tip of his tongue as it sought entrance to the honeyed sweetness of her mouth.

The hardness of him pressed against her lower abdomen, and Gillian reached down to stroke his throbbing manhood.

"Oh, Gillian," he groaned raggedly.

Pressing her gently back against the pillows, Philip began to kiss every inch of her silky flesh, lingering over her taut nipples until Gillian softly cried out against the tension building up within her. By the time his mouth found the most secret part of her, Gillian's need was as raging as his own. She thrashed wildly, her fingers digging into the hard muscles of his back.

Just when she thought she could bear no more of his teasing, probing tongue, she felt his fullness within her.

With a gasp of delight, Gillian felt herself swept along on a tidal wave of raw pleasure that she wished would never end.

When it had finally crested and subsided, Gillian was too exhausted even to open her eyes and slipped gratefully into the welcoming abyss of sleep.

Helene Lehr

* * *

A bright sun glinting through the window and onto his face woke Philip the following morning.

Turning his head, he looked at his wife. Gillian was sitting up, arms clasped around her raised knees. Though she had the sheet pulled up over her breasts, it fell away at her side, providing a tantalizing view of her back and buttocks.

Her gray eyes were viewing him solemnly.

"Have you been awake long?" Philip asked quietly.

"A while," she answered in an equally restrained voice. "I've been thinking."

"Always a good pastime," he noted, resisting the urge to touch her.

Gillian viewed him uncertainly. She wasn't at all convinced that last night had not been a dream. The last thing she remembered with any real clarity was being in the tub with Katie fussing over her. She didn't remember getting out of the tub or getting into bed. She did, however, remember Philip making love to her. What she didn't know was whether it had been real or whether she had dreamed it.

"What have you been thinking about?" Philip prompted.

"I know you didn't want to marry me," she began. Her fingers plucked nervously at the sheet covering her knees. "I know you did it just to get me released." She took a deep breath and looked at him again. "However, you are a lawyer. I'm sure you know of a way to . . . to dissolve it. I can go to Halifax and stay there until this war is over. They'll never find me up there."

Getting up, Philip donned a robe and headed for the dresser. Picking up the ewer that was on top of it, he poured water into the basin beside it. Dipping his hands in the cool liquid, he splashed it on his face.

"You've certainly been doing a lot of thinking since you woke up," he commented as he reached for a towel. He dried his face and hands, then threw the towel on a chair.

"It seemed to me to be the best solution." Gillian was still toying with the sheet.

"You still don't understand, do you?" he murmured softly.

Her eyes swung to him. He stared at her for such a length of time that Gillian felt a chill of apprehension.

Going to the bed, Philip sat down. "I have loved you from the first moment I saw you. It was as though I had been waiting all my life for you to come to me. I didn't know who you were or even what you looked like. Then, suddenly, you were standing before me. And though my mind at first questioned, my heart knew."

Her eyes filled with tears, and her lower lip trembled. "But, you said . . ."

Philip put a finger to her lips. "We both said a lot of things we didn't mean. Let us promise each other now that we will never do it again."

Her arms went around his neck, and as his mouth brushed her cheek Philip could taste the salt of her tears.

"I promise," she murmured shakily. "I love you so much."

He drew back slightly, so that he could look at her face. "Say that again," he whispered with a catch in his voice.

She smiled, and though the tears still fell, they were not expressions of sadness but rather of the joy that filled her to overflowing. "I plan to say it every day for the rest of my life. And that's a promise, too."

He crushed her to him in a fierce embrace.

After a time, Philip drew back, startled by the sound of her small laugh. She raised her head to look at him.

"I was recalling the night you told me that you intended to make me yours."

"Well," he chuckled, "I kept my word, did I not?"

"Indeed you did," she agreed, kissing the tip of his nose.

Philip viewed her a moment before again speaking. "What was the name of the guard who struck you?" he asked casually, adding a smile to conceal his murderous thoughts.

Gillian wasn't fooled. "I don't know," she answered easily, then grinned in a way that wrenched his heart. "Besides, it wasn't a very hard slap. And I think I repaid him more than even he deserved."

Philip was certain she had, but his hands itched to break the man's jaw.

Gillian tilted her head. "You were angry about Rob, too," she said candidly, with the honesty that had always thrown him off guard. "You needn't have been."

"I wasn't angry," he objected quickly, then sighed. "I'm ashamed to admit that I was jealous."

"You needn't have been that either," she murmured softly, touching his cheek. She was amazed by her feelings for this man. Suddenly, her cheeks flushed a soft pink. "I must confess that you made me jealous once, though I would never have admitted to it at the time."

Philip was more than puzzled. Since he had met Gillian, he hadn't even looked at another woman.

The Passionate Rebel

Gillian wet her lips. "That night you told Delia she had hair like spun gold."

"Delia!" he exclaimed, brow furrowing. "Who the hell is Delia?"

Gillian's laughter sounded like wind chimes.

Removing his robe, Philip threw it carelessly to the floor. Then he reached for her. "And now, Mistress Meredith," he said huskily, "I believe the time for talk is over."

Chapter Twenty-six

From Gillian's Diary:

> *August 5, 1779*
> *The British are showing concern over the increased fortifications at West Point, which is our strongest defense of the Hudson River Valley. A massive iron chain has been laid across the river, linking the Point with Constitution Island. British ships have been unable to pass this formidable barrier. There are rumors, unconfirmed at this time, that the command of this most important garrison is to be given to one of our most able and experienced military leaders: General Benedict Arnold.*

The day was uncomfortably hot and humid. Her yellow silk dress felt like a fur cloak to Gillian

The Passionate Rebel

on this summer morning. At her dressing table, she sat patiently while Katie pinned up her hair in a high chignon, but when the young woman brought forth the white cap, Gillian waved it away.

"No, no," she said, getting up. "I can't remember it being this hot last year." She glanced outside. No breeze stirred the leaves. Though the sky was clear, if hazy, Gillian wondered whether a storm was brewing. The stillness was such that nature seemed to be holding its breath in that moment before unleashing a hurricane. "Perhaps it will rain," she speculated, turning away from the window.

Katie gave a small laugh as she put the rejected cap on a shelf in the wardrobe. "If it does, I hope William found the time to fix the roof. The leak in the corner of my room is getting worse."

Gillian looked surprised. Katie had never before mentioned that problem. "Did you tell him about it?"

"Oh, yes," Katie said quickly. "But I don't know if he's done it."

"Well," Gillian sighed, "I suppose I should stop by the house in the next day or two and make certain everything is in order for Gram's return. I'm really looking forward to seeing her again." She began to walk to the door.

"Nine months is a long time." Katie nodded, then smiled. "But thank goodness her sister is fully recovered." She hesitated, then asked, "You've told her that you're married?"

Slowly, Gillian shook her head. "No. I know I should have," she added quickly. "It just seemed too involved to put into a letter. And when she sent word that she was on her way home, I thought it would be best to wait and tell her in person."

Leaving the room, Gillian went downstairs.

She frowned, as she always did, when she entered the dining room. Although it held a table and eight chairs, that was about all that was in it. The doors leading to the ballroom remained closed. There was nothing at all in that room.

Gillian had been devoting most of her days to the process of redecorating. It was maddeningly slow. In the past, every ship that put into port was bursting at the seams with goods from foreign countries. Now, one had to wait for months on end or have it made to order.

Philip was already seated at the table, eating his breakfast. Bending forward to give him a light kiss on the cheek, Gillian smiled inwardly, thinking of their shared intimacy the night before.

The smile faded as she sat down. "I had expected the sideboard to be here by now," she said, picking up her cup and sipping the hot liquid. When he made no answer, she felt a prickle of annoyance. "I cannot understand why you haven't ordered these things before."

Philip shrugged. "I thought the war would be over in a year or two. I hadn't expected to be here this long." He grinned and squeezed her hand. "Then I met you, and . . ."

Gillian made a face. "What if we had gotten married as planned?" she demanded. "Did you expect me to move into a house without furniture?"

Philip looked a bit sheepish at that. Of all his expressions, this was the one that always melted her heart.

"Well, my love," he said, raising her hand to his lips, "if you recall, we were at first not to

The Passionate Rebel

be married for a year. I figured that would give me plenty of time, and I did indeed begin the process. This room..." He waved a hand in a vague gesture, as if to bring to her attention the fact that it held a table and chairs. "Then, after that..." His voice trailed off.

Gillian sighed. Though she understood that Philip, due to the nature of his activities, saw fit to have as few servants around as possible, she had been astonished to learn just to what extent the house was understaffed. There was, in fact, only one servant. Matthew served as valet, butler, driver and occasional cook, all in one.

By the time Philip finished eating and headed for his office, giving her a long and deliciously lingering kiss before he did so, Gillian was in better spirits. Gram had certainly been right when she said marriage would be an antidote for tedium, Gillian reflected as she left the dining room. She no longer went to the Blue Swan, unless it was to visit Edwina or Claudia, and she had been so busy in these past weeks that she hadn't done much of that, either.

In the kitchen now, Gillian briefly discussed the day's menu with the new cook, a free woman named Margaret Seales. A widow whose husband had been killed at Dartmouth, Margaret had three children to support. She was also a patriot, something Gillian had made certain of before she hired the woman.

When she was through with Margaret, Gillian went back into the hall to see Matthew coming toward her.

"A lady to see you, Miz Meredith," he said with a smile. It pleased him to know his employer had chosen as his wife a lady who was capable of taking charge. Matthew did not mind any of his chores, except cooking and washing dishes. A man shouldn't have to do things like that.

"Thank you." Gillian quickened her steps. She knew that Matthew had directed her guest to the library, which was the only room adequately furnished right now. Gillian was certain her caller was Edwina, and she hoped her sister had brought the children with her. She knew it couldn't be Alice. Though the latest letter from her grandmother indicated that she was by now on her way home, Gillian didn't expect her for at least a week.

When she entered the library, her eyes widened.

"Claudia!"

The other woman immediately got up from the chair in which she had been seated. Her eyes darted nervously to the door.

"Is your husband home?"

A bit startled by the question, Gillian shook her head. "No."

Claudia visibly relaxed. "Could we talk in private?" At Gillian's perplexed look, she added, "I mean, where no one can hear our conversation."

A small smile, one she tried to hide, quivered at the corners of Gillian's lips when she suddenly realized that Claudia didn't know about Philip's loyalties. Crossing the room, she quietly closed the door.

"I'm sure we'll not be disturbed," she assured, heading for the settee. "Come. Sit beside me. Now," she said when Claudia settled herself, "what's all this about?"

Claudia moistened her lips. "I've come to say good-bye. I'm going away. With Franz. We were

The Passionate Rebel

married yesterday." A twinge of guilt left her with an uncomfortable feeling, for she had told Gillian nothing about her relationship with Franz. In fact, she had only recently told Edwina and Tom and happily had received their blessing.

Gillian blinked. "The Hessian?" She had known that Claudia was attracted to the handsome German lieutenant, but she couldn't imagine Claudia actually married to him.

"He's going to defect," Claudia confided in a low voice and clasped her trembling hands tightly. She was frightened to a point that deprived her of coherent thought. She had found a happiness she had thought would forever be beyond her. To lose it would be unbearable.

"Oh, Claudia!" Gillian put her arms around her friend. Next to Edwina and Gram, Claudia was the woman most dear to her heart. "I'm so pleased. I wish you every happiness." Gillian studied her friend. In spite of the warm day, she looked crisp and cool in her silk dress. Gillian wondered how she managed that on a day like this. Claudia's beauty, always unique, was now tinged with a radiance that put her in the realm of the exotic.

Gillian frowned as the full impact of Claudia's words became clear. "How are you going to accomplish this?" she asked in a low voice. "Franz speaks excellent English, but he does have a noticeable accent," she pointed out. "If he should ever be recognized . . ." She shook her head. "And, my God, the list is endless—British, Hessians, Tories. Every one of them is a danger to you."

Slowly, Claudia nodded. "We both recognize the risk. There is really only one safe place." She gave a little laugh. "If it can be called that."

She looked at Gillian. "Franz will have to join the Continentals. He won't be the first Hessian to do so."

Gillian saw the wisdom of that. Then she bit her lip. "If you can only get there safely," she murmured, more to herself than to Claudia.

Each day it was becoming more hazardous to leave the city. Patrols had been increased. If travelers were caught without a pass, they were hauled off to prison, no questions asked. Then she brightened. There was one person who could see Franz and Claudia to safety and also vouch for Franz. Gillian felt certain Philip would do it, once he had met Franz and verified his good intentions.

"Where is Franz now?" she asked Claudia.

"He's waiting in my room. We've already packed, but we thought it best to wait until dark."

Taking hold of Claudia's slim hand, she said, "I want you both to come here tonight. Bring all your things with you." She paused at the shocked look she was seeing. "Please," she whispered, squeezing Claudia's hand. "Trust me."

"What about your husband?"

Gillian's smile emerged as a grin. "Claudia, you were the one who told me there was something deceitful about Philip. Well, you were right. He's no more a Tory than I am." She got up. "I'm going to have Matthew drive you to the Blue Swan. He will bring you both back here. There are very few redcoats who don't recognize Philip Meredith's carriage and driver. It's for certain you will not be stopped. Then, when it's dark, Philip can take you both to the American camp."

Feeling a bit dazed, Claudia got to her feet. Doubt left a cold feeling down her spine. It wasn't Gillian

The Passionate Rebel

she mistrusted. But Philip Meredith? Suppose he had fooled Gillian into thinking he was something he was not?

Gillian saw and recognized the play of emotion on Claudia's face.

"Do you remember when I went to Elizabethtown to see General Washington?"

Claudia nodded. Actually, Gillian hadn't said much about the trip, only that she had met the general and been most impressed by the man.

"Well, someone got there with the news before I did. In fact, he was in the study with the general when I arrived."

Claudia's lips parted. "Mr. Meredith?" It took a moment for that news to register. Now she looked confused. "But why did you break your engagement then?"

Gillian flushed. "Well, that had nothing to do with politics." She took Claudia's arm. "Come. I'll call Matthew."

Arriving back at the Blue Swan a while later, Claudia entered her room, conscious that the carriage was waiting outside.

Though they had both wanted to leave sooner, the time had been inopportune. Franz wanted to make certain that things were quiet before he left, so as to give them as much of a head start as possible.

Everything had been all set, as much as it was able to be under the circumstances.

Now Gillian had offered assistance that, if it worked, would be more than welcome.

If it didn't, all was lost.

In a breathless fashion, unusual for her, Claudia related her conversation with Gillian to Franz.

He was silent for a time while he considered the possibilities.

"Do you trust her?" he asked finally.

"With my life," Claudia replied readily. "But her husband..."

"We are not all what we seem," he reminded her with a smile.

"Oh, Franz." She threw her arms around him, and he could feel her heart beating rapidly against his chest. "I'm just not sure." Her voice caught in a sob.

"My love?" Gently, he stroked her back in a soothing gesture. "Do you think a woman can live with a man and not know him for what he is?"

Claudia looked up at him, and he smiled at her. He held her at arm's length, peering deeply into her eyes. "It would be improbable, wouldn't it?"

Claudia gave a sound of despair. She had never known a man who was so trusting. He was like a child. Five years. That's how long it had gone on. Five years! Did it really matter who was for or against? Where could they hide? Where could they live their lives in peace?

"If it doesn't go right," she said slowly, "can we live in Hanover?"

His grip tightened, and Franz spoke sternly. "All will go well. And we will live here in America."

Claudia made herself relax. "As long as you love me, nothing else matters."

"Oh, what a life we will have." He swung her off her feet. "And our children will reap the rewards." Arms around her waist, he allowed her body to slide down his until her feet again touched the floor. Claudia could feel every hard muscle as she made the short journey.

The Passionate Rebel

"Our children..." Claudia's green eyes misted at the thought.

He laughed, a hearty, delighted sound. "And our grandchildren. We must not forget them."

His kiss left no room for discussion. Claudia didn't want any.

Black clouds were gathering by the time they arrived back at the Meredith house. Claudia and Franz barely made it inside the house before the rain came pouring down.

"If this keeps up," Gillian said, viewing the worsening weather, "you'll not be going anywhere tonight."

"Weather or no, we cannot delay our departure," Franz said firmly. "By morning my absence will be noted."

Gillian nodded, then motioned to the stairs. "I've had Katie prepare a room for you, just in case." She led them up the stairs. "We'll eat in about an hour. Philip will be home by then."

"Did you speak to him yet?" Claudia asked, sounding worried.

"No," Gillian replied. Seeing Claudia's suddenly anxious look, she put an arm around the slim shoulders. "Don't worry. Everything will be all right."

Coming down the stairs, Gillian's face lit up as she saw Philip handing his hat to Matthew.

"I thought I'd beat the rain," he said to her, bending forward to receive her kiss, "but I didn't make it."

Matthew assisted Philip out of his jacket, clucking as he saw the dampened shoulders and sleeves. Then he eyed Philip's shirt.

"It's all right," Philip assured him. "It didn't soak through. Mr. Bissel was in the office today, and he kindly drove me home." He put an arm around Gillian's waist as they walked into the library. "And what have you been doing all day, Mistress Meredith?"

She grinned up at him, thinking how much she loved him. "Well, I've ordered new material for the draperies in the parlor. The green was too dark a shade. I've selected a new carpet for the library since the Persian was far too bright—and we have guests." At Philip's surprised look, she hastily explained the situation. As surprise slid into doubt, she placed a hand on his arm. "Oh, Philip, you must help them."

"How well do you know this man?" he asked cautiously.

Gillian caught the tone of doubt in his voice. "Darling, if it hadn't been for Franz, Tom might have died. He saw to it that Tom received extra food and clothing. I'm convinced that Claudia would never have married him if she didn't believe in his sincerity."

Viewing his wife's beautiful face, Philip grinned ruefully, knowing there was little he could deny her. "Very well," he said. "I will speak to him."

Watching her hurry from the room, Philip shook his head. Now, he thought with a sigh, all we have to hope for is that the Hessian himself is sincere.

Matthew entered, bringing with him another jacket and holding it out to enable Philip to shrug his arms into the sleeves.

A few minutes later, Gillian returned, Claudia and Franz close on her heels.

Once in the room, Claudia paused and viewed this man whom she had always thought of as a Tory. Nothing about his appearance changed her mind. He was wearing a jacket of dark gray taffeta, trimmed in silver braid. A waistcoat of pearl satin partially concealed his white lawn shirt. Close-fitting breeches of blue satin, white silk stockings and black leather shoes adorned with silver buckles completed his attire. That he was handsome, Claudia could not deny and never had.

Nevertheless, her heart sank. Surely, Gillian's judgment had been clouded by love. The man looked like he would be a welcome visitor at King George's Court.

"You remember Claudia?" Gillian said to Philip in the awkward silence that had fallen. At his nod she added, "And this is Franz Heideman."

Another nod. Neither man attempted to shake hands.

"May I offer you a drink, Mr. Heideman?" Philip asked, heading for the decanter on a table.

"Franz, please. And yes, I would like a brandy, if you have it."

Philip filled two glasses. Both Gillian and Claudia declined. The two women now seated themselves side by side on the settee. Franz and Philip remained standing.

"I hope you arrived before the rain," Philip commented as he recapped the decanter.

"It was just beginning when we arrived," Franz said. "Though I must admit, it is welcome. Perhaps the weather will cool down once the storm is over."

"It has been an unduly hot summer," Philip agreed, surreptitiously studying his guest. The man had the appearance of a prosperous merchant. He was not wearing a jacket, but a richly ornamented waistcoat covered his cambric shirt and was fitted with pearl buttons. His satin breeches were fastened on the outside of each knee by a black velvet ribbon.

Gillian and Claudia exchanged anxious looks, perplexed by the conversation of their men. Why were they skirting the issue?

Philip, however, wasn't taking any chances. He was not about to deliver a spy in the guise of a defect to the American camp. There was, of course, no way to make absolutely certain. However, he trusted his own intuition and his capacity for judging a man's worth.

"Have you been in New York long?" Philip asked as he handed Franz his drink.

"Long enough to know that I would like to remain here."

"If the British win, that might be difficult," Philip observed, draining his glass.

Franz had taken no more than a sip of his brandy and now put the glass down on a nearby table. He was beginning to wonder whether Claudia had been right in her doubts about Philip Meredith.

"If they win, it would be impossible," he stated finally. "However, I do not think that will happen. The British have foolishly ignored every opportunity offered to them to end this war. I was here when General Howe routed the Americans from Manhattan. Right then and there, the Continentals could have been defeated, the rebellion crushed. Since I have never found the British to be cowards, I can only assess their actions as stupid." Franz saw the level look directed at him by his host, and he relaxed. A true loyalist would not let that pass unchallenged.

Philip allowed himself a small smile. "I wish I could be as certain of that as you seem to be.

The Passionate Rebel

There is a real possibility that the Continentals will lose this war."

Franz took a step closer and spoke with an earnestness he had no difficulty in summoning. "America cannot lose this war, not now, not with the French army at her side. The British know it. I suspect they have known it for some time."

Outside, the wind increased in intensity, the rain now coming down in a deluge.

Clasping his hands behind his back, Philip went to the window and thoughtfully viewed the worsening weather.

"You want to defect?" he asked finally, without turning.

"I do," Franz replied simply.

Slowly, Philip turned and viewed him squarely. "Why?"

Franz smiled at the blunt question. He needed no time to form his answer; it came quickly, and he spoke with ease and conviction. "Because when it is finally over, this will be a land where a man can be anything he chooses to be. Only his skills and his determination will set any limit to his goals."

Claudia sat up straighter at these words from her husband. Her eyes were moist, but her lips were set in a soft smile.

Philip, too, smiled. He walked closer to Franz. "You're right about one thing. America cannot lose. Not when men like you come forward to fight at our side."

Franz gripped the outstretched hand. "In the future, I hope to be not only a man who fights at your side but to be, in fact, an American."

Matthew appeared at the door, waiting discreetly until he caught Gillian's eye; then he announced that supper was served.

Getting up, Gillian led the way to the dining room.

As Gillian had suspected earlier in the day, the storm that raged across Manhattan was fierce. By midnight, however, it had lost some of its severity. The rain still fell, but it was steady and monotonous, containing none of the fury it had displayed at its peak.

Just before one o'clock, Philip decided the time was right for them to leave. While Franz was changing into clothes more suitable for travel, Philip studied Claudia's heart-shaped face. Once he had thought her beauty frozen, much as one would see in a painting or a statue; now he saw how wrong he had been.

Feeling that somehow he was speaking out of line and yet feeling that he would be remiss if he did not speak, Philip said to Claudia, "It might be wise if you were to remain here. You could always—"

He got no further. Claudia's head snapped up, and she viewed him in something that bordered on astonishment, as if he had suggested that she could sprout wings and fly.

"That's out of the question," she said, then smiled to soften her unintentionally sharp tone. "After all," she pointed out, "Molly Pitcher followed her husband into battle and even worked the cannon when he was injured. If she can do that, so can I."

Philip couldn't think of any argument to that, so he didn't even try.

What few possessions Claudia and Franz had were rolled into bundles and placed on the horses by Matthew, while Gillian and Claudia tried to

The Passionate Rebel

find the words to say good-bye to each other.

"It's time," Philip said finally. Now dressed in buckskin, a cloak around his broad shoulders, he led the way to the door.

Claudia and Gillian clung to each other in a tearful farewell.

"Write to me," Gillian whispered as they finally drew away from each other.

Words were beyond her, but Claudia managed a quick nod as she hurried outside.

Going to a window, Gillian watched them go, saying a prayer for their safety. And she wondered if she and Claudia would ever meet again.

Chapter Twenty-seven

From Gillian's Diary:

> *June 30, 1781*
> *For the first time since this war started, I begin to despair. Since our devastating defeat at Charleston last year, the British seem to be firmly entrenched in the South, particularly the Carolinas. My hopes had risen when the young Marquis de Lafayette returned from France to lead our allies in the battle against the British; so far, little progress has been made. There seems to be no end in sight.*

A warm and welcoming light shone from the windows of the Meredith house. Everyone of any importance was in attendance. The ladies were dazzling, the gentlemen bewigged.

During the past two years, Gillian had discovered

The Passionate Rebel

that she had as much talent for entertaining as did the British, and she put it to good use. She was now considered to be The Hostess of New York. No one refused an invitation to Gillian Meredith's gala banquets unless duty precluded acceptance.

This Saturday evening was no exception.

The ballroom glittered beneath crystal chandeliers fitted with multicolored beeswax candles. Music played, wine flowed, and tables were laden with every imaginable delicacy. Though the household staff now numbered seven, Gillian always hired extra help for these occasions, and liveried servants hurried to and fro to see to the needs of the guests.

In her dressing room, which adjoined the bedroom shared by her and Philip, Gillian was now completing the final touches of her toilette. Katie was no longer with her. She had married Edward, and, true to his word, her husband had opened his own shop in Hanover Square.

Katie's replacement was a young woman named Lisa Hobbs. Like all the servants in the Meredith house, Lisa was a rebel at heart, though she paid lip service to loyalism.

Though she had not seen Claudia since that summer night almost two years ago when she and Franz had gone to New Jersey, Gillian had received an occasional letter from her. So far she had been unable to answer any of the letters because Claudia never stayed in one place for any length of time. Wherever Franz went with the army, she followed. That, however, would probably change soon. The last word Gillian had from Claudia contained the happy news that she was now pregnant.

"Ahh, you look so lovely, my dear."

Seated in a comfortable cushioned chair, Alice Wharton nodded in approval at the sight of her granddaughter. Tonight Gillian was garbed in a lavish hooped sacque gown of amber satin, with an underskirt fashioned from cloth of silver. The elaborate creation was embellished with black velvet bowknots. Her golden tresses were artfully arranged in a high pompadour, with one long, lush curl draped seductively over a shoulder.

How right she had been, Alice thought, immensely satisfied with herself. Gillian had finally come to her senses. Her marriage had relieved her of all her seditious activities, and she was now a model wife and hostess, not to mention the adoring mother of a ten-month-old son named Adam. Although Alice had been more than surprised upon her return from Halifax to discover that Philip and Gillian had married, when she had learned of Gillian's arrest and the conditions upon which she would be released, Alice could only approve of General Clinton's wise decision.

All for the best. Gillian had finally settled down, and that was all that was important.

Alice still lived in her house on Berkley Street, though she attended many of Gillian's parties and occasionally spent the night when the festivities wended their way into the wee hours of the morning.

Gillian turned from the mirror and smiled. "Shall we go downstairs?" she asked. "I do wish Edwina and Thomas could have come with you," she added, clasping her grandmother's hand.

Alice squeezed the slim hand that held her own. "Now you know they come as often as they can." She cast a glance at Lisa, who was straightening Gillian's dressing table, then lowered her voice to a whisper. "But you know, my dear, they're not entirely at ease in the company of your guests." She sighed. "It's not

The Passionate Rebel

Edwina's fault, of course. She must adhere to her husband's . . . inclinations."

"I imagine you're right, Gram." Someday, she supposed, she would have to tell Alice the truth. For now, however, it was out of the question.

Looking about her, Gillian smiled in pleasure as they descended the stairs. The interior of the house bore little resemblance to the one in which she had spent her wedding night. Damask, brocade, velvets and handsomely carved furniture now decorated every room. Tables were resplendent with crystal, gleaming silverware, and fine linen and lace. In the library, books bound in leather now filled shelves heretofore empty, and a magnificent billiard table graced the center of that room.

They entered the ballroom, and Alice immediately moved forward to greet some friends. Gillian stood there a moment longer, surveying her guests. Even General Sir Henry Clinton was in attendance. She saw Philip speaking to Colonel Harcroft and began to head in their direction.

As she moved forward, Gillian paused every few steps to smile a welcome. However, even she balked at greeting the rather short Brigadier General she found standing in her path. He was, until just a year ago, a general in the Continental army and a trusted and valued friend of George Washington. For the past year this man had been plundering the coast of New England with a savagery even the British eyed with alarm.

She was unable to avoid him.

"Mistress Meredith . . ."

Leaning on a cane fitted with a jeweled hilt, the man limped forward and bowed.

Gillian's nod was curt. No need to worry that her cool greeting would be misconstrued. Just about everyone, including the British, treated this man with a reservation edged with ice. And as far as Gillian was concerned, he deserved no less.

"General Arnold," she acknowledged coldly. She kept on walking. Benedict Arnold, placed in command of West Point, had promptly tried to turn it over to the British. He had failed, but his accomplice, Major Andre, had been caught and hung.

Gillian sincerely wished Arnold's fate had been the same. Only one comfort offered itself, if it could be called that. While not shunned by British officers, Arnold was treated with a coolness that was noticeable to all. While they would accept a deserter with open arms, a traitor was an entirely different matter. A man who would betray his country, especially during time of war, was simply not to be trusted.

For once, Gillian agreed with the British.

Gillian reached Philip just in time to hear him say to Harcroft, "I've been hearing disturbing rumors that Washington is planning to attack New York."

Colonel Harcroft nodded solemnly. "I know."

Gillian slipped her arm through Philip's and viewed the colonel with wide and pleading eyes. "You won't let that happen, will you?"

"He will never recapture the city, Mistress Meredith," the colonel quickly assured. "Please do not alarm yourself with such a possibility."

"How can you be sure?" she asked in a small voice.

His smile was benevolent. "General Clinton has already sent for reinforcements from the Carolinas and Delaware. Once they arrive, our position here will be impregnable."

Philip smiled in approval, though in a direction Colonel Harcroft would not have supposed.

Gillian knew why. On direct orders from Washington, Philip had been the one who started the

The Passionate Rebel

rumor of the attack on New York, and the plan was working beautifully. Soon, half the British troops would be here in Manhattan, but Washington had no intention of coming here. He was on his way with the French to Virginia, there to join forces with Lafayette. Gillian returned her attention to Colonel Harcroft, who apparently was still trying to set her mind at ease.

"For the past four years we have been increasing and strengthening our fortifications for just such an event. Washington knows this." Then he laughed heartily and nudged Philip with an elbow, as if he were sharing a joke. "Certainly he spends enough time viewing us from across the river through his spyglass. We could only blame his failing eyesight if he didn't know what we are doing."

"We, too, have our spyglasses, Colonel," Philip noted gravely. "And it is easy to see that their camp is growing larger every day."

Gillian managed to look apprehensive. This, too, was part of the plan. Everything new being constructed on the Palisades was, in fact, no more than a facade.

Colonel Harcroft took a sip of his Madeira. He didn't look at all apprehensive. "Believe me, Philip, if they are foolish enough to attempt to cross the river, they will be blown out of the water. Every one of our ships has been put on alert."

Gillian lightly touched Harcroft's hand. "That's very reassuring, Colonel."

Feeling a slight pressure on her arm, Gillian turned to her husband and accepted his request for a dance.

The party lasted until two o'clock in the morning. Gillian stifled a yawn as the last of the guests finally took their leave. Alice had returned home hours ago.

When the front door closed, Gillian sighed with relief and gratefully followed Philip upstairs. As they always did each evening, regardless of the hour, they went first to the nursery. Assured that their son was sleeping soundly, they retired to their bedroom.

Lisa had left a solitary candle burning in the silver candelabra atop the dresser.

"There are days when I am convinced you look as beautiful as you can," Philip whispered as Gillian closed the door. "Then comes a night like this, and I know I was wrong."

She smiled as his strong arms went around her.

His kiss sent rippling tremors of delight through her. Gillian still had not yet grown accustomed to his touch or his kiss. Each time it was new, setting off a spark of excitement that intensified rather than diminished with time.

"I love you more today than I did yesterday," Gillian whispered breathlessly when he released her. And it was true, she thought happily. Edwina had been right. Gram had been right. How could she have ever doubted? Gillian wondered, mentally shaking her head at the foolish girl she had been.

In the flickering light, Gillian disrobed, then put on a silk nightgown, the diaphanous material revealing more of her than it concealed.

Philip had taken off his jacket and shirt but still wore his breeches.

"Gillian," he said, taking her hand, "please sit down. I want to talk to you."

Regarding his suddenly serious expression, a cold prickle of fear tightened her nerves, and Gillian shivered as she sat on the edge of the bed.

Philip stood there, looking down at her, seeing

The Passionate Rebel

how the candlelight played in her hair. She had said she loved him more today than yesterday. For him, it was even more so. He loved this woman more than life itself, even more than his own son. If any harm befell her, it would destroy him.

"I can be of no further use here," he explained quietly. "I am going back to Williamsburg."

Relief washed over her, and Gillian relaxed. "Of course," she quickly agreed. "Just let me know when we are to leave, and I will be ready."

Philip wet his lips and raised a hand to rub the back of his neck. He knew this wasn't going to be easy, and he willed himself to be strong.

"Gillian, you don't understand. I want you and Adam to remain here in New York. You may either stay in this house, or you can stay with your grandmother."

Gillian jumped to her feet, eyes blazing. "I will do neither!"

"I beg your pardon?" The force of her outburst took Philip by surprise. A moment before, she had been compliant and serene. Now, anger shaded her eyes to cold steel, tightened her mouth and tilted her chin at an angle he knew all too well.

"Both Adam and I will be going to Williamsburg with you," she stated firmly.

"That's out of the question," he shot back, just as firmly. "You'll do no such thing."

Gillian raised a brow and folded her arms across her breasts, fuller now since the birth of her son. "I hardly think you can stop me," she pointed out. "If you don't take us with you, I'll follow you any way I can."

She didn't raise her voice when she stated that. Philip wished she had. He could deal with a woman who ranted, raved or even cried. Gillian was impossible when she went into one of her quietly stubborn moods. Philip always felt that he had no defense against it.

His jaw clenched. "By Christ, you'd do it, too," he muttered. He raked an agitated hand through his hair, took a breath and decided to try reason. "Listen to me, Gillian. There's bound to be fighting. I have an idea that Virginia will be in the thick of it."

"Your home is in Williamsburg. Your mother is there."

"And who's to say the fighting will not take place in Williamsburg?" he shouted. Panic was making an uncomfortable appearance in the pit of his stomach. With effort, Philip softened his tone. "Sweetheart, I know how you feel—"

"I doubt it," she interrupted in the same tone that was so maddening to him.

"Use your head." He was growing angry again. "It's too dangerous. If you don't care about your own safety, at least think of our child."

Gillian was viewing him through narrowed eyes; not a good sign, Philip thought uneasily.

"When you return to your home, your wife and your son will be with you." Her chin went up a notch. "If necessary, I will walk to Williamsburg."

Philip shook his head, knowing he had lost. He sighed deeply. He could argue for hours, and all he would be doing was wasting his breath. Gillian would not budge. "I cannot believe that this means that much to you."

Gillian's face softened. "*You* mean that much to me." Her arms went around his neck. "Oh, Philip, I'd die if anything happened to you. I cannot bear to be away from you." She smiled at him with eyes that had now filled with tears. He was holding her so tight that Gillian was certain she couldn't take

The Passionate Rebel

a breath, but still she pressed into him, as if she could somehow fuse their bodies into one entity. "Please, whatever awaits us, let's face it together." She clutched him fiercely. "Promise me. Say it!" she demanded when he did not immediately respond.

"I promise," Philip whispered at last, and in his heart he vowed to keep that promise.

Chapter Twenty-eight

From Gillian's Diary:

> *August 2, 1781*
> *Though it grieves me to pen these words, victory is still beyond our reach. Most of New England together with Maryland, Delaware, Pennsylvania and New Jersey remains in the hands of the Continentals. The British, however, now control the Carolinas, New York and a good part of Maine. Virginia appears to be the key. If we lose this richest and largest of our sovereign states, all will be lost.*

Gillian woke to the pleasant sound of chattering birds, stretched, then rolled over to embrace her husband. Her hands encountered only the smoothness of sheets.

Sitting up, she brushed the tousled hair from her

The Passionate Rebel

face, disappointed that Philip had not been here to kiss her awake as he usually did. Drawing her knees up, she clasped her arms around them, taking a moment to revel in her happiness.

She had thought there would be a bittersweet quality to relocating in Virginia. New York had been her home all her life. She couldn't have been more wrong. She loved Williamsburg, loved the plantation, and had become deeply fond of her new family. Philip's mother had welcomed her with open arms and was thrilled with her new grandson. Adam even had his own personal servant, but then, servants seemed to well outnumber everyone else on plantations.

Surprisingly, Lisa had agreed to accompany Gillian to her new home. And just as surprisingly, Matthew had declined, saying he preferred to remain in Manhattan. Though his bond still had two more months to go, Philip had graciously released Matthew and had given him a glowing letter of recommendation.

Finally, Gillian swung her long legs to the floor and got up. She ran to the window, hoping to catch a glimpse of Philip.

A warm sun embraced the land in the soft, hazy glow of summer. Bees droned monotonously in the still air. Gillian could see the workers in the field but there was no sign of Philip.

The fact that Philip had gotten up earlier than she did caused her no undue concern. He did that frequently. Running a tobacco plantation required constant attention, especially in the summer. Weeds had to be removed as soon as they appeared, caterpillars were painstakingly removed by hand, and eyes constantly scanned the horizon for the slightest warning of a summer storm in the making, for in only minutes a crop could be devastated by hailstones. And tobacco, Gillian had learned, was not an ordinary crop. Its value was such that it was actually used, on occasion, as a medium of exchange. Almost everyone accepted tobacco in place of hard coin.

Gillian summoned Lisa, and after donning a cool cotton dress, patterned by perky violet flowers, she went downstairs, a bit surprised to learn that Philip had already left the house.

Gillian smiled at the woman seated at the dining room table.

"Good morning, Isobel." She planted a light kiss on her mother-in-law's cool, dry cheek.

Isobel Meredith returned the greeting and motioned for the servants to bring Gillian's breakfast. She was a small, petite woman who stood only an inch or so over five feet. At 54, she was still slim, with dainty hands and feet. Gillian thought she looked a bit like the fashion doll her father had sent to her some years ago.

"Where is Philip?" she asked, taking a sip of the hot coffee a servant had just poured into her cup.

Isobel frowned and spoke slowly. "We have received reports of British ships landing at Yorktown. I believe Philip went to check on the veracity of the sightings."

Gillian felt the blood leave her cheeks. These past weeks had been a quiet interlude, one which she had hoped would continue indefinitely. In fact, since the battle of Monmouth in June, 1778, things had been relatively quiet; indeed, it seemed at times as if both sides had slipped into inertia.

Now it was to begin again. Gillian put down her cup and sighed.

The Passionate Rebel

* * *

On the bluff overlooking Yorktown, Philip stood with Lafayette and a few aides to reconnoiter the situation. Patiently, he listened to one of the fishermen who had sighted the British. The man was so excited that he was babbling.

"I was the first to see them," the man cried, plucking at Philip's sleeve. "The whole damn British navy is out there."

Philip glanced at the gathered forces. "I don't expect there's more than eight thousand soldiers aboard those transports." He had intended his words to be comforting, but they were not.

"Jesus," the fisherman groaned, "the town's only got three hundred militiamen. We'll be swamped."

Philip watched as the man edged away. Yorktown no longer had any militia. Together with most of the citizens they had fled to Williamsburg. Philip had passed them on his way here.

He walked to the edge of the 35-foot bluff and looked down. About 60 houses were scattered along the river. Another 250 residences were on the bluff itself. Most of the houses were now empty. Lafayette came to stand at Philip's side. The marquis was so elated he could hardly contain himself.

"The earl has placed himself and his men in a bottle," he declared happily. "There is no escape."

As he spoke, he moved restlessly. The marquis was rarely still. He exuded energy, an exuberance that suggested to Philip, at times, a childish glee. But then, he was only 23. After almost six years in this war, Philip felt every one of his own 28 years.

"I admit I cannot understand his move," Philip finally responded.

"Ahh! His Lordship is overconfident. They all are." He poked Philip in the chest with a slender fingertip.

Helene Lehr

"I tell you, Meredith, this is the confrontation that will end the war."

The display of ebullience drew a smile from Philip. The marquis was one of those rare individuals who appealed to both men and women alike. More importantly, the influential Marie Antoinette found him charming—so much so that the young marquis had captured her interest in the American cause. And what captured Marie Antoinette's interest, ultimately interested the whole of France. Notwithstanding the fact that England and France were not the best of friends, Philip was willing to concede that the marquis had been most instrumental in bringing about the aid of their French allies.

The idea that the ensuing battle would end the war, however, was one Philip viewed with caution. Depending on whether one included the Hessians in the count, Cornwallis's 8,000 men could represent anywhere from a quarter to a third of the enemy forces. That still left a lot of soldiers to fight this endless war.

Again viewing the scene below, Philip shook his head. He couldn't believe that Cornwallis had made such a foolish move. The earl had positioned himself on a narrow strip of land, flanked on each side by wide rivers with the ocean at his back. Across the river, in Gloucester, British Colonel Tarleton was providing a semblance of support. But if Cornwallis should need reinforcements at any point, he could receive them only by sea. If he should run out of food or ammunition, he would be in the worst kind of trouble.

"Well, we can do nothing until His Excellency arrives with Rochambeau," the marquis declared, getting onto his horse. "But when he does, we'll teach the British a lesson they'll never forget."

The Passionate Rebel

Philip loosened the reins from the bush to which he had tethered his horse. That could take weeks, he thought worriedly. What if Cornwallis decided to move before Washington reached Williamsburg? If he did, they'd be overrun in no time. Washington and Rochambeau would find only rubble when they rode into town.

Later that day, Philip directed his horse onto the road that led to the family plantation. The sight always calmed him. He had been born here. In his most secret heart, he hoped to die here. His parents had sent him to England to be educated, rejoicing in the fact that their son would be a lawyer. And to please them, he had gone.

Deep inside, however, Philip had his father's blood; he was a planter, a farmer and a worker of the soil. Here were his roots. Here was where he wanted to raise his children.

Here was where he would make his stand.

The horse ambled up the drive. Philip made no attempt to hurry him. The animal had ridden the 14 miles to Yorktown at a fast pace and at only a slightly slower one on the return trip.

Gillian was standing in the driveway in front of the house. Philip was certain she had been waiting a long time, and it grieved him to know that he had caused her worry.

Gillian indeed had been standing there for more than an hour. She had spent the morning with her son, cuddling his warm soft body against her own, trying to reassure herself that this was a normal day. In her heart she knew it wasn't so.

Philip dismounted and turned the reins over to a servant, then came toward his wife. The anxiety was there in her eyes, clutching at his heart. His arms reached out, and he held her close.

"There's nothing to be alarmed about right now," he soothed.

"Will the militia return to Yorktown?" She knew he would go if they did.

"No. We can do nothing until General Washington gets here."

Arm draped around her shoulders, he led her back into the house.

The days of August passed in heavy heat. Gillian tried to keep busy. Like every other woman in town, she baked and cooked, trying to feed the swelling horde of men that increased the population every day.

Gillian was at once amazed and filled with pride as each day saw small groups of men arriving from Maryland and all parts of Virginia as word spread throughout the countryside of the imminent British threat.

As did every other family in the area, Isobel welcomed the newcomers into her home, and she and Gillian spent most of their time cooking in an effort to keep the men well-fed.

Her days fell into a routine. Gillian was up at dawn to help in the kitchen.

"Lord," she exclaimed to Isobel during the first week in September, "I wonder how many loaves of bread I have baked in these past weeks."

Isobel laughed and wiped her hands on her apron. "Quite a few, I'd say. But at least the weather is cooler now."

"A blessing," Gillian agreed. She sat at the table, put a bowl on her lap and began to snap the beans Isobel had just washed.

The Passionate Rebel

Both women gave a start a few minutes later when Philip burst into the kitchen with the news that the French fleet under the command of Comte de Grasse was now anchored in the Chesapeake. With the French admiral were more than 3,000 marines.

"Cornwallis cannot possibly escape," he went on enthusiastically. He poured himself a glass of milk and downed it before he continued. "Not only does de Grasse's position cut off any retreat by Cornwallis, if he is expecting reinforcements from New York they won't be able to get through the French blockade. He's trapped!"

Putting the bowl on the table, Gillian got up and hugged her husband, just as elated with the news as he was. At last she drew back. "But when will Washington be here?" she asked, knowing that nothing could be done until the Continental army arrived.

"Any day now," Philip assured. He grabbed a piece of freshly baked seed cake and hurried from the room, anxious to tell everyone of this latest development.

Despite Philip's assurance, however, it wasn't until September 14th when Washington arrived with his Continentals, all of them as ill-clad as ever. Close behind them was the Comte de Rochambeau in command of the French army.

The whole town turned out to greet the new arrivals.

Gillian was more than impressed at the sight of the French soldiers. She had never before gotten a close look at their allies. Used to the ragtail appearance of the Continentals, she was stunned by the magnificence of the French. Their waistcoasts and leggings were snowy white. Their jackets, too, were white, but the lapels and collar bands were a riot of color. Each regiment had their own hue, being either crimson, yellow, blue or green. Sergeants sported white plumes in their hats; grenadiers, red; infantrymen, called chasseurs, green.

Four days after Washington and Rochambeau met with de Grasse aboard his huge, three-deck flagship, the *Ville de Paris*, Philip received word that his commander-in-chief wanted to see him. Philip made arrangements to leave at once to see Washington who was staying in the same house as Lafayette, a rambling plantation on the water's edge.

When he arrived, Philip was immediately ushered into the drawing room.

"It's good to see you again, my friend," Washington said warmly. "I want to commend you for a job well done. And," he added with a twinkle in his eye, "to raise your rank to captain." He waved aside Philip's murmured appreciation. "It's only what you deserve. I've not been unaware of your contributions during these trying years. Because of men like you, Clinton has been deceived into thinking that we will attack New York. It gave us the time we needed and enabled de Grasse to position his ships."

"Then we will be attacking Cornwallis soon?" Philip asked.

Washington gave a slow nod. "It will have to be soon. De Grasse wants to return to the West Indies by the middle of November."

Philip frowned. "That means he has to leave by the middle of October."

"Yes. Though he has indicated he might give us another week or two."

The Passionate Rebel

Philip was dismayed by that. They badly needed de Grasse's ships, not only to prevent Cornwallis from escaping, but to assure that no reinforcements could reach him by sea.

"Surely his business cannot be that pressing that he could not stay if needed."

Washington sighed but spoke mildly. "The French admiral has his commitments. His fleet is needed to escort an important convoy from the West Indies back to France."

Leaving the house a while later, Philip mounted his horse. The roads were crowded with soldiers and militia. Beneath him, the stallion danced and side-stepped in nervous excitement at the unusual commotion. Patting the animal's neck, Philip managed to calm him with a few reassuring words.

As he rode home, the thought occurred to Philip that Cornwallis must know by now that he was soon to be attacked. He also must know that he was heavily outnumbered. Obviously the earl was pinning his hopes on Clinton's promised reinforcements.

Philip wondered whether they would arrive in time.

On September 28th, as she watched her husband don his uniform, Gillian felt as though her very soul was turning to jelly. At last all was ready for the attack. The Continental army of 9,000 men had swelled to 31,000 as French soldiers and sailors had joined their ranks. Though she had fought for the cause for more than five years and still believed fervently in its goals and ideals, the thought of Philip in the midst of cannon and musket fire was more than she could bear. If there was any way on God's earth that she could now offer her own flesh, Gillian would have gladly done so.

"Don't go."

The breathless plea was out before any conscious thought directed Gillian's tongue.

Philip paused to gave her a long, searching look that sent her flying into his arms.

"You've done enough," she cried, her voice coming muffled as she pressed her face against his broad chest.

He made no immediate answer but just held her close. Her body was past trembling. She was shaking to the point where he could hear her teeth chattering.

The relief of tears was beyond Gillian. Fear had her wrapped in a cocoon of dread that left her shivering. She felt Philip's hand caressing her hair in a soothing gesture that afforded no comfort.

Finally, he gently pushed her from him. Hands on her upper arms, he looked deeply into those gray eyes that had for so long held him enchanted.

"You know I must go," he said softly.

Gillian did know. She also suspected that the battle about to take place in Yorktown would be a last-ditch effort. Both sides were becoming weary. A war that was supposed to have been decided by one or two skirmishes was now in its sixth year. Three countries were in the fray, with Spain and the Netherlands making overtures to join the fracas. Brave men had fought, and brave men had died.

"No . . ." she moaned. "Not this time." Her eyes brimmed and spilled over. At this moment she would have agreed to return to England, if Philip had asked.

"This time more than any other," Philip countered. "This time we must, we will win! We have more men now than we've ever had. Rochambeau is here with his soldiers. So is Lafayette. Can we do less?"

The Passionate Rebel

The tears came, unbidden and unwanted, but no sobs accompanied their flow. Deep inside, Gillian knew she would have despised him had he decided to hide until it was over. That didn't mitigate her terror that he might be killed. Torn between what she knew was right and what her selfish heart desired, she put her hands to her face and wept her frustration.

Abruptly, Philip released her. "Would you have me stay home?" he asked quietly. "I will allow you to make the decision."

Her hands dropped away from her face, and she gaped at him in astonishment. From the look on his face, she knew he spoke the truth. It was within her power to keep him here, keep him safe. She knew him well enough to know that he would honor his word.

The moment lengthened. The baby cried and was soon silenced by a servant who picked him up and rocked him in her arms. In only moments, the house was again quiet.

Gillian turned away from her husband, unable to think with those dark eyes on her.

Philip would be safe here. She would be safe here. Their son would be safe here.

And what kind of life would they have? Would it be free, or would it be under the domination of a distant country with laws instigated by men who had never been in this land and known real liberty?

At last she turned.

"Go," she said simply.

His angular face creased with his smile. "I love you, Gillian. I always will."

As she watched him leave, she wished she could have drawn more comfort from that declaration.

Gillian made no attempt to see him off; that response was beyond her. She knew if she accompanied him outside, even to the front drive, she would weaken.

Chapter Twenty-nine

From Gillian's Diary:

> *October 1, 1781*
> *For more than 24 hours now I have been listening to the sound of cannon; it is particularly noticeable at night. Low on the horizon, I can see red clouds, produced by bursting shells. Despite its fierce beauty, it is a chilling sight. The bombardment has not ceased since the siege began. Cornwallis is outnumbered four to one. Clinton's reinforcements are nowhere in sight. One can only wonder why the earl is putting his men at such risk.*

Dawn found the bright October sky black with smoke. For the moment, the guns were silent.

Slowly, Philip stood up in the trench in which he had spent the night. Beside him, a lanky militiaman from Maryland did the same. His name was Jon Prescott, and he was all of 19 years old.

"What the hell . . . ?" Jon muttered, staring in disbelief at the scene that greeted his eyes. "What do you suppose it means?" he asked Philip, who was registering every bit as much surprise.

"Damned if I know," Philip responded. He climbed out of the trench and extended a hand to assist his companion in doing the same.

Both men stood there regarding the British trenches ahead of them.

They were empty. All of them were empty!

"Why do you think they pulled back?" Jon asked.

Philip shrugged. Regardless of the reason, he thought it was a bad move. "They are expecting Clinton's ships to bring them reinforcements any day now," he said finally. "Perhaps Cornwallis wants to regroup his men until their arrival. I admit I'm surprised they're not here already."

Jon snorted at that. "De Grasse about tore those ships apart. They won't set out again until they're repaired. That could take weeks."

A group of American and French officers, including Washington and Lafayette, came forward to assess this unexpected development. All looked puzzled. Philip went to join them.

"Sir," Philip inquired of his commander-in-chief, "shall we move forward?"

"Yes." As if having sudden doubts, Washington cast another speculative glance at the empty trenches. Trickery? Ambush? "However, wait a few hours before you move your men, Captain," he added, again viewing Philip. "It pays to be cautious. If by noon there is still no sign of activity, you may proceed."

Glad for the respite, Philip and Jon went to get

The Passionate Rebel

their morning meal. Cold meat and cheese constituted the simple, but filling repast. The food had been purchased with French gold.

As he ate, Philip listened to the jovial banter of the men around him. All of them were in good spirits.

Things were going well, Philip reflected as he popped the last morsel into his mouth. Losses so far were minimal. Twelve French soldiers had been killed, three Americans wounded.

Getting to his feet, Philip glanced toward the enemy camp. Once they moved forward to claim the abandoned works, only 360 yards would separate them from the inner fortifications of the British.

With a sigh, Gillian put down the book, realizing that she had read the same paragraph several times and still had no idea what she was reading.

Seated in a nearby chair, Isobel Meredith was working on a piece of embroidery.

The final rays of the afternoon sun streamed in through the parlor window, but the light was fast fading. Soon it would be dark.

Gillian was beginning to dread the night. Sleep was all but impossible. She had never wanted for courage when she herself had been at risk. Now she felt vulnerable and afraid. Each boom of the cannon, each flare in the sky could be the one that might injure or even kill Philip. It was a thought too horrible to contemplate; yet it was a thought Gillian could not drive from her mind.

Feeling restless, exhausted and unnerved, Gillian got up, went to the window and closed it.

It did no good. It did not mask the sounds that made her want to cover her ears and scream.

Isobel had let her hands fall idle. "You did not sleep again last night?" she asked Gillian in a low voice.

Gillian spun around. "Did you? Did anyone? Oh, God!" She clasped her hands. "It must be worse for the soldiers."

"I'm sure it is. Perhaps a few glasses of wine might allow you to rest," she suggested.

Gillian attempted a smile. Isobel was a godsend. All day long the two of them had tried to comfort each other, but it was difficult when their words were constantly being punctuated by flaring rockets and the thunderous impact of cannonballs. As if to emphasize her thoughts, a particularly shattering blast caused the windows to rattle.

"They are beginning to use their heavy artillery," Isobel noted with a sigh. She put her handiwork on the table beside her chair.

Gillian rubbed her throbbing temples. "What if something happens to him?"

"Don't think such things," Isobel said quickly.

"But what if it does?"

Isobel took a breath. "Then you will raise your son and go on with your life."

With a strangled sob, Gillian ran toward the older woman. Sinking down before her, Gillian placed her head in Isobel's lap. "There is no life for me without him," she said, weeping.

Isobel stroked the golden hair, listening to the heart-wrenching sobs of her daughter-in-law. Finally, she put her arms around Gillian and rocked her as though she were a child.

The sun finally slipped below the horizon, and soon after stars began to dot the ebony sky.

Isobel made no attempt to light the lamps and waved away a servant who attempted to do so. It

The Passionate Rebel

was, she thought to herself, going to be another endless night.

Wet and miserable, Philip and Jon huddled in a trench. There was no shelter from either the wind or rain. Lightning tore against the sky, rending the blackness with searing light.

Raising himself slightly, Philip peered over the edge of the trench. The British army was a mere 200 yards away.

Philip sat back again. By his reckoning today was October 16th. For the past two weeks the British had kept up their ceaseless bombardment of Yorktown. Hardly a building was now left standing.

Despite their aggressiveness, Philip knew that the British were in trouble. They were firing better than 100,000 rounds a day on what was left of Yorktown. At that rate their ammunition would soon be depleted. And, cornered as they were, their food supply by now must be dangerously low.

Philip shifted his weight and looked up at the sudden flash of light. Against the dark sky the bombshells looked like fiery meteors streaking through the air before they finally fell to the ground, there to burst with deadly impact. The American and French lines were situated, for the most part, out of range of the enemy cannon. But the British, under siege of the superior French heavy artillery, were not, and they were suffering grievous losses.

"I could use a cup of something hot," Philip shouted to Jon over the incessant rumble of thunder and cannon. "How about you?"

The young man nodded wearily. It was near to impossible to sleep with the unremitting din, and he, like everyone else, was feeling sluggish from exhaustion.

Helene Lehr

Slipping and sliding in the mud, both of them scrambled out of the trench.

"Damn! I didn't think they'd hold out this long," Jon grumbled as he finally stood upright.

Slowly, they sloshed to the rear of the line, where a large tent had been set up. About them, as they had been doing every day, men and horses strained against the terrain in an effort to drag the heavy artillery forward, foot by foot.

"We'll be breathin' down their necks in no time," Jon announced in no little satisfaction as they entered the tent.

Both men availed themselves of food and drink. Even in here, the dirt floor was damp and muddy. Pools of water had collected by the entrance, reflecting the yellow light of the lanterns.

Jon scowled at Philip, who was appreciatively draining his mug of sweet, hot tea.

"How come you drink that stuff?" he muttered, putting his mug, half full of strong black coffee, back on the trestle table.

Philip grinned. "I like it. I've been a tea drinker all my life. I see no reason to change now."

"It's unpatriotic," Jon complained as they headed back into the wet night.

Philip laughed and clapped his companion on the shoulder. "I guess it is," he agreed, "but if there's one thing I can thank the British for, it's their tea. I can't see that—"

Philip broke off as a resounding clap of thunder blotted out his words. It was followed by a searing flash of lightning that lit up the landscape like a bright, new moon.

His eyes narrowed. "Did you see that?" he asked Jon.

"What?"

The Passionate Rebel

"On the river," Philip said, pointing.

Jon looked, but it was so dark now, nothing could be seen. "I can't see anything." Shoulders hunched against the rain, he began to walk again, then halted when Philip grabbed his arm.

"Wait a minute."

Not too long a time passed before another flash of lightning came, casting a silver sheen on the river.

"Well, I'll be damned," Jon exclaimed, now seeing what Philip had seen only moments ago.

Flatboats, at least 15 of them, were putting out from Yorktown, presumably headed across the river to Gloucester. All were filled with British soldiers.

"They're trying to escape." Philip turned and began to run as fast as he could over the slippery ground, heading for the tent that had been set up as headquarters.

The general was not asleep. After listening to Philip's reports the order quickly went out. Every cannon and every gun was to be trained on the fleeing British army.

Returning to his post and bracing himself against the wind, Philip held his musket as steady as possible.

Beside him, Jon had paused to reload. "The wind's getting worse," he shouted to Philip, then glanced at the river. The water was churning to the extent that it was threatening the stability of the flatboats.

Philip lowered his gun as he saw the flatboats turn back to the relative safety of Yorktown.

They waited for a time, then wearily trudged back to their trench.

Philip was still awake when dawn lightened the sky. The clouds had at last passed, taking the storm with them. He took a deep breath. The air felt cleaner and fresher than it had been before the storm.

Settling himself as best as he could in the still muddy dirt, Philip tried to sleep. He was dozing fitfully when Jon shook him awake.

"What is it?" he mumbled, trying to clear his foggy brain. It was quiet—too quiet. Quickly, he got up.

Jon pointed to one of the battered British parapets.

In some amazement, Philip viewed the small redcoated figure who stood alone, a perfect target. He was only a lad. A leather strap over his shoulder supported a small drum, which he was beating in a measured, almost hypnotic cadence.

Philip slowly shook his head in admiration. He wondered whether he himself would be brave enough to so expose himself under such conditions as had prevailed since this siege started.

Except for the staccato sounds produced by the drummerboy, it was silent.

It seemed like a long time, but in fact it was only a few minutes later when a British officer began walking slowly across the battlefield. In his right hand he was holding a white handkerchief.

Gillian was lying on her bed, fully clothed, trying to rest after yet another sleepless night.

Though the draperies were closed, the room was far from dark, and Gillian flung an arm over her eyes in an effort to blot out the light. She had actually begun to doze, when her mind became aware of the silence.

With a gasp, Gillian sat bolt upright, heart slamming against her ribs with a sound that seemed louder than a cannon to her.

After all these weeks, the silence seemed unnatural, even ominous. Birds could suddenly be heard. A child's laughter came to her. A door slammed.

The Passionate Rebel

What did it mean? she wondered fearfully. Was it over, or was this sudden quiet merely a cessation?

Getting up, Gillian ran to the window on legs that felt unsteady and threw the draperies aside with a force that nearly tore them from the rods. From this vantage point she could see the road. She saw women, some running, some walking slowly, almost as if they didn't want to reach their destination.

Where were they going? Gillian wondered frantically.

At that moment, the door flew open, and Isobel rushed into the room.

"It's over," she cried. "We've won!"

Gillian looked out the window again, now realizing why the women were heading up the road. How many of them would find only grief at the end of their journey?

Gillian felt rooted to the floor. She was afraid to join them; she was afraid to stay.

"Go," Isobel urged quietly, seeing her indecision. "Don't torment yourself by waiting."

"Come with me," Gillian said, reaching out a hand.

The older woman shook her head. "Yours is the first face he'll want to see."

They clung to each other for a moment, neither of them willing to voice the dark uncertainty uppermost in both their minds.

Gillian trudged up the dirt road at a considerably slower pace than she had started out. She had forgotten to put on her cap. The sun felt hot on her head, even though the air was cool.

A few of the men were returning, presumably, Gillian thought, those who lived nearby.

When she judged she had gone about half the

distance, Gillian sat down on a fallen log to rest. She hadn't realized how far it was. Taking off her shoes, she gave a small groan as she viewed them. The soft material was beginning to wear. Her left foot was beginning to throb with the beginnings of a blister.

Looking up, she saw a man coming slowly along the road. Even at this distance she could see the weariness that marked his passage. When he was within hailing distance, Gillian pushed herself up, fighting the dizziness that threatened to defeat her.

"What is happening?" she called out to him. Her hands clasped her skirt and, in her stockinged feet, she moved toward him, trying not to wince as her feet encountered pebbles and stones.

He paused. "The redcoats have surrendered," he replied. "Their officers are at the Moore house now, signing the papers."

Gillian didn't know where the Moore house was, and right now it was of no importance to her. "Do you know a captain named Philip Meredith?"

The man shook his head. "No." He started to move forward again.

"Please . . ." Her hand halted him. "You must have seen him. He's very tall," she added helpfully.

"I don't know him, ma'am," the man mumbled, shrugging off the grip on his arm. "Sorry."

With a sigh, Gillian sat down on the log again. She was so tired.

Sunlight shimmered on the land, pointing up light and shadow in sharp contrast. Images danced before her eyes, and Gillian stared, trying to focus her eyes to no avail. A soft breeze set the leaves to dancing. The quiet was mesmerizing, lulling her into a stupor.

Feeling numb, Gillian picked up her shoes. Instead

of putting them on, she let them fall into her lap. A few minutes rest, she thought, then she would continue.

Sliding to the ground, her slippers tumbling to the soft grass, Gillian used the log as a pillow and promptly fell asleep.

It was only by chance that Philip saw her as he came down the road. Pausing, he smiled tenderly as he saw his wife. That he saw her here, halfway to Yorktown, did not surprise him. He had expected to see her on the road. He had not, however, expected to find her asleep, using a log as a pillow.

Going to her side, he sat down and filled his eyes with the sight of her.

This, he thought, was what it was all about. His hand went out, and he stroked her hair.

Immediately, her eyes opened, and she sat up. For a moment, Gillian made no move, feeling dazed and disoriented. Then her gray eyes widened as she saw her husband. A joy that was almost past bearing flooded Gillian with its heady sweetness. Impatient with the tears that blurred her vision, she hastily dashed them away. Her eyes quickly traveled the length of his lean, muscular form, and she sighed in profound relief.

"Oh, my love," she cried, clutching at him. "Thank God you're safe."

"With you to come home to, I wasn't about to take unnecessary chances," he replied softly.

Her hand went to his suntanned cheek. How was it possible to love this much? she wondered. Unable to help herself, she began to weep, hard, racking sobs that Philip made no effort to stifle. He realized she needed the relief.

Finally, she quieted.

"Did you plan to sleep the day away?" he teased, kissing her brow.

Filled with sudden remorse, Gillian bit her lip. "Every other woman kept walking," she wept, chagrined. "And I..."

"...stopped to take a nap." He kissed her. "And so you should have. You can't have slept much during these past weeks."

Gillian looked up at him. "I love you."

"Oh, Gillian," he murmured, holding her close. She snuggled contentedly within the security of his arms. Gillian felt she could stay here forever. He buried his face in her silky hair and inhaled deeply. "I didn't realize that roses were still in bloom," he murmured.

She looked up at him. "Roses?"

Philip didn't bother to answer. Bending his head, he captured her lips in a kiss of such intensity, she moaned with the sudden languor that swept over her. When he at last drew away, they clung to each other for long moments.

Then Gillian sat up straighter. "Your mother..." she said quickly, realizing how selfish she was being. "We must get back. She'll want to know you're safe."

They both got to their feet. Gillian found her shoes and put them on. Supported by Philip's strong arm, she began to trudge the miles back to Williamsburg.

"It is over, isn't it?" Gillian asked after a while.

Philip sighed deeply. He felt as if he could sleep a week. "I sometimes wonder if it will ever end," he said tiredly.

Gillian frowned. It was not the answer she wanted to hear. "But surely now that Cornwallis has surrendered..."

Philip looked down at her. With his fingertip,

The Passionate Rebel

he brushed away a smudge of dirt from her chin. "There are British camps strung out from Halifax to Charleston," he explained. "Clinton is still firmly entrenched in New York. And now that de Grasse is taking his fleet back to the Indies; the British are once again in control of our waters."

Without speaking, content that they were together, they made their way home.

Chapter Thirty

From Gillian's Diary:

> *November 22, 1783*
> *I confess that I grow more apprehensive with each passing day, fearful that in some way the British will renege and resume this conflict, even though a peace treaty has been signed. Everyone seems to feel the war has been won. This has generated an apathy that fills me with fear. Each state, heretofore united in our time of crisis, is now turning inward, concerned only with their own affairs. Our French allies have returned to their own country. The Continental army is in such disrepair that should the British decide once more to march, the Americans would be all but helpless. I will not be at peace until the British vacate our shores.*

The Passionate Rebel

"Well, of course, I have mixed feelings about it." Alice sighed. She was, as usual, dressed in black, and she considered the somber color to be particularly appropriate on this day. "One can only hope that it will all turn out for the best."

She smiled at everyone, and the smile, despite her cautious words, was genuine. A long time had passed since she had had her family gathered around her all at one time. Seated to her right at the breakfast table were Gillian and Philip and to her left were Edwina and Tom. The Blue Swan was closed on this auspicious day. At the far end of the rectangular table sat six-year-old Constance, who considered herself to be a young lady. Her younger brother Tom and Gillian's son Adam were upstairs in the care of a servant.

Gillian and Philip had arrived from Williamsburg two days ago. Their trip was not only for the purpose of visiting Gillian's family. It was to witness the dénouement of eight long years of conflict. Today was the day the British were finally to evacuate New York.

"It will be for the best, Gram," Gillian said firmly. Unlike her grandmother, Gillian had worn her brightest dress. Of red silk, it had a low, square neckline and elbow-length sleeves. The full skirt was drawn up a few inches on either side to reveal her white lace petticoat. Gillian had removed the red satin ribbons that held the gatherings secure and had replaced them with blue velvet bowknots.

"Perhaps," Alice murmured, sounding unconvinced. She couldn't believe the rebels had actually won the war; to the end of her days, Alice would think of them as rebels. Even now, it was inconceivable to her that this small, thinly populated country had faced the mighty British Empire and won.

Edwina gently chided Constance for not sitting up straight, then addressed her grandmother. "I think it's exciting to be able to govern ourselves. We're starting fresh. We needn't make the mistakes other countries have made."

Alice looked dubious. "I don't suppose you've given any thought as to where the money will come from to support our new government, not to mention our army."

"Federal taxation is the only solution," Tom said quickly, before his wife could respond. Then he sighed and shook his head. "I can't imagine that it will come about, though. The individual sovereignty of our states is guaranteed under the Articles of Confederation."

"But surely the state legislatures see the need for it." Edwina looked earnestly at her husband. "They must only vote it into being."

Tom laughed. He looked well and fit and had developed the beginnings of a paunch in the last two years. "I have yet to see them all agree on anything. It would take only one negative vote to destroy a bill like that."

"It wouldn't even take a negative vote," Philip observed as he sipped his tea. "One abstention would do it."

Alice cast a speculative glance at this man she had chosen to marry her beloved granddaughter. That he was a rebel—had been all along—she now knew. The information caused mixed emotions, even now when it no longer mattered. On one hand, she felt deceived, inclined toward anger. Yet with her own eyes she could see how happy Gillian was, how much she had settled down to the role of wife and mother.

The Passionate Rebel

Alice shook her head. Perhaps in the end that was all that mattered.

"We will learn as we go along," Tom said confidently. "We'll have to. Once they have gone, we're on our own."

Philip got up. "And we'd better get going, or we're going to miss it all."

"Believe me," Tom said grimly as he got to his feet, "it's something I don't want to miss."

"Are you coming with us, Gram?" Edwina asked, as she pushed her chair back.

Alice waved a hand. "No, no. A person could get trampled to death out there. I'll stay here with the children."

In the foyer, Gillian and Edwina donned heavy cloaks, for the November day was cold.

Taking a carriage was out of the question. Even a solitary horse and rider would be hard-pressed to get through the crowded streets.

Gillian and Philip, with Edwina and Tom close behind, walked to the harbor, where the British transports were anchored.

The city was festooned as Gillian had never before seen it. Streets had been swept clean of all refuse and garbage. Shops, houses and taverns were all draped in red, white and blue cloth. Over doorways, flags of 13 stars and 13 stripes flapped smartly in the breeze.

"I've never seen so many people all in one place," Edwina exclaimed in amazement when they finally reached the harbor. She clung tightly to Tom's arm.

Gillian laughed at her sister's observation, though she herself was of the same opinion. "Well," she noted, "more than thirty thousand of them will be soon be gone."

Philip managed to elbow his way to an advantageous spot, and the four of them settled down to wait.

Hours passed, but the people stayed to watch. Evacuating 30,000 men was no easy task and would probably not be accomplished in one day. Not only soldiers were taking their leave. Among the evacuees were Tories and their families. Although she could not find them in the crowd, Gillian knew that the Cartwrights and their daughter, Melanie Bennicot, were among that group. Also departing—though deported might have been a better word—were prisoners of war captured by the Americans, all of whom had been set free on the condition that they leave the country.

One man was missing from the British ranks. Sir Henry Clinton had been ousted the year before. Sir Guy Carleton had taken his place.

Gillian smiled to herself as she thought of that. England had sent three of its finest men to act as commander-in-chief. All had failed.

And we have had only one, she thought in satisfaction. But then again it took only one, if that man was George Washington.

"The first ship is leaving," Edwina cried, craning her neck for a better view.

Gillian directed her eyes to the forest of masts. Then she saw it. Her colors hoisted high, her decks crowded with scarlet-coated figures, the ship began to pull away, its white sails quickly catching the breeze.

Now, one after another, British ships began to sail down the bay, heading for the open sea.

They stayed until late afternoon. The tide had turned, and the rest of the ships were scheduled to leave the following day.

The Passionate Rebel

Slowly, the four of them made their way back home.

On the corner of Berkley and Broad Way, Tom left them and went to open the tavern. Certainly there was cause for celebration on this day.

Edwina continued with Gillian and Philip along the street to the Wharton house. It was even crowded here. Bells were ringing, people were cheering, and somewhere someone was setting off rockets.

Hearing her name called suddenly over the noise and confusion, Gillian turned around. For a moment, all she could see was a crowd of faces. Then one stood out.

"Claudia!"

Gillian erupted into happy tears as she saw her friend. Both of them ran forward at the same time to embrace each other.

Franz, holding his son in his arms, advanced at a more sedate pace. He clasped Philip's outstretched hand.

The booming sound of cannons now joined the cacaphony, and though Franz spoke, Philip couldn't hear a word he said. Gillian and Claudia seemed not to have noticed the increased din.

"Come inside," Philip shouted.

In the foyer, William took their outer wraps. Coming down the stairs, a startled Alice conveyed greetings and hastened to the kitchen to tell Polly they would be having guests for supper.

"When did you arrive?" Gillian asked excitedly when they had seated themselves in the parlor. "Why didn't you come to see me?"

Claudia laughed and raised a hand. "We arrived late this morning. We had hoped to be here sooner, but our wagon lost a wheel." She gave an exaggerated sigh. "It took forever to fix it."

Gillian smiled, studying her friend. Clad in an aquamarine silk dress, Claudia looked lovely. Her thick dark hair was braided and coiled around her head in the fashion of a coronet, entwined with a satin ribbon that was exactly the same shade as her gown. "Was it very bad?" she asked, referring to the years that Claudia had followed her husband from camp to camp.

"The life was difficult," Claudia admitted. "To say otherwise would be foolish. I was not the only woman there, and that made it easier. Thankfully, there wasn't much fighting." She paused. "Winters were the worst," she added as an afterthought.

"And where are you living now?" Philip asked.

"We have a bakery shop in Trenton," Franz replied.

"Were you at Yorktown?" Philip asked, handing Franz a glass of wine.

Franz shifted his now sleeping child to his other knee and took the glass. "No. I was with the small force General Washington left behind on the Palisades." He laughed. "If the British had ever decided to attack, they would have found no more than a few of us, trying to look like a thousand!"

Claudia took her sleeping son from her husband's arms. Settling herself, she displayed him for Gillian's view. The child was adorable, and Gillian said so. He was still asleep, and Claudia placed him on the couch, carefully positioning pillows around him so that he would not tumble off.

Edwina came in, holding Constance by the hand. "Young Tom is sleeping so soundly, I cannot bear to awaken him. He will spend the night here."

"You are not leaving?" Gillian cried. "Please stay for supper."

Edwina laughingly declined. "I have an idea that

once it gets dark Tom will be needing all the help he can get. Claudia, will you be in town for a few days?" At Claudia's nod, Edwina added, "Then please come to visit me tomorrow."

When she left, Claudia said, "Edwina hasn't changed at all."

Gillian turned to her. "And I have?" she demanded with mock accusation.

"Indeed you have," Claudia asserted with a laugh. "And all for the better, I might add. Marriage certainly agrees with you."

Hearing the men debating the pros and cons of the war, Gillian led Claudia upstairs to view the children. Both Adam and Tom were asleep.

Going to the bed, Claudia gently touched the fringe of young Tom's reddish brown hair.

"He once resembled my first son so much, I couldn't bear to look at him," Claudia confessed with a glance at Gillian. "Now he looks like his father."

"Claudia, are you happy?" Gillian whispered.

"Yes. I don't deserve the happiness I have."

"You do."

Claudia gave a soft laugh. "Whether I do or not, I have it." She slipped her arm through Gillian's as they made their way downstairs.

Claudia and Franz stayed for several days, then departed for their home.

Gillian was anxious to return home, too. Surprisingly, Philip demurred. There was one more event he wanted to witness.

Philip stood on the corner of Broad and Pearl in front of the Fraunces Tavern and watched as what remained of the Continental Army came down the street on this fourth day of December. The display was an indication that they were formally taking possession of the city.

Philip smiled as his eye lit on George Washington. Astride a white charger and resplendent in the uniform he had worn so proudly all these years, the general looked every inch the commander-in-chief. Behind Washington, his troops were as ill-clad as ever.

Turning, Philip entered the tavern and viewed the men inside. It was not a large crowd, but they had one thing in common. All had been officers in the army. They had gathered here today because Washington had indicated that he wished to say farewell to these men who had served him so faithfully.

A man of medium height with thinning brown hair approached Philip, hand outstretched. General Henry Knox was one of the few officers who still wore his uniform. Most, like Philip, were no longer in service.

"Good to see you again, Philip." Knox heartily shook Philip's hand. "I thought you would be back in Virginia by now."

"I'll be leaving in the morning," Philip admitted. He paused, seeing that all the men in the room were standing up as George Washington made his entrance.

Though he nodded at them all, Washington did not speak as he took his seat at the head of the long table.

Bowls and platters of food were being placed on the table, and Philip took his seat with the others. He studied the face of his former commander-in-chief, expecting to see triumph or at least satisfaction. He saw neither. He was looking at the face of a sad and troubled man. Philip knew, as did

The Passionate Rebel

every man in the room, that Washington had made a monumental effort to gain for his men their just due in the form of back pay. His efforts so far had been in vain.

Barmaids were now filling the glasses with wine. Everyone, including Philip, waited for Washington to begin eating. Instead, he pushed aside his plate and picked up his wineglass.

No one spoke. Philip got the impression that the general was too overcome by emotion to speak. At last, Washington raised his glass in a silent toast, and Philip was close enough to see the tears that shone in his eyes.

Finally, Washington got to his feet.

With the others, Philip stepped forward to shake the hand of the man who had, almost single-handedly, held the army together during the long years of conflict.

General Henry Knox made no effort to brush away the tears that streamed down his face. He turned to Philip, who was standing at his side.

"We could not have done it without him," he said in a voice choked with emotion.

Philip, whose throat felt tight with his own repressed emotion, made no answer. None was necessary.

When he left the tavern some time later, Philip did not immediately go home. Instead, he walked, trying to compose himself after the emotionally draining encounter.

It was quiet now. Things were returning to normal. He smiled sardonically at the refuse and clutter that was once more making an appearance in the streets. A few of the shops were still displaying the flag, but most had been taken down.

It was dark by the time Philip finally headed for the Wharton house. He didn't know what the future held; none of them did. Had it all been worthwhile? he wondered. And what a waste if it had not been.

Gillian greeted him at the door.

"We've waited supper for you," she said with a smile.

"I didn't mean to be so late," he apologized. Removing his cloak and hat, he hung them on the coatrack. Turning to Gillian, he touched her silky cheek. "We'll return to Williamsburg in the morning."

"Whenever you say," she whispered, giving him a hug.

Understandably, Alice was unhappy when she learned that they were leaving; however, after it was decided that she would come to Williamsburg for Christmas, her good spirits were restored.

In their room later that night, Gillian made certain their bags were packed and the clothes they intended to wear the following day were laid out and ready. Philip was already in bed. Gillian extinguished the lamp and left only the candle burning on top of the writing table.

Seating herself, she removed the leather-bound diary from the drawer in which she had placed it. There were only a few pages left, but no matter. She didn't need any more.

"Come to bed," Philip urged, watching her. She always scribbled a few words in her diary. Philip hadn't the faintest idea of what she felt compelled to report. He didn't care. Women did things like that.

"In a moment, love," she murmured.

Picking up the quill, Gillian dipped it into the

The Passionate Rebel

brass inkpot and in her neat script penned her last entry:

December 4, 1783: Praise God! Victory is at last ours!

ATTENTION PREFERRED CUSTOMERS!

SPECIAL TOLL-FREE NUMBER
1-800-481-9191

Call Monday through Friday
**12 noon to 10 p.m.
Eastern Time**
*Get a free catalogue
and order books using your
Visa, MasterCard,
or Discover®*

Leisure Books

Love Spell